HOMERIC HYMNS
HOMERIC APOCRYPHA
LIVES OF HOMER

LCL 496

HOMERIC HYMNS
HOMERIC APOCRYPHA
LIVES OF HOMER

EDITED AND TRANSLATED BY

MARTIN L. WEST

HARVARD UNIVERSITY PRESS
CAMBRIDGE, MASSACHUSETTS
LONDON, ENGLAND
2003

LOEB CLASSICAL LIBRARY® is a registered trademark
of the President and Fellows of Harvard College

Library of Congress Catalog Card Number 2002031814
CIP data available from the Library of Congress

ISBN 0-674-99606-2

CONTENTS

CONTENTS

HOMERIC APOCRYPHA

CONTENTS

PREFACE

In the old Loeb Classical Library edition by H. G. Evelyn-White, which originally appeared in 1914, the poems and fragments of Hesiod were coupled with the Homeric Hymns and Epigrams, the remains of the Epic Cycle and of other poems associated with Homer's name (including the *Battle of Frogs and Mice*), and the *Contest of Homer and Hesiod*. This material is now being distributed across three new volumes, each of which will contain a considerable amount of extra matter. The present one contains the Hymns and the other Homerica. Besides the *Battle of Frogs and Mice* I have included a fragment of a perhaps earlier poem of the same type, a *Battle of the Weasel and the Mice*. To accompany the *Contest of Homer and Hesiod* I have gathered in the whole collection of ancient Lives of Homer. The so-called Homeric Epigrams, which Evelyn-White printed on their own, are here given in the contexts in which they are preserved, dispersed through the pseudo-Herodotean Life.

I have edited and arranged the texts according to my own judgment, but relied on existing editions for information about manuscript readings. The nature of the Loeb series precludes the provision of the fullest philological detail about variant readings or scholars' conjectures. I have nevertheless tried to ensure that the reader is alerted to the significant textual uncertainties. In places I have made minor orthographical changes without signalling the fact.

It is a pleasant duty to thank Dr. Nikolaos Gonis for bringing to my attention an unpublished Oxyrhynchus papyrus containing parts of two of the Homeric Hymns.

Martin L. West
Oxford, May 2002

ABBREVIATIONS AND SYMBOLS

CAG	M. Hayduck and others, *Commentaria in Aristotelem Graeca* (Berlin, 1882–1909)
CEG	P. A. Hansen, *Carmina Epigraphica Graeca* (Berlin and New York, 1983–1989)
CQ	*Classical Quarterly*
FGrHist	Felix Jacoby, *Die Fragmente der griechischen Historiker* (Berlin and Leiden, 1923–1958)
FHG	Carolus et Theodorus Müller, *Fragmenta Historicorum Graecorum* (Paris, 1841–1873)
GRBS	*Greek, Roman and Byzantine Studies*
HSCP	*Harvard Studies in Classical Philology*
JHS	*Journal of Hellenic Studies*
LIMC	*Lexicon Iconographicum Mythologiae Classicae* (Zurich and Munich, 1981–1999)
Mus. Helv.	*Museum Helveticum*
NGG	*Nachrichten der Gesellschaft der Wissenschaften zu Göttingen*
OCD[3]	*The Oxford Classical Dictionary*, third edition (Oxford, 1996)

ABBREVIATIONS AND SYMBOLS

PMG	*Poetae Melici Graeci,* ed. D. L. Page (Oxford, 1962)
PMGF	*Poetarum Melicorum Graecorum Fragmenta,* ed. M. Davies (Oxford, 1991)
RE	*Paulys Real-Encyclopädie der klassischen Altertumswissenschaft* (Stuttgart, 1894–1980)
Rh. Mus.	*Rheinisches Museum*
SVF	H. von Arnim, *Stoicorum Veterum Fragmenta* (Leipzig, 1903–1905)
TAPA	*Transactions of the American Philological Association*
ZPE	*Zeitschrift für Papyrologie und Epigraphik*
[ ]	words restored where the manuscript is damaged
⟦ ⟧	letters deleted by scribe
⟨ ⟩	editorial insertion
{ }	editorial deletion
† †	corruption in text
*	(attached to a fragment number) uncertain attribution

HOMERIC HYMNS

INTRODUCTION

Nature and Purpose of the Hymns

When a rhapsode gave a performance of epic poetry in a formal setting—a complete short epic, or an episode from a longer one—it was the custom to begin with a hymnic address to a god or goddess. There is an allusion to the practice in the *Odyssey* (8.499), where Demodocus, in fulfilling Odysseus' request for the story of the Wooden Horse, "began from the god." Hesiod's *Theogony* and *Works and Days* each begin with a hymn (to the Muses and to Zeus respectively), followed by a transition to the main matter of the poem. Crates knew a copy of the *Iliad* that had a prefatory hymn to the Muses and Apollo attached.[1] Pindar compares an athlete's victorious debut at the Nemean Games, which were sacred to Zeus, with the fact that "the Homeridai, the singers of stitched words, generally begin from a *prohoimion* to Zeus."[2] *Prohoimion* means what precedes the *hoimē*, a term used in the *Odyssey* (8.74, 481; 22.347) for the theme of an epic singer's narrative.

The so-called Homeric Hymns are a collection of thirty-three such *prohoimia*. In fact when Thucydides

[1] See the Appendix Romana B, edited in this volume after the Lives.

[2] *Nemean* 2.1.

3

(3.104.4) quotes from the *Hymn to Apollo*, he calls it not a hymn but a *prohoimion*. Socrates is said to have composed a *prohoimion* to Apollo in prison, besides versifying some Aesopic fables (Plato, *Phaedo* 60d). Later authors, however, cite poems from the collection as "hymns," and their title in the manuscripts is Ὁμήρου ὕμνοι, "the Hymns of Homer." Their original prefatory function is confirmed by internal evidence. Nine of them (2, 11, 13, 16, 22, 25, 26, 28, 31) refer at the outset to "beginning" from the deity, that is, to celebrating him or her first. Most of them end with a salute to the deity, often followed by the announcement that the singer will now pass on to another subject: "I will take heed both for you and for other singing," or some such formula. In the late Hymns 31 and 32 it is made explicit that the transition will be to narrative about the deeds of heroes. Sometimes (2, 6, 10, 11, 13, 15, 20, 22, 24–26, 30–31) the ending includes a brief prayer for assistance, favor, or prosperity.

The first thing that strikes the reader of the Hymns is the enormous disparity in their length. A few of them run to hundreds of lines; there are two of intermediate length, Hymn 7 of fifty-nine verses and Hymn 19 of forty-nine; of the rest, none exceeds twenty-two lines, and fifteen are of under ten. There is, then, a basic distinction between long and short Hymns. What distinguishes the long ones is the inclusion of an extended narrative about the deity's birth or some other mythical episode in which he or she was involved. The short ones limit themselves to summary mythical references, indications of the god's spheres of influence, or description of his or her typical activity. A few of them are essentially mere excerpts from longer poems: Hymns 13, 17, and 18 from the longer Hymns to Demeter, the Dioscuri, and Hermes respectively, and Hymn 25 from Hesiod's *Theogony*.[3]

Thucydides quotes the *Hymn to Apollo* as the work of Homer, and with one exception (to be considered presently) no other author is ever named for any of the Hymns. However, the third Anonymous Life of Homer preserves an ancient scholarly opinion that the only genuine works of Homer were the *Iliad* and *Odyssey*, and that "the *Hymns* and the rest of the poems attributed to him are to be reckoned alien." To the modern critic it is clear from differences of language, political reference, and geographical outlook that the Hymns were composed by various authors in various places, at dates ranging probably from the second half of the seventh century BC to at least the fifth century, possibly even later. Their authors' names were not recorded because rhapsodes did not claim individual credit for what they added to the inherited stock of hexameter poetry. They dealt in traditional matter, and those of them at least who called themselves Homeridai, the Sons of Homer, regarded it as all coming down to them from their supposed ancestor "Homer."[4] The authors of the Hymns often show their acquaintance with the *Iliad*, the *Odyssey*, and Hesiod, and sometimes with other poems in the Hymn collection itself. This is not surprising in view of the Hymns' creation and transmission among a professional rhapsode class.

Most of them, we may suppose, were originally com-

[3] Hymn 13.1–2 ~ 2.1–2, 493; Hymn 17.2–5 ~ 33.2–5, 18; Hymn 18.2–9 ~ 4.2–9; Hymn 25.2–5 ~ Hes. *Th.* 94–97.

[4] See M. L. West, "The Invention of Homer," *CQ* 49 (1999), 364–382.

posed for recitation in a particular setting, at some particular festival or gathering. Sometimes a specific local reference is apparent from the poem itself. Of the long Hymns, that to Demeter obviously stands in intimate relationship to the Eleusinian Mysteries, while that to Apollo contains a vivid depiction of the Delian festival at which the poet is participating. Other local references will be mentioned below. In some cases the rhapsode was in competition for a prize; the poet of Hymn 6 prays to Aphrodite to "grant me victory in this contest, and order my singing."

Individual Hymns

In first place stand four fragments of what was evidently a long *Hymn to Dionysus*. Two come from ancient quotations, one of them overlapped by a papyrus; a third is given by another papyrus; the fourth, from the conclusion of the poem, survives in a manuscript of the Hymns, preceding the *Hymn to Demeter*.[5] It apparently contained the story, well known to poets and vase painters from around 600 BC, of how Dionysus came to be received in Olympus and accepted by Hera. When she gave birth to Hephaestus she was disgusted at the crippled child she had borne and threw him down from heaven into the sea. There he stayed for years with the Nereids, perfecting his engineering skills. Then he sent his mother a fine throne, in which he had incorporated a secret mechanism. When she sat down in it, she found herself trapped. None of the other gods was

[5] For the connection of the fragments and a reconstruction of the content see M. L. West, "The Fragmentary Homeric Hymn to Dionysus," *ZPE* 134 (2001), 1–11.

able to free her. It was clear that Hephaestus had to be induced to come back and undo what he had done. Ares undertook to go and fetch him by force. He went off, but failed to achieve his object, because Hephaestus defended himself with fire, which Ares could not face. Then Dionysus went equipped with wine, made Hephaestus drunk, and brought him back to Olympus in jolly mood, riding on a donkey or mule. He set Hera free, and she rewarded Dionysus by persuading the other Olympians to admit him to their number.

There is nothing in the fragments inconsistent with a dating to the later seventh century, so that the popularity of the story may be due to the currency of the hymn. The denial of Naxos' claim to be the god's birthplace (fr. A 3 ff.) is against a Naxian origin for the poem. On the other hand, the emphasis on Drakanos and Ikaros as claimants, the one a promontory in Cos, the other an island near Samos, does indicate the southeast Aegean as the poet's vantage point.

The *Hymn to Demeter* (2) remained unknown to the world until C. F. Matthaei's discovery of the manuscript M in Moscow in 1777 and Ruhnkenius' editions of 1780 and 1782. It is actually a hymn to both Demeter and Persephone, the presiding goddesses of the Eleusinian Mysteries, and it contains the Mysteries' foundation myth. It relates how Persephone was carried off to the lower world by Hades; how her grieving mother Demeter searched for her, came in the guise of an old woman to the house of Keleos the king of Eleusis, and was engaged to nurse the infant Demophon; how she was caught putting him in the fire at night, which would have made him immortal, and then revealed her divinity; how her continuing grief held the world barren, until Zeus commanded Hades to release Persephone; and how, before Demeter returned to Olympus, she instructed the Eleusinians to build her a temple and taught their lords her secret rites, which enable the initiate to enjoy a happier fate after death than the rest of us. Various details of the mythical narrative implicitly foreshadow ritual usages or taboos: Demeter's wandering with torches (48), her fasting and abstention from washing (49–50, 200), her sitting at the Maiden's Well (98 f.), her silent sitting on a stool covered by a fleece (195–199), the ribald jesting of Iambe (the eponymous representative of the *iambos*, 202–205), the breaking of the fast with a specially prepared barley potion, the *kykeōn* (208–211).[6]

The Hymn was clearly composed for recitation at Eleusis, perhaps at the Eleusinian Games which were held three years out of every four. Later it may have been taken up as a sacred text. In a papyrus of the first century BC (P.Berol. 13044) we find a prose narrative of the Persephone myth with verse quotations from "Orpheus": the prose account diverges from that of the Homeric Hymn, but the verses are all oral variants of the Hymn, which had evidently been adopted (perhaps also adapted) as an official scripture and put under Orpheus' name to enhance its authority. We know that Eleusis adopted Orpheus as the revealer and founder of the Mysteries not later than the fourth century BC.[7]

But the Hymn is a good deal older than that. As it con-

[6] See N. J. Richardson's commentary on these passages.

[7] Fritz Graf, *Eleusis und die orphische Dichtung Athens in vorhellenistischer Zeit* (Berlin and New York, 1974), 22–39; Richardson, 12, 77–86; M. L. West, *The Orphic Poems* (Oxford, 1983), 24.

tains no mention of Athens, it is assumed to date from before the time of Pisistratus, when the Mysteries came under Athenian control. On the other hand its poet seems to make use, not only of Hesiod and the Homeric epics, but also of the *Hymn to Aphrodite*. The poem may be dated with some probability to the first half of the sixth century.

The *Hymn to Apollo* (3) is a work of exceptional literary-historical interest for several reasons. Firstly, as has been almost universally accepted since Ruhnkenius (1782), it is a pantomime horse, a combination of two originally separate poems: a Delian hymn, performed at Delos and concerned with Apollo's birth there, ending at line 178; and a Pythian hymn, concerned with his arrival and establishment at Delphi. The two parts differ markedly in their geographical outlook, and to some extent in language. Secondly, the singer of the Delian hymn refers to himself as a blind man who lives on Chios, and boasts that all of his songs are acknowledged as supreme (172–3); from at least the time of Thucydides (3.104.5) this was taken to be a statement of Homer himself. Thirdly, it is reported that this hymn (whether the whole, or the Delian part only, is unclear) was displayed on a white painted panel (λεύκωμα) in the Delian temple of Artemis (*Certamen* 18). And fourthly, for this alone of all the Hymns[8] an author other than Homer is named. A scholiast on Pindar, explaining that poet's reference to Homeridai (*Nemean* 2.1), writes: "'Homeridai' was the name given anciently to the members of Homer's family, who also sang

[8] To disregard the appropriation of the *Hymn to Demeter* for Orpheus.

his poetry in succession. But later it was also given to the rhapsodes, who no longer traced their descent back to Homer. Particularly prominent were Cynaethus and his school, who, they say, composed many of the verses and inserted them into Homer's work. This Cynaethus came from a Chian family, and, of the poems that bear Homer's name, it was he who wrote the *Hymn to Apollo* and laid it to his credit. And this Cynaethus was the first to recite Homer's poems at Syracuse, in the 69th Olympiad (= 504/ 501 BC), as Hippostratus says" (*FGrHist* 568 F 5).[9]

Scholars have interpreted and combined these data in many different ways. No survey of the controversy can be attempted here.[10] The present editor's view of the matter is as follows.

The Pythian hymn is the older of the two, composed in central Greece shortly after the First Sacred War, when the Delphic sanctuary was wrested from Crisa's control by an alliance of Phocians and others and Crisa itself was destroyed (591/590 BC): the warning in lines 540–543 is a *post eventum* prophecy referring to the change of governance.[11] The hymn was perhaps recited at the first Pythian Games in 586.

[9] Hippostratus was a Hellenistic historian who specialized in Sicilian history.

[10] Karl Förstel, *Untersuchungen zum Homerischen Apollonhymnus* (Diss. Bochum, 1979), 20–62, gives a full account up to 1975. See further Walter Burkert, *Homerica* (*Kleine Schriften* i, Göttingen, 2001), 189–197; Richard Janko, *Homer, Hesiod, and the Hymns* (Cambridge, 1982), 99–132.

[11] See especially Pierre Guillon, *Le Bouclier d'Héraclès et l'histoire de la Grèce centrale dans la période de la première guerre sacrée* (Aix-en-Provence, 1963), 85–101.

Half a century later the Chian poet Cynaethus composed a hymn for a Delian festival that was attended by Ionians from far and wide. He knew the Pythian hymn and to some extent used it as a model. His poem comprised lines 1–18, 30–94, 97, 96, 102–104, 107–143, 179–180, and 146–178 of our hymn, with a couple of verses between 18 and 30 to initiate the narrative of Leto's wanderings. As a member of the Homeridai, who were just starting to promulgate the legend of their great imaginary ancestor Homer, Cynaethus claimed that his own poetry had been handed down from Homer: the verses about the blind Chian were supposed to be Homer's own utterance at a much earlier Delian festival. The Delians were delighted to learn this, and had the poem set up in the temple for public contemplation.

In 523 BC Polycrates, the great ruler of Samos, announced that he was going to celebrate a combined Delian and Pythian festival on Delos in honour of Apollo. For this occasion Cynaethus produced a combined Delian–Pythian hymn by conflating the older Pythian hymn with his own Delian one. He suppressed the beginning of the Pythian poem and tacked the remainder on to the Delian, making an awkward join.[12] The Pythian poet had prefaced his narrative with a review of various options: "How shall I sing of you? Shall it be how Leto gave birth to you in Delos; or how you courted various girls; or how you travelled in search of a place for your oracle?" Cynaethus could not

[12] It may be, as some have thought, that he omitted the passage about the Delian festival (147–176), passing from 142 or 145 to 179. This makes the join with 182 easier, though it remains clumsy.

leave the first of these options in place; he transferred it to serve as the introduction to his Delian birth narrative (19–29; the rest remained at 207–215). He made a place in his story for Hera, the great goddess of Polycrates' island, who had been ignored in the first version (95–101,[13] 105–106). He also brought her into the Pythian part by means of an interpolated episode (305–356) which crassly interrupts the narrative about Apollo and is of no relevance to him.

Because these changes were not made by oral recomposition in performance but by cutting and splicing written texts, the joints and discontinuities remain plainly visible, and it is comparatively easy to analyse the composite hymn into its constituent parts.

It looks very much as if Thucydides still knew the Delian hymn as an independent poem. Some rhapsodes may have learned it from the Delian inscription and kept it in circulation for a time. Sometime before the final redaction of the Homeric Hymns, a version of this Delian poem was collated with the Delian–Pythian composite and certain variants incorporated.

The *Hymn to Hermes* (4) is distinctive in other ways. Of all the earlier Greek hexameter poems, it is without doubt the most amusing. It is also the most untraditional in its language, with many late words and expressions, and many used in slapdash and inaccurate ways; and it is the most incompetent in construction, with many narrative inconsistencies and redundancies and no command of the even tempo appropriate to epic storytelling.

[13] Reversing the original order of 97 and 96.

The narrative begins with Hermes' birth in the mountains of Arcadia and ends with his establishment as an honored member of the divine company on Olympus and a special friend of Apollo. The story in between, like that of the fragmentary Dionysus hymn, or Demodocus' tale of Ares and Aphrodite in *Odyssey* 8, or Hera's seduction of Zeus in *Iliad* 14, is one that portrays the gods in a humorous light, playing tricks on one another for their own purposes. Here the trickery is basic to Hermes' nature as god of thieving and deception as well as of pastoralism. As a newborn baby not yet a day old, he slips out from his crib, bent on mischief. Finding a tortoise, he at once sees its potentialities, kills it, and makes its shell into the first lyre. Then he crosses half Greece and steals fifty of Apollo's cattle. Concealing their tracks by a cunning artifice, he brings them to the river Alpheios, where he slaughters and roasts two of them, incidentally inventing the method of creating fire from firesticks. Before the night is over he slips back into his crib and plays the innocent. But Apollo tracks him down and hales him to judgment before Zeus, who is heartily amused and commands the two of them to be reconciled. Hermes gives Apollo the lyre in exchange for the cows; he thus becomes the god of the lyre, while Hermes is confirmed as god of the pastures.

Besides accounting for some of the two gods' functions and the inventions of the lyre and the firesticks, the Hymn also contains an aetiological element relating to cult.[14] In killing the two cows by the Alpheios, Hermes uses sacrificial procedures, and when he has roasted the meat he lays it out in twelve portions, to each of which a fixed rank is as-

[14] Burkert, *Homerica*, 178–188.

signed by lot. He refrains from eating any of it, appetizing
though it is. All this must be connected with the sacrifices
at Olympia, which is by the Alpheios, to the Twelve Gods.
Pindar speaks of Heracles, the founder of the Olympic
Games, "honoring the stream of Alpheios with the twelve
ruler gods" (*Olympian* 10.48). Hermes was associated with
Apollo there, for the two shared one of the six altars
(Herodorus, fr. 34 Fowler). It seems likely, therefore, that
the Hymn was composed for performance at Olympia. It
alludes in lines 124–126 to the hides of the slaughtered
cows being still visible where Hermes spread them out on
a rock: presumably the reference is to some rock formation
that looked like a pair of spread hides.

It is generally agreed on grounds of style and diction
that it must be the latest of the major Hymns. The subject
matter was already familiar to Alcaeus, whose lyric hymn
to Hermes covered similar ground.[15] Alcaeus very likely
knew a "Homeric" hymn on the subject. But to date our
Hymn as early as 600 is implausible: it contains too many
words and expressions that are not paralleled before the
fifth century. The likelihood is that it is a later descendant
of the hymn that Alcaeus knew.[16]

The *Hymn to Aphrodite* (5), by contrast, is probably the
oldest of the long Hymns, and it is the closest in style to
the epics. In fact it has a special connection with the sub-

[15] See D. L. Page, *Sappho and Alcaeus* (Oxford, 1955), 252–
258.

[16] For further arguments for a fifth-century dating see Herwig
Görgemanns, "Rhetorik und Poetik im homerischen Hermes-
hymnus," in H. Görgemanns and E. A. Schmidt (ed.), *Studien
zum antiken Epos* (Meisenheim, 1976), 113–128.

ject matter of the epics about Troy, for the myth told in it relates to the birth of one of the major Trojan heroes, Aeneas, and it does not serve to document the goddess's divine power but rather a temporary weakness to which she succumbed and of which she is somewhat ashamed. Previously she had enjoyed making other gods compromise their dignity by falling in love with a mortal; but by making her fall for Anchises, Zeus has put a stop to that for the future. However, the union that is an embarrassment for the goddess is a matter of glory for the heroic family that issues from it, and this is the real point of the poem. Aphrodite tells Anchises that "you are to have a dear son who will rule among the Trojans, as will the children born to his children continually" (196 f.). The inference is that there was a princely family in the Troad in the poet's time that claimed descent from Aeneas and suzerainty over "Trojans." The Hymn was composed for the gratification of this family rather than of the goddess.[17]

There is a very similar prophecy about the descendants of Aeneas in the *Iliad* (20.307 f.), and that poet too must have been in contact with the same aristocratic family. There cannot be a huge difference in time, probably a generation at most, between these two celebrations of the Aeneadae. Karl Reinhardt even argued that the *Hymn to*

[17] This widely accepted conclusion has been forcefully contested by P. M. Smith, "Aineiadai as Patrons of *Iliad* XX and the Homeric *Hymn to Aphrodite*," *HSCP* 85 (1981), 17–58. What his arguments do show is that the Aineiadai implied in the Hymn and the *Iliad* cannot be identified with any mentioned by later historical sources, such as those in Scepsis (Strabo 13.1.52–53, following Demetrius of Scepsis).

Aphrodite was by the poet of the *Iliad* himself.[18] It was not a preposterous idea, but subsequent scholars have given good grounds for seeing the poet of the Hymn as an epigone with his own narrative style, a slightly more developed vocabulary, and a derivative use of the Homeric epics and Hesiod. We shall not go far wrong if we place him in the last third of the seventh century.

Hymn 6, again to Aphrodite, is notable for its explicit reference to a rhapsodic contest which the poet hopes to win. The emphasis on the goddess's power in Cyprus suggests that island as the venue; the panegyris at Old Paphos (Strabo 14.6.3) might be a plausible occasion. The description of Aphrodite's dressing and adornment resembles fragments 5–6 of the *Cypria*, an epic that also came from Cyprus.

Hymn 7 relates a story about Dionysus' capture by pirates which is otherwise first alluded to by Pindar (fr. 236 Snell). The conjunction of Egypt and the Hyperboreans (28–29) also makes a link with that poet (*Isthmian* 6.23), and the Hymn is not likely to be very much earlier than Pindar in date. It is difficult not to see some connection with the famous black-figure cup by Exekias, dating from about 530 BC, which depicts Dionysus reclining at ease on shipboard, with a grape vine growing up above the mast,

---

[18] *Die Ilias und ihr Dichter* (Göttingen, 1961), 507–521. Detailed studies in reaction to Reinhardt: Ernst Heitsch, *Aphroditehymnos, Aeneas und Homer* (*Hypomnemata* 15, Göttingen, 1965); Henryk Podbielski, *La structure de l'Hymne homérique à Aphrodite* (Polish Academy, 1971); L. H. Lenz, *Der homerische Aphroditehymnus und die Aristie des Aineias in der Ilias* (Bonn, 1975).

enormous grape clusters hanging from it over the ship, and a number of dolphins in the sea round about. The painting need not presuppose the myth, as the dolphins can be understood as a conventional feature of the sea, and the vine as a mark of the god's sacred ship, which played a part in his cult. On the other hand it is possible to imagine that the myth was inspired by the painting.

Hymn 8 (Ares) is a late intruder among the Homeric Hymns, as has long been recognized. It is probably the work of the Neoplatonist Proclus (fifth century AD), and has through some accident migrated here from the collection of his *Hymns*, which in the Middle Ages were transmitted in company with the Homeric Hymns, the Orphic Hymns, and the Hymns of Callimachus.[19]

Hymn 9 (Artemis) describes the goddess driving her chariot through Smyrna to her brother's shrine at Claros. The poem no doubt comes from that area, and it should date from before Alyattes' destruction of Smyrna around 600 BC.

Hymn 10 (Aphrodite), like Hymn 6, dwells on the goddess's power in Cyprus, and in this case the city of Salamis is specifically mentioned. That is where the poem is likely to have been performed.

Hymn 12 may possibly have been composed for one of Hera's festivals on Samos, the principal centre of her cult in classical times.

Hymn 15 (Heracles) is not likely to antedate the sixth

[19] See M. L. West, "The Eighth Homeric Hymn and Proclus," *CQ* 20 (1970), 300–304. Thomas Gelzer, *Museum Helveticum* 44 (1987), 150–167, argues that the hymn predates Proclus and is from Porphyry or his circle.

century, as there is no earlier evidence for the cult of Heracles as a god. It was held to have been an Attic innovation. There was a major Heracles festival at Marathon every four years, and this would be one possible setting for the Hymn. Some scholars have conjectured that it was designed as a prelude to an epic about Heracles.

Hymn 16 is made up of conventional elements that continued to appear for centuries in hymns and paeans to Asclepius. Matthiae thought it might have been composed for the Epidaurian Asclepieia; Epidaurus is certainly the major center of the cult, but there were many others.

Hymn 18 is abstracted, as noted above, from the long *Hymn to Hermes*. In the last line the god is addressed with the unusual title χαριδώτης, "bestower of favor." There was a Samian festival at which he was so styled (Plutarch, *Greek Questions* 303d).

Hymn 19 celebrates the Arcadian god Pan, who did not become widely known until the early fifth century. The language of the Hymn and the romantic imaginative description of Pan dancing with the nymphs suit a fifth-century dating.

Hymn 20 associates Hephaestus as god of crafts with Athena, and sees these crafts as the means by which the human race has raised itself from living in caves to a civilized way of life. This concept of human progress from a primitive state was an invention of the mid fifth century, associated with the sophist Protagoras. The pairing of Hephaestus and Athena is Athenian, and the little poem was probably composed for the Attic Hephaestia sometime in the second half of the fifth century.

Hymn 22 praises Poseidon as lord of Helicon and Aegae. This is an error for Helice and Aegae, the two towns in Achaea sacred to Poseidon (*Iliad* 8.203). The source of the error is the title *Helikōnios*, under which the god was worshipped in several Ionian cities, and especially at the Panionian festival on Mt. Mycale until its cessation in the early fifth century; the ancients tried to derive *Helikōnios* from Helice. The Hymn may have been composed for the Panionia.

Hymn 24 (Hestia) refers to the goddess's association with Apollo at Delphi, but asks her to come to "this house" together with Zeus. Allen and Sikes suggested that the occasion was the dedication of a temple—of Zeus, presumably.

Hymn 26 (Dionysus) was performed at a festival of an annual nature, as appears from the closing prayer. It agrees with Hymn 1 in locating the god's birth on Mt. Nysa; whether this is an indication that it comes from the same area is questionable.

Hymns 31 and *32*, to the Sun and Moon, are a matching pair and clearly the work of one poet. They must be among the latest poems in the collection. There is a clue to their origin in the reference to a daughter of the Moon called Pandia (32.15), for this obscure figure featured in an Attic genealogy: she was the wife of Antiochos, the eponymous hero of the Antiochid *phylē*.[20]

Hymn 33, to the Dioscuri, is one of three Hymns (the others being 1 and 4) whose content was paralleled in lyric hymns by Alcaeus. He evidently knew a hexameter hymn to the Dioscuri which had some similarity to ours. Matthiae conjectured that this Hymn was the prelude to a

[20] Apollodorus, *FGrHist* 244 F 162 as corrected by Albert Henrichs, *Cronache Ercolanesi* 5 (1975), 13 n. 40.

19

longer narrative about the Dioscuri. He compared Theocritus, *Idyll* 22, where a similar arrangement is seen.[21]

The Formation of the Collection. Transmission

The passages cited from Pindar and Thucydides at the beginning of this Introduction show that the fifth-century public was familiar with the *prohoimion* as a genre, and that at least some specimens of it had achieved wide currency. Perhaps it was already possible to find books in which a number of "the Hymns of Homer" had been gathered together. But in pre-Alexandrian times there was probably no agreement in respect of which poems were included or in what order.

The earliest extant references to the Hymns as a collection come from Philodemus and Diodorus in the first century BC. Philodemus' citations perhaps go back to the great work of Apollodorus *On the Gods*, written a century earlier. So far as we can see, the collection of "Hymns of Homer" that these authors cite is the same one that has come down to us. A standard edition had emerged, perhaps from the hand of one of the Alexandrian scholars, though Aristarchus at least seems to have had no interest in the Hymns. Evidence of the editorial process is to be seen in the presence, at several places in the Hymns, of alternative versions side by side in the text.[22] The editor must have found divergent rhapsodes' recensions in different copies

[21] For comparison of the Hymn with the poems of Alcaeus and Theocritus, see Page, *Sappho and Alcaeus*, 265–268.

[22] The clearest examples are: 1.4–6/7 and 8–10/11–12; 3.136–138/139; 5.97/98 and 274–275/276–277; 18.10–11/12.

and, rather than choose one to the exclusion of the other, included both, with appropriate critical signs in the margin. A remnant of these signs survives in one group of manuscripts at 3.136–139.

The order in which the Hymns are arranged is not random, though not governed by any single principle. The long Hymns precede the short ones, but the latter sequence is somewhat disturbed by the forty-nine-line *Hymn to Pan* (19). From 9 to 14 we have a series of goddesses, and they are followed in 15–17 by deified men (Heracles, Asclepius, the Dioscuri). In 27–30 come another group of goddesses (again following a hymn to Dionysus). The last of these, Earth as the universal mother, is followed up by two more deities of a cosmic nature (Sun and Moon), and finally by the Dioscuri considered especially in their meteorological aspect.

The Hymns were not widely read. The number of ancient quotations and allusions is not large, and apart from the "Orphic" version of the *Hymn to Demeter* only four papyrus fragments have been identified. The medieval tradition is not a strong one. None of the extant manuscripts is earlier than the fifteenth century, and the text is much less well preserved than that of the *Iliad* or *Odyssey*. There are many corrupt readings (some of them incurable), verses have fallen out in about a dozen places, and a couple of times the order of lines is disturbed.

Sometime in late antiquity, or more likely in the early Middle Ages, the Homeric Hymns were gathered together in one codex with the Orphic *Argonautica* and Hymns and the Hymns of Callimachus and Proclus. The order, to judge from the majority of the surviving manuscripts of these works, was Orpheus, Proclus, Homer, Callimachus.

21

At some stage, as noted above, Proclus' hymn to Ares became displaced and continued its career as the eighth Homeric Hymn. All our manuscripts are descended from a copy which had this displacement.

There is a clear division within the tradition between M, the manuscript discovered by Matthaei in Moscow in 1777,[23] and all the other manuscripts, twenty-eight in number, which derive from a lost archetype designated as Ψ. M alone preserves the *Hymn to Demeter*, and it would have preserved the long *Hymn to Dionysus* too if a quinion had not fallen out, leaving only the last few lines on the page on which the Demeter hymn begins. These two poems were absent from Ψ. The texts of M and Ψ often diverge quite strikingly up to 18.4, where M ceases.

Ψ is thought to have been a paper codex of the thirteenth century; it may have been brought from Constantinople to Italy in 1423 by Ioannes Aurispa.[24] Its descendants fall into three families, designated *f*, *p*, and *x*. The hyparchetype of the *x* manuscripts contained a number of marginal variants drawn from a source apparently independent of Ψ; this source is designated *y*.[25]

[23] Now in Leiden, University Library, cod. BPG 33H; written by Ioannes Eugenikos, probably in Constantinople sometime after 1439. See Thomas Gelzer, "Zum *Codex Mosquensis* und zur Sammlung der *Homerischen Hymnen*," *Hyperboreus* 1 (1994), 113–136.

[24] See Rudolf Pfeiffer, *Callimachus* II (Oxford, 1953), lxxxi f.

[25] For more detailed accounts see P. S. Breuning, *De Hymnorum Homericorum memoria* (Traiecti ad Rhenum, 1929); Allen–Halliday, xi–lviii; Jean Humbert, *Homère: Hymnes* (Paris, 1937), 12–15; Filippo Càssola, *Inni omerici* (Milan, 1975), 593–613.

SIGLA AND BIBLIOGRAPHY

Manuscript sigla

Π1 Berlin papyrus 13044 (first century BC)
Π2 P. Oxy. 2379 (third century)
Π3 P. Oxy., forthcoming (third century)
Ω   The consensus of the medieval manuscripts
M   Leiden, University Library, cod. BPG 33H
    (fifteenth century)
M^2 A scholarly corrector of M (sixteenth century)
Ψ   The lost archetype of f, p, and x (thirteenth
    century?)
f, p, x Manuscript families (fourteenth–fifteenth
    centuries)
a, b Subgroups of x
y Marginal variants transmitted in the x group

Editions, Commentaries

Chalcondyles, Demetrius. ἡ τοῦ Ὁμήρου ποίησις ἅπα-
σα. Florence, 1488. The *editio princeps*.

Barnes, Joshua. *Homeri Ilias, Odyssea,* etc. Cambridge,
1711.

Ruhnkenius, David. *Homeri Hymnus in Cererem*. Leiden,
1780, 1782.

Wolf, F. A. *Homeri Odyssea cum Batrachomyomachia,
hymnis,* etc. Halle, 1784.

————*Homeri et Homeridarum opera et reliquiae*, v. Leipzig, 1807.

Ilgen, C. D. *Hymni Homerici cum reliquis carminibus minoribus*. Halle, 1796.

Matthiae, August. *Hymni Homerici et Batrachomyomachia*. Leipzig, 1805.

Hermann, Gottfried. *Homeri Hymni et Epigrammata*. Berlin, 1806.

Franke, L. G. F. *Homeri hymni epigrammata fragmenta et Batrachomyomachia*. Leipzig, 1828.

Baumeister, Augustus. *Hymni Homerici*. Leipzig, 1860.

Gemoll, Albert. *Die homerischen Hymnen*. Leipzig, 1886.

Goodwin, Arthur. *Hymni Homerici*. Oxford, 1893.

Allen, T. W., and E. E. Sikes. *The Homeric Hymns*. London, 1904.

Allen, T. W. *Homeri Opera*, v. Oxford Classical Texts, 1912.

Evelyn-White, H. G. *Hesiod, The Homeric Hymns and Homerica*. Loeb Classical Library, 1914.

Radermacher, Ludwig. *Der homerische Hermeshymnus*. Vienna and Leipzig, 1931.

Allen, T. W., W. R. Halliday, E. E. Sikes. *The Homeric Hymns*, Second Edition. Oxford, 1936.

Humbert, Jean. *Homère, Hymnes*. Paris (Budé), 1937.

Richardson, N. J. *The Homeric Hymn to Demeter*. Oxford, 1974.

Càssola, Filippo. *Inni omerici*. Milan, 1975.

van Eck, J. *The Homeric Hymn to Aphrodite. Introduction, Commentary and Appendices*. Diss. Utrecht, 1978; critical comment by N. van der Ben, *Mnemosyne*, 39 (1986), 1–41.

Foley, Helene P., and others. *The Homeric Hymn to*

Demeter. Translation, Commentary, and Interpretive Essays. Princeton, 1993.

Zanetto, Giuseppe. *Inni omerici*. Milan, 1996.

Other Studies

Breuning, P. S. *De Hymnorum Homericorum memoria*. Traiecti ad Rhenum, 1929.

Clay, Jenny S. *The Politics of Olympus. Form and Meaning in the Major Homeric Hymns*. Princeton, 1989.

Hoekstra, Arie. *The Sub-epic Stage of the Formulaic Tradition. Studies in the Homeric Hymns to Apollo, Aphrodite, and Demeter*. Amsterdam and London, 1969.

Janko, Richard. *Homer, Hesiod, and the Hymns*. Cambridge, 1982.

Martin(us), Bernard. *Variarum Lectionum libri IV*. Paris, 1605.

Matthiae, August. *Animadversiones in Hymnos Homericos*. Leipzig, 1800.

Parker, Robert. "The *Hymn to Demeter* and the *Homeric Hymns*." *Greece and Rome*, 38 (1991), 1–17.

Ruhnkenius, David. *Epistola critica ad Valckenarium*. Leiden, 1749.

Zumbach, Otto. *Neuerungen in der Sprache der homerischen Hymnen*. Diss. Zürich, 1955.

HYMNS

1. ΕΙΣ ΔΙΟΝΥΣΟΝ

A (Pap. Genav. 432; lines 2–10 Diod. 3.66.3; lines 9–10 also Diod. 1.15.7, 4.2.4, schol. Ap. Rhod. 2.1211)

]παπαθ[
οἱ μὲν γὰρ Δρακάνωι σ᾽, οἱ δ᾽ Ἰκάρωι ἠνεμοέσσηι
φᾶσ᾽, οἱ δ᾽ ἐν Νάξωι, δῖον γένος Εἰραφιῶτα,
οἱ δέ σ᾽ ἐπ᾽ Ἀλφειῶι ποταμῶι βαθυδινήεντι
5 {κυσαμένην Σεμέλην τεκέειν Διὶ τερπικεραύνωι},
ἄλλοι δ᾽ ἐν Θήβηισιν ἄναξ σε λέγουσι γενέσθαι,
ψευδόμενοι· σὲ δ᾽ ἔτικτε πατὴρ ἀνδρῶν τε θεῶν τε
πολλὸν ἀπ᾽ ἀνθρώπων, κρύπτων λευκώλενον Ἥρην.
ἔστι δέ τις Νύση ὕπατον ὄρος, ἀνθέον ὕληι,
10 τηλοῦ Φοινίκης, σχεδὸν Αἰγύπτοιο ῥοάων·
ἔνθ᾽ οὔ τις σὺν νηὶ] περ[ᾶι] μερόπων ἀνθρώπων·
οὐ γάρ οἱ ἔστι λι]μήν, νηῶν ὄχος ἀμφιελισσέων,
ἀλλά οἱ ἠλίβα]τος πέτρη περιδέδρομε πάντηι
ὑψηλή, τά τε κα]λὰ φύει μενοεικέα πολλά
15   ]. κατέχει βαθὺτ[....]πλο[
                     ]. τεταν υ....[
                      ]...τεκα[

26

HYMNS

1. TO DIONYSUS

(A) . . . For some say it was at Drakanos, some on windy Ikaros, some on Naxos, O scion of Zeus, Bull god, and some at Alpheios the deep-swirling river {that Semele conceived and bore you to Zeus whose sport is the thunderbolt}, while others, Lord, say that it was at Thebes you were born. All false! The father of gods and men gave you birth far from humankind, to conceal you from white-armed Hera. There is a place Nysa, a mountain most high, burgeoning with forest, in a distant part of Phoenicia, almost at the waters of the Nile. No one crosses there by ship, for it has no harbor where curly-tipped ships can ride: a steep cliff encloses it all round to a great height. But it grows lovely and delicious things in abundance . . . occu-

---

A 2 σ’ om. pap.
5 om. pap. et Diod. codd. pars
6 post 3 pap.
9 ὄρος pap., Diod.: κέρας schol.
11–14 ex Orph. *Arg.* 1199–1202 restituti
13 περιδέδρομε West: -δεδραμε pap.

ἀ]πὸ φλοίσ[β
]κτον ἀποβλ[
20   ]..την πε.[
]πολων ν..[
]ι παλάμηι δα[
]ων ἔρατοι νομο[ί
]. ὑπὸ δρυ.διο[

B (Crates ap. Ath. 653b, ἐν τοῖς ὕμνοις τοῖς ἀρχαίοις)

αὐτῆισι σταφυλῆισι μελαίνηισιν κομόωντες

C (Pap. Oxy. 670)

ἐθέ]λεις· τί δ᾽ ἂν ἄλλο πά[θοι
ἀασάμη]ν δὲ καὶ αὐτός, ἀπ[
].[..] αὐτόματος λίπεν[
]ως [εἰ]κάζουσιν ἀειγε[
5 ἔμβα]λε Ταρταρίηισιν ἀλυκτ[οπέδηισι δολώσας.
τίς σ]ε, φίλη, λύσειεν; ἐπιζώ[στρη δ᾽ ἀλεγεινή
πάν]τοθεν [ἀμ]φιβέβηκε τ[εὸν δέμας· αὐτὰρ ὅ γ᾽
    ἄλλως
οὔτ᾽ ἄ]ρ᾽ ἐφη[μοσύ]νης μεμν[ημένος οὔτε λιτάων
βουλὴ]ν ἀστυ[φέλι]κτον ἑῶι σ[υμφράσσατο θυμῶι.
10 ὠμό]ν, ἀδελ[φειή,] τέκες υἱέα·
τεχ]νήεις [καὶ] χωλὸς ἐὼν.[
]ς πρό[σθε π]οδῶν ἀγαθ[
]μενω[...]τεεις κοτε.[
]ν μη[....]ων σε τεὸς.[

1. TO DIONYSUS

pied by a deep . . . extended . . . away from the surge . . . by skill . . . lovely pas[tures . . .

(B) (Vine rows) luxuriant with their own dark grape clusters . . .

(C) (*Zeus speaks to Hera*) ". . . you wish. What else could happen to [you worse than this? I was stupi]d myself, from [. . .] left of his own accord [. . .] as they [sur]mise ever [. . . he tricked you and pu]t you in hellish fett[ers. Who] could set y[ou] free, my dear? [A painful b]elt encircles y[our body, while he], heed[ing neither co]mmand [nor entreaty, has formed] an unshakeable r[esolve in his heart. It's a cruel] son you have borne, sis[ter . . . craf]ty, even though a cripple [. . .] in front [of . . .] feet good [. . .]

C suppl. Grenfell–Hunt (5 ἀλυκτ[οπέδηισι, 7 πάν]τοθεν [ἀμ]φιβέβηκε, 9 ἀστυ[φέλι]κτον, 11–12), Ganszyniec (8 ἐφη-[μοσύ]νης μεμν[ημένος, 21 ἰδέε[ιν]), J. U. Powell (6 ἐπιζώ-[στρα δ' ἀλεγεινή, 19 πινυτόφ[ρονες), West

15   ]ο καὶ [. . .]έουσα φιλο[
      ]σι χωομε[ν . .] καὶ μ.[
      θυμὸ]ν ἄρ᾽ εἰσώμεσθα σιδήρ[εον εἴ τι μαλάξει.
      δοιοὶ] γὰρ πάρεασι τεοῖς [καμάτοισιν ἀρωγοί
      υἱέες] ἡμέτεροι πι̣ν̣υ̣τόφ[ρονες· ἔστι μὲν Ἄρης,
20   ὃς θοὸ]ν ἔγχος ἀ̣νέσχε τα̣[λαύρινος πολεμιστής
      ]ην ἰδέε̣[ιν] καὶ παλ[
      ἔστι δὲ] καὶ Διόνυσος, ε.[
      αὐτὰρ] ἐμοὶ μὴ δῆριν ἐγει̣[ρέτω· ἥ τε κεραυνοῖς
      εἶσι]ν ὑφ᾽ ἡμετέροις πε̣[πληγμένος οὐ κατὰ κόσμον.
25   ]ασθε γλυκερῶν επ[
      ]εως πάϊς οὗτος ἐμο̣[

D (codex M)

"καί οἱ ἀναστήσουσιν ἀγάλματα πόλλ᾽ ἐνὶ νηοῖς.
ὡς δὲ †τὰ μὲν τριάσοι πάντως† τριετηρίσιν αἰεί
ἄνθρωποι ῥέξουσι τελη έσσας ἑκατόμβας."

      ἦ, καὶ κυανέῃσιν ἐπ᾽ ὀφρύσι νεῦσε Κρονίων·
5   ἀμβρόσιαι δ᾽ ἄρα χαῖται ἐπερρώσαντο ἄνακτος
    κρατὸς ἀπ᾽ ἀθανάτοιο, μέγαν δ᾽ ἐλέλιξεν Ὄλυμπον.
    {ὣς εἰπὼν ἐπένευσε καρήατι μητίετα Ζεύς.}

      ἵληθ᾽, Εἰραφιῶτα γυναιμανές· οἱ δέ σ᾽ ἀοιδοί
      ᾄδομεν ἀρχόμενοι λήγοντές τ᾽· οὐδέ πῃ ἔστιν
10   σεῖ᾽ ἐπιληθόμενον ἱερῆς μεμνῆσθαι ἀοιδῆς.
     {καὶ σὺ μὲν οὕτω χαῖρε, Διώνυσ᾽ εἰραφιῶτα,
     σὺν μητρὶ Σεμέλῃ, ἥν περ καλέουσι Θυώνην.}

30

wrathful [. . .] . . . angry [. . .] Let us find out [if he will soften his hear]t of iron. For there are [two] clever [sons] of mine at hand [to help with] your [suffering. There is Ares, who] has raised his [keen] spear, a th[ick-hide fighter . . .] to look and bra[ndish . . .; and there is] also Dionysus [. . . But let him] not stir up a quarrel with me, [otherwise he will be on his way belab]ored by my [thunderbolts in no tidy style . . .] of sweet [. . .] this lad [. . . "

(D) ". . . And they will set up many effigies in his shrines; and as there are three . . ., so at triennial festivals people will ever sacrifice perfect hecatombs."

So spoke the son of Kronos, and confirmed it with a nod of his sable brows; and the lord's ambrosial locks danced up from his immortal head, and he sent a tremor through great Olympus.

Be propitious, Bull god, women-frenzier! We singers sing of you as we begin and as we end; there is no way to take heed for holy singing while heedless of you.[1]

---

[1] The text in M incorporates two alternative endings to the hymn; the first looks the more authentic. The second reads: "So saying, wise Zeus confirmed it with a nod of his head. So I salute you, Dionysus, Bull god, together with your mother Semele, whom they call Thyone."

D 2 τάμεν Allen–Sikes   τρία, σοὶ Ruhnkenius
4–6 (= Il. 1.528–530) damn. Ilgen, 7 Càssola
7 ἐπένευσε Ruhnkenius: ἐκέλευσε M
8–10 damn. Hermann, 11–12 West

2. ΕΙΣ ΔΗΜΗΤΡΑΝ

Δήμητρ᾽ ἠΰκομον σεμνὴν θεὸν ἄρχομ᾽ ἀείδειν,
αὐτὴν ἠδὲ θύγατρα τανίσφυρον, ἣν Ἀϊδωνεὺς
ἥρπαξεν, δῶκεν δὲ βαρύκτυπος εὐρύοπα Ζεύς,
νόσφιν Δήμητρος χρυσαόρου ἀγλαοκάρπου
5 παίζουσαν κούρηισι σὺν Ὠκεανοῦ βαθυκόλποις
ἄνθεά τ᾽ αἰνυμένην ῥόδα καὶ κρόκον ἠδ᾽ ἴα καλά
λειμῶν᾽ ἂμ μαλακὸν καὶ ἀγαλλίδας ἠδ᾽ ὑάκινθον
νάρκισσόν θ᾽, ὃν φῦσε δόλον καλυκώπιδι κούρηι
Γαῖα Διὸς βουλῆισι, χαριζομένη Πολυδέκτηι,
10 θαυμαστὸν γανόωντα, σέβας τό γε πᾶσιν ἰδέσθαι
ἀθανάτοις τε θεοῖς ἠδὲ θνητοῖς ἀνθρώποις.
τοῦ καὶ ἀπὸ ῥίζης ἑκατὸν κάρα ἐξεπεφύκει
κηώδης τ᾽ ὀδμή· πᾶς δ᾽ οὐρανὸς εὐρὺς ὕπερθεν
γαῖά τε πᾶσ᾽ ἐγέλασσε καὶ ἁλμυρὸν οἶδμα
θαλάσσης.
15 ἡ δ᾽ ἄρα θαμβήσασ᾽ ὠρέξατο χερσὶν ἅμ᾽ ἄμφω
καλὸν ἄθυρμα λαβεῖν· χάνε δὲ χθὼν εὐρυάγυια
Νύσιον ἂμ πεδίον, τῆι ὄρουσεν ἄναξ Πολυδέγμων
ἵπποις ἀθανάτοισι, Κρόνου πολυώνυμος υἱός.
ἁρπάξας δ᾽ ἀέκουσαν ἐπὶ χρυσέοισιν ὄχοισιν
20 ἦγ᾽ ὀλοφυρομένην· ἰάχησε δ᾽ ἄρ᾽ ὄρθια φωνῆι
κεκλομένη πατέρα Κρονίδην ὕπατον καὶ ἄριστον.
οὐδέ τις ἀθανάτων οὐδὲ θνητῶν ἀνθρώπων

1 θεὸν Voss: θεὰν M
2 τανίσφυρον Richardson: τανύ- M

2. TO DEMETER

Of Demeter the lovely-haired, the august goddess first I sing, of her and her slender-ankled daughter, whom Aïdoneus[2] seized by favor of heavy-booming, wide-sounding Zeus as she frolicked, away from Demeter of the golden sword and resplendent fruit, with the deep-bosomed daughters of Ocean, picking flowers across the soft meadow, roses and saffron and lovely violets, iris and hyacinth, and narcissus, that Earth put forth as a snare for the maiden with eyes like buds by the will of Zeus, as a favor to the Hospitable One.[3] It shone wondrously, an awe-inspiring thing to see both for the immortal gods and for mortal men. From its root a hundred heads grew out, and a perfumed odor; the whole broad sky above and the whole earth smiled, and the salty swell of the sea.

In amazement she reached out with both hands to take the pretty plaything. But the broad-wayed earth gaped open on the plain of Nysa,[4] and there the Hospitable Lord rushed forth with his immortal steeds, Kronos' son whose names are many. Seizing her by force, he began to drive her off on his golden chariot, with her wailing and screaming as she called on her father Zeus, the highest and noblest. But no one heard her voice, none of the immortals

---

[2] Hades.   [3] A name for Hades, who takes everyone into his house. He is also called the Major General, because he has so many under his command.   [4] This mythical locality, variously located, is normally associated with Dionysus, as in Hymn 1 fr. A 9.

---

10 τό γε Goodwin: τότε Π1 M
13 κηώδης τ' Ludwich: κώδιστ' M

ἤκουσεν φωνῆς, οὐδ' ἀγλαόκαρποι ἐλαῖαι,
εἰ μὴ Περσαίου θυγάτηρ ἀταλὰ φρονέουσα
25 ἄϊεν ἐξ ἄντρου, Ἑκάτη λιπαροκρήδεμνος,
Ἥλιός τε ἄναξ Ὑπερίονος ἀγλαὸς υἱός,
κούρης κεκλομένης πατέρα Κρονίδην· ὁ δὲ νόσφιν
ἧστο θεῶν ἀπάνευθε πολυλλίστωι ἐνὶ νηῶι
δέγμενος ἱερὰ καλὰ παρὰ θνητῶν ἀνθρώπων.
30   τὴν δ' ἀεκαζομένην ἦγεν Διὸς ἐννεσίηισιν
πατροκασίγνητος πολυσημάντωρ Πολυδέγμων
ἵπποις ἀθανάτοισι, Κρόνου πολυώνυμος υἱός.
ὄφρα μὲν οὖν γαῖάν τε καὶ οὐρανὸν ἀστερόεντα
λεῦσσε θεὰ καὶ πόντον ἀγάρροον ἰχθυόεντα
35 αὐγάς τ' ἠελίου, ἔτι δ' ἤλπετο μητέρα κεδνήν
ὄψεσθαι καὶ φῦλα θεῶν αἰειγενετάων,
τόφρα οἱ ἐλπὶς ἔθελγε μέγαν νόον ἀχνυμένης περ.
ἤχησαν δ' ὀρέων κορυφαὶ καὶ βένθεα πόντου
φωνῆι ὑπ' ἀθανάτηι· τῆς δ' ἔκλυε πότνια μήτηρ,
40 ὀξὺ δέ μιν κραδίην ἄχος ἔλλαβεν, ἀμφὶ δὲ χαίταις
ἀμβροσίαις κρήδεμνα δαΐζετο χερσὶ φίλησιν.
κυάνεον δὲ κάλυμμα κατ' ἀμφοτέρων βάλετ' ὤμων,
σεύατο δ' ὥς τ' οἰωνὸς ἐπὶ τραφερήν τε καὶ ὑγρήν
μαιομένη. τῆι δ' οὔ τις ἐτήτυμα μυθήσασθαι
45 ἤθελεν οὔτε θεῶν οὔτε θνητῶν ἀνθρώπων,
οὔτ' οἰωνῶν τις τῆι ἐτήτυμος ἄγγελος ἦλθεν.
    ἐννῆμαρ μὲν ἔπειτα κατὰ χθόνα πότνια Δηώ
στρωφᾶτ', αἰθομένας δαΐδας μετὰ χερσὶν ἔχουσα·

24 Περσαίη West

or of mortal men, nor yet the olive trees with their resplendent fruit—except that Perses' daughter still innocent of heart, Hecate of the glossy veil, heard from her cave, and so did the lord Helios, Hyperion's resplendent son, as the maiden called on her father Zeus: he, however, was seated apart, away from the gods, in his prayerful temple, receiving fine offerings from mortals.

So, despite her resistance, her father's brother was carrying her off by Zeus' design, the Major General, the Hospitable One, Kronos' son whose names are many, with his immortal steeds. Now so long as the goddess could still see the earth and the starry sky and the strong-flowing fishy sea and the light of the sun, and yet expected to see her good mother again and the families of gods who are for ever, so long her great mind had the comfort of hope, despite her distress. The mountain peaks and the sea deeps rang with the sound of her divine voice; and her lady mother heard it, and a sharp pain seized her heart, and the veil over her ambrosial locks tore apart under her hands. Throwing a dark covering over her shoulders, she sped like a bird over land and water in her search. But there was no one prepared to tell her the truth, either of gods or mortals, nor did any of the birds come to her with reliable news.

For nine days then did the lady Deo[5] roam the earth with burning torches in her hands, and in her grief she did

[5] A name of Demeter.

28 πολυλλίστωι Ruhnkenius: πολυκλίστω M
35 δ' om. Π1

οὐδέ ποτ᾽ ἀμβροσίης καὶ νέκταρος ἡδυπότοιο
50 πάσσατ᾽ ἀκηχεμένη, οὐδὲ χρόα βάλλετο λουτροῖς.
ἀλλ᾽ ὅτε δὴ δεκάτη οἱ ἐπήλυθε φαινόλις ἠώς,
ἤντετό οἱ Ἑκάτη, σέλας ἐν χείρεσσιν ἔχουσα,
καί ῥά οἱ ἀγγελέουσα ἔπος φάτο φώνησέν τε·
    "πότνια Δημήτηρ ὡρηφόρε ἀγλαόδωρε,
55 τίς θεῶν οὐρανίων ἠὲ θνητῶν ἀνθρώπων
ἥρπασε Περσεφόνην καὶ σὸν φίλον ἤκαχε θυμόν;
φωνῆς γὰρ ἤκουσ᾽, ἀτὰρ οὐκ ἴδον ὀφθαλμοῖσιν
ὅς τις ἔην· σοὶ δ᾽ ὦκα λέγω νημερτέα πάντα."
    ὣς ἄρ᾽ ἔφη Ἑκάτη· τὴν δ᾽ οὐκ ἠμείβετο μύθωι
60 Ῥείης ἠυκόμου θυγάτηρ, ἀλλ᾽ ὦκα σὺν αὐτῆι
ἤιξ᾽ αἰθομένας δαΐδας μετὰ χερσὶν ἔχουσα.
Ἥλιον δ᾽ ἵκοντο θεῶν σκοπὸν ἠδὲ καὶ ἀνδρῶν,
στὰν δ᾽ ἵππων προπάροιθε καὶ εἴρετο δῖα θεάων·
    "Ἥλι᾽, αἴδεσσαί με †θέας ὕπερ, εἴ ποτε δή σεο
65 ἢ ἔπει ἢ ἔργωι κραδίην καὶ θυμὸν ἴηνα.
κούρην τὴν ἔτεκον, γλυκερὸν θάλος, εἴδεϊ κυδρήν,
τῆς ἀδινὴν ὄπ᾽ ἄκουσα δι᾽ αἰθέρος ἀτρυγέτοιο
ὥς τε βιαζομένης, ἀτὰρ οὐκ ἴδον ὀφθαλμοῖσιν.
ἀλλὰ σὺ γὰρ δὴ πᾶσαν ἐπὶ χθόνα καὶ κατὰ πόντον
70 αἰθέρος ἐκ δίης καταδέρκεαι ἀκτίνεσσιν,
νημερτέως μοι ἔνισπε φίλον τέκος εἴ που ὄπωπας
ὅς τις νόσφιν ἐμεῖο λαβὼν ἀέκουσαν ἀνάγκηι
οἴχεται ἠὲ θεῶν ἢ καὶ θνητῶν ἀνθρώπων."
    ὣς φάτο, τὴν δ᾽ Ὑπεριονίδης ἠμείβετο μύθωι·
75 "Ῥείης ἠυκόμου θύγατερ, Δήμητερ ἄνασσα,
εἰδήσεις· δὴ γὰρ μέγα ‹σ᾽› ἅζομαι ἠδ᾽ ἐλεαίρω

not once taste ambrosia and the nectar sweet to drink, nor did she splash her body with washing water. But when the tenth bright dawn came upon her, Hecate met her with a light in her hand, and spoke to give her news:

"Lady Demeter, bringer of resplendent gifts in season, who of the heavenly gods or of mortal men has seized Persephone and grieved your dear heart? I heard her voice, but I did not see who it was. I am telling you promptly the whole truth of it."

So spoke Hecate; but lovely-haired Rhea's daughter said nothing in answer, but quickly ran with her, with burning torches in her hands. They came to Helios, the watcher of gods and men, and stood in front of his chariot, and the goddess asked:

"Helios, have regard for me, if ever I have gladdened your heart either by word or deed. The maiden I bore, my sweet sprig, with looks to be proud of—I heard her voice loud through the fathomless air as if she was being taken by force, but I did not see it. You, however, look down from the sky with your rays over the whole earth and sea: so tell me truly if perchance you have seen who it is, of gods or mortals, that has taken her away from me by force against her will and gone off with her."

So she spoke, and Hyperion's son answered, "Daughter of lovely-haired Rhea, lady Demeter, you shall know, for I greatly revere you, and I pity you in your sorrow over your

---

49 ἡδυπότοιο Ruhnkenius: ἥδε πότοιο M
51 φαινόλις Ruhnkenius: φαινόλη M
70–1 καταδέρκεται ... ὅπωπεν M: corr. Ruhnkenius
75 θύγατερ Wolf: θυγάτηρ M
76 σ᾽ add. quidam ap. Ruhnkenium

ἀχνυμένην περὶ παιδὶ τανισφύρωι. οὐδέ τις ἄλλος
αἴτιος ἀθανάτων εἰ μὴ νεφεληγερέτα Ζεύς,
ὅς μιν ἔδωκ᾽ Ἀΐδηι θαλερὴν κεκλῆσθαι ἄκοιτιν
80 αὐτοκασιγνήτωι· ὃ δ᾽ ὑπὸ ζόφον ἠερόεντα
ἁρπάξας ἵπποισιν ἄγεν μεγάλα ἰάχουσαν.
ἀλλά, θεά, κατάπαυε μέγαν γόον· οὐδέ τί σε χρή
μὰψ αὔτως ἄπλητον ἔχειν χόλον. οὔ τοι ἀεικής
γαμβρὸς ἐν ἀθανάτοις πολυσημάντωρ Ἀϊδωνεύς,
85 αὐτοκασίγνητος καὶ ὁμόσπορος· ἀμφὶ δὲ τιμήν,
ἔλλαχεν ὡς τὰ πρῶτα διάτριχα δασμὸς ἐτύχθη·
τοῖς μεταναιετάει, τῶν ἔλλαχε κοίρανος εἶναι."
    ὣς εἰπὼν ἵπποισιν ἐκέκλετο, τοὶ δ᾽ ὑπ᾽ ὀμοκλῆς
ῥίμφα φέρον θοὸν ἅρμα τανύπτεροι ὥς τ᾽ οἰωνοί·
90 τὴν δ᾽ ἄχος αἰνότερον καὶ κύντερον ἵκετο θυμόν.
    χωσαμένη δήπειτα κελαινεφέϊ Κρονίωνι
νοσφισθεῖσα θεῶν ἀγορὴν καὶ μακρὸν Ὄλυμπον
ὤιχετ᾽ ἐπ᾽ ἀνθρώπων πόλιας καὶ πίονα ἔργα,
εἶδος ἀμαλδύνουσα πολὺν χρόνον· οὐδέ τις ἀνδρῶν
95 εἰσορόων γίνωσκε βαθυζώνων τε γυναικῶν,
πρίν γ᾽ ὅτε δὴ Κελεοῖο δαΐφρονος ἵκετο δῶμα,
ὃς τότ᾽ Ἐλευσῖνος θυοέσσης κοίρανος ἦεν.
ἕζετο δ᾽ ἐγγὺς ὁδοῖο φίλον τετιημένη ἦτορ
Παρθενίωι φρέατι, ὅθεν ὑδρεύοντο πολῖται,
100 ἐν σκιῆι, αὐτὰρ ὕπερθε πεφύκει θάμνος ἐλαίης,

77 τανυσφύρω M
87 μεταναιετάει Voss, -άειν Valckenaer: μετάναίεται M
98 τετιημένος M: corr. Ruhnkenius

slender-ankled child. No other of the immortals is to
blame but the cloud-gatherer Zeus, who has given her to
Hades, his own brother, to be known as his buxom wife. He
seized her, and was taking her on his chariot down to the
misty darkness, while she screamed loudly. So goddess,
end your loud lamenting; there is no call for you to rage for
ever like this to no purpose. Aïdoneus, the Major General,
is not an unsuitable son-in-law to have among the gods,
your own brother, of the same seed. As for privileges, he
has the portion he was allotted originally in the threefold
division;[6] he dwells among those whose ruler he was allot-
ted to be."

With these words he urged on his horses, and they at his
command quickly bore on the swift chariot, like spread-
winged birds, while a harsher and crueller grief struck her
to the heart.

Then in her anger at the dark-cloud son of Kronos she
turned away from the gods' assembly and long Olympus,
and for a long time she travelled to the communities of
men and their rich farmlands, effacing her beauty, and no
man or deep-girt woman looking upon her knew who she
was, until the time when she came to the house of wise
Keleos, who was then the ruler of fragrant Eleusis. She had
sat down at the roadside, sick at heart, at the Maiden's
Well, from where the people of the community used to
draw water; she was in the shade, with a bushy olive grow-

---

[6] The universe was divided by lot among the three sons of
Kronos; Zeus got the sky, Poseidon the sea, and Hades the under-
world (*Iliad* 15.187–192).

γρηὶ παλαιγενέϊ ἐναλίγκιος, ἥ τε τόκοιο
εἴργηται δώρων τε φιλοστεφάνου Ἀφροδίτης,
οἷαί τε τροφοί εἰσι θεμιστοπόλων βασιλήων
παίδων καὶ ταμίαι κατὰ δώματα ἠχήεντα.

105   τὴν δὲ ἴδον Κελεοῖο Ἐλευσινίδαο θύγατρες
ἐρχόμεναι μεθ' ὕδωρ εὐήρυτον, ὄφρα φέροιεν
κάλπισι χαλκείηισι φίλα πρὸς δώματα πατρός,
τέσσαρες, ὥς τε θεαὶ κουρήιον ἄνθος ἔχουσαι,
Καλλιδίκη καὶ Κλεισιδίκη Δημώ τ' ἐρόεσσα
110 Καλλιθόη θ', ἣ τῶν προγενεστάτη ἦεν ἁπασῶν·
οὐδ' ἔγνον· χαλεποὶ δὲ θεοὶ θνητοῖσιν ὁρᾶσθαι.
ἀγχοῦ ⟨δ'⟩ ἱστάμεναι ἔπεα πτερόεντα προσηύδων·
   "τίς πόθεν ἐσσί, γρηῦ, παλαιγενέων ἀνθρώπων;
τίπτε δὲ νόσφι πόληος ἀπέστιχες, οὐδὲ δόμοισιν
115 πίλνασαι; ἔνθα γυναῖκες ἀνὰ μέγαρα σκιόεντα
τηλίκαι ὡς σύ περ ὧδε καὶ ὁπλότεραι γεγάασιν,
αἵ κέ σε φίλωνται ἠμὲν ἔπει ἠδὲ καὶ ἔργωι."
   ὣς ἔφαθ', ἢ δ' ἐπέεσσιν ἀμείβετο πότνα θεάων·
"τέκνα φίλ', αἵ τινές ἐστε γυναικῶν θηλυτεράων,
120 χαίρετ', ἐγὼ δ' ὑμῖν μυθήσομαι· οὔ τοι ἀεικές
ὑμῖν εἰρομένηισιν ἀληθέα μυθήσασθαι.
Δὼς ⟨μὲν⟩ ἐμοί γ' ὄνομ' ἐστί· τὸ γὰρ θέτο πότνια
   μήτηρ·
νῦν αὖτε Κρήτηθεν ἐπ' εὐρέα νῶτα θαλάσσης
ἤλυθον οὐκ ἐθέλουσα, βίηι δ' ἀέκουσαν ἀνάγκηι
125 ἄνδρες ληϊστῆρες ἀπήγαγον. οἳ μὲν ἔπειτα
νηὶ θοῆι Θορικόνδε κατέσχεθον, ἔνθα γυναῖκες
ἠπείρου ἐπέβησαν ἀολλέες ἠδὲ καὶ αὐτοί

ing overhead, and she looked like an ancient crone, debarred from motherhood and the blessings of garland-loving Aphrodite: a woman like those that are nurses to the children of lawgiver kings, or housekeepers in their bustling mansions.

The daughters of Keleos the Eleusinid caught sight of her as they came to draw water and carry it in bronze pails to their father's dear house—four of them, like goddesses in the flower of their girlhood, Callidice, Clisidice, lovely Demo, and Callithoe, the eldest of them all. They did not recognize her, for gods are hard for mortals to see, but stood close to her and spoke winged words:

"Who are you, old woman, of those born long ago? Where are you from? And why have you walked so far from the town, instead of going to the houses, where there are women of your age and others younger in the shady halls, who might greet you and treat you kindly?"

So she spoke, and the lady goddess answered: "My dears, good day to you, whoever of womankind you are. I will tell you; it is not improper, since you ask, to tell you the truth. Bounty is my name that my lady mother gave me. But now I have come from Crete over the sea's broad back, not from choice, but by force, against my will, some free-booters took me away. They put in at Thorikos in their swift ship; the women all disembarked, and they themselves set

---

111 ἔγνον Cobet: ἔγνων M   112 δ᾽ add. Ruhnkenius

115 πίλνασαι Voss: πιλνᾶς M   118 ἔφαν Voss

119 φίλα· τίνες M: corr. Fontein   120 τοι Fontein: τι M

121 εἰρομένοισιν M: corr. Ruhnkenius

122 μὲν add. Brunck

δεῖπνον ἐπηρτύνοντο παρὰ πρυμνήσια νηός·
ἀλλ' ἐμοὶ οὐ δόρποιο μελίφρονος ἤρατο θυμός,
130 λάθρηι δ' ὁρμηθεῖσα δι' ἠπείροιο μελαίνης
φεῦγον ὑπερφιάλους σημάντορας, ὄφρα κε μή με
ἀπριάτην περάσαντες ἐμῆς ἀποναίατο τιμῆς.
οὕτω δεῦρ' ἱκόμην ἀλαλημένη, οὐδέ τι οἶδα
ἥ τις δὴ γαῖ' ἐστὶ καὶ οἵ τινες ἐγγεγάασιν.
135 ἀλλ' ὑμῖν μὲν πάντες Ὀλύμπια δώματ' ἔχοντες
δοῖεν κουριδίους ἄνδρας καὶ τέκνα τεκέσθαι,
ὡς ἐθέλουσι τοκῆες· ἔμ' αὖτ' οἰκτίρατε, κοῦραι,

. . . .

προφρονέως, φίλα τέκνα, τέων πρὸς δώμαθ' ἵκωμαι
ἀνέρος ἠδὲ γυναικός, ἵνά σφισιν ἐργάζωμαι
140 πρόφρων, οἷα γυναικὸς ἀφήλικος ἔργα τέτυκται.
καί κεν παῖδα νεογνὸν ἐν ἀγκοίνηισιν ἔχουσα
καλὰ τιθηνοίμην, καὶ δώματα τηρήσαιμι,
καί κε λέχος στορέσαιμι μυχῶι θαλάμων εὐπήκτων
δεσπόσυνον, καί κ' ἔργα διδασκήσαιμι γυναῖκας."
145 φῆ ῥα θεά· τὴν δ' αὐτίκ' ἀμείβετο παρθένος ἀδμής
Καλλιδίκη, Κελεοῖο θυγατρῶν εἶδος ἀρίστη·
"μαῖα, θεῶν μὲν δῶρα καὶ ἀχνύμενοί περ ἀνάγκηι
τέτλαμεν ἄνθρωποι· δὴ γὰρ πολὺ φέρτεροί εἰσιν.
ταῦτα δέ τοι σαφέως ὑποθήσομαι ἠδ' ὀνομήνω
150 ἀνέρας, οἷσιν ἔπεστι μέγα κράτος ἐνθάδε τιμῆς
δήμου τε προὔχουσιν ἰδὲ κρήδεμνα πόληος
εἰρύαται βουλῆισι καὶ ἰθείηισι δίκηισιν.
ἠμὲν Τριπτολέμου πυκιμήδεος ἠδὲ Διόκλου
ἠδὲ Πολυξείνου καὶ ἀμύμονος Εὐμόλποιο

about preparing their supper by the ship's stern cables. But I had no appetite for dinner's delights: I slipped away over the dark land and fled from those imperious ruffians to stop them selling me unbought and profiting from my sale value. That is how I have come wandering here. I don't know what country it is or who are its people. So, may all the Olympians grant you husbands and childbearing as your parents wish, only take pity on me, girls < . . . And tell me > kindly, my dears, whose house I am to go to, what man's and wife's, so that I can do for them with a will such work as suits a woman past her prime. I could hold a baby in my arms and nurse him well, I could look after the house, and make the master's bed in the sturdy chamber's recess, and teach the women their tasks."

So said the goddess; and straightway the virgin Callidice, fairest of Keleos' daughters, replied: "Nanna, what the gods give, we humans endure, painful as it is, for they are far our superiors. But I will give you this sure advice and tell you the names of the men who control privilege here, who stand out from the people and protect the city's ramparts by their counsel and straight judgments. Wise Triptolemus and Diocles, Polyxenus and worthy

---

134 ἐγγεγάασιν Ruhnkenius: ἐκγεγάασιν M
137 ἔμ' Fontein: ἐμὲ δ' M   lacunam stat. Allen
144 διδασκήσαιμι γυναῖκας Voss: διαθήσαιμι γυναικὸς M

155 καὶ Δολίχου καὶ πατρὸς ἀγήνορος ἡμετέροιο,
τῶν πάντων ἄλοχοι κατὰ δώματα πορσαίνουσιν·
τάων οὐκ ἄν τίς σε κατὰ πρώτιστον ὀπωπήν
εἶδος ἀτιμήσασα δόμων ἀπονοσφίσσειεν,
ἀλλά σε δέξονται· δὴ γὰρ θεοείκελός ἐσσι.
160 εἰ δ᾽ ἐθέλεις, ἐπίμεινον, ἵνα πρὸς δώματα πατρός
ἔλθωμεν καὶ μητρὶ βαθυζώνωι Μετανείρηι
εἴπωμεν τάδε πάντα διαμπερές, αἴ κέ σ᾽ ἀνώγηι
ἡμέτερόνδ᾽ ἰέναι, μηδ᾽ ἄλλων δώματ᾽ ἐρευνᾶν.
τηλύγετος δέ οἱ υἱὸς ἐνὶ μεγάρωι εὐπήκτωι
165 ὀψίγονος τρέφεται, πολυεύχετος ἀσπάσιός τε.
εἰ τόν γ᾽ ἐκθρέψαιο καὶ ἥβης μέτρον ἵκοιτο,
ἦ ῥά κέ τίς σε ἰδοῦσα γυναικῶν θηλυτεράων
ζηλώσαι· τόσα κέν τοι ἀπὸ θρεπτήρια δοίη."
    ὣς ἔφαθ᾽· ἡ δ᾽ ἐπένευσε καρήατι, ταὶ δὲ φαεινά
170 πλησάμεναι ὕδατος φέρον ἄγγεα κυδιάουσαι.
ῥίμφα δὲ πατρὸς ἵκοντο μέγαν δόμον, ὦκα δὲ μητρί
ἔννεπον ὡς εἶδόν τε καὶ ἔκλυον· ἡ δὲ μάλ᾽ ὦκα
ἐλθούσας ἐκέλευε καλεῖν ἐπ᾽ ἀπείρονι μισθῶι.
αἱ δ᾽ ὥς τ᾽ ἢ ἔλαφοι ἢ πόρτιες εἴαρος ὥρηι
175 ἄλλοντ᾽ ἂν λειμῶνα κορεσσάμεναι φρένα φορβῆς,
ὣς αἱ ἐπισχόμεναι ἑανῶν πτύχας ἱμεροέντων
ἤιξαν κοίλην κατ᾽ ἀμαξιτόν, ἀμφὶ δὲ χαῖται
ὤμοις ἀίσσοντο κροκηίωι ἄνθει ὁμοῖαι.
τέτμον δ᾽ ἐγγὺς ὁδοῦ κυδρὴν θεόν, ἔνθα πάρος περ
180 κάλλιπον· αὐτὰρ ἔπειτα φίλα πρὸς δώματα πατρός

167 ἦ ῥα Matthiae (cf. 222): ῥεῖά Μ

44

Eumolpus, Dolichus and our own noble father all have wives managing in the house, not one of whom would scorn your appearance on sight and send you away; no, they will take you in, for really, there is something almost divine about you. Or if you like, wait here while we go home and tell our mother, deep-girt Metaneira, this whole story, and see if she will say you should come to our house and not go searching out other people's. She has a darling late-born son being nursed in the sturdy mansion, the happy answer to many prayers: if you were to raise him and see him to young manhood's measure, then any woman who saw you might well envy you, so richly would she[7] repay you for his nurturing."

So she spoke; and Demeter nodded her agreement. So they filled their gleaming pails with water and carried them away with heads held high. They soon reached their father's mansion, and quickly told their mother what they had seen and heard. She told them to go quickly and invite the woman to come, at an unstinting wage. They then, like deer or heifers in springtime who frisk over the meadow after feeding their fill, drew up the folds of their lovely dresses and ran along the rutted carriageway, their saffron-yellow hair flying about their shoulders. They found the glorious goddess by the roadside where they had left her, and then they led the way to their father's dear house,

---

[7] Or perhaps "he," the child when grown up.

---

174 τ᾽ ἢ Brunck: τοι M
175 φορβῆς Voss: φορβῇ M
179 θεόν Hermann: θεὰν M

45

ἡγέονθ᾽, ἣ δ᾽ ἄρ᾽ ὄπισθε φίλον τετιημένη ἦτορ
στεῖχε, κατὰ κρῆθεν κεκαλυμμένη, ἀμφὶ δὲ πέπλος
κυάνεος ῥαδινοῖσι θεῆς ἐλελίζετο ποσσίν.
  αἶψα δὲ δώμαθ᾽ ἵκοντο διοτρεφέος Κελεοῖο,

185 βὰν δὲ δι᾽ αἰθούσης, ἔνθά σφισι πότνια μήτηρ
ἧστο παρὰ σταθμὸν τέγεος πύκα ποιητοῖο,
παῖδ᾽ ὑπὸ κόλπωι ἔχουσα, νέον θάλος· αἱ δὲ παρ᾽
    αὐτήν
ἔδραμον. ἣ δ᾽ ἄρ᾽ ἐπ᾽ οὐδὸν ἔβη ποσί, καί ῥα
    μελάθρου
κῦρε κάρη, πλῆσεν δὲ θύρας σέλαος θείοιο.

190 τὴν δ᾽ αἰδώς τε σέβας τε ἰδὲ χλωρὸν δέος εἷλεν·
εἶξε δέ οἱ κλισμοῖο καὶ ἑδριάασθαι ἄνωγεν.
ἀλλ᾽ οὐ Δημήτηρ ὡρηφόρος ἀγλαόδωρος
ἤθελεν ἑδριάασθαι ἐπὶ κλισμοῖο φαεινοῦ,
ἀλλ᾽ ἀκέουσα ἔμιμνε κατ᾽ ὄμματα καλὰ βαλοῦσα,

195 πρίν γ᾽ ὅτε δή οἱ ἔθηκεν Ἰάμβη κέδν᾽ εἰδυῖα
πηκτὸν ἕδος, καθύπερθε δ᾽ ἐπ᾽ ἀργύφεον βάλε
    κῶας⟨ς⟩.
ἔνθα καθεζομένη προκατέσχετο χερσὶ καλύπτρην·
δηρὸν δ᾽ ἄφθογγος τετιημένη ἧστ᾽ ἐπὶ δίφρου,
οὐδέ τιν᾽ οὔτ᾽ ἔπεϊ προσπτύσσετο οὔτέ τι ἔργωι,

200 ἀλλ᾽ ἀγέλαστος ἄπαστος ἐδητύος ἠδὲ ποτῆτος
ἧστο, πόθωι μινύθουσα βαθυζώνοιο θυγατρός,
πρίν γ᾽ ὅτε δὴ χλεύηις μιν Ἰάμβη κέδν᾽ εἰδυῖα
πολλὰ παρασκώπτουσ᾽ ἐτρέψατο πότνιαν ἁγνήν
μειδῆσαι γελάσαι τε καὶ ἵλαον σχεῖν θυμόν·

205 ἣ δή οἱ καὶ ἔπειτα μεθύστερον εὔαδεν ὀργαῖς.

and she walked behind with sorrowing heart, a veil over her head, while the dark robe fluttered about the goddess's slender calves.

Soon they came to the house of Keleos, nursling of Zeus, and passed through the portico to where their lady mother sat by a pillar of the strong-built roof with her young sprig of a child in her bosom, and they ran to join her. Then Demeter stepped onto the threshold: her head reached to the rafter, and she filled the doorway with divine radiance. The queen was seized by awe and reverence and sallow fear; she gave up her couch for her, and invited her to sit down. But Demeter, bringer of resplendent gifts in season, did not want to be seated on the gleaming couch, but stood in silence, her lovely eyes downcast, until dutiful Iambe set a jointed stool for her and laid a shining white fleece over it. There she sat, holding her veil before her face, and for a long time she remained there on the seat in silent sorrow. She greeted no one with word or movement, but sat there unsmiling, tasting neither food nor drink, pining for her deep-girt daughter, until at last dutiful Iambe with ribaldry and many a jest diverted the holy lady so that she smiled and laughed and became benevolent— Iambe who ever since has found favor with her moods.[8]

[8] Or perhaps "in her ceremonies." On the significance of the stool with the fleece and of Iambe's behavior see the Introduction.

205 εὔαδ' ἑορταῖς Voss

47

τῆι δὲ δέπας Μετάνειρα δίδου μελιηδέος οἴνου
πλήσασ᾽, ἢ δ᾽ ἀνένευσ᾽· οὐ γὰρ θεμιτόν οἱ ἔφασκεν
πίνειν οἶνον ἐρυθρόν, ἄνωγε δ᾽ ἄρ᾽ ἄλφι καὶ ὕδωρ
δοῦναι μείξασαν πιέμεν γληχῶνι τερείνηι.
210 ἡ δὲ κυκεῶ τεύξασα θεᾶι πόρεν, ὡς ἐκέλευεν·
δεξαμένη δ᾽ ὁσίης ἕνεκεν πολυπότνια Δηώ

.   .   .   .

τῆισι δὲ μύθων ἦρχεν ἐΰζωνος Μετάνειρα·
"χαῖρε, γύναι, ἐπεὶ οὔ σε κακῶν ἄπ᾽ ἔολπα τοκήων
ἔμμεναι, ἀλλ᾽ ἀγαθῶν· ἐπί τοι πρέπει ὄμμασιν
αἰδώς
215 καὶ χάρις, ὡς εἴ πέρ τε θεμιστοπόλων βασιλήων.
ἀλλὰ θεῶν μὲν δῶρα καὶ ἀχνύμενοί περ ἀνάγκηι
τέτλαμεν ἄνθρωποι· ἐπὶ γὰρ ζυγὸν αὐχένι κεῖται.
νῦν δ᾽ ἐπεὶ ἵκεο δεῦρο, παρέσσεται ὅσσά τ᾽ ἐμοί
περ.
παῖδα δέ μοι τρέφε τόνδε, τὸν ὀψίγονον καὶ ἄελπτον
220 ὤπασαν ἀθάνατοι, πολυάρητος δέ μοί ἐστιν.
εἰ τόν γ᾽ ἐκθρέψαιο καὶ ἥβης μέτρον ἵκοιτο,
ἦ ῥά κέ τίς σε ἰδοῦσα γυναικῶν θηλυτεράων
ζηλώσαι· τόσα κέν τοι ἀπὸ θρεπτήρια δοίην."
τὴν δ᾽ αὖτε προσέειπεν ἐϋστέφανος Δημήτηρ·
225 "καὶ σύ, γύναι, μάλα χαῖρε, θεοὶ δέ τοι ἐσθλὰ
πόροιεν.

207 οἱ Matthiae: τοι M   208 ἄλφι Ruhnkenius: ἀμφὶ M
post 211 lacunam stat. Bücheler
217 ζυγὸν West: -ὸς M

2. TO DEMETER

Metaneira filled a cup with honey-sweet wine and of-
fered it to her. But she declined, saying that it was not
proper for her to drink red wine; she told her to mix barley
and water with the graceful pennyroyal and give it to her to
drink. So she made the *kykeon*[9] and gave it to the goddess,
as she requested, and the lady Deo took it for custom's sake
and . . .[10]

Then fair-girt Metaneira opened the conversation:
"Greetings, lady, for I do not expect you come from low
parents, but ones of standing; your eyes have a striking
modesty and charm, as might come from lawgiver princes.
But what the gods give, we humans endure, painful as it is,
for our necks are under the yoke. However, now that you
have come here, you shall have as much as I have myself.
Just rear this boy for me, whom the immortals have
granted me, late and beyond expectation, but in answer to
many a prayer. If you were to raise him and see him to
young manhood's measure, then any woman who saw you
might well envy you, so richly would I repay you for his
nurturing."

Fair-garlanded Demeter addressed her in turn:
"Greetings to you too, lady, and may the gods give you

---

[9] *Kykeon*, literally 'stir-up,' was the name of the barley drink
ritually consumed by the initiates at Eleusis. It had to be stirred
before drinking so that the barley grains did not settle.

[10] One or more lines are missing at this point.

---

220 πολυήρατος M: corr. Ruhnkenius
221 γ᾽ ἐκθρέψαιο Hermann: γε θρέψαιο M
223 δοίη Matthiae

παῖδα δέ τοι πρόφρων ὑποδέξομαι, ὥς με κελεύεις·
θρέψω, κού μιν, ἔολπα, κακοφραδίηισι τιθήνης
οὔτ᾽ ἄρ᾽ ἐπηλυσίη δηλήσεται οὔθ᾽ ὑποτάμνων·
οἶδα γὰρ ἀντίτομον μέγα φέρτερον ὑλοτόμοιο,
230 οἶδα δ᾽ ἐπηλυσίης πολυπήμονος ἐσθλὸν ἐρυσμόν.”
     ὣς ἄρα φωνήσασα θυώδεϊ δέξατο κόλπωι
χερσίν τ᾽ ἀθανάτηισι· γεγήθει δὲ φρένα μήτηρ.
ὣς ἣ μὲν Κελεοῖο δαΐφρονος ἀγλαὸν υἱόν
Δημοφόωνθ᾽, ὃν ἔτικτεν ἐΰζωνος Μετάνειρα,
235 ἔτρεφεν ἐν μεγάροις· ὃ δ᾽ ἀέξετο δαίμονι ἶσος,
οὔτ᾽ οὖν σῖτον ἔδων, οὐ θησάμενος ‹γάλα μητρός.
236a ἠματίη μὲν γὰρ καλλιστέφανος› Δημήτηρ
χρίεσκ᾽ ἀμβροσίηι ὡς εἰ θεοῦ ἐκγεγαῶτα,
ἡδὺ καταπνείουσα καὶ ἐν κόλποισιν ἔχουσα,
νύκτας δὲ κρύπτεσκε πυρὸς μένει ἠΰτε δαλόν
240 λάθρα φίλων γονέων. τοῖς δὲ μέγα θαῦμ᾽ ἐτέτυκτο,
ὡς προθαλὴς τελέθεσκε, θεοῖσι δὲ ἄντα ἐῴκει.
     καί κέν μιν ποίησεν ἀγήρων τ᾽ ἀθάνατόν τε,
εἰ μὴ ἄρ᾽ ἀφραδίηισιν ἐΰζωνος Μετάνειρα
νύκτ᾽ ἐπιτηρήσασα θυώδεος ἐκ θαλάμοιο
245 σκέψατο· κώκυσεν δὲ καὶ ἄμφω πλήξατο μηρώ,
δείσασ᾽ ὧι περὶ παιδί, καὶ ἀάσθη μέγα θυμῶι.
καί ῥ᾽ ὀλοφυρομένη ἔπεα πτερόεντα προσηύδα·
     “τέκνον Δημοφόων, ξείνη σε πυρὶ ἔνι πολλῶι
κρύπτει, ἐμοὶ δὲ γόον καὶ κήδεα λυγρὰ τίθησιν.”

228 ὑποτάμνων Ignarra: ὑποταμνὸν M
229 ὑποτόμοιο Kledt

50

blessings. As for your boy, I will gladly take him over, as you request. I will rear him, and I do not anticipate that any supernatural visitation or cutter of roots will harm him through any negligence by his nurse. For I know a powerful counter-cut to beat the herb-cutter, and I know a good inhibitor of baneful visitation."

With these words she took him into her fragrant bosom and immortal arms, and his mother was delighted. So she proceeded to rear in the mansion wise Keleos' resplendent son Demophon, whom fair-girt Metaneira had borne, and he grew like a divine being, though he ate no food and sucked no ‹mother's milk. For by day fair-garlanded› Demeter would anoint him with ambrosia, as if he were the son of a god, breathing her sweet breath over him as she held him in her bosom, while each night she would hide him away in the burning fire, like a brand, without his dear parents' knowledge. To them it was a great wonder how precociously he flourished; he was like the gods to behold.

Indeed she would have made him ageless and deathless, if in her folly fair-girt Metaneira had not waited for the nighttime and spied from her fragrant chamber: she shrieked and clapped her two thighs in alarm for her son, for she was greatly misled, and she addressed him with winged words of lament:

"Demophon my child, the visitor is hiding you away in the blazing fire, causing me groaning and grief."

---

232 ἀθανάτηισι Ilgen: -οισι M
236 suppl. Hermann, 236a Voss
248 πυρη ενι πο]λλη Π1

250 &ὼς φάτ᾽ ὀδυρομένη· τῆς δ᾽ ἄϊε δῖα θεάων,
τῆι δὲ χολωσαμένη καλλιστέφανος Δημήτηρ
παῖδα φίλον, τὸν ἄελπτον ἐνὶ μεγάροισιν ἔτικτεν,
χείρεσσ᾽ ἀθανάτηισιν ἀπὸ ἕο θῆκε πέδονδε
ἐξανελοῦσα πυρός, θυμῶι κοτέσασα μάλ᾽ αἰνῶς.
255 καί ῥ᾽ ἄμυδις προσέειπεν ἐΰζωνον Μετάνειραν·
    "νήϊδες ἄνθρωποι καὶ ἀφράδμονες οὔτ᾽ ἀγαθοῖο
αἶσαν ἐπερχομένου προγνώμεναι οὔτε κακοῖο·
καὶ σὺ γὰρ ἀφραδίηισι τεῆις νήκεστον ἀάσθης.
ἴστω γὰρ θεῶν ὅρκος, ἀμείλικτον Στυγὸς ὕδωρ·
260 ἀθάνατόν κέν τοι καὶ ἀγήραον ἤματα πάντα
παῖδα φίλον ποίησα καὶ ἄφθιτον ὤπασα τιμήν·
νῦν δ᾽ οὐκ ἔσθ᾽ ὥς κεν θάνατον καὶ κῆρας ἀλύξαι.
τιμὴ δ᾽ ἄφθιτος αἰὲν ἐπέσσεται, οὕνεκα γούνων
ἡμετέρων ἐπέβη καὶ ἐν ἀγκοίνηισιν ἴαυσεν.
265 ὥρηισιν δ᾽ ἄρα τῶι γε περιπλομένων ἐνιαυτῶν
παῖδες Ἐλευσινίων πόλεμον καὶ φύλοπιν αἰνήν
αἰὲν ἐν ἀλλήλοισι συνάξουσ᾽ ἤματα πάντα.
εἰμὶ δὲ Δημήτηρ τιμάοχος, ἥ τε μέγιστον
ἀθανάτοις θνητοῖσί τ᾽ ὄνεαρ καὶ χάρμα τέτυκται.
270 ἀλλ᾽ ἄγε μοι νηόν τε μέγαν καὶ βωμὸν ὑπ᾽ αὐτῶι
τευχόντων πᾶς δῆμος ὑπαὶ πόλιν αἰπύ τε τεῖχος,
Καλλιχόρου καθύπερθεν ἐπὶ προύχοντι κολωνῶι·
ὄργια δ᾽ αὐτὴ ἐγὼν ὑποθήσομαι, ὡς ἂν ἔπειτα

256–7 αφρονε[ς] ανθ[ρω]ποι δυστλημονες [ουτε κακοιο
αισαν επ]ερ[χομενου πρ]ογνωμενες Π1   προγνώμεναι Mat-
thiae: -μενοι M

So she lamented; and the goddess heard her. Angry with her, fair-garlanded Demeter took her dear son, whom she had borne beyond expectation in the mansion, in her immortal arms and laid him down away from her on the ground, removing him out of the fire in her heart's great wrath, and at the same time she spoke to fair-girt Metaneira:

"Ignorant humans and witless to recognize a dispensation of coming good or ill! You are another one irremediably misled by your folly. For may the implacable Water of Shuddering[11] on which the gods swear their oaths be my witness, I would have made your dear son deathless and ageless for ever, and granted him unfading privilege; but now there is no way he can avoid death and mortality. Yet a privilege unfading shall always be his, because he came onto my lap and slept in my arms: in his honor, at the due season of the revolving years, the sons of the Eleusinians shall evermore make battle and affray among themselves.[12] For I am Demeter the honored one, who is the greatest boon and joy to immortals and mortals. Now, let the whole people build me a great temple with an altar below it, under the citadel's sheer wall, above Kallichoron, where the hill juts out. As to the rites, I myself will instruct

[11] "Shuddering" is the literal meaning of the Greek name Styx.
[12] This refers to a ritual mock battle, the *Balletys*.

---

258 νήκεστον Voss: μήκιστον M
263 ἄφθιτος Ruhnkenius: -ον M
267 συνάξουσ' Ignarra: συναυξήσουσ' M
269 θνητοῖσί τ' Ruhnkenius: -οῖσιν M

εὐαγέως ἔρδοντες ἐμὸν νόον ἱλάσκοισθε."

275 ὣς εἰποῦσα θεὰ μέγεθος καὶ εἶδος ἄμειψεν
γῆρας ἀπωσαμένη, περί τ' ἀμφί τε κάλλος ἄητο·
ὀδμὴ δ' ἱμερόεσσα θυηέντων ἀπὸ πέπλων
σκίδνατο, τῆλε δὲ φέγγος ἀπὸ χροὸς ἀθανάτοιο
λάμπε θεῆς, ξανθαὶ δὲ κόμαι κατενήνοθεν ὤμους,
280 αὐγῆς δ' ἐπλήσθη πυκινὸς δόμος ἀστεροπῆς ὥς.
βῆ δὲ διὲκ μεγάρων, τῆς δ' αὐτίκα γούνατ' ἔλυντο,
δηρὸν δ' ἄφθογγος γένετο χρόνον, οὐδέ τι παιδός
μνήσατο τηλυγέτοιο ἀπὸ δαπέδου ἀνελέσθαι.
τοῦ δὲ κασίγνηται φωνὴν ἐσάκουσαν ἐλεινήν,
285 κὰδ δ' ἄρ' ἀπ' εὐστρώτων λεχέων θόρον· ἣ μὲν
  ἔπειτα
παῖδ' ἀνὰ χερσὶν ἑλοῦσα ἑῶι ἐγκάτθετο κόλπωι,
ἣ δ' ἄρα πῦρ ἀνέκαι', ἣ δ' ἔσσυτο πόσσ' ἁπαλοῖσιν
μητέρ' ἀναστήσουσα θυώδεος ἐκ θαλάμοιο.
ἀγρόμεναι δέ μιν ἀμφὶς ἐλούεον ἀσπαίροντα
290 ἀμφαγαπαζόμεναι· τοῦ δ' οὐ μειλίσσετο θυμός·
χειρότεραι γὰρ δή μιν ἔχον τροφοὶ ἠδὲ τιθῆναι.

αἳ μὲν παννύχιαι κυδρὴν θεὸν ἱλάσκοντο
δείματι παλλόμεναι· ἅμα δ' ἠοῖ φαινομένηφιν
εὐρυβίηι Κελεῶι νημερτέα μυθήσαντο,
295 ὡς ἐπέτελλε θεὰ καλλιστέφανος Δημήτηρ.
αὐτὰρ ὅ γ' εἰς ἀγορὴν καλέσας πολυπείρονα λαόν
ἤνωγ' ἠϋκόμωι Δημήτερι πίονα νηόν
ποιῆσαι καὶ βωμὸν ἐπὶ προύχοντι κολωνῶι.
οἳ δὲ μάλ' αἶψ' ἐπίθοντο καὶ ἔκλυον αὐδήσαντος,
300 τεῦχον δ' ὡς ἐπέτελλ'· ὃ δ' ἀέξετο δαίμονος αἴσηι.

you on how in future you can propitiate me with holy performance."

With these words the goddess changed her form and stature, thrusting old age away; beauty wafted all about her, a lovely fragrance spread from her scented dress, and a radiance shone afar from her immortal body; flaxen locks bestrewed her shoulders, and the sturdy house was filled with a brilliance as of lightning as she went out through the hall. The queen at once gave way at the knees, and remained speechless for a long time, not thinking to pick her darling child up from the floor. His sisters heard his piteous crying, and jumped down from their well-bedecked beds: one of them picked the child up in her arms and took him to her bosom, another stoked up the fire, while another dashed on tender young feet to help her mother up from the scented chamber. Then, gathering round him, they cuddled him and washed him as he squirmed, but he was not to be comforted: these were inferior rearers and nurses that held him now.

They then throughout the night tried to propitiate the glorious goddess, trembling with fear. As soon as dawn appeared, they told wide-ruling Keleos everything exactly, as the goddess, fair-garlanded Demeter, had instructed. He summoned his far-flung people to assembly, and told them to build a rich temple for lovely-haired Demeter, and an altar where the hill juts out. They promptly obeyed and hearkened to his words, and made it as he instructed, and it grew by divine dispensation. When they had finished it and

---

274 νόον Ruhnkenius: νηὸν M
280 αὐγῆς Ruhnkenius: αὐτῆς M

αὐτὰρ ἐπεὶ τέλεσαν καὶ ἐρώησαν καμάτοιο,
βάν ῥ' ἴμεν οἴκαδ' ἕκαστος. ἀτὰρ ξανθὴ Δημήτηρ
ἔνθα καθεζομένη μακάρων ἀπὸ νόσφιν ἀπάντων
μίμνε πόθωι μινύθουσα βαθυζώνοιο θυγατρός.

305   αἰνότατον δ' ἐνιαυτὸν ἐπὶ χθόνα πουλυβότειραν
ποίησ' ἀνθρώποις καὶ κύντατον· οὐδέ τι γαῖα
σπέρμ' ἀνίει· κρύπτεν γὰρ ἐϋστέφανος Δημήτηρ·
πολλὰ δὲ καμπύλ' ἄροτρα μάτην βόες εἷλκον
      ἀρούραις,
πολλὸν δὲ κρῖ λευκὸν ἐτώσιον ἔμπεσε γαίηι.

310   καί νύ κε πάμπαν ὄλεσσε γένος μερόπων ἀνθρώπων
λιμοῦ ὕπ' ἀργαλέης, γεράων τ' ἐρικυδέα τιμήν
καὶ θυσιῶν ἤμερσεν Ὀλύμπια δώματ' ἔχοντας,
εἰ μὴ Ζεὺς ἐνόησεν, ἑῶι δ' ἐφράσσατο θυμῶι.
Ἶριν δὲ πρῶτον χρυσόπτερον ὦρσε καλέσσαι

315   Δήμητρ' ἠΰκομον πολυήρατον εἶδος ἔχουσαν.
ὣς ἔφαθ'· ἡ δὲ Ζηνὶ κελαινεφέϊ Κρονίωνι
πείθετο καὶ τὸ μεσηγὺ διέδραμεν ὦκα πόδεσσιν.
ἵκετο δὲ πτολίεθρον Ἐλευσῖνος θυοέσσης,
ηὗρεν δ' ἐν νηῶι Δημήτερα κυανόπεπλον,

320   καί μιν φωνήσασ' ἔπεα πτερόεντα προσηύδα·
   "Δήμητερ, καλέει σε πατὴρ Ζεὺς ἄφθιτα εἰδώς
ἐλθέμεναι μετὰ φῦλα θεῶν αἰειγενετάων.
ἀλλ' ἴθι, μηδ' ἀτέλεστον ἐμὸν ἔπος ἐκ Διὸς ἔστω."
   ὣς φάτο λισσομένη· τῆς δ' οὐκ ἐπεπείθετο θυμός.

325   αὖτις ἔπειτα <πατὴρ> μάκαρας θεοὺς αἰὲν ἐόντας

302 ῥ' Wyttenbach: δ' M

paused from their toil, they went to their various homes; but flaxen Demeter took her seat in it and remained there, apart from all the blessed gods, pining for her deep-girt daughter.

The most dreadful and abominable year she made it for mankind across the nurturing earth. The land allowed nothing sown to come up, for fair-garlanded Demeter kept it hidden. Many were the bent ploughs that the oxen dragged in vain over the fields, and much the white barley seed that fell into the soil without result. Indeed, she would have destroyed humankind altogether by grievous famine, and deprived the Olympians of their honorific privileges and their sacrifices, had Zeus not taken notice, and counselled with his heart. As a first step he sent gold-winged Iris to summon Demeter the lovely-haired, whose form is beautiful. So he instructed her, and she in obedience to Zeus, the dark-cloud son of Kronos, swiftly darted across the intervening space and arrived at the fragrant town of Eleusis. She found dark-robed Demeter in her temple, and addressed her with winged words:

"Demeter, father Zeus whose counsels do not fade summons you to join the families of gods who are for ever. So come, and let the word I have from Zeus not go unfulfilled."

So she entreated her, but her heart was not persuaded. Next the Father sent all the blessed eternal gods, one after

---

309 γαίηι Ruhnkenius: γαῖα M
314 Ἶριν Ruhnkenius: ἥρην M
317 τὸ μεσηγὺ Ilgen: μεσσηγγὺ M
325 πατὴρ add. Valckenaer

πάντας ἐπιπροΐαλλεν· ἀμοιβηδὶς δὲ κιόντες
κίκλησκον καὶ πολλὰ δίδον περικαλλέα δῶρα,
τιμὰς τάς κε βόλοιτο μετ᾽ ἀθανάτοισιν ἑλέσθαι·
ἀλλ᾽ οὔ τις πεῖσαι δύνατο φρένας οὐδὲ νόημα
330 θυμῷ χωομένης, στερεῶς δ᾽ ἠναίνετο μύθους.
οὐ μὲν γάρ ποτ᾽ ἔφασκε θυώδεος Οὐλύμποιο
πρίν γ᾽ ἐπιβήσεσθαι, οὐ πρὶν γῆς καρπὸν ἀνήσειν,
πρὶν ἴδοι ὀφθαλμοῖσιν ἑὴν εὐώπιδα κούρην.
    αὐτὰρ ἐπεὶ τό γ᾽ ἄκουσε βαρύκτυπος εὐρύοπα
      Ζεύς,
335 εἰς Ἔρεβος πέμψε χρυσόρραπιν Ἀργειφόντην,
ὄφρ᾽ Ἀΐδην μαλακοῖσι παραιφάμενος ἐπέεσσιν
ἁγνὴν Περσεφόνειαν ἀπὸ ζόφου ἠερόεντος
ἐς φάος ἐξαγάγοι μετὰ δαίμονας, ὄφρα ἑ μήτηρ
ὀφθαλμοῖσιν ἰδοῦσα μεταλλήξειε χόλοιο.
340 Ἑρμῆς δ᾽ οὐκ ἀπίθησεν, ἄφαρ δ᾽ ὑπὸ κεύθεα γαίης
ἐσσυμένως κατόρουσε λιπὼν ἕδος Οὐλύμποιο.
τέτμε δὲ τόν γε ἄνακτα δόμων ἔντοσθεν ἐόντα,
ἥμενον ἐν λεχέεσσι σὺν αἰδοίῃ παρακοίτι
πόλλ᾽ ἀεκαζομένῃ μητρὸς πόθῳ· †ἣ δ᾽ ἐπ᾽ ἀτλήτων
345 ἔργοις θεῶν μακάρων μητίσετο βουλῇ.†
ἀγχοῦ δ᾽ ἱστάμενος προσέφη κρατὺς Ἀργειφόντης·
    "Ἀΐδη κυανοχαῖτα καταφθιμένοισιν ἀνάσσων,
Ζεύς με πατὴρ ἤνωγεν ἀγαυὴν Περσεφόνειαν
ἐξαγαγεῖν Ἐρέβεσφι μετὰ σφέας, ὄφρα ἑ μήτηρ
350 ὀφθαλμοῖσιν ἰδοῦσα χόλου καὶ μήνιος αἰνῆς
ἀθανάτοις λήξειεν· ἐπεὶ μέγα μήδεται ἔργον,
φθεῖσαι φῦλ᾽ ἀμενηνὰ χαμαιγενέων ἀνθρώπων

another: they went in turn to summon her, offering many resplendent gifts, the choice of whatever privileges she wanted among the immortals. But none was able to bend her will, angry in heart as she was, and she firmly rejected their speeches. She said she would never set foot on fragrant Olympus, or allow the earth's fruit to come up, until she set eyes on her fair-faced daughter.

When heavy-booming, wide-sounding Zeus heard that, he sent the gold-wand Argus-slayer[13] to the Lower Darkness to persuade Hades with soft words and bring chaste Persephone out from the misty dark to the daylight to join the gods, so that her mother might set eyes on her and cease from her wrath. Hermes did not demur, but straightway left the seat of Olympus and sped down under the recesses of the earth. He found its lord within his mansions, seated on his couch with his modest consort, who was full of resistance from longing for her mother . . . [*unintelligible*] . . . Standing close to him, the strong Argus-slayer addressed him:

"Hades of the sable hair, lord over the dead, Zeus the father has instructed me to bring illustrious Persephone out from the Darkness to them, so that her mother may set eyes on her and cease from her wrath and her dreadful resentment against the immortals. For she is purposing a grave thing, to destroy the feeble stock of earthborn

13 Hermes.

---

328 τάς West, κε βόλοιτο Allen: θ᾽ ἅς κ᾽ ἐθέλοιτο M
348 με Wyttenbach: σε M
349 Ἐρέβεσφι Franke: -ευσφι M
351 λήξειεν Burney: παύσειεν M

σπέρμ' ὑπὸ γῆς κρύπτουσα, καταφθινύθουσα δὲ
    τιμάς
ἀθανάτων. ἢ δ' αἰνὸν ἔχει χόλον, οὐδὲ θεοῖσιν
355 μίσγεται, ἀλλ' ἀπάνευθε θυώδεος ἔνδοθι νηοῦ
ἧσται, Ἐλευσῖνος κραναὸν πτολίεθρον ἔχουσα."
    ὣς φάτο· μείδησεν δὲ ἄναξ ἐνέρων Ἀϊδωνεύς
ὀφρύσιν, οὐδ' ἀπίθησε Διὸς βασιλῆος ἐφετμῆς.
ἐσσυμένως δ' ἐκέλευσε δαΐφρονι Περσεφονείῃ·
360 "ἔρχεο, Περσεφόνη, παρὰ μητέρα κυανόπεπλον
ἤπιον ἐν στήθεσσι μένος καὶ θυμὸν ἔχουσα,
μηδέ τι δυσθύμαινε λίην περιώσιον ἄλλων.
οὔ τοι ἐν ἀθανάτοισιν ἀεικὴς ἔσσομ' ἀκοίτης
αὐτοκασίγνητος πατρὸς Διός· ἔνθα δ' ἐοῦσα
365 δεσπόσσεις πάντων ὁπόσα ζώει τε καὶ ἕρπει,
τιμὰς δὲ σχήσησθα μετ' ἀθανάτοισι μεγίστας,
τῶν δ' ἀδικησάντων τίσις ἔσσεται ἤματα πάντα,
οἵ κεν μὴ θυσίῃσι τεὸν μένος ἱλάσκωνται
εὐαγέως ἔρδοντες, ἐναίσιμα δῶρα τελοῦντες."
370 ὣς φάτο· γήθησεν δὲ περίφρων Περσεφόνεια,
καρπαλίμως δ' ἀνόρουσ' ὑπὸ χάρματος· αὐτὰρ ὅ γ'
    αὐτῆι
ῥοιῆς κόκκον ἔδωκε φαγεῖν μελιηδέα λάθρῃ,
ἀμφὶ ἓ νωμήσας, ἵνα μὴ μένοι ἤματα πάντα
αὖθι παρ' αἰδοίῃ Δημήτερι κυανοπέπλωι.
375 ἵππους δὲ προπάροιθεν ὑπὸ χρυσέοισιν ὄχεσφιν
ἔντυεν ἀθανάτους πολυσημάντωρ Ἀϊδωνεύς·
ἢ δ' ὀχέων ἐπέβη, παρὰ δὲ κρατὺς Ἀργειφόντης
ἡνία καὶ μάστιγα λαβὼν μετὰ χερσὶ φίλῃσιν

humankind by keeping the seed hidden under the soil, and so diminishing the immortals' tribute. Her wrath is dreadful, and she is not mingling with the gods but stays apart, seated in her fragrant temple, occupying Eleusis' rugged citadel."

So he spoke; and the lord of those below, Aïdoneus, smiled with his brows, but did not demur from the command of Zeus the king. Quickly he told wise Persephone: "Go, Persephone, to your dark-robed mother's side, keeping a gentle temper in your heart, and be not too excessively aggrieved. I shall not make you an unsuitable husband to have among the gods, own brother to your father Zeus; by being here, you will be mistress of everything that lives and moves, and have the greatest privileges among the immortals, while there will ever be punishment for those who act unrighteously and fail to propitiate your fury with sacrifices, in holy performance, making the due offerings."

So he spoke, and prudent Persephone was delighted, and promptly jumped up in joy. But he gave her a honey-sweet pomegranate seed to eat, surreptitiously, peering about him, to prevent her from staying up there for ever with reverend Demeter of the dark robe.

Then the Major General Aïdoneus harnessed his immortal steeds at the front under the golden chariot. She got into it, while beside her the strong Argus-slayer took the reins and the goad in his hands and urged the horses

---

364 ἐοῦσα Ruhnkenius: ἰοῦσα M
371 αὐτῆι Voss: αὐτὸς M

σεῦε διὲκ μεγάρων· τὼ δ' οὐκ ἄκοντε πετέσθην.
380 ῥίμφα δὲ μακρὰ κέλευθα διήνυσαν, οὐδὲ θάλασσα
οὔθ' ὕδωρ ποταμῶν οὔτ' ἄγκεα ποιήεντα
ἵππων ἀθανάτων οὔτ' ἄκριες ἔσχεθον ὁρμήν,
ἀλλ' ὑπὲρ αὐτάων βαθὺν ἠέρα τέμνον ἰόντες·
στῆσε δ' ἄγων ὅθι μίμνεν ἐϋστέφανος Δημήτηρ
385 νηοῖο προπάροιθε θυώδεος. ἡ δὲ ἰδοῦσα
ἤϊξ' ἠΰτε μαινὰς ὄρος κάτα δάσκιον ὕληι,
Περσεφόνη δ' ἑτέρ[ωθεν, ἐπεὶ ἴδεν ὄμματα καλά]
μητρὸς ἑῆς, κατ' [ἄρ' ἥ γ' ὄχεα προλιποῦσα καὶ
    ἵππους]
ἆλτο θέει[ν, δειρῆι δέ οἱ ἔμπεσεν ἀμφιχυθεῖσα.]
390 τῆι δὲ [φίλην ἔτι παῖδα ἑῆς μετὰ χερσὶν ἐχούσηι]
α[ἶψα δόλον θυμός τιν' ὀΐσατο, τρέσσε δ' ἄρ' αἰνῶς]
πα‹υ›ομ[ένη φιλότητος, ἄφαρ δ' ἐρεείνετο μύθωι·]
"τέκνον, μή ῥά τί μοι σ[ύ γε πάσσαο νέρθεν ἐοῦσα]
βρώμης; ἐξαύδα, [μὴ κεῦθ', ἵνα εἴδομεν ἄμφω·]
395 ὡς μὲν γάρ κεν ἐοῦσα π[αρ' ἄλλοις ἀθανάτοισιν]
καὶ παρ' ἐμοὶ καὶ πατρὶ κελ[αινεφέϊ Κρονίωνι]
ναιετάοις πάντεσσι τετιμ[ένη ἀθανάτοι]σιν·
εἰ δ' ἐπάσω, πάλιν ‹αὖτις› ἰοῦσ' ὑπ[ὸ κεύθεσι
    γαίης]
οἰκήσεις ὡρέων τρίτατον μέρ[ος εἰς ἐνιαυτόν,]
400 τὰς δὲ δύω παρ' ἐμοί τε καὶ [ἄλλοις ἀθανάτοισιν.]
ὁππότε δ' ἄνθεσι γαῖ' εὐώδε[σιν] εἰαρινο[ῖσιν]
παντοδαποῖς θάλλει, τότ' ἀπὸ ζόφου ἠερόεντος
αὖτις ἄνει, μέγα θαῦμα θεοῖς θνητοῖς τ' ἀνθρώποις.

out through the halls, and they flew forward without demur. Swiftly they accomplished the long legs of their journey: neither sea nor flowing rivers nor grassy glens nor mountain peaks stayed the immortal steeds' impetus, but they passed over them cleaving the deep air. He brought them to a halt where fair-garlanded Demeter was waiting, in front of her fragrant temple, and when she saw them she rushed forward like a maenad on the shady-forested mountain. Persephone on her side, [when she saw] her mother's [lovely eyes], leaped down [from the chariot] and ran [and fell about her neck in embrace].

[But even as she held her child in her arms, her heart suddenly suspected some trick, and she was very afraid,] endi[ng the embrace, and quickly she asked:] "My child, I hope you didn't [taste] any food [when you were down there? Tell me, [don't hide it, let's both know about it]. For if you didn't, you can be w[ith the rest of the immortals] and live with me and your father, the dark-cloud son of Kronos, with all the immortals honoring you; but if you tasted anything, you will go back down and dwell in the recesses of the earth for a third of the year, until the due date, spending the other two thirds with me and the other gods; and when the earth blooms with sweet-smelling spring flowers of every kind, then you will come back up from the misty dark, a great wonder to the gods and to mortals. < But

---

386 ὕληι Ruhnkenius: ὕλης M

387–93 e.g. suppl. Goodwin, 394 Hermann, 395 Bücheler, 396–404 M²

398 ἐπάσω Wyttenbach: πτᾶσα M   αὖτις add. Ruhnkenius

403a ⟨εἰπὲ δέ, πῶς σ' ἥρπαξεν ὑπὸ ζόφον ἠερόεντα,⟩
καὶ τίνι σ' ἐξαπάτησε δόλωι κρατερ[ὸς
Πολυδ]έγμων;"
405 τὴν δ' αὖ Περσεφόνη περικαλλὴς ἀντίον ηὔδα·
"τοιγὰρ ἐγώ τοι, μῆτερ, ἐρέω νημερτέα πάντα.
εὖτέ μοι Ἑρμῆς ἦ[λθ]' ἐριούνιος ἄγγελος ὠκύς
πὰρ πατέρος Κρονίδαο καὶ ἄλλων οὐρανιώνων
ἐλθεῖν ἐξ Ἐρέβεος, ἵνα μ' ὀφθαλμοῖσιν ἰδοῦσα
410 λήξαις ἀθανάτοισι χόλου καὶ μήνιος αἰνῆς,
αὐτίκ' ἐγὼν ἀνόρουσ' ὑπὸ χάρματος, αὐτὰρ ὁ
λάθρηι
ἔμβαλέ μοι ῥοιῆς κόκκον, μελιηδέ' ἐδωδήν,
ἄκουσαν δὲ βίηι με προσηνάγκασσε πάσασθαι.
ὡς δέ μ' ἀναρπάξας Κρονίδεω πυκινὴν διὰ μῆτιν
415 ὤιχετο πατρὸς ἐμοῖο φέρων ὑπὸ κεύθεα γαίης,
ἐξερέω, καὶ πάντα διΐξομαι ὡς ἐρεείνεις.
ἡμεῖς μὲν μάλα πᾶσαι ἀν' ἱμερτὸν λειμῶνα,
Λευκίππη Φαινώ τε καὶ Ἠλέκτρη καὶ Ἰάνθη
καὶ Μελίτη Ἰάχη τε Ῥό⟨δ⟩ειά τε Καλλιρόη τε
420 Μηλόβοσίς τε Τύχη τε καὶ Ὠκυρόη καλυκῶπις
Χρυσηΐς τ' Ἰάνειρά τ' Ἀκάστη τ' Ἀδμήτη τε
καὶ Ῥοδόπη Πλουτώ τε καὶ ἱμερόεσσα Καλυψώ
καὶ Στὺξ Οὐρανίη τε Γαλαξαύρη τ' ἐρατεινή
Παλλάς τ' ἐγρεμάχη καὶ Ἄρτεμις ἰοχέαιρα,
425 παίζομεν ἠδ' ἄνθεα δρέπομεν χείρεσσ' ἐρόεντα,
μίγδα κρόκον τ' ἀγανὸν καὶ ἀγαλλίδας ἠδ' ὑάκινθον
καὶ ῥοδέας κάλυκας καὶ λείρια, θαῦμα ἰδέσθαι,
νάρκισσόν θ', ὃν ἔφυσ' ὥς περ κρόκον εὐρεῖα χθών.

tell me, how did he snatch you down to the misty dark, >
and what did he trick you with, the mighty Hospitable
One?"

Beautiful Persephone spoke to her in reply: "Well,
mother, I will tell you everything just as it was. When
coursing Hermes came swift with the message from father
Zeus and the other Heavenly Ones that I should leave the
Darkness, so that you might set eyes on me and cease from
your wrath and your dreadful resentment against the im-
mortals, I at once jumped up in joy; but he surreptitiously
got a pomegranate seed into me, a honey-sweet food, and
made me taste it against my will. As to how he snatched me
up through the crafty design of Zeus my father, and took
me off to the recesses of the earth, I will explain and go
through it all, just as you ask. We were all frolicking in the
lovely meadow—Leucippe and Phaeno and Electra and
Ianthe, and Melite and Iache and Rhodeia and Callirhoe,
and Melobosis and Tyche and Ocyrhoe with eyes like buds,
and Chryseis and Ianeira and Acaste and Admete, and
Rhodope and Plouto and captivating Calypso, and Styx and
Ourania and lovely Galaxaura, and Pallas the battle-rouser
and Artemis profuse of arrows—and we were picking
lovely flowers, a mixture of gentle saffron and iris and hya-
cinth and rosebuds and lilies, wondrous to behold, and
narcissus that the broad earth put out like saffron. I was

403a e.g. suppl. Goodwin, lac. statuerat Ruhnkenius
405 Φερσεφον[η Π2
407 ευτε μ]οι αγγελος ηλ[θ εριουνιος Αργειφοντης Π2
411 αὐτίκ' Ilgen: αὐτὰρ M
419 om. Π1 et Paus. 4.30.4
427 ῥοδέας Heyne: ῥόδα ἐς M

αὐτὰρ ἐγὼ δρεπόμην περὶ χάρματι, γαῖα δ' ἔνερθεν
430 χώρησεν, τῆι δ' ἔκθορ' ἄναξ κρατερὸς Πολυδέγμων,
βῆ δὲ φέρων ὑπὸ γαῖαν ἐν ἅρμασι χρυσείοισιν
πόλλ' ἀεκαζομένην, ἐβόησα δ' ἄρ' ὄρθια φωνῆι.
ταῦτά τοι ἀχνυμένη περ ἀληθέα πάντ' ἀγορεύω."
    ὡς τότε μὲν πρόπαν ἦμαρ ὁμόφρονα θυμὸν
        ἔχουσαι
435 πολλὰ μάλ' ἀλλήλων κραδίην καὶ θυμὸν ἴαινον
ἀμφαγαπαζόμεναι, ἀχέων δ' ἀπεπαύετο θυμός·
γηθοσύνας δὲ δέχοντο παρ' ἀλλήλων ἔδιδ[όν τε.]
τῆισιν δ' ἐγγύθεν ἦλθ' Ἑκάτη λιπαροκρήδεμνος,
πολλὰ δ' ἄρ' ἀμφαγάπησε κόρην Δήμητερος ἁγνῆς·
440 ἐκ τοῦ οἱ πρόπολος καὶ ὀπάων ἔπλετ' ἄνασσα.
    ταῖς δὲ μετάγγελον ἧκε βαρύκτυπος εὐρύοπα Ζεύς
Ῥείην ἠΰκομον, Δήμητερα κυανόπεπλον
ἀξέμεναι μετὰ φῦλα θεῶν· ὑπέδεκτο δὲ τιμάς
δωσέμεν, ἅς κεν ἕλοιτο μετ' ἀθανάτοισι θεοῖσιν·
445 νεῦσε δέ οἱ κούρην ἔτεος περιτελλομένοιο
τὴν τριτάτην μὲν μοῖραν ὑπὸ ζόφον ἠερόεντα,
τὰς δὲ δύω παρὰ μητρὶ καὶ ἄλλοις ἀθανάτοισιν.
ὡς ἔφατ'· οὐδ' ἀπίθησε θεὰ Διὸς ἀγγελιάων,
ἐσσυμένως δ' ἤϊξε κατ' Οὐλύμποιο καρήνων,
450 ἐς δ' ἄρα ⟨Ῥά⟩ριον ἷξε, φερέσβιον οὖθαρ ἀρούρης
τὸ πρίν, ἀτὰρ τότε γ' οὔ τι φερέσβιον, ἀλλὰ ἔκηλον
ἑστήκει πανάφυλλον· ἔκευθε δ' ἄρα κρῖ λευκόν
μήδεσι Δήμητρος καλλισφύρου· αὐτὰρ ἔπειτα
μέλλεν ἄφαρ ταναοῖσι κομήσειν ἀσταχύεσσιν
455 ἦρος ἀεξομένοιο, πέδωι δ' ἄρα πίονες ὄγμοι

66

picking away happily, when the ground beneath gave way, and there the lord, the mighty Hospitable One, leaped forth. He went off below the earth with me in his golden chariot, for all my resistance, and I screamed aloud. I'm sorry, but that's the whole truth I'm telling you."

So they then all day long, at one in their feelings, greatly warmed each other's hearts with embraces, and assuaged their sorrows, giving each other joy and receiving it. And Hecate of the glossy veil joined them, and gave the daughter of holy Demeter many an embrace; because of that the goddess became her attendant and servant.

Then heavy-booming, wide-sounding Zeus sent lovely-haired Rhea with a message for them, to bring dark-robed Demeter to join the families of the gods, and he promised to give her what privileges among the immortal gods she might choose. And he gave his approval that her daughter, in the course of the year, should go for a third of it down to the misty dark, spending the other two thirds with her mother and the other immortals. So he spoke, and Rhea did not demur to take Zeus' message, but swiftly sped down from Olympus' peaks, and came to Rarion:[14] in the past a life-giving ploughland to be milked, but not life-giving then, for it stood still and leafless, hiding its white barley by the designs of fair-ankled Demeter, though afterwards it would soon come to wave with long ears of corn as the spring developed, and on the ground its rich furrows

---

14 An arable plain somewhere near the Eleusinian sanctuary.

---

437 γηθοσύνας Ruhnkenius: γηθόσυναι M
442 Δημήτερα Fontein: ἦν μ(ητέ)ρα M

βρισέμεν ἀσταχύων, τὰ δ' ἐν ἐλλεδανοῖσι δίδεσθαι.
ἔνθ' ἐπέβη πρώτιστον ἀπ' αἰθέρος ἀτρυγέτοιο·
ἀσπασίως δ' ἴδον ἀλλήλας, κεχάρηντο δὲ θυμῶι.
τὴν δ' ὧδε προσέειπε Ῥέη λιπαροκρήδεμνος·
460   "δεῦρο, τέκος, καλέει σε βαρύκτυπος εὐρύοπα
        Ζεύς
ἐλθέμεναι μετὰ φῦλα θεῶν, ὑπέδεκτο δὲ τιμάς
[δωσέμεν, ἅς κ' ἐθέλησθα] μετ' ἀθανάτοισι θεοῖσιν·
[νεῦσε δέ τοι κούρην ἔτεος π]εριτελλομένοιο
[τὴν τριτάτην μὲν μοῖραν ὑπὸ ζόφον ἠ]εροέντα,
465   [τὰς δὲ δύω παρὰ σοί τε καὶ ἄλλοις] ἀθανάτοισιν.
[ὣς ἄρ' ἔφη τελέ]εσθαι, ἑῶι δ' ἐπένευσε κάρητι.
[ἀλλ' ἴθι, τέκνον] ἐμόν, καὶ πείθεο, μηδέ τι λίην
ἀ[ζηχὲς μεν]έαινε κελαινεφέϊ Κρονίωνι·
α[ἶψα δὲ κα]ρπὸν ἄεξε φερέσβιον ἀνθρώποισιν."
470   ὣ[ς ἔφατ', οὐ]δ' ἀπίθησεν ἐϋστέφανος Δημήτηρ,
αἶψα δὲ καρπὸν ἀνῆκεν ἀρουράων ἐριβώλων.
πᾶσα δὲ φύλλοισίν τε καὶ ἄνθεσιν εὐρεῖα χθὼν
ἔβρισ'· ἡ δὲ κιοῦσα θεμιστοπόλοις βασιλεῦσιν
δεῖξεν, Τριπτολέμωι τε Διοκλεῖ τε πληξίππωι
475   Εὐμόλπου τε βίηι Κελεῶι θ' ἡγήτορι λαῶν,
δρησμοσύνην ἱερῶν, καὶ ἐπέφραδεν ὄργια καλά
Τριπτολέμωι τε Πολυξείνωι ‹τ'›, ἐπὶ τοῖς δὲ
        Διοκλεῖ,
σεμνά, τά τ' οὔ πως ἔστι παρεξ[ίμ]εν οὔ[τε]
        πυθέσθαι
οὔτ' ἀχέειν· μέγα γάρ τι θεῶν σέβας ἰσχάνει
        αὐδήν.

would be heavy with them, with others already being tied in sheaves. That was where she first set foot as she descended from the fathomless air. They were glad to see each other, and rejoiced at heart. This is how Rhea of the glossy veil addressed her:

"Come, my child, heavy-booming, wide-sounding Zeus summons you to join the families of the gods, and he promised to give you what privileges among the immortal gods you may wish. And he gave his approval that your daughter, in the course of the year, should go for a third of it down to the misty dark, spending the other two thirds with you and the other immortals. [This is how he said it] would be, and he confirmed it with a nod of his head. So go, my child, do what he says, and don't go too far by maintaining your wrath uninterrupted against the dark-cloud son of Kronos. Quickly make the life-giving produce grow for humankind."

So she spoke, and fair-garlanded Demeter did not demur, but quickly made the produce of the loam-rich ploughlands come up; and the whole broad earth grew heavy with leafage and bloom. She went to the lawgiver kings, Triptolemos and horse-goading Diocles, strong Eumolpos and Keleos leader of hosts, and taught them the sacred service, and showed the beautiful mysteries to Triptolemos, Polyxenos, and also Diocles—the solemn mysteries which one cannot depart from or enquire about or broadcast, for great awe of the gods restrains us from

---

456 δίδεσθαι Voss: δεδέσθαι M   462–470 suppl. M², praeter quod 465 Ruhnkenius, 466 Goodwin

476 δρησμοσύνην Paus. 2.14.3: χρησμοσύνην θ' M   καλὰ M: πᾶσιν Paus.   478 τ' Ilgen: γ' M

480 ὄλβιος ὃς τάδ' ὄπωπεν ἐπιχθονίων ἀνθρώπων·
ὃς δ' ἀτελὴς ἱερῶν ὅς τ' ἄμμορος, οὔ ποθ' ὁμοίων
αἶσαν ἔχει φθίμενός περ ὑπὸ ζόφωι εὐρώεντι.
αὐτὰρ ἐπεὶ δὴ πάνθ' ὑπεθήκατο δῖα θεάων,
βάν ῥ' ἴμεν Οὐλυμπόνδε θεῶν μεθ' ὁμήγυριν ἄλλων.
485 ἔνθα δὲ ναιετάουσι παραὶ Διὶ τερπικεραύνωι,
σεμναί τ' αἰδοῖαί τε· μέγ' ὄλβιος, ὅν τιν' ἐκεῖναι
προφρονέως φίλωνται ἐπιχθονίων ἀνθρώπων·
αἶψα δέ οἱ πέμπουσιν ἐφέστιον ἐς μέγα δῶμα
Πλοῦτον, ὃς ἀνθρώποις ἄφενος θνητοῖσι δίδωσιν.
490 ἀλλ' ἄγ', Ἐλευσῖνος θυοέσσης δῆμον ἔχουσαι
καὶ Πάρον ἀμφιρύτην Ἀντρῶνά τε πετρήεντα,
πότνια ἀγλαόδωρ' ὡρηφόρε Δηοῖ ἄνασσα
αὐτὴ καὶ κούρη περικαλλὴς Περσεφόνεια,
πρόφρονες ἀντ' ὠιδῆς βίοτον θυμήρε' ὀπάζειν.
495 αὐτὰρ ἐγὼ καὶ σεῖο καὶ ἄλλης μνήσομ' ἀοιδῆς.

3. ΕΙΣ ΑΠΟΛΛΩΝΑ

Μνήσομαι οὐδὲ λάθωμαι Ἀπόλλωνος ἑκάτοιο,
ὅν τε θεοὶ κατὰ δῶμα Διὸς τρομέουσιν ἰόντα·
καί ῥά τ' ἀναΐσσουσιν ἐπὶ σχεδὸν ἐρχομένοιο
πάντες ἀφ' ἑδράων, ὅτε φαίδιμα τόξα τιταίνει.
5 Λητὼ δ' οἴη μίμνε παραὶ Διὶ τερπικεραύνωι,
ἥ ῥα βίόν τ' ἐχάλασσε καὶ ἐκλήϊσε φαρέτρην,
καί οἱ ἀπ' ἰφθίμων ὤμων χείρεσσιν ἑλοῦσα
τόξον ἀνεκρέμασε πρὸς κίονα πατρὸς ἑοῖο

speaking. Blessed is he of men on earth who has beheld them, whereas he that is uninitiated in the rites, or he that has had no part in them, never enjoys a similar lot down in the musty dark when he is dead.

After the goddess had instructed them in everything, she and Persephone went to Olympus to join the congregation of the other gods. There they dwell beside Zeus whose sport is the thunderbolt, august and reverend. Greatly blessed is he of men on earth whom they love and favor: they soon send Wealth to lodge in his mansion, the god who bestows affluence on mortals.

So come, you that preside over the people of fragrant Eleusis, and seagirt Paros, and rocky Antron—Lady, bringer of resplendent gifts in season, mistress Deo, both you and your daughter, beautiful Persephone: be favorable, and grant comfortable livelihood in return for my singing. And I will take heed both for you and for other singing.

3. TO APOLLO

Let me call to mind and not neglect Apollo the far-shooter, at whose coming the gods tremble in Zeus' house. They all spring up from their seats as he approaches, when he draws his shining bow. Leto alone remains beside Zeus whose sport is the thunderbolt; she unstrings his bow and closes his quiver, and taking the bow from his strong shoulders she hangs it up on a pillar of his father's house from a

---

490 ἀλλὰ θελευσῖνος M: corr. Ruhnkenius
494 ὀπάζειν Voss: ὄπαζε M   3 τ' Hermann: γ' Ω

πασσάλου ἐκ χρυσέου· τὸν δ' ἐς θρόνον εἶσεν
ἄγουσα.

10 τῶι δ' ἄρα νέκταρ ἔδωκε πατὴρ δέπαϊ χρυσείωι
δεικνύμενος φίλον υἱόν, ἔπειτα δὲ δαίμονες ἄλλοι
ἔνθα καθίζουσιν· χαίρει δέ τε πότνια Λητώ,
οὕνεκα τοξοφόρον καὶ καρτερὸν υἱὸν ἔτικτεν.

χαῖρε μάκαιρ' ὦ Λητοῖ, ἐπεὶ τέκες ἀγλαὰ τέκνα,
15 Ἀπόλλωνά τ' ἄνακτα καὶ Ἄρτεμιν ἰοχέαιραν,
τὴν μὲν ἐν Ὀρτυγίηι, τὸν δὲ κραναῆι ἐνὶ Δήλωι,
κεκλιμένη πρὸς μακρὸν ὄρος καὶ Κύνθιον ὄχθον,
ἀγχοτάτω φοίνικος, ὑπ' Ἰνωποῖο ῥεέθροις.

πῶς τάρ σ' ὑμνήσω, πάντως εὔυμνον ἐόντα;
20 πάντηι γάρ τοι, Φοῖβε, νομὸς βεβλήαται ὠιδῆς,
ἠμὲν ἀν' ἤπειρον πορτιτρόφον ἠδ' ἀνὰ νήσους.
πᾶσαι δὲ σκοπιαί τοι ἅδον καὶ πρώονες ἄκροι
ὑψηλῶν ὀρέων ποταμοί θ' ἅλαδε προρέοντες
ἀκταί τ' εἰς ἅλα κεκλιμέναι λιμένες τε θαλάσσης.

25 ἦ ὥς σε πρῶτον Λητὼ τέκε χάρμα βροτοῖσιν,
κλινθεῖσα πρὸς Κύνθου ὄρος κραναῆι ἐνὶ νήσωι,
Δήλωι ἐν ἀμφιρύτηι, ἑκάτερθε δὲ κῦμα κελαινόν
ἐξήιει χέρσονδε λιγυπνοίοις ἀνέμοισιν;
ἔνθεν ἀπορνύμενος πᾶσι θνητοῖσιν ἀνάσσεις.

30 ὅσσους Κρήτη ⟨τ'⟩ ἐντὸς ἔχει καὶ δῆμος
Ἀθηνέων
νῆσός τ' Αἰγίνη ναυσικλειτή τ' Εὔβοια
Αἰγαί τ' Εἰρεσίαι τε καὶ ἀγχιάλη Πεπάρηθος

19 τ' ἄρ Barnes: γάρ Ω

peg of gold, leads him to a chair, and seats him on it. His father gives him nectar in a golden cup, toasting his dear son, and then the other deities do likewise from where they sit, while the mistress Leto rejoices at having borne a powerful archer son.

I salute you, O blessed Leto, for you bore splendid children, the lord Apollo and Artemis profuse of arrows: her you bore in Ortygia, him in rocky Delos, leaning against the long eminence of Cynthus, hard by the palm-tree, below the streams of Inopos.

How shall I hymn you, fit subject as you are in every respect? For in every direction, Phoibos, you have laid down a field for song, both on the heifer-rearing mainland and across the islands. All the peaks find favor with you, and the upper ridges of the high mountains, and the rivers flowing on to the sea, and the headlands that lean toward the main, and the sea harbors. Shall it be how in the beginning Leto bore you for mortals' delight, leaning against Cynthus' mountain on a rocky island, seagirt Delos, while on both sides the dark waves came up on the shores under the keening winds? From where you went forth and are become lord over all humankind.

All whom Crete has within it, and the people of Athens, the island of Aegina and Euboea famed for its shipping, Aegae, Iresiae, and maritime Peparethos, Thracian Athos

---

20 νομοὶ Barnes
βεβλήατ᾽ ἀοιδῆς Ilgen
23–73 om. M
26 Κύνθου Holstein: Κύνθος Ψ
30 τ᾽ add. Hermann
32 Πειρεσιαί Ruhnkenius

Θρηΐκιός τ᾽ Ἀθ‹ό›ως καὶ Πηλίου ἄκρα κάρηνα
34 Θρηϊκίη τε Σάμος Ἴδης τ᾽ ὄρεα σκιόεντα,
36 Ἴμβρος ἐϋκτιμένη καὶ Λῆμνος ἀμιχθαλόεσσα
37 Λέσβος τ᾽ ἠγαθέη, Μάκαρος ἕδος Αἰολίωνος,
35 Σκῦρος καὶ Φώκαια καὶ Αὐτοκάνης ὄρος αἰπύ
   καὶ Χίος, ἣ νήσων λιπαρωτάτη εἰν ἁλὶ κεῖται,
   παιπαλόεις τε Μίμας καὶ Κωρύκου ἄκρα κάρηνα
40 καὶ Κλάρος αἰγλήεσσα καὶ Αἰσαγέης ὄρος αἰπύ
   καὶ Σάμος ὑδρηλὴ Μυκάλης τ᾽ αἰπεινὰ κάρηνα
   Μίλητός τε Κόως τε, πόλις Μερόπων ἀνθρώπων,
   καὶ Κνίδος αἰπεινὴ καὶ Κάρπαθος ἠνεμόεσσα
   Νάξος τ᾽ ἠδὲ Πάρος Ῥήναιά τε πετρήεσσα·
45 τόσσον ἔπ᾽ ὠδίνουσα Ἑκηβόλον ἵκετο Λητώ,
   εἴ τίς οἱ γαιέων υἱεῖ θέλοι οἰκία θέσθαι.
   αἱ δὲ μάλ᾽ ἐτρόμεον καὶ ἐδείδισαν, οὐδέ τις ἔτλη
   Φοῖβον δέξασθαι καὶ πιοτέρη περ ἐοῦσα,
   πρίν γ᾽ ὅτε δή ῥ᾽ ἐπὶ Δήλου ἐβήσετο πότνια Λητώ,
50 καί μιν ἀνειρομένη ἔπεα πτερόεντα προσηύδα·
   "Δῆλ᾽, εἰ γάρ κ᾽ ἐθέλοις ἕδος ἔμμεναι υἷος ἐμοῖο
   Φοίβου Ἀπόλλωνος, θέσθαι τ᾽ ἔνι πίονα νηόν.
   ἄλλος δ᾽ οὔ τις σεῖό ποθ᾽ ἅψεται, οὐδέ σε τίσει·
   οὐδ᾽ εὔβων σέ ‹γ᾽› ἔσεσθαι ὀίομαι οὐδ᾽ εὔμηλον,
55 οὐδὲ τρύγην οἴσεις, οὔτ᾽ ἂρ φυτὰ μυρία φύσεις.
   αἱ δέ κ᾽ Ἀπόλλωνος ἑκαέργου νηὸν ἔχῃσθα,
   ἄνθρωποί τοι πάντες ἀγινήσουσ᾽ ἑκατόμβας
   ἐνθάδ᾽ ἀγειρόμενοι, κνίση δέ τοι ἄσπετος αἰεὶ
   δημοῦ ἀναΐξει, βοσκήσεις θ᾽ οἵ κέ σ᾽ ἔχωσιν
60 χειρὸς ἄπ᾽ ἀλλοτρίης, ἐπεὶ οὔ τοι πῖαρ ὑπ᾽ οὖδας."

and the summits of Pelion, Samothrace and Ida's shaded mountains, well-cultivated Imbros and inhospitable Lemnos, fair Lesbos, settlement of Macar the Aeolid, Scyros, Phocaea, and steep Autocane, Chios, sleekest of islands set in the sea, rugged Mimas and the summits of Corycus, splendid Claros and steep Aisagea, well-watered Samos and Mycale's steep summits, Miletus and Cos, home of the Merop people, steep Cnidos and windy Carpathos, Naxos and Paros and rocky Rhenaea—all that way Leto travelled when pregnant with the Far-shooter, to see if any of those lands would be willing to give her son a home. But they were very tremulous and afraid, and none, however rich, ventured to accept Phoibos, until at last the mistress Leto set foot on Delos, and asked her with winged words:

"Delos, if only you would be willing to be the seat of my son, Phoibos Apollo, and establish his rich temple on your soil! No one else is ever going to engage with you or honor you, for I do not see you ever being rich in cattle or sheep, nor will you bring forth a harvest or grow abundant fruit trees. But if you have the temple of Apollo the far-shooter, all men will bring you hecatombs as they congregate here, and you will have the savor of the fat ever going up beyond measure, and you will feed your inhabitants from the hand of others, for you do not have richness under your soil."

---

35 post 37 trai. Humbert

36 ἐϋκτ- Hermann: τ᾽ εὐκτ- Ψ

53 τίσει Ernesti: λίπτει Ψ

54 γ᾽ add. Hermann

59 δημοῦ Baumeister, ἀναΐξει Schneidewin, βοσκήσεις Stoll: δηρὸν (δημὸν) ἄναξ εἰ βόσκοις fere codd.

ὣς φάτο· χαῖρε δὲ Δῆλος, ἀμειβομένη δὲ
    προσηύδα·
"Λητοῖ κυδίστη, θύγατερ μεγάλοιο Κοίοιο,
ἀσπασίη κεν ἐγώ γε γονὴν Ἑκάτοιο ἄνακτος
δεξαίμην· αἰνῶς γὰρ ἐτήτυμόν εἰμι δυσηχής
65 ἀνδράσιν, ὧδε δέ κεν περιτιμήεσσα γενοίμην.
ἀλλὰ τόδε τρομέω, Λητοῖ, ἔπος, οὐδέ σε κεύσω·
λίην γάρ τινά φασιν ἀτάσθαλον Ἀπόλλωνα
ἔσσεσθαι, μέγα δὲ πρυτανευσέμεν ἀθανάτοισιν
καὶ θνητοῖσι βροτοῖσιν ἐπὶ ζείδωρον ἄρουραν.
70 τώ ῥ᾽ αἰνῶς δείδοικα κατὰ φρένα καὶ κατὰ θυμόν,
μὴ ὁπότ᾽ ἂν τὸ πρῶτον ἴδῃ φάος ἠελίοιο
νῆσον ἀτιμήσας, ἐπεὶ ἦ κραναήπεδός εἰμι,
ποσσὶ καταστρέψας ὤσῃ ἁλὸς ἐν πελάγεσσιν·
ἔνθ᾽ ἐμὲ μὲν μέγα κῦμα κατὰ κρατὸς ἅλις αἰεί
75 κλύσσει, ὁ δ᾽ ἄλλην γαῖαν ἀφίξεται, ᾗ κεν ἅδῃ οἱ
τεύξασθαι νηόν τε καὶ ἄλσεα δενδρήεντα·
πουλύποδες δ᾽ ἐν ἐμοὶ θαλάμας φῶκαί τε μέλαιναι
οἰκία ποιήσονται ἀκηδέα χήτεϊ λαῶν.
ἀλλ᾽ εἴ μοι τλαίης γε, θεά, μέγαν ὅρκον ὀμόσσαι,
80 ἐνθάδε μιν πρῶτον τεύξειν περικαλλέα νηόν
ἔμμεναι ἀνθρώπων χρηστήριον, αὐτὰρ ἔπειτα
πάντας ἐπ᾽ ἀνθρώπους, ἐπεὶ ἦ πολυώνυμος ἔσται."
    ὣς ἄρ᾽ ἔφη· Λητὼ δὲ θεῶν μέγαν ὅρκον ὄμοσσεν·
"ἴστω νῦν τάδε Γαῖα καὶ Οὐρανὸς εὐρὺς ὕπερθεν
85 καὶ τὸ κατειβόμενον Στυγὸς ὕδωρ, ὅς τε μέγιστος
ὅρκος δεινότατός τε πέλει μακάρεσσι θεοῖσιν·
ἦ μὴν Φοίβου τῇδε θυώδης ἔσσεται αἰεί

So she spoke; and Delos was glad, and answered her:
"Leto most glorious, daughter of great Koios, I should be
happy to accept the birth of lord Far-shooter, for I am in-
deed terribly ill-famed among men, and in this way I can
become highly esteemed. But I am apprehensive about
one thing I have heard, Leto, I won't conceal it from you:
they say Apollo will be an all too wild sort, and lord it
greatly over immortals and mortals across the grain-giving
land. So my heart is terribly afraid that as soon as he sees
the light of the sun he may spurn this island, as I am indeed
rocky of soil, and kick it over into the sea's expanses. Then I
shall have the mighty waves surging over my head in a mass
for evermore, and he will go to another land, wherever it
pleases him to make his temple and his wooded groves,
while it will be the octopuses and the dark seals that make
their homes in me, all untroubled in the absence of people.
But suppose you could bring yourself, goddess, to swear a
powerful oath that this will be the first place he makes his
beautiful temple to be an oracular site for men, and that
(only) after that (will he go) all over the world, since indeed
his name will be widely known?"

So she spoke, and Leto swore the gods' powerful oath:
"So may Earth be my witness, and the broad Heaven
above, and the trickling Water of Shuddering—the most
powerful and dreadful oath that the blessed gods can
swear—truly Phoibos' fragrant altar and precinct will for

---

62 Κοίοιο Barnes: Κρόνοιο Ψ
82 ante h.v. lac. stat. Hermann   ἔσται M: ἐστιν Ψ
87 αἰεί Barnes: αἰὲν Ω

βωμὸς καὶ τέμενος, τίσει δέ σέ γ' ἔξοχα πάντων."
αὐτὰρ ἐπεί ῥ' ὅμοσέν τε τελεύτησέν τε τὸν ὅρκον,
90 Δῆλος μὲν μάλα χαῖρε γόνωι Ἑκάτοιο ἄνακτος·
Λητὼ δ' ἐννῆμάρ τε καὶ ἐννέα νύκτας ἀέπτοις
ὠδίνεσσι πέπαρτο. θεαὶ δ' ἔσαν ἔνδοθι πᾶσαι,
ὅσσαι ἄρισται ἔασι, Διώνη τε Ῥείη τε
Ἰχναίη τε Θέμις καὶ ἀγάστονος Ἀμφιτρίτη,
95 ἄλλαί τ' ἀθάναται, νόσφιν λευκωλένου Ἥρης·
ἧστο γὰρ ἐν μεγάροισ⟨ι⟩ Διὸς νεφεληγερέταο.
μούνη δ' οὐκ ἐπέπυστο μογοστόκος Εἰλείθυια·
ἧστο γὰρ ἄκρωι Ὀλύμπωι ὑπὸ χρυσέοισι νέφεσσιν
Ἥρης φραδμοσύνηις λευκωλένου, ἥ μιν ἔρυκεν
100 ζηλοσύνηι, ὅ τ' ἄρ' υἱὸν ἀμύμονά τε κρατερόν τε
Λητὼ τέξεσθαι καλλιπλόκαμος τότ' ἔμελλεν.
αἱ δ' Ἶριν προύπεμψαν ἐϋκτιμένης ἀπὸ νήσου
ἀξέμεν Εἰλείθυιαν, ὑποσχόμεναι μέγαν ὅρμον
χρυσείοισι λίνοισιν ἐερμένον, ἐννεάπηχυν·
105 νόσφιν δ' ἤνωγον καλέειν λευκωλένου Ἥρης,
μή μιν ἔπειτ' ἐπέεσσιν ἀποστρέψειεν ἰοῦσαν.
αὐτὰρ ἐπεὶ τό γ' ἄκουσε ποδήνεμος ὠκέα Ἶρις,
βῆ ῥα θέειν, ταχέως δὲ διήνυσε πᾶν τὸ μεσηγύ.
αὐτὰρ ἐπεί ῥ' ἵκανε θεῶν ἕδος αἰπὺν Ὄλυμπον,
110 αὐτίκ' ἄρ' Εἰλείθυιαν ἀπὸ μεγάροιο θύραζε
ἐκπροκαλεσσαμένη ἔπεα πτερόεντα προσηύδα
πάντα μάλ' ὡς ἐπέτελλον Ὀλύμπια δώματ' ἔχουσαι·
τῆι δ' ἄρα θυμὸν ἔπειθεν ἐνὶ στήθεσσι φίλοισιν,
βὰν δὲ ποσὶ τρήρωσι πελειάσιν ἴθμαθ' ὁμοῖαι.
115 εὖτ' ἐπὶ Δήλου ἔβαινε μογοστόκος Εἰλείθυια,

ever be here, and he will honor you above all others."

When she had sworn and completed the oath, Delos rejoiced over the birth of lord Far-shooter, while Leto for nine days and nine nights was pierced by unutterable birth pangs. All the goddesses of highest degree were in with her: Dione, Rhea, Themis of Ichnai, and loud-groaning Amphitrite, and the other goddesses apart from white-armed Hera, for she was seated in the halls of Zeus the cloud-gatherer. The only one who had not learned of it was the goddess of birth labor, Eileithyia, for she was seated atop Olympus under golden clouds by the designs of white-armed Hera, who was holding her back out of jealousy, because lovely-haired Leto was about to give birth to a fine strong son.

The others sent Iris off from the well-cultivated island to fetch Eileithyia, promising her a great necklace strung with golden threads, nine cubits long; and they told her to summon her without reference to white-armed Hera, in case she should call her back. When windfoot-swift Iris heard that, she went off at a run, and quickly crossed the whole intervening space. Arriving at the gods' seat, steep Olympus, she at once called Eileithyia out from the hall and spoke to her winged words, all that the Olympian goddesses had instructed her, and persuaded her heart within her breast; and they went forth, stepping like anxious doves.

Once the goddess of birth labor, Eileithyia, was on

---

91 ἀέπτοις Wackernagel: ἀέλπτοις Ω
93 ἔασι Wolf: ἔσαν Ω   96 om. M*a*
99 φραδμοσύνης M: -νη Ψ
104 ἐερμένον Barnes: ἐεργμένον Ω

τὴν τότε δὴ τόκος εἷλε, μενοίνησεν δὲ τεκέσθαι.
ἀμφὶ δὲ φοίνικι βάλε πήχεε, γούνα δ᾽ ἔρεισεν
λειμῶνι μαλακῶι, μείδησε δὲ γαῖ᾽ ὑπένερθεν·
ἐκ δ᾽ ἔθορε πρὸ φόωσδε, θεαὶ δ᾽ ὀλόλυξαν ἅπασαι.
120 ἔνθα σέ, ἤϊε Φοῖβε, θεαὶ λόον ὕδατι καλῶι
ἁγνῶς καὶ καθαρῶς, σπάρξαν δ᾽ ἐν φάρεϊ λευκῶι
λεπτῶι νηγατέωι· περὶ δὲ χρύσεον στρόφον ἧκαν.
οὐδ᾽ ἄρ᾽ Ἀπόλλωνα χρυσάορα θήσατο μήτηρ,
ἀλλὰ Θέμις νέκταρ τε καὶ ἀμβροσίην ἐρατεινήν
125 ἀθανάτηισιν χερσὶν ἐπήρξατο· χαῖρε δὲ Λητώ.
{οὕνεκα τοξοφόρον καὶ καρτερὸν υἱὸν ἔτικτεν.}
    αὐτὰρ ἐπεὶ δή, Φοῖβε, κατέβρως ἄμβροτον εἶδαρ,
οὔ σέ γ᾽ ἔπειτ᾽ ἴσχον χρύσεοι στρόφοι ἀσπαίροντα
οὐδ᾽ ἔτι δέσματ᾽ ἔρυκε, λύοντο δὲ πείρατα πάντα.
130 αὐτίκα δ᾽ ἀθανάτηισι μετηύδα Φοῖβος Ἀπόλλων·
"εἴη μοι κίθαρίς τε φίλη καὶ καμπύλα τόξα,
χρήσω τ᾽ ἀνθρώποισι Διὸς νημερτέα βουλήν."
    ὣς εἰπὼν ἐβίβασκεν ἐπὶ χθονὸς εὐρυοδείης
Φοῖβος ἀκερσεκόμης ἑκατηβόλος· αἱ δ᾽ ἄρα πᾶσαι
135 θάμβεον ἀθάναται· χρυσῶι δ᾽ ἄρα Δῆλος ἅπασα
βεβρίθει, καθορῶσα Διὸς Λητοῦς τε γενέθλην,
γηθοσύνηι ὅτι μιν θεὸς εἵλετο οἰκία θέσθαι
νήσων ἠπείρου τε, φίλησε δὲ κηρόθι μᾶλλον.
ἤνθησ᾽, ὡς ὅτε τε ῥίον οὔρεος ἄνθεσιν ὕλης.

126 (= 13) del. Matthiae
133 ἐπὶ Matthiae: ἀπὸ Ω
136–8 praebet y: om. ΜΨ

Delos, Leto was seized with birthing and strove to be delivered. She clasped her arms round the palm tree, and braced her knees against the soft meadow grass, and the earth beneath her smiled; out he sprang into the light, and all the goddesses gave a yell.[15] There they washed you in clear water, Eïan[16] Phoibos, in pure and holy fashion, wrapped you in a white cloth, fine-woven and unsullied(?), and tied a golden cord round it. Apollo of the golden sword was not breast-fed by his mother: Themis served him nectar and lovely ambrosia with her immortal hands, and Leto rejoiced {at having borne a powerful archer son}.

Once you had eaten the divine food, Phoibos, then the golden cords no longer restrained your wriggling, the fastenings no longer held you back, but all the ties came undone. At once Phoibos Apollo spoke among the goddesses: "I want the lyre and the crooked bow as my things. And I shall prophesy Zeus' unerring will to humankind."

So saying, he began to walk on the broad-wayed earth as Phoibos the far-shooter of unshorn locks. All the goddesses looked on in wonder, and all Delos[17] was laden with golden growth as it beheld the offspring of Zeus and Leto, in joy that the god had chosen her to make his home out of all the islands and mainland, and had given her his affection from the heart.

[15] A ritual cry of emotional release uttered by women at the climax of a sacrifice or otherwise when the presence of divinity is manifested.

[16] Adjective formed from the ritual shout "Ē!" or "Iē!"

[17] Two alternative versions of the text are transmitted for the remainder of this sentence. The other reads: "blossomed with gold, as when a mountain slope blossoms with wild flowers."

140 αὐτὸς δ᾽, ἀργυρότοξε ἄναξ ἑκατηβόλ᾽ Ἄπολλον,
ἄλλοτε μέν τ᾽ ἐπὶ Κύνθου ἐβήσαο παιπαλόεντος,
ἄλλοτε δ᾽ αὖ νήσους τε καὶ ἀνέρας ἠλάσκαζες.
πολλοί τοι νηοί τε καὶ ἄλσεα δενδρήεντα,
πᾶσαι δὲ σκοπιαί τε φίλαι καὶ πρώονες ἄκροι

145 ὑψηλῶν ὀρέων ποταμοί θ᾽ ἅλαδε προρέοντες·
ἀλλὰ σὺ Δήλωι, Φοῖβε, μάλιστ᾽ ἐπιτέρπεαι ἦτορ,
ἔνθά τοι ἑλκεχίτωνες Ἰάονες ἠγερέθονται
αὐτοῖς σὺν παίδεσσι γυναιξί τε σὴν ἐς ἄγυιαν·
οἳ δέ σε πυγμαχίηι τε καὶ ὀρχηστυῖ καὶ ἀοιδῆι

150 μνησάμενοι τέρπουσιν, ὅταν καθέσωσιν ἀγῶνα.
φαίη κ᾽ ἀθανάτους καὶ ἀγήρως ἔμμεναι ἀνήρ,
ὃς τότ᾽ ἐπαντιάσει᾽, ὅτ᾽ Ἰάονες ἀθρόοι εἶεν·
πάντων γάρ κεν ἴδοιτο χάριν, τέρψαιτο δὲ θυμόν
ἄνδράς τ᾽ εἰσορόων καλλιζώνους τε γυναῖκας

155 νῆάς τ᾽ ὠκείας ἠδ᾽ αὐτῶν κτήματα πολλά.
πρὸς δὲ τόδε μέγα θαῦμα, ὅου κλέος οὔ ποτ᾽
   ὀλεῖται,
κοῦραι Δηλιάδες Ἑκατηβελέταο θεράπναι·
αἵ τ᾽ ἐπεὶ ἂρ πρῶτον μὲν Ἀπόλλων᾽ ὑμνήσωσιν,
αὖτις δ᾽ αὖ Λητώ τε καὶ Ἄρτεμιν ἰοχέαιραν,

160 μνησάμεναι ἀνδρῶν τε παλαιῶν ἠδὲ γυναικῶν
ὕμνον ἀείδουσιν, θέλγουσι δὲ φῦλ᾽ ἀνθρώπων.
πάντων δ᾽ ἀνθρώπων φωνὰς καὶ βαμβαλιαστύν
μιμεῖσθ᾽ ἴσασιν· φαίη δέ κεν αὐτὸς ἕκαστος
φθέγγεσθ᾽· οὕτω σφιν καλὴ συνάρηρεν ἀοιδή.

165 ἀλλ᾽ ἄγεθ᾽ ἱλήκοι μὲν Ἀπόλλων Ἀρτέμιδι ξύν,

3. TO APOLLO

You yourself, lord Silverbow, far-shooting Apollo, went sometimes on rugged Cynthus, and sometimes you roamed the islands and the world of men. Many are your temples and wooded groves, and all the peaks find favor with you, and the upper ridges of the high mountains, and the rivers flowing on to the sea. But it is in Delos, Phoibos, that your heart most delights, where the Ionians with trailing robes assemble with their children and wives on your avenue, and when they have seated the gathering they think of you and entertain you with boxing, dancing, and singing. A man might think they were the unaging immortals if he came along then when the Ionians are all together: he would take in the beauty of the whole scene, and be delighted at the spectacle of the men and the fair-girt women, the swift ships and the people's piles of belongings. And besides, this great wonder, the fame of which will never perish: the Maidens of Delos, the servants of the Far-shooter, who, after first hymning Apollo, and then in turn Leto and Artemis profuse of arrows, turn their thoughts to the men and women of old and sing a song that charms the peoples. They know how to mimic all people's voices and their babble; anyone might think it was he himself speaking, so well is their singing constructed.

But now, may Apollo be favorable, together with Arte-

---

148 αὐτοῖς σὺν Ω: σὺν σφοῖσιν Thuc. 3.104   γυναιξί τε
σὴν ἐς ἄγυιαν Thuc.: καὶ αἰδοίῃς ἀλόχοισιν Ω
149 οἳ δέ Ω: ἔνθα Thuc.   ὀρχηστυῖ Thuc.: ὀρχηθμῶι Ω
150 καθέσωσιν Thuc.: στήσωνται Ω
151 ἀθάνατος M   ἀνὴρ fx: αἰεὶ Mp
162 βαμβαλιαστὺν y: κρεμβ- MΨ
165 ἀλλ' ἄγεθ' ἱλήκοι Thuc.: ἀλλά γε (δὴ) Λητὼ Ω

83

χαίρετε δ᾽ ὑμεῖς πᾶσαι· ἐμεῖο δὲ καὶ μετόπισθε
μνήσασθ᾽, ὁππότε κέν τις ἐπιχθονίων ἀνθρώπων
ἐνθάδ᾽ ἀνείρηται ξεῖνος ταλαπείριος ἐλθών·
"ὦ κοῦραι, τίς δ᾽ ὔμμιν ἀνὴρ ἥδιστος ἀοιδῶν
170 ἐνθάδε πωλεῖται, καὶ τέωι τέρπεσθε μάλιστα;"
ὑμεῖς δ᾽ εὖ μάλα πᾶσαι ὑποκρίνασθαι ἀφήμως·
"τυφλὸς ἀνήρ, οἰκεῖ δὲ Χίωι ἔνι παιπαλοέσσηι·
τοῦ πᾶσαι μετόπισθεν ἀριστεύουσιν ἀοιδαί."
ἡμεῖς δ᾽ ὑμέτερον κλέος οἴσομεν, ὅσσον ἐπ᾽ αἶαν
175 ἀνθρώπων στρεφόμεσθα πόλεις εὖ ναιεταώσας·
οἳ δ᾽ ἐπὶ δὴ πείσονται, ἐπεὶ καὶ ἐτήτυμόν ἐστιν.
αὐτὰρ ἐγὼν οὐ λήξω ἑκηβόλον Ἀπόλλωνα
ὑμνέων ἀργυρότοξον, ὃν ἠΰκομος τέκε Λητώ.
ὦ ἄνα, καὶ Λυκίην καὶ Μηιονίην ἐρατεινήν
180 καὶ Μίλητον ἔχεις ἔναλον πόλιν ἱμερόεσσαν,
αὐτὸς δ᾽ αὖ Δήλοιο περικλύστου μέγ᾽ ἀνάσσεις·
εἶσι δὲ φορμίζων Λητοῦς ἐρικυδέος υἱός
φόρμιγγι γλαφυρῆι πρὸς Πυθὼ πετρήεσσαν,
ἄμβροτα εἵματ᾽ ἔχων τεθυωμένα· τοῖο δὲ φόρμιγξ
185 χρυσέου ὑπὸ πλήκτρου καναχὴν ἔχει ἱμερόεσσαν.
ἔνθεν δὲ πρὸς Ὄλυμπον ἀπὸ χθονὸς ὥς τε νόημα
εἶσι Διὸς πρὸς δῶμα θεῶν μεθ᾽ ὁμήγυριν ἄλλων·
αὐτίκα δ᾽ ἀθανάτοισι μέλει κίθαρις καὶ ἀοιδή.
Μοῦσαι μέν θ᾽ ἅμα πᾶσαι ἀμειβόμεναι ὀπὶ καλῆι
190 ὑμνέουσίν ῥα θεῶν δῶρ᾽ ἄμβροτα ἠδ᾽ ἀνθρώπων
τλημοσύνας, ὅσ᾽ ἔχοντες ὑπ᾽ ἀθανάτοισι θεοῖσιν
ζώουσ᾽ ἀφραδέες καὶ ἀμήχανοι, οὐδὲ δύνανται

mis, and hail, all you Maidens! Think of me in future, if ever some long-suffering stranger comes here and asks, "O Maidens, which is your favorite singer who visits here, and who do you enjoy most?" Then you must all answer with one voice(?), "It is a blind man, and he lives in rocky Chios; all of his songs remain supreme afterwards."[18] And we will carry your reputation wherever we go as we roam the well-ordered cities of men, and they will believe it, because it is true. And myself, I shall not cease from hymning the far-shooter Apollo of the silver bow, whom lovely-haired Leto bore.

O Lord, Lycia too is yours, and lovely Lydia, and Miletus the beautiful town by the sea; and you again, none other, are the great lord of wave-washed Delos; and playing on his scooped-out lyre glorious Leto's son goes also to rocky Pytho, his divine garments scented, while his lyre under the golden plectrum makes a delightful clangor. From there he goes up from earth to Olympus, swift as thought, to the house of Zeus, to join the congregation of the other gods; and at once the immortals devote themselves to lyre music and song. The Muses, responding all together with lovely voice, sing of the gods' divine gifts and of human sufferings—all that they have from the immortal gods and yet live witless and helpless, unable to find a rem-

---

[18] On this passage see the Introduction.

---

168 ξεῖνος ταλαπείριος ἐλθών Ω: ταλαπείριος ἄλλος ἐπελθών Thuc.

171 ἀφήμως Thuc.: ἀφ' ἡμέων Mfb, ἀφ' ὑμέων a, ἀφ' ὑμῶν p

181 περικλύστου M: -ης Ψ

184 τεθνωμένα Barnes: τεθνώδεα Ω

εὑρέμεναι θανάτοιό τ' ἄκος καὶ γήραος ἄλκαρ.
αὐτὰρ ἐϋπλόκαμοι Χάριτες καὶ εὔφρονες Ὧραι
195 Ἁρμονίη θ' Ἥβη τε Διὸς θυγάτηρ τ' Ἀφροδίτη
ὀρχέοντ' ἀλλήλων ἐπὶ καρπῶι χεῖρας ἔχουσαι·
τῆισι μὲν οὔτ' αἰσχρὴ μεταμέλπεται οὔτ' ἐλάχεια,
ἀλλὰ μάλα μεγάλη τε ἰδεῖν καὶ εἶδος ἀγητή
Ἄρτεμις ἰοχέαιρα ὁμότροφος Ἀπόλλωνι·
200 ἐν δ' αὖ τῆισιν Ἄρης καὶ ἐΰσκοπος Ἀργειφόντης
παίζουσ'· αὐτὰρ ὁ Φοῖβος Ἀπόλλων ἐγκιθαρίζει
καλὰ καὶ ὕψι βιβάς, αἴγλη δέ μιν ἀμφιφαείνει
μαρμαρυγαί τε ποδῶν καὶ ἐϋκλώστοιο χιτῶνος.
οἱ δ' ἐπιτέρπονται θυμὸν μέγαν εἰσορόωντες
205 Λητώ τε χρυσοπλόκαμος καὶ μητίετα Ζεύς
υἷα φίλον παίζοντα μετ' ἀθανάτοισι θεοῖσιν.
πῶς τάρ σ' ὑμνήσω, πάντως εὔυμνον ἐόντα;
ἠέ σ' ἐνὶ μνηστῆισιν ἀείδω καὶ φιλότητι,
ὅππως μνωόμενος ἔκιες Ἀζαντίδα κούρην
210 Ἴσχυ' ἅμ' ἀντιθέωι Ἐλατιονίδηι εὐίππωι;
†ἢ ἅμα Φόρβαντι Τριόπεω γένος, ἢ ἅμ' Ἐρευθεῖ,
ἢ ἅμα Λευκίππωι καὶ Λευκίπποιο δάμαρτι
πεζός, ὁ δ' ἵπποισιν; οὐ μὴν Τρίοπός γ' ἐνέλειπεν.†
ἢ ὡς τὸ πρῶτον χρηστήριον ἀνθρώποισιν
215 ζητεύων κατὰ γαῖαν ἔβης, ἑκατηβόλ' Ἄπολλον;
Πιερίην μὲν πρῶτον ἀπ' Οὐλύμποιο κατῆλθες·

198 ἀγητὴ Ψ: ἀγαυὴ Μ
209 ὅππως Wolf, μνωόμενος Martin: ὁππόσ' ἀνωόμενος Ψ,
ὁππόταν ἱέμενος Μ

edy for death or a defence against old age. The lovely-
haired Graces and the cheerful Horai, and Harmonia,
Hebe, and Zeus' daughter Aphrodite, dance, holding each
other's wrists; among them performs one neither plain nor
short of stature, but tall and fair to behold, Artemis profuse
of arrows, fellow nursling of Apollo. Among them also Ares
and the keen-sighted Argus-slayer sport; while he, Phoibos
Apollo, plays his lyre in the middle, stepping fine and high,
and splendor shines about him, and the flashing of his feet
and his tunic of quality thread. Leto of the golden locks
and resourceful Zeus are delighted in their great hearts as
they watch their dear son sporting among the immortal
gods.

How shall I hymn you, fit subject as you are in every
respect? Shall I sing of you as a wooer and lover, of how
you went to court the Azantid maid[19] in rivalry with god-
like Ischys, Elatos' cavalier son, or with Phorbas born
of Triopas, or with Ereutheus, or with Leucippus and
Leucippus' wife, you on foot and he on chariot—and he
did not fall behind Triops?[20] Or of how you first went over
the earth, far-shooting Apollo, in search of a place for your
oracle for humankind?

To Pieria first you came down from Olympus; you

[19] Coronis, who gave birth to Asclepius. See Hymn 16.
[20] These lines are deeply obscure. Phorbas the son of Triopas
is elsewhere mentioned as a youth whom Apollo loved.

---

211 Τριόπεω Ilgen: τριοπῶ M, τριόπω Ψ (τριοπόω b marg.)
ἅμ᾽ ἐρευθεῖ Ψ (ἀμαρύνθω b marg.): ἅμ᾽ ἐρεχθεῖ M

Λέκτον τ᾽ ἠμαθόεντα παρέστιχες ἠδ᾽ Αἰνιῆνας
καὶ διὰ Περραιβούς· τάχα δ᾽ εἰς Ἰωλκὸν ἵκανες,
Κηναίου τ᾽ ἐπέβης ναυσικλειτῆς Εὐβοίης·
220 στῆς δ᾽ ἐπὶ Ληλάντωι πεδίωι, τό τοι οὐχ ἅδε θυμῶι
τεύξασθαι νηόν τε καὶ ἄλσεα δενδρήεντα.
ἔνθεν δ᾽ Εὔριπον διαβάς, ἑκατηβόλ᾽ Ἄπολλον,
βῆς ἀν᾽ ὄρος ζάθεον Χλωρόν· τάχα δ᾽ ἷξες ἀπ᾽
αὐτοῦ
ἐς Μυκαλησσὸν ἰὼν καὶ Τευμησσὸν λεχεποίην.
225 Θήβης δ᾽ εἰσαφίκανες ἕδος καταειμένον ὕληι·
οὐ γάρ πώ τις ἔναιε βροτῶν ἱερῆι ἐνὶ Θήβηι,
οὐδ᾽ ἄρα πω τότε γ᾽ ἦσαν ἀταρπιτοὶ οὐδὲ κέλευθοι
Θήβης ἂμ πεδίον πυρηφόρον, ἀλλ᾽ ἔχεν ὕλη.
ἔνθεν δὲ προτέρω ἔκιες, ἑκατηβόλ᾽ Ἄπολλον,
230 Ὀγχηστὸν δ᾽ ἷξες, Ποσιδήϊον ἀγλαὸν ἄλσος·
ἔνθα νεοδμὴς πῶλος ἀναπνέει ἀχθόμενός περ
ἕλκων ἅρματα καλά, χαμαὶ δ᾽ ἐλατὴρ ἀγαθός περ
ἐκ δίφροιο θορὼν ὁδὸν ἔρχεται· οἳ δὲ τέως μέν
κείν᾽ ὄχεα κροτέουσιν ἀνακτορίην ἀφιέντες.
235 εἰ δέ κεν ἅρματ᾽ ἀγῆισιν ἐν ἄλσεϊ δενδρήεντι,
ἵππους μὲν κομέουσι, τὰ δὲ κλίναντες ἐῶσιν·
ὣς γὰρ τὰ πρώτισθ᾽ ὁσίη γένεθ᾽· οἳ δὲ ἄνακτι
εὔχονται, δίφρον δὲ θεοῦ τότε μοῖρα φυλάσσει.
ἔνθεν δὲ προτέρω ἔκιες, ἑκατηβόλ᾽ Ἄπολλον·
240 Κηφισὸν δ᾽ ἄρ᾽ ἔπειτα κιχήσαο καλλιρέεθρον,
ὅς τε Λιλαίηθεν προχέει καλλίρροον ὕδωρ·
τὸν διαβάς, Ἑκάεργε, καὶ Ὠκαλέην πολύπυρον

passed by sandy Lektos, and the Aenianes, and through the Perrhaebians. Soon you reached Iolcus, and landed on Kenaion in Euboea famed for shipping, and stood on the Lelantine Plain; but it did not find favor with you for making your temple and wooded groves. From there you crossed the Euripus, far-shooting Apollo, and stepped upon the holy Green Mountain. From that you quickly reached Mycalessus and grassy Teumessus, and arrived at the site of Thebes, which was cloaked in vegetation, for no mortal yet dwelt in holy Thebes and there were not yet any paths or roads crossing the wheat-bearing Theban plain, but it was occupied by wild growth.

From there you went on, far-shooting Apollo, and reached Onchestus, Poseidon's bright grove, where the new-broken colt takes breath from the burden of pulling a fine chariot: the driver, good as he is, jumps down from the car and walks, while they continue to rattle the empty vehicle along, having discarded their master. If the chariot gets smashed in the wooded grove, they take care of the horses but tip the chariot down and leave it; for so the rule was established in the beginning. They pray to the deity, and the chariot is kept as the god's property.

From there you went on, far-shooting Apollo, and you next reached the fair streams of the Cephisus, which sends its fair-flowing water forth from Lilaia. You crossed it, Far-shooter, and Ocalea rich in wheat, and from there

---

217 Ἠμαθίην τε Matthiae   ἠδ' Αἰνιῆνας Fick: ἠδ' ἀγνιήνας M: ἠ μαγνιήνας y: ἠ μαγνηίδας Ψ

227 τότε fp: ποτε Mx   228 ὔλη Barnes: ὔλην Ω

233 οἱ δὲ p: οὐδὲ Mfx

242 πολύπυρον Barnes: -πυργον Ω

ἔνθεν ἄρ' εἰς Ἁλίαρτον ἀφίκεο ποιήεντα.
βῆς δ' ἐπὶ Τελφούσης· τόθι τοι ἅδε χῶρος ἀπήμων
245 τεύξασθαι νηόν τε καὶ ἄλσεα δενδρήεντα.
στῆς δὲ μάλ' ἄγχ' αὐτῆς καί μιν πρὸς μῦθον ἔειπες·
"Τελφοῦσ', ἐνθάδε δὴ φρονέω περικαλλέα νηόν
ἀνθρώπων τεῦξαι χρηστήριον, οἵ τέ μοι αἰεί
πολλοὶ ἀγινήσουσι τεληέσσας ἑκατόμβας,
250 ἠμὲν ὅσοι Πελοπόννησον πίειραν ἔχουσιν
ἠδ' ὅσοι Εὐρώπην τε καὶ ἀμφιρύτας κατὰ νήσους,
χρησόμενοι· τοῖσιν δέ κ' ἐγὼ νημερτέα βουλήν
πᾶσι θεμιστεύοιμι χρέων ἐνὶ πίονι νηῶι."
ὣς εἰπὼν διέθηκε θεμείλια Φοῖβος Ἀπόλλων
255 εὐρέα καὶ μάλα μακρὰ διηνεκές· ἡ δ' ἐσιδοῦσα
Τελφοῦσα κραδίην ἐχολώσατο εἶπέ τε μῦθον·
"Φοῖβε ἄναξ ἑκάεργε, ἔπος τί τοι ἐν φρεσὶ θήσω,
ἐνθάδ' ἐπεὶ φρονέεις τεῦξαι περικαλλέα νηόν
ἔμμεναι ἀνθρώποις χρηστήριον, οἳ δέ τοι αἰεί
260 ἐνθάδ' ἀγινήσουσι τεληέσσας ἑκατόμβας·
ἀλλ' ἔκ τοι ἐρέω, σὺ δ' ἐνὶ φρεσὶ βάλλεο σῆισιν·
πημανέει σ' αἰεὶ κτύπος ἵππων ὠκειάων
ἀρδόμενοί τ' οὐρῆες ἐμῶν ἱερῶν ἀπὸ πηγέων·
ἔνθά τις ἀνθρώπων βουλήσεται εἰσοράασθαι
265 ἅρματά τ' εὐποίητα καὶ ὠκυπόδων κτύπον ἵππων
ἢ νηόν τε μέγαν καὶ κτήματα πόλλ' ἐνεόντα.
ἀλλ' εἰ δή τι πίθοιο (σὺ δὲ κρέσσων καὶ ἀρείων
ἐσσὶ ἄναξ ἐμέθεν, σέο δὲ σθένος ἐστὶ μέγιστον)·
ἐν Κρίσηι ποίησαι, ὑπὸ πτυχὶ Παρνησσοῖο.
270 ἔνθ' οὔθ' ἅρματα καλὰ δονήσεται, οὔτέ τοι ἵππων

you arrived at grassy Haliartus. And you approached
Telphousa: there the innocuous site found favor with you
for making your temple and wooded groves. You stood up
close to her and spoke to her:

"Telphousa, here I am minded to make my beautiful
temple as an oracle for humankind, who will ever come in
crowds bringing me perfect hecatombs, both those who
live in the fertile Peloponnese and those who live in the
Mainland and the seagirt islands, wishing to consult me;
and I would dispense unerring counsel to them all, issuing
oracles in my rich temple."

So saying, Phoibos Apollo laid out his foundations in
broad and very long, unbroken lines. Telphousa, looking
on, grew angry and said:

"Phoibos, far-shooting lord, I am going to say some-
thing for you to take to heart, as it is here you are minded to
make your beautiful temple as an oracle for humankind,
who will ever come in crowds bringing you perfect heca-
tombs. I will speak out, and you must take it to heart. You
will always be bothered by the clatter of racehorses, and of
mules being watered from my divine springs; here people
will want to gaze at well-built chariots and the clatter of
racing horses, rather than at a big temple with a mass of
wealth inside it. No, if you would take my advice (of course
you are nobler and more powerful than I, lord, and your
strength is supreme), make it at Crisa, in the hollow of
Parnassus: there there will be no noise of chariots or clatter

---

249 πολλοὶ M: ἐνθάδ᾽ (= 260, 289) Ψ
251 ἀμφιρύτας Ψ: -τους M
252 κ᾽ Ilgen: τ᾽ Ω

ὠκυπόδων κτύπος ἔσται ἐΰδμητον περὶ βωμόν.
ἀλλὰ καὶ ὧς προσάγοιεν Ἰηπαιήονι δῶρα
ἀνθρώπων κλυτὰ φῦλα, σὺ δὲ φρένας ἀμφὶ γεγηθώς
δέξαι᾽ ἱερὰ καλὰ περικτιόνων ἀνθρώπων."

275 ὧς εἰποῦσ᾽ Ἑκάτου πέπιθε φρένας, ὄφρα οἱ αὐτῆι
Τελφούσηι κλέος εἴη ἐπὶ χθονί, μηδ᾽ Ἑκάτοιο.
ἔνθεν δὲ προτέρω ἔκιες, ἑκατηβόλ᾽ Ἄπολλον,
ἷξες δ᾽ ἐς Φλεγύων ἀνδρῶν πόλιν ὑβριστάων,
οἳ Διὸς οὐκ ἀλέγοντες ἐπὶ χθονὶ ναιετάασκον
280 ἐν καλῆι βήσσηι Κηφισίδος ἐγγύθι λίμνης.
ἔνθεν καρπαλίμως προσέβης πρὸς δειράδα θυίων,
ἵκεο δ᾽ ἐς Κρίσην ὑπὸ Παρνησσὸν νιφόεντα,
κνημὸν πρὸς Ζέφυρον τετραμμένον, αὐτὰρ ὕπερθεν
πέτρη ἐπικρέμαται, κοίλη δ᾽ ὑποδέδρομε βήσσα
285 τρηχεῖ᾽· ἔνθα ἄναξ τεκμήρατο Φοῖβος Ἀπόλλων
νηὸν ποιήσασθαι ἐπήρατον, εἶπέ τε μῦθον·
"ἐνθάδε δὴ φρονέω τεῦξαι περικαλλέα νηὸν
ἔμμεναι ἀνθρώποις χρηστήριον, οἵ τέ μοι αἰεί
ἐνθάδ᾽ ἀγινήσουσι τεληέσσας ἑκατόμβας,
290 ἠμὲν ὅσοι Πελοπόννησον πίειραν ἔχουσιν,
ἠδ᾽ ὅσοι Εὐρώπην τε καὶ ἀμφιρύτας κατὰ νήσους,
χρησόμενοι· τοῖσιν δ᾽ ἄρ᾽ ἐγὼ νημερτέα βουλήν
πᾶσι θεμιστεύοιμι χρέων ἐνὶ πίονι νηῶι."
ὧς εἰπὼν διέθηκε θεμείλια Φοῖβος Ἀπόλλων
295 εὐρέα καὶ μάλα μακρὰ διηνεκές· αὐτὰρ ἐπ᾽ αὐτοῖς
λάϊνον οὐδὸν ἔθηκε Τροφώνιος ἠδ᾽ Ἀγαμήδης,
υἱέες Ἐργίνου, φίλοι ἀθανάτοισι θεοῖσιν·
ἀμφὶ δὲ νηὸν ἔνασσαν ἀθέσφατα φῦλ᾽ ἀνθρώπων

of racing horses round your well-built altar, but just the same the thronging peoples would bring their gifts for Ie-Paieon, and your heart would be glad as you received the fine offerings from the surrounding peoples."

So saying she persuaded the Far-shooter, intending that renown in the land should be her own, Telphousa's, and not his. From there you went on, far-shooting Apollo, and reached the community of the Phlegyes, ruffians who lived there disregarding Zeus, in a pretty valley near the Cephisus Marshes. From there you rushed speedily on up towards the ridge, and you arrived at Crisa, under snowy Parnassus, a west-facing spur with the cliff hanging over it and a hollow, rugged glen extending below. There the lord Phoibos Apollo decided to make his lovely temple, and he said:

"Here I am minded to make my beautiful temple as an oracle for humankind, who will ever come in crowds bringing me perfect hecatombs, both those who live in the fertile Peloponnese and those who live in the Mainland and the seagirt islands, wishing to consult me; and I would dispense unerring counsel to them all, issuing oracles in my rich temple."

So saying, Phoibos Apollo laid out his foundations in broad and very long, unbroken lines. Upon them Trophonios and Agamedes, the sons of Erginus, favorites of the immortal gods, laid a stone floor; and about it the teem-

---

272 καὶ Ψ: τοι Μ
287 τεῦξαι Abel: τεύξειν Ω
291 ἀμφιρύτας Barnes: -τους Ω
295 μακρὰ διαμπερές Ψ: καλὰ διηνεκές Μ

κτιστοῖσιν λάεσσιν, ἀοίδιμον ἔμμεναι αἰεί.

300   ἀγχοῦ δὲ κρήνη καλλίρροος, ἔνθα δράκαιναν
κτεῖνεν ἄναξ Διὸς υἱὸς ἀπὸ κρατεροῖο βιοῖο
ζατρεφέα μεγάλην, τέρας ἄγριον, ἣ κακὰ πολλά
ἀνθρώπους ἔρδεσκεν ἐπὶ χθονί, πολλὰ μὲν αὐτούς,
πολλὰ δὲ μῆλα ταναύποδ', ἐπεὶ πέλε πῆμα
    δαφοινόν.

305   καί ποτε δεξαμένη χρυσοθρόνου ἔτρεφεν Ἥρης
δεινόν τ' ἀργαλέον τε Τυφάονα πῆμα βροτοῖσιν,
ὅν ποτ' ἄρ' Ἥρη ἔτικτε χολωσαμένη Διὶ πατρί,
εὖτ' ἄρα δὴ Κρονίδης ἐρικυδέα γείνατ' Ἀθήνην
ἐκ κορυφῆς. ἣ δ' αἶψα χολώσατο πότνια Ἥρη,

310   ἠδὲ καὶ ἀγρομένοισι μετ' ἀθανάτοισιν ἔειπεν·
    "κέκλυτέ μεο, πάντές τε θεοὶ πᾶσαί τε θέαιναι,
ὡς ἔμ' ἀτιμάζειν ἄρχει νεφεληγερέτα Ζεύς
πρῶτος, ἐπεί μ' ἄλοχον ποιήσατο κέδν' εἰδυῖαν,
καὶ νῦν νόσφιν ἐμεῖο τέκε γλαυκῶπιν Ἀθήνην,

315   ἣ πᾶσιν μακάρεσσι μεταπρέπει ἀθανάτοισιν·
αὐτὰρ ὅ γ' ἠπεδανὸς γέγονεν μετὰ πᾶσι θεοῖσιν
παῖς ἐμὸς Ἥφαιστος ῥικνὸς πόδας, ὃν τέκον αὐτή.
⟨τὸν μὲν   . . . . . .⟩
ῥῖψ' ἀνὰ χερσὶν ἑλοῦσα καὶ ἔμβαλον εὐρέϊ πόντωι·
ἀλλά ἑ Νηρῆος θυγάτηρ Θέτις ἀργυρόπεζα

320   δέξατο καὶ μετὰ ἧισι κασιγνήτηισι κόμισσεν·
ὡς ὄφελ' ἄλλο θεοῖσι χαρίσσασθαι μακάρεσσιν.
σχέτλιε, ποικιλομῆτα, τί νῦν μητίσεαι ἄλλο;
πῶς ἔτλης οἶος τεκέειν γλαυκῶπιν Ἀθήνην;
οὐκ ἂν ἐγὼ τεκόμην; καὶ σὴ κεκλημένη ἔμπης

ing peoples built the temple with blocks set in place, to be a theme of song for ever.

Nearby is the fair-flowing spring where the lord, the son of Zeus, shot the serpent from his mighty bow, a great bloated creature, a fierce prodigy that caused much harm to people in the land—much to them, and much to their long-shanked flocks, for she was a bloody affliction.

And once she accepted for nurture from gold-throned Hera the dreadful and problematic Typhaon to be an affliction to mortals; Hera once bore him in anger at father Zeus, when he gave birth to glorious Athena out of his head. She, lady Hera, at once grew angry, and spoke among the assembled immortals:

"Hear from me, all you gods and all you goddesses, how Zeus the cloud-gatherer is taking steps to dishonor me, without provocation. For he made me his wife—a dutiful one—and now he has given birth without me to steely-eyed Athena, who stands out among all the blessed immortals, while my son has turned out a weakling among the gods, Hephaestus of the withered legs, whom I myself bore. I picked him up and threw him in the broad sea, but Nereus' daughter, Thetis silverfoot, took him in and looked after him together with her sisters; I wish she had done the gods some different service. You cunning wretch, what will you devise next? How could you bring yourself to father steely-eyed Athena on your own? Couldn't I have given birth to her? She would still have been called your child

---

309 ἐκ κορυφῆς rec.: ἐν κορυφῇ Ω
post 317 lac. stat. Chalcondyles
322 μητίσεαι M: μήσεαι fx, ἔτι μήσεαι p
323 γλαυκῶπιν Abel: γλαυκώπιδ᾽ Ω

325　ἦ‹ν ἄ›ρ' ἐν ἀθανάτοισιν οἳ οὐρανὸν εὐρὺν ἔχουσιν.
325a　φράζεο νῦν, μή τοί τι κακὸν μητίσομ' ὀπίσσω.
　　καὶ νῦν μέν τοι ἐγὼ τεχνήσομαι ὥς κε γένηται
　　παῖς ἐμός, ὅς κε θεοῖσι μεταπρέποι ἀθανάτοισιν,
　　οὔτε σὸν αἰσχύνασ' ἱερὸν λέχος οὔτ' ἐμὸν αὐτῆς·
　　οὐδέ τοι εἰς εὐνὴν πωλήσομαι, ἀλλ' ἀπὸ σεῖο
330　τηλόθ' ἐοῦσα θεοῖσι μετέσσομαι ἀθανάτοισιν."
　　ὣς εἰποῦσ' ἀπονόσφι θεῶν κίε χωομένη κῆρ.
　　αὐτίκ' ἔπειτ' ἠρᾶτο βοῶπις πότνια Ἥρη,
　　χειρὶ καταπρηνεῖ δ' ἔλασε χθόνα καὶ φάτο μῦθον·
　　"κέκλυτε νῦν μοι, Γαῖα καὶ Οὐρανὸς εὐρὺς ὕπερθεν
335　Τιτῆνές τε θεοί, τοὶ ὑπὸ χθονὶ ναιετάουσιν
　　Τάρταρον ἀμφὶ μέγαν, τῶν ἐξ ἄνδρές τε θεοί τε·
　　αὐτοὶ νῦν μεο πάντες ἀκούσατε, καὶ δότε παῖδα
　　νόσφι Διός, μηδέν τι βίην ἐπιδευέα κείνου,
　　ἀλλ' ὅ γε φέρτερος εἴη, ὅσον Κρόνου εὐρύοπα
　　　Ζεύς."
340　ὣς ἄρα φωνήσασ' ἵμασε χθόνα χειρὶ παχείηι,
　　κινήθη δ' ἄρα γαῖα φερέσβιος· ἡ δὲ ἰδοῦσα
　　τέρπετο ὃν κατὰ θυμόν, ὀίετο γὰρ τελέεσθαι.
　　ἐκ τούτου δήπειτα τελεσφόρον εἰς ἐνιαυτόν
　　οὔτε ποτ' εἰς εὐνὴν Διὸς ἤλυθε μητιόεντος
345　οὔτε ποτ' ἐς θῶκον πολυδαίδαλον, ὡς τὸ πάρος περ
　　αὐτῶι ἐφεζομένη πυκινὰς φραζέσκετο βουλάς·
　　ἀλλ' ἥ γ' ἐν νηοῖσι πολυλλίστοισι μένουσα
　　τέρπετο οἷς ἱεροῖσι βοῶπις πότνια Ἥρη.
　　ἀλλ' ὅτε δὴ μῆνές τε καὶ ἡμέραι ἐξετελέοντο

3. TO APOLLO

among the immortals who dwell in the broad heaven.
Mind I don't devise some harm for you sometime. And
right now I am going to contrive to have a son who may
stand out among the immortal gods, without disgracing
your holy bed or my own. I won't visit your bed, but stay
well away from you and keep company with the immortal
gods."

So saying, she went apart from the gods, angry at heart.
Then straightway she prayed, did the mild-eyed lady Hera,
and struck the earth with the flat of her hand and said,
"Hear me now, Earth and broad Heaven above, and you
Titan gods who dwell below the earth around great Tar-
tarus, and from whom gods and men descend: all of you
now in person, hear me and grant me a son without Zeus'
help, in no way falling short of him in strength, but as much
superior as wide-sounding Zeus is to Kronos."

So saying, she beat the ground with her stout hand, and
the life-giving earth shifted. When she saw that, her heart
was delighted, for she guessed that her prayer would be
fulfilled. From then on for a full year she never went to re-
sourceful Zeus' bed, nor to the richly carved throne, as in
the past sitting at his side she used to consider her coun-
sels. She stayed in her prayerful temples, did the mild-
eyed lady Hera, enjoying the offerings made to her. But
when the months and the days were fulfilled as the year

---

325 ἦν ἄρ' Chalcondyles: ἢ ῥ' fere Ω

325a praebet y: om. MΨ   330 τηλόθ' ἐοῦσα Hermann:
τηλόθεν οὖσα Ω   331 κῆρ Barnes: περ Ω

335 ναιετάουσιν Ilgen: ναιετάοντες Ω

339 εἴη ὅσον Hermann: ἐστιν ὅσον M: ἢ πόσσον Ψ
(παρόσον p)   349 μῆνές M: νύκτες Ψ

97

350 ἂψ περιτελλομένου ἔτεος καὶ ἐπήλυθον ὧραι,
ἣ δ' ἔτεκ' οὔτε θεοῖς ἐναλίγκιον οὔτε βροτοῖσιν,
δεινόν τ' ἀργαλέον τε Τυφάονα, πῆμα θεοῖσιν.
αὐτίκα τόν γε λαβοῦσα βοῶπις πότνια Ἥρη
δῶκεν ἔπειτα φέρουσα κακῶι κακόν, ἣ δ' ὑπέδεκτο.

355 ἣ κακὰ πόλλ' ἔρδεσκε κατὰ κλυτὰ φῦλ' ἀνθρώπων·
ὃς τῆι γ' ἀντιάσειε, φέρεσκέ μιν αἴσιμον ἦμαρ,
πρίν γέ οἱ ἰὸν ἐφῆκεν ἄναξ ἑκάεργος Ἀπόλλων
καρτερόν· ἣ δ' ὀδύνηισιν ἐρεχθομένη χαλεπῆισιν
κεῖτο μέγ' ἀσθμαίνουσα, κυλινδομένη κατὰ χῶρον.

360 θεσπεσίη δ' ἐνοπὴ γένετ' ἄσπετος· ἣ δὲ καθ' ὕλην
πυκνὰ μάλ' ἔνθα καὶ ἔνθα ἑλίσσετο, λεῖπε δὲ θυμόν,
φοινὸν ἀποπνείουσ'. ὃ δ' ἐπηύξατο Φοῖβος
    Ἀπόλλων·
"ἐνταυθοῖ νῦν πύθε' ἐπὶ χθονὶ βωτιανείρηι·
οὐδὲ σύ γ' ἐν ζωοῖσι κακὸν δήλημα βροτοῖσιν

365 ἔσσεαι, οἳ γαίης πολυφόρβου καρπὸν ἔδοντες
ἐνθάδ' ἀγινήσουσι τεληέσσας ἑκατόμβας,
οὐδέ τί τοι θάνατόν γε δυσηλεγέ' οὔτε Τυφωεύς
ἀρκέσει οὐδὲ Χίμαιρα δυσώνυμος, ἀλλὰ σέ γ' αὐτοῦ
πύσει γαῖα μέλαινα καὶ ἠλέκτωρ Ὑπερίων."

370 ὣς φάτ' ἐπευχόμενος, τὴν δὲ σκότος ὄσσε
    κάλυψεν.
τὴν δ' αὐτοῦ κατέπυσ' ἱερὸν μένος Ἠελίοιο·
ἐξ οὗ νῦν Πυθὼ κικλήσκεται, οἱ δὲ ἄνακτα

came round again, and the seasons came on, she gave birth to one resembling neither gods nor mortals, the dreadful and problematic Typhaon, to be an affliction to the gods. At once the mild-eyed lady Hera picked him up and took him and gave the one bane to the other;[21] and she accepted him.

She used to do much harm to the teeming peoples—whoever encountered her was carried off by his day of doom—until the far-shooting lord Apollo discharged his powerful arrow at her. Racked by sore pain she lay, loudly gasping, rolling about the place; an extraordinary hissing arose without measure, as she kept writhing this way and that among the trees, and quit her spirit with bloody exhalations. Phoibos Apollo exulted over her:

"Now rot away here on the earth that feeds mankind! You will not be an evil bane among the living to the mortals who will eat the fruits of the nurturing soil and bring perfect hecatombs here. Neither Typhoeus nor the accursed Chimaera will save you from grisly death, but you will be rotted away here by the dark earth and the blazing sun."

So he exulted, while darkness covered her eyes. And there the sun's divine force rotted her down; hence the place is now called Pytho,[22] and the people give the god the

---

[21] That is, to the serpent at Delphi, to which the narrative now returns.

[22] The verb for 'to rot' being *pytho*.

---

352 θεοῖσιν M: βροτοῖσιν Ψ
353 τόν γε West: τόνδε Ω
355 ἥ Wolf: ὃς Ω
364 γ᾽ ἐν West: γε Ω

Πύθιον ⟨αὖ⟩ καλέουσιν ἐπώνυμον, οὕνεκα κεῖθι
αὐτοῦ πῦσε πέλωρ μένος ὀξέος Ἠελίοιο.
375 καὶ τότ᾽ ἄρ᾽ ἔγνω ᾗσιν ἐνὶ φρεσὶ Φοῖβος
  Ἀπόλλων,
οὕνεκά μιν κρήνη καλλίρροος ἐξαπάφησεν·
βῆ δ᾽ ἐπὶ Τελφούσῃ κεχολωμένος, αἶψα δ᾽ ἵκανεν·
στῆ δὲ μάλ᾽ ἄγχ᾽ αὐτῆς καί μιν πρὸς μῦθον ἔειπεν·
"Τελφοῦσ᾽, οὐκ ἄρ᾽ ἔμελλες ἐμὸν νόον ἐξαπαφοῦσα
380 χῶρον ἔχουσ᾽ ἐρατὸν προρέειν καλλίρροον ὕδωρ.
ἐνθάδε δὴ καὶ ἐμὸν κλέος ἔσσεται, οὐδὲ σὸν οἴης."
ἦ, καὶ ἐπὶ ῥίον ὦσεν ἄναξ ἑκάεργος Ἀπόλλων
πέτρῃσι προχυτῇσιν, ἀπέκρυψεν δὲ ῥέεθρα,
καὶ βωμὸν ποιήσατ᾽ ἐν ἄλσεϊ δενδρήεντι
385 ἄγχι μάλα κρήνης καλλιρρόου· ἔνθα δ᾽ ἄνακτι
πάντες ἐπίκλησιν Τελφουσίῳ εὐχετόωνται,
οὕνεκα Τελφούσης ἱερῆς ᾔσχυνε ῥέεθρα.
 καὶ τότε δὴ κατὰ θυμὸν ἐφράζετο Φοῖβος
  Ἀπόλλων,
οὕς τινας ἀνθρώπους ὀργήονας εἰσαγάγοιτο,
390 οἳ θεραπεύσονται Πυθοῖ ἔνι πετρηέσσῃ.
ταῦτ᾽ ἄρα ὁρμαίνων ἐνόησ᾽ ἐνὶ οἴνοπι πόντῳ
νῆα θοήν· ἐν δ᾽ ἄνδρες ἔσαν πολέες τε καὶ ἐσθλοί,
Κρῆτες ἀπὸ Κνωσοῦ Μινωΐου, οἵ ῥά τ᾽ ἄνακτι
ἱερά τε ῥέζουσι καὶ ἀγγέλλουσι θέμιστας
395 Φοίβου Ἀπόλλωνος χρυσαόρου, ὅττι κεν εἴπῃ
χρείων ἐκ δάφνης γυάλων ὑπὸ Παρνησσοῖο.
οἱ μὲν ἐπὶ πρῆξιν καὶ χρήματα νηῒ μελαίνῃ
ἐς Πύλον ἠμαθόεντα Πυλοιγενέας τ᾽ ἀνθρώπους

title Pythios, because it was just there that the keen sun's
force rotted the monster away.

Then Phoibos Apollo realized that the (other) fair-
flowing spring had tricked him. He set off for Telphousa in
anger, and soon he was there. He stood up close to her and
spoke to her: "Telphousa, you were not after all going to
get away with tricking me and keeping your lovely place to
pour forth your fair water. I too am going to be renowned
here, not you alone." So saying, the far-shooting lord
Apollo overturned a crag onto her in an avalanche of rocks,
and covered up her waters. And he made himself an altar
in a wooded grove close to the fair-flowing spring; there
everyone prays to the lord under the title Telphousios,
because he disfigured holy Telphousa's streams.

Then Phoibos Apollo started to consider what men he
should bring in as ministers to serve him at rocky Pytho.
While he was pondering this, he noticed a swift ship on the
wine-faced sea, and in it were many fine men, Cretans
from Cnossos the city of Minos, the ones who perform
sacrifices for the god, and who announce the rulings of
Phoibos Apollo of the golden sword, whatever he says
when he gives his oracles from the bay tree down in the
glens of Parnassus. They were sailing on business in their
dark ship towards sandy Pylos and Pylos' folk. But he,

---

373 αὖ add. West
391 ἐνὶ West: ἐπὶ Ω
398 (et 424) Πυλοιγενέας Fick: πυληγ- Ω

ἔπλεον· αὐτὰρ ὃ τοῖσι συνήνετο Φοῖβος Ἀπόλλων,
400 ἐν πόντωι δ' ἐπόρουσε δέμας δελφῖνι ἐοικώς
νηῒ θοῆι, καὶ κεῖτο πέλωρ μέγα τε δεινόν τε·
τῶν δ' ὅς τις κατὰ θυμὸν ἐπιφράσσαιτο †νοῆσαι,
πάντοσ' ἀνασσείσασκε, τίνασσε δὲ νήϊα δοῦρα.
οἳ δ' ἀκέων ἐνὶ νηῒ καθείατο δειμαίνοντες,
405 οὐδ' οἵ γ' ὅπλ' ἔλυον κοίλην ἀνὰ νῆα μέλαιναν,
οὐδ' ἔλυον λαῖφος νηὸς κυανοπρώιροιο,
ἀλλ' ὡς τὰ πρώτιστα κατεστήσαντο βοεῦσιν,
ὣς ἔπλεον· κραιπνὸς δὲ Νότος κατόπισθεν ἔπειγεν
νῆα θοήν. πρῶτον δὲ παρημείβοντο Μάλειαν,
410 πὰρ δὲ Λακωνίδα γαῖαν ἁλιστέφανον πτολίεθρον
ἷξον καὶ χῶρον τερψιμβρότου Ἠελίοιο
Ταίναρον, ἔνθά τε μῆλα βαθύτριχα βόσκεται αἰεί
Ἠελίοιο ἄνακτος, ἔχει δ' ἐπιτερπέα χῶρον.
οἳ μὲν ἄρ' ἔνθ' ἔθελον νῆα σχεῖν ἠδ' ἀποβάντες
415 φράσσασθαι μέγα θαῦμα καὶ ὀφθαλμοῖσιν ἰδέσθαι,
εἰ μενέει νηὸς γλαφυρῆς δαπέδοισι πέλωρον,
ἢ εἰς οἶδμ' ἅλιον πολυΐχθυον ἀμφὶς ὀρούσει·
ἀλλ' οὐ πηδαλίοισιν ἐπείθετο νηῦς ἐυεργής,
ἀλλὰ πάρεκ Πελοπόννησον πίειραν ἔχουσα
420 ἤϊ' ὁδόν· πνοιῆι δὲ ἄναξ ἑκάεργος Ἀπόλλων
ῥηϊδίως ἴθυν'. ἣ δὲ πρήσσουσα κέλευθον
Ἀρήνην ἵκανε καὶ Ἀργυφέην ἐρατεινήν
καὶ Θρύον, Ἀλφειοῖο πόρον, καὶ ἔυκτιτον Αἰπύ
καὶ Πύλον ἠμαθόεντα Πυλοιγενέας τ' ἀνθρώπους·
425 βῆ δὲ παρὰ Κρουνοὺς καὶ Χαλκίδα καὶ παρὰ
Δύμην

Phoibos Apollo, intercepted them, and out at sea he leaped
onto the swift ship in the likeness of a dolphin, and lay
there, a huge and fearsome beast. If any of them took it in
mind to (touch him?), he would toss him off in any direc-
tion, shaking the ship's timbers. So they sat quiet in the
ship in terror; they did not slacken the sheets along the
hollow ship, or slacken the sail of the dark-prowed craft,
but as they had originally rigged it, so they sailed on, with a
brisk southerly speeding the vessel from astern. First they
passed Cape Malea, and along the Laconian coast they
reached that sea-garlanded town and place sacred to the
Sun god who delights mortals, Taenarum, where the lord
Helios' fleecy sheep ever graze in a lovely place.

They wanted to halt the ship there and disembark
to consider the wondrous creature, and see whether the
beast would stay on the deck of the hollow ship or plunge
off into the salt swell that teems with fish. But the well-
built craft would not obey the rudder, but continued to
hold its course past the rich Peloponnese; the far-shooting
lord Apollo was steering it effortlessly with his breath.
Journeying on, it reached Arene and lovely Argyphea,
Thryon where the Alpheios is forded and well-cultivated
Aipy, and sandy Pylos and Pylos' folk; it went past the
Krounoi and Chalcis and past Dyme, and past fair Elis,

---

408 ἔπειγε Ruhnkenius: ἔγειρε Ω

ἠδὲ παρ' Ἤλιδα δῖαν, ὅθι κρατέουσιν Ἐπειοί.
   εὖτε Φεὰς ἐπέβαλλεν ἀγαλλομένη Διὸς οὔρωι,
καί σφιν ὕπεκ νεφέων Ἰθάκης τ' ὄρος αἰπὺ πέφαντο
Δουλίχιόν τε Σάμη τε καὶ ὑλήεσσα Ζάκυνθος·
430 ἀλλ' ὅτε δὴ Πελοπόννησον παρενίσατο πᾶσαν,
καὶ δὴ ἐπὶ Κρίσης κατεφαίνετο κόλπος ἀπείρων,
ὅς τε διὲκ Πελοπόννησον πίειραν ἐέργει,
ἦλθ' ἄνεμος Ζέφυρος μέγας αἴθριος ἐκ Διὸς αἴσης
λάβρος ἐπαιγίζων ἐξ αἰθέρος, ὄφρα τάχιστα
435 νηῦς ἀνύσειε θέουσα θαλάσσης ἁλμυρὸν ὕδωρ.
ἄψορρον δῆπειτα πρὸς ἠῶ τ' ἠέλιόν τε
ἔπλεον, ἡγεμόνευε δ' ἄναξ Διὸς υἱὸς Ἀπόλλων·
ἷξον δ' ἐς Κρίσην εὐδείελον ἀμπελόεσσαν
ἐς λιμέν', ἡ δ' ἀμάθοισιν ἐχρίμψατο ποντοπόρος
   νηῦς.
440   ἔνθ' ἐκ νηὸς ὄρουσεν ἄναξ ἑκάεργος Ἀπόλλων
ἀστέρι εἰδόμενος μέσωι ἤματι· τοῦ δ' ἀπὸ πολλαί
σπινθαρίδες πωτῶντο, σέλας δ' εἰς οὐρανὸν ἷκεν·
ἐς δ' ἄδυτον κατέδυσε διὰ τριπόδων ἐριτίμων.
ἔνθ' ἄρ' ὅ γε φλόγα δαῖε πιφαυσκόμενος τὰ ἃ
   κῆλα,
445 πᾶσαν δὲ Κρίσην κάτεχεν σέλας· αἱ δ' ὀλόλυξαν
Κρισαίων ἄλοχοι καλλίζωνοί τε θύγατρες
Φοίβου ὑπὸ ῥιπῆς· μέγα γὰρ δέος ἔμβαλ' ἑκάστωι.
ἔνθεν δ' αὖτ' ἐπὶ νῆα νόημ' ὣς ἆλτο πέτεσθαι,
ἀνέρι εἰδόμενος αἰζηῶι τε κρατερῶι τε
450 πρωθήβηι, χαίτηις εἰλυμένος εὐρέας ὤμους,
καί σφεας φωνήσας ἔπεα πτερόεντα προσηύδα·

where the Epeians rule.

As it headed for Pheia, exulting in the divine tailwind, from under the clouds there appeared to them Ithaca's steep mountain, Doulichion and Same and wooded Zacynthus. But when it had rounded the whole of the Peloponnese, and the vast gulf leading to Crisa came into view, that cuts through the rich Peloponnese and divides it off, there came a strong clearing westerly through Zeus' dispensation, rushing furious in from the sky to make the ship cross the briny sea with all speed. So then they sailed back eastwards, guided by the son of Zeus, lord Apollo; and they came to Crisa with its sunny vine slopes, into the harbor, and the seagoing ship grounded on the sands.

There the far-shooting lord Apollo darted off the ship, looking like a star in broad daylight, with countless sparks flying off him, and the brilliance was heaven-high. He disappeared into the sanctum through the precious tripods, and there he lit a flame to manifest his divine force. The whole of Crisa was filled with the radiance, and the Crisaeans' wives and fair-girt daughters yelled aloud under Phoibos' impulse, for he had put terror into everyone. From there again he flew back to the ship, fast as thought, in the likeness of a sturdy yeoman in his first prime, his hair falling over his broad shoulders, and he addressed them in winged words:

---

427 Φεὰς Eberhard: φερὰς Ψ, φέρας M
431 ἐπὶ M: ἐπεὶ Ψ
444 ἔνθ᾽ Hermann: ἐν δ᾽ Ω
447 ἔμβαλ᾽ ἑκάστῳ M: εἷλεν ἕκαστον Ψ

"ὦ ξεῖνοι, τίνες ἐστέ; πόθεν πλεῖθ' ὑγρὰ κέλευθα;
ἤ τι κατὰ πρῆξιν, ἦ μαψιδίως ἀλάλησθε
οἷά τε ληϊστῆρες ὑπεὶρ ἅλα, τοί τ' ἀλόωνται
455 ψυχὰς παρθέμενοι, κακὸν ἀλλοδαποῖσι φέροντες;
τίφθ' οὕτως ἧσθον τετιηότες, οὐδ' ἐπὶ γαῖαν
ἔκβητ', οὐδὲ καθ' ὅπλα μελαίνης νηὸς ἔθεσθε;
αὕτη μέν γε δίκη πέλει ἀνδρῶν ἀλφηστάων,
ὁππότ' ἂν ἐκ πόντοιο ποτὶ χθονὶ νηῒ μελαίνηι
460 ἔλθωσιν καμάτωι ἀδηκότες, αὐτίκα δέ σφεας
σίτοιο γλυκεροῖο περὶ φρένας ἵμερος αἱρεῖ."
    ὣς φάτο, καί σφιν θάρσος ἐνὶ στήθεσσιν ἔθηκεν.
τὸν καὶ ἀμειβόμενος Κρητῶν ἀγὸς ἀντίον ηὔδα·
"ξεῖν', ἐπεὶ οὐ μὲν γάρ τι καταθνητοῖσιν ἔοικας,
465 οὐ δέμας οὐδὲ φυήν, ἀλλ' ἀθανάτοισι θεοῖσιν,
οὐλέ τε καὶ μέγα χαῖρε, θεοὶ δέ τοι ὄλβια δοῖεν.
καί μοι τοῦτ' ἀγόρευσον ἐτήτυμον, ὄφρ' ἐῢ εἴδω·
τίς δῆμος; τίς γαῖα; τίνες βροτοὶ ἐγγεγάασιν;
ἄλληι γὰρ φρονέοντες ἐπεπλέομεν μέγα λαῖτμα
470 ἐς Πύλον ἐκ Κρήτης, ἔνθεν γένος εὐχόμεθ' εἶναι·
νῦν δ' ὧδε ξὺν νηῒ κατήλθομεν οὔ τι ἑκόντες,
νόστου ἱέμενοι, ἄλλην ὁδόν, ἄλλα κέλευθα,
ἀλλά τις ἀθανάτων δεῦρ' ἤγαγεν οὐκ ἐθέλοντας."
    τοὺς δ' ἀπαμειβόμενος προσέφη ἑκάεργος
        Ἀπόλλων·
475 "ξεῖνοι, τοὶ Κνωσὸν πολυδένδρεον ἀμφινέμεσθε
τὸ πρίν, ἀτὰρ νῦν οὐκέθ' ὑπότροποι αὖτις ἔσεσθε
ἔς τε πόλιν ἐρατὴν καὶ δώματα καλὰ ἕκαστος
ἔς τε φίλας ἀλόχους, ἀλλ' ἐνθάδε πίονα νηόν

"Who are you, sirs? From where do you sail the watery ways? Are you on business, or roaming at random over the sea as freebooters do, who gamble their lives abroad to bring trouble to other folk? Why do you sit so downcast without disembarking or stowing your ship's tackle? That's the usual way of civilized men when they reach land in their dark ship, weary with effort, and their hearts are at once seized with appetite for sweet food."

So he spoke, giving them confidence. The leader of the Cretans answered him: "Sir, as you don't seem at all like a mortal in body and stature, but like the immortal gods, I bid you all hail, and may the gods grant you blessings. Now tell me this for truth so that I can be sure: what folk is this, what country? What people are native here? You see, we were sailing the main with a different purpose, to Pylos from Crete, which is where we declare ourselves to originate from, but now we have landed here without meaning to, when we were seeking safe passage, by another course, other ways; some god has brought us here without us wishing it."

The far-shooter Apollo answered them: "Sirs, who dwelt in wooded Cnossos before, now you will return no more to your lovely city and your fine individual homes and your dear wives: you will occupy my rich temple here,

---

452 τίνες Chalcondyles: πόθεν Ω

ἕξετ' ἐμὸν πολλοῖσι τετιμένον ἀνθρώποισιν.
480 εἰμι δ' ἐγὼ Διὸς υἱός, Ἀπόλλων δ' εὔχομαι εἶναι,
ὑμέας δ' ἤγαγον ἐνθάδ' ὑπὲρ μέγα λαῖτμα
    θαλάσσης
οὔ τι κακὰ φρονέων, ἀλλ' ἐνθάδε πίονα νηόν
ἕξετ' ἐμὸν πᾶσιν μάλα τίμιον ἀνθρώποισιν,
βουλάς τ' ἀθανάτων εἰδήσετε· τῶν ἰότητι
485 αἰεὶ τιμήσεσθε διαμπερὲς ἤματα πάντα.
ἀλλ' ἄγεθ', ὡς ἂν ἐγὼ εἴπω, πείθεσθε τάχιστα·
ἱστία μὲν πρῶτον κάθετον λύσαντε βοῆας,
νῆα δ' ἔπειτα μέλαιναν ἐπ' ἠπείρου ἐρύσασθε,
ἐκ δὲ κτήμαθ' ἕλεσθε καὶ ἔντεα νηὸς ἐΐσης,
490 καὶ βωμὸν ποιήσατ' ἐπὶ ῥηγμῖνι θαλάσσης·
πῦρ <δ'> ἐπικαίοντες ἐπί τ' ἄλφιτα λευκὰ θύοντες
εὔχεσθαι δήπειτα παριστάμενοι περὶ βωμόν.
ὡς μὲν ἐγὼ τὸ πρῶτον ἐν ἠεροειδέι πόντωι
εἰδόμενος δελφῖνι θοῆς ἐπὶ νηὸς ὄρουσα,
495 ὣς ἐμοὶ εὔχεσθαι Δελφινίωι· αὐτὰρ ὁ βωμὸς
αὐτὸς Δέλφειος καὶ ἐπόψιος ἔσσεται αἰεί.
δειπνῆσαί τ' ἄρ' ἔπειτα θοῆι παρὰ νηὶ μελαίνηι,
καὶ σπεῖσαι μακάρεσσι θεοῖς οἳ Ὄλυμπον ἔχουσιν.
αὐτὰρ ἐπὴν σίτοιο μελίφρονος ἐξ ἔρον ἧσθε,
500 ἔρχεσθαί θ' ἅμ' ἐμοὶ καὶ ἰηπαιήον' ἀείδειν,
εἰς ὅ κε χῶρον ἵκησθον, ἵν' ἕξετε πίονα νηόν."
    ὣς ἔφαθ'· οἳ δ' ἄρα τοῦ μάλα μὲν κλύον ἠδ'
        ἐπίθοντο.
ἱστία μὲν πρῶτον κάθεσαν, λῦσαν δὲ βοῆας,
ἱστὸν δ' ἱστοδόκηι πέλασαν προτόνοισιν ὑφέντες,

which is widely honored by men. For I am Zeus' son, I declare myself Apollo; and I brought you here over the mighty main not with any ill intent, but you are to occupy my rich temple here, which is greatly honored by all men, and you shall know the gods' intentions. By their will you shall be held in honor for all time. But come, do as I tell you without delay. First slacken the sheets and lower the sails, and then haul the dark ship up on land, take out your belongings and the ship's tackle, and build an altar on the seashore. Light a fire on it, offer white barley groats on it, and then stand round the altar and pray. Even as I originally leapt onto your ship in the misty sea in the form of a dolphin, so you are to pray to me as 'the Dolphin god,'[23] and the altar itself will be 'Delphian,' and a permanent landmark. Then have your meal beside your swift dark ship, and make libation to the blessed gods in Olympus. And when you have satisfied your appetite for delicious food, come with me, singing Ie Paieon, till you arrive at the place where you will occupy the rich temple."

So he spoke, and they readily hearkened to him and did as he said. First they slackened the sheets and lowered the sails, and brought the mast down to its rest by paying out

---

[23] A common cult title of Apollo.

---

479 τετιμένοι Hermann
487 (et 503) βοῆας Buttmann: βοείας Ω
488 μέλαιναν (*Il.* 1.485) Matthiae: θοὴν Ω
491 δ' add. Ilgen

505 ἐκ δὲ καὶ αὐτοὶ βαῖνον ἐπὶ ῥηγμῖνι θαλάσσης,
ἐκ δ' ἁλὸς ἤπειρόνδε θοὴν ἀνὰ νῆ' ἐρύσαντο
ὑψοῦ ἐπὶ ψαμάθοις, παρὰ δ' ἕρματα μακρὰ
τάνυσσαν,
καὶ βωμὸν ποίησαν ἐπὶ ῥηγμῖνι θαλάσσης·
πῦρ δ' ἐπικαίοντες ἐπί τ' ἄλφιτα λευκὰ θύοντες
510 ηὔχονθ' ὡς ἐκέλευε παριστάμενοι περὶ βωμόν.
δόρπον ἔπειθ' εἵλοντο θοῆι παρὰ νηὶ μελαίνηι,
καὶ σπεῖσαν μακάρεσσι θεοῖς οἳ Ὄλυμπον ἔχουσιν.
αὐτὰρ ἐπεὶ πόσιος καὶ ἐδητύος ἐξ ἔρον ἔντο,
βάν ῥ' ἴμεν· ἦρχε δ' ἄρά σφιν ἄναξ Διὸς υἱὸς
Ἀπόλλων
515 φόρμιγγ' ἐν χείρεσσιν ἔχων, ἐρατὸν κιθαρίζων,
καλὰ καὶ ὕψι βιβάς· οἱ δὲ ῥήσσοντες ἕποντο
Κρῆτες πρὸς Πυθὼ καὶ ἰηπαιήον' ἄειδον,
οἷοί τε Κρητῶν παιήονες, οἷσί τε Μοῦσα
ἐν στήθεσσιν ἔθηκε θεὰ μελίγηρυν ἀοιδήν.
520 ἄκμητοι δὲ λόφον προσέβαν ποσίν, αἶψα δ'
ἵκοντο
Παρνησσὸν καὶ χῶρον ἐπήρατον, ἔνθ' ἄρ' ἔμελλεν
οἰκήσειν πολλοῖσι τετιμένος ἀνθρώποισιν·
δεῖξε δ' ἄγων ἄδυτον ζάθεον καὶ πίονα νηόν.
τῶν δ' ὠρίνετο θυμὸς ἐνὶ στήθεσσι φίλοισιν·
525 τὸν καὶ ἀνειρόμενος Κρητῶν ἀγὸς ἀντίον ηὔδα·
"ὦ ἄν', ἐπεὶ δὴ τῆλε φίλων καὶ πατρίδος αἴης
ἤγαγες· οὕτω που τῶι σῶι φίλον ἔπλετο θυμῶι·
πῶς καὶ νῦν βιώμεσθα; τό σε φράζεσθαι ἄνωγμεν.
οὔτε τρυγηφόρος ἥδε γ' ἐπήρατος οὔτ' εὐλείμων,

the forestays. They themselves disembarked onto the sea-
shore, and from the water they hauled the swift ship up on
land, high up the beach, and set a long line of props along
its sides. They built an altar on the seashore, lit a fire on it,
offered white barley groats on it, and then stood round the
altar and prayed, according to his instructions. Then they
had their meal beside their swift dark ship, and made liba-
tion to the blessed gods in Olympus. And when they had
satisfied their appetite for food and drink, they set off, and
Zeus' son, lord Apollo, led the way with his lyre in his
hands, playing delightfully, stepping fine and high, while
the Cretans followed to Pytho, dancing in time, and sing-
ing Ie Paieon—like the paeans of the Cretans in whose
breasts the Muse has placed honey-voiced singing.

Unwearied, they climbed the hill, and soon arrived at
Parnassus and the lovely place where he was to dwell,
widely honored by men. He led them and showed them
the holy sanctum and the rich temple, and their hearts
were stirred within them. The leader of the Cretans turned
to him and asked:

"Lord, as you have brought us far from our dear ones
and our native land—so it must have pleased your heart—
how are we going to feed ourselves now? That's what we
want you to consider. This land is not attractive as a bearer

---

510 περὶ rec. in marg.: παρὰ Ω
515 ἐρατὸν M: ατὸν x, ἀγατὸν f, χρυσῆν p: χαρίεν Ath. 22c
521–2 ἔμελλον . . . τετιμένοι Pierson
523 ἄδυτον ζάθεον y: αὐτοῦ δάπεδον MΨ
528 βώμεσθα Janko: βιόμεσθα Ω

530 ὥς τ᾽ ἀπό τε ζώειν καὶ ἅμ᾽ ἀνθρώποισιν ὀπηδεῖν."
   τοὺς δ᾽ ἐπιμειδήσας προσέφη Διὸς υἱὸς Ἀπόλλων·
"νήπιοι ἄνθρωποι, δυστλήμονες, οἳ μελεδώνας
βούλεσθ᾽ ἀργαλέους τε πόνους καὶ στείνεα θυμῶι·
ῥηΐδιον ἔπος ὔμμ᾽ ἐρέω καὶ ἐπὶ φρεσὶ θήσω.
535 δεξιτερῆι μάλ᾽ ἕκαστος ἔχων ἐν χειρὶ μάχαιραν
σφάζειν αἰεὶ μῆλα· τὰ δ᾽ ἄφθονα πάντα παρέσται,
ὅσσα κ᾽ ἐμοὶ ἀγάγωσι περικλυτὰ φῦλ᾽ ἀνθρώπων.
νηὸν δὲ προφύλαχθε, δέδεχθε δὲ φῦλ᾽ ἀνθρώπων
ἐνθάδ᾽ ἀγειρομένων· καὶ ἐμὴν ἰθύν τε μάλιστα
· · · · · · · · ·
540 ἠέ τι τηΰσιον ἔπος ἔσσεται ἠέ τι ἔργον
ὕβρις θ᾽, ἣ θέμις ἐστὶ καταθνητῶν ἀνθρώπων,
ἄλλοι ἔπειθ᾽ ὑμῖν σημάντορες ἄνδρες ἔσονται,
τῶν ὑπ᾽ ἀναγκαίηι δεδμήσεσθ᾽ ἤματα πάντα.
εἴρηταί τοι πάντα, σὺ δὲ φρεσὶ σῆισι φύλαξαι."
545   καὶ σὺ μὲν οὕτω χαῖρε, Διὸς καὶ Λητοῦς υἱέ·
αὐτὰρ ἐγὼ καὶ σεῖο καὶ ἄλλης μνήσομ᾽ ἀοιδῆς.

4. ΕΙΣ ΕΡΜΗΝ

Ἑρμῆν ὕμνει, Μοῦσα, Διὸς καὶ Μαιάδος υἱόν,
Κυλλήνης μεδέοντα καὶ Ἀρκαδίης πολυμήλου,
ἄγγελον ἀθανάτων ἐριούνιον, ὃν τέκε Μαῖα
νύμφη ἐϋπλόκαμος Διὸς ἐν φιλότητι μιγεῖσα
5 αἰδοίη· μακάρων δὲ θεῶν ἠλεύαθ᾽ ὅμιλον
ἄντρον ἔσω ναίουσα παλίσκιον, ἔνθα Κρονίων
νύμφηι ἐϋπλοκάμωι μισγέσκετο νυκτὸς ἀμολγῶι,

of harvest, nor rich in grassland, so as for us to live off it and serve the public at the same time."

Zeus' son Apollo smiled at them and said, "O foolish men of misplaced suffering, who want anxiety, hard toil, and heartache! I will give you a simple answer to bear in mind. Each of you must just keep a knife in his right hand and keep slaughtering sheep: they will be available in abundance, as many as the thronging peoples bring for me. Watch over my temple, and welcome the peoples as they gather here, and ⟨regard⟩ my will above all and ⟨my . . . But if on your part⟩ anything wanton is said or done, any insolence, as is the manner of mortal folk, then you shall have other men as your masters, under whose compulsion you will be subjugated for ever. You have your instructions; it is for you to remember them."

So I salute you, son of Zeus and Leto. And I will take heed both for you and for other singing.

4. TO HERMES

Sing of Hermes, Muse, the son of Zeus and Maia, the lord of Cyllene and Arcadia rich in flocks, the immortals' coursing messenger, whom Maia bore, that nymph of lovely tresses, in shared intimacy with Zeus; modest one, who shunned the company of the blessed gods, dwelling within a cave's shadow. There the son of Kronos used to unite with the nymph of lovely tresses in the depth of the night, so

---

530 τε Cobet: τ' εὖ Ω
537 κ' ἐμοὶ West: ἐμοί κ' Ω
post 539 lac. stat. Wolf

ὄφρα κατὰ γλυκὺς ὕπνος ἔχοι λευκώλενον Ἥρην,
λήθων ἀθανάτους τε θεοὺς θνητούς τ' ἀνθρώπους.
10 ἀλλ' ὅτε δὴ μεγάλοιο Διὸς νόος ἐξετελεῖτο,
τῆι δ' ἤδη δέκατος μεὶς οὐρανῶι ἐστήρικτο,
ἔς τε φόως ἄγαγεν, ἀρίσημά τε ἔργα τέτυκτο.
καὶ τότ' ἐγείνατο παῖδα πολύτροπον, αἱμυλομήτην,
ληϊστῆρ', ἐλατῆρα βοῶν, ἡγήτορ' ὀνείρων,
15 νυκτὸς ὀπωπητῆρα, πυληδόκον, ὃς τάχ' ἔμελλεν
ἀμφανέειν κλυτὰ ἔργα μετ' ἀθανάτοισι θεοῖσιν·
ἠῶιος γεγονὼς μέσωι ἤματι ἐγκιθάριζεν,
ἑσπέριος βοῦς κλέψεν ἑκηβόλου Ἀπόλλωνος,
τετράδι τῆι προτέρηι, τῆι μιν τέκε πότνια Μαῖα.
20 ὃς καὶ ἐπεὶ δὴ μητρὸς ἀπ' ἀθανάτων θόρε γυίων,
οὐκέτι δηρὸν ἔκειτο μένων ἱερῶι ἐνὶ λίκνωι,
ἀλλ' ὅ γ' ἀναΐξας ζήτει βόας Ἀπόλλωνος,
οὐδὸν ὑπερβαίνων ὑψηρεφέος ἄντροιο.
ἔνθα χέλυν εὑρὼν ἐκτήσατο μυρίον ὄλβον·
25 Ἑρμῆς τοι πρώτιστα χέλυν τεκτήνατ' ἀοιδόν·
ἥ ῥά οἱ ἀντεβόλησεν ἐπ' αὐλείηισι θύρηισιν
βοσκομένη προπάροιθε δόμων ἐριθηλέα ποίην,
σαῦλα ποσὶν βαίνουσα. Διὸς δ' ἐριούνιος υἱὸς
ἀθρήσας ἐγέλασσε καὶ αὐτίκα μῦθον ἔειπεν·
30 "σύμβολον ἤδη μοι μέγ' ὀνήσιμον, οὐκ ὀνοτάζω.
χαῖρε, φυὴν ἐρόεσσα, χοροιτύπε δαιτὸς ἑταίρη,
ἀσπασίη προφανεῖσα. πόθεν τόδε καλὸν ἄθυρμα,
αἰόλον ὄστρακον ἔσσο, χέλυς ὄρεσι ζώουσα;
ἀλλ' οἴσω σ' ἐς δῶμα λαβών· ὄφελός τί μοι ἔσσηι,
35 οὐδ' ἀπατιμήσω· σὺ δ' ἐμὲ πρώτιστον ὀνήσεις.

114

long as sweet sleep held white-armed Hera fast, and neither immortal gods nor mortal men knew of it. And when great Zeus' purpose came to fulfilment, and her tenth moon was set in the sky, she brought forth, and notable things came to pass. And she gave birth to a son resourceful and cunning, a robber, a rustler of cattle, a bringer of dreams, a night watcher, a gate-lurker, who was soon to display deeds of renown among the immortal gods: born in the morning, by midday he was playing the lyre, and in the evening he stole the cattle of far-shooting Apollo—on the fourth of the month, the day the lady Maia bore him.

Once he had sprung from his mother's immortal legs, he did not stay long lying in his holy cradle, but jumped up and started to look for Apollo's cattle, crossing the threshold of the high-roofed cave. There he found a tortoise, and so gained a priceless treasure: Hermes it was who first crafted the singing tortoise.[24] He encountered it at the yard entrance as it grazed on the lush grass in front of the dwelling, sidling along on its legs. Zeus' courser son laughed when he saw it, and said at once:

"Here's a portent of good fortune for me, I don't mind this! Hello, my lovely, my dance-beat dinner companion, welcome apparition! Where did you get this fine plaything, this blotchy shell that you wear, you tortoise living in the mountains? I shall take you indoors; you will be of some use to me, and I shan't undervalue you, I shall be the very

[24] The lyre; *chelys* denotes both the tortoise and the lyre made from its shell.

---

33 ἔσσο Matthiae: ἐσσὶ Ω
35 ἀπατιμήσω Matthiae: ἀποτ- Ω

οἴκοι βέλτερον εἶναι, ἐπεὶ βλαβερὸν τὸ θύρηφιν.
ἦ γὰρ ἐπηλυσίης πολυπήμονος ἔσσεαι ἔχμα
ζώουσ᾽· ἦν δὲ θάνῃς, τότε ⟨δ᾽⟩ ἂν μάλα καλὸν
    ἀείδοις."
    ὣς ἄρ᾽ ἔφη· καὶ χερσὶν ἅμ᾽ ἀμφοτέρῃσιν ἀείρας
40 ἂψ εἴσω κίε δῶμα φέρων ἐρατεινὸν ἄθυρμα.
ἔνθ᾽ ἀναμηλώσας γλυφάνῳ πολιοῖο σιδήρου
αἰῶν᾽ ἐξετόρησεν ὀρεσκώοιο χελώνης.
ὣς δ᾽ ὁπότ᾽ ὠκὺ νόημα διὰ στέρνοιο περήσῃ
ἀνέρος ὅν τε θαμειαὶ ἐπιστρωφῶσι μέριμναι,
45 ἠ᾽ ὅτε δινηθῶσιν ἀπ᾽ ὀφθαλμῶν ἀμαρυγαί,
ὣς ἅμ᾽ ἔπος τε καὶ ἔργον ἐμήδετο κύδιμος Ἑρμῆς.
πῆξε δ᾽ ἄρ᾽ ἐν μέτροισι ταμὼν δόνακας καλάμοιο,
πειρήνας διὰ νῶτα λιθορρίνοιο χελώνης·
ἀμφὶ δὲ δέρμα τάνυσσε βοὸς πραπίδεσσιν ἑῇσιν,
50 καὶ πήχυς ἐνέθηκ᾽, ἐπὶ δὲ ζυγὸν ἤραρεν ἀμφοῖν,
ἑπτὰ δὲ συμφώνους ὀΐων ἐτανύσσατο χορδάς.
αὐτὰρ ἐπεὶ δὴ τεῦξε, φέρων ἐρατεινὸν ἄθυρμα
πλήκτρῳ ἐπειρήτιζε κατὰ μέλος, ἣ δ᾽ ὑπὸ χειρός
σμερδαλέον κονάβησε· θεὸς δ᾽ ὑπὸ καλὸν ἄειδεν
55 ἐξ αὐτοσχεδίης πειρώμενος, ἠΰτε κοῦροι
ἡβηταὶ θαλίῃσι παραιβόλα κερτομέουσιν,
ἀμφὶ Δία Κρονίδην καὶ Μαιάδα καλλιπέδιλον,
ὡς πάρος ὠρίζεσκον ἑταιρείῃ φιλότητι,
ἥν τ᾽ αὐτοῦ γενεὴν ὀνομάκλυτον ἐξονομάζων·

37 ἔχμα Ruhnkenius: αἶχμα M, αἰχμὰ Ψ
38 δ᾽ add. Matthiae

first to profit from you. 'Better to be in the house, it's dangerous outside.'[25] For you will be a check against baneful visitation while you live, and if you die, then you may be a beautiful singer."

So he spoke, and picking it up in both hands he went back inside the dwelling, carrying the lovely plaything. There he probed with a chisel of grey iron and gouged out the life-stuff of the mountain-couching tortoise. And as when a sudden notion passes through the breast of a man who is constantly visited by thoughts, or when sparkling glances spin from someone's eyes, so glorious Hermes made his action as quick as his word. Cutting reed stalks to measure, he fixed them in, piercing the back of the stony-hided tortoise. Over them he cleverly stretched oxhide; he attached two arms, and fastened a crossbar on them, and stretched out seven sheep-gut strings to sound in concord. When he had made it, he carried the lovely plaything and tried it out with a plectrum in a tuned scale, and it rang out impressively under his hand. The god sang beautifully to it, impromptu, experimentally, as young men at dinners make ribald interjections: (he sang) about Zeus son of Kronos and fair-shod Maia, how they used to talk love in companionable intimacy, and declaring his own renowned

25 A humorous quotation of Hesiod, *Works and Days* 365.

---

41 ἀναμηλώσας Ruhnkenius: ἀναπηλήσας Ω
44 θαμειναὶ Wackernagel: θαμιναὶ Ω
48 λιθορρίνοιο Pierson: διὰ ῥινοῖο Ω
51 συμφώνους Ω: θηλυτέρων Antig. *Mir.* 7
53 μέλος (cf. 419, 501) Allen: μέρος Ω
58 ὥς rec. in marg.: ὃν Ω

60 ἀμφιπόλους τ᾽ ἐγέραιρε καὶ ἀγλαὰ δώματα νύμφης
   καὶ τρίποδας κατὰ οἶκον ἐπηετανούς τε λέβητας.
   καὶ τὰ μὲν οὖν ἤειδε, τὰ δὲ φρεσὶν ἄλλα μενοίνα·
   καὶ τὴν μὲν κατέθηκε φέρων ἱερῶι ἐνὶ λίκνωι
   φόρμιγγα γλαφυρήν, ὃ δ᾽ ἄρα κρειῶν ἐρατίζων
65 ἄλτο κατὰ σκοπιὴν εὐώδεος ἐκ μεγάροιο,
   ὁρμαίνων δόλον αἰπὺν ἐνὶ φρεσίν, οἷά τε φῶτες
   φιληταὶ διέπουσι μελαίνης νυκτὸς ἐν ὥρηι.
   Ἥλιος μὲν ἔδυνε κατὰ χθονὸς Ὠκεανόνδε
   αὐτοῖσίν θ᾽ ἵπποισι καὶ ἅρμασιν, αὐτὰρ ἄρ᾽ Ἑρμῆς
70 Πιερίης ἀφίκανε θεῶν ὄρεα σκιόεντα,
   ἔνθα θεῶν μακάρων βόες ἄμβροτοι αὖλιν ἔχεσκον,
   βοσκόμεναι λειμῶνας ἀκηρασίους ἐρατεινούς·
   τῶν τότε Μαιάδος υἱὸς ἐύσκοπος Ἀργειφόντης
   πεντήκοντ᾽ ἀγέλης ἀπετάμνετο βοῦς ἐριμύκους.
75 πλανοδίας δ᾽ ἤλαυνε διὰ ψαμαθώδεα χῶρον
   ἴχνι᾽ ἀποστρέψας, δολίης δ᾽ οὐ λήθετο τέχνης,
   ἀντία ποιήσας ὁπλάς, τὰς πρόσθεν ὄπισθεν,
   τὰς δ᾽ ὄπιθεν πρόσθεν, κατὰ δ᾽ ἔμπαλιν αὐτὸς
     ἔβαινεν.
   σάνδαλα δ᾽ αὐτίκα ῥιψὶν ἐπὶ ψαμάθοις ἁλίηισιν
80 ἄφραστ᾽ ἠδ᾽ ἀνόητα διέπλεκε, θαυματὰ ἔργα,
   συμμίσγων μυρίκας καὶ μυρσινοειδέας ὄζους·
   τῶν τότε συνδήσας νεοθηλέος ἀγκαλὸν ὕλης
   ἀβλαβέως ὑπὸ ποσσὶν ἐδήσατο σάνδαλα κοῦφα
   αὐτοῖσιν πετάλοισι, τὰ κύδιμος Ἀργειφόντης
85 ἔσπασε Πιερίηθεν ὁδοιπορίην ἀλεγύνων,
   οἷά τ᾽ ἐπειγόμενος δολιχὴν ὁδὸν αὐτοτροπήσας.

lineage. He also celebrated the servants of the nymph, and her splendid home, the tripods disposed about it and the unending cauldrons.

As he sang of all that, his mind was already on other things. He took the scooped-out lyre and laid it down in his holy cradle. Craving meat, he sprang out from the fragrant mansion to the peak, meditating a piece of sheer trickery such as thieves carry out in the dark nighttime.

The Sun was dipping below the earth towards Ocean with his horses and chariot, when Hermes came running to Pieria's shadowed mountains, where the blessed gods' deathless cows had their steading, grazing the lovely virgin meadows. From them Maia's son, the keen-sighted Argus-slayer, cut fifty lowing cows off from their herd, and drove them by offroad ways, over a sandy region, turning their footprints round, for his skill in deception did not fail him; he turned their hooves opposite ways, fore to back and hinder to front, while he himself walked backwards. At the sands of the coast he at once used wicker to plait sandals beyond description or imagination, wondrous work, combining tamarisk and myrtle twigs. Tying together an armful of their fresh growth, he bound the light sandals securely on his feet, foliage and all, which the glorious Argus-slayer had plucked from Pieria as he prepared his journeying, improvising as one does when hastening on a long journey.

---

70 θέων f: θεῶν Mxp
75 πληνοδίας Schneider: πλαν- Ω
76 ἴχνι' Hermann: ἴχνη Ω
79 ῥῖψιν Postgate: ἔριψεν Ω
85 ἀλεγύνων Windisch: ἀλεείνων Ω
86 αὐτοπρεπὴς ὣς yf

119

τὸν δὲ γέρων ἐνόησε δέμων ἀνθοῦσαν ἀλωήν
ἱέμενον πεδίονδε δι' Ὀγχηστὸν λεχεποίην.
τὸν πρότερος προσέφη Μαίης ἐρικυδέος υἱός·
90   "ὦ γέρον, ὅς τε φυτὰ σκάπτεις ἐπικαμπύλος
    ὤμους,
ἦ πολυοινήσεις, εὖτ' ἂν τάδε πάντα φέρησιν

  .   .   .   .

καί τε ἰδὼν μὴ ἰδὼν εἶναι καὶ κωφὸς ἀκούσας,
καὶ σιγᾶν, ὅτε μή τι καταβλάπτῃ τὸ σὸν αὐτοῦ."
τόσσον φὰς ἔσσευε βοῶν ἴφθιμα κάρηνα.
95 πολλὰ δ' ὄρη σκιόεντα καὶ αὐλῶνας κελαδεινοὺς
καὶ πεδί' ἀνθεμόεντα διήλασε κύδιμος Ἑρμῆς.
ὀρφναίη δ' ἐπίκουρος ἐπαύετο δαιμονίη νὺξ
ἡ πλείων, τάχα δ' ὄρθρος ἐγίνετο δημιοεργός,
ἡ δὲ νέον σκοπιὴν προσεβήσατο δῖα Σελήνη
100 Πάλλαντος θυγάτηρ Μεγαμηδείδαο ἄνακτος·
τῆμος ἐπ' Ἀλφειὸν ποταμὸν Διὸς ἄλκιμος υἱός
Φοίβου Ἀπόλλωνος βοῦς ἤλασεν εὐρυμετώπους,
ἀδμῆτες δ' ἵκανον ἐς αὔλιον ὑψιμέλαθρον
καὶ ληνοὺς προπάροιθεν ἀριπρεπέος λειμῶνος.
105   ἔνθ' ἐπεὶ εὖ βοτάνης ἐπεφόρβει βοῦς ἐριμύκους,
καὶ τὰς μὲν συνέλασσεν ἐς αὔλιον ἀθρόας οὔσας,
λωτὸν ἐρεπτομένας ἠδ' ἑρσήεντα κύπειρον,
σὺν δ' ἐφόρει ξύλα πολλά, πυρὸς δ' ἐπεμαίετο
    τέχνην.
δάφνης ἀγλαὸν ὄζον ἑλὼν ἐπέλεψε σιδήρῳ

  .   .   .   .

110 ἄρμενον ἐν παλάμῃ, ἄμπνυτο δὲ θερμὸς ἀϋτμή·

An old man who was tilling a vineyard in bud saw him as
he hurried towards the plain through grassy Onchestus.
Glorious Maia's son spoke to him first:

"Old sir with bent shoulders, digging your vines, you
will indeed be well in wine when these all bear fruit, ‹pro-
vided you do as I say: keep your own counsel,› and don't
see what you've seen, and don't hear what you've heard,
and keep silent so long as it isn't harming your own affairs."

Saying no more, he urged on the doughty cattle. Many
were the shadowed mountains and echoing valleys and
flowered plains that glorious Hermes drove through. His
ally, the dark divine night, was coming to an end, the
greater part, and soon it would be lightening and arousing
people to work; the lady Moon had just reached her height,
daughter of Megamedes' son, lord Pallas. Then it was that
Zeus' brave son drove Phoibos Apollo's broad-browed
cattle to the river Alpheios, and they came, still innocent of
the yoke, to the high-roofed steading and the water
troughs in front in the magnificent meadow.

There, after he had given the lowing cows a good feed
on the vegetation, and driven them together into the stead-
ing in a mass, still cropping the clover and dewy galingale,
he gathered a lot of wood and essayed the art of fire. He
took a fine bay branch and whittled it with a knife, ‹and
twirled it in a hollowed-out piece of ivy wood,› held firmly
in his hand, and the heat came blowing up: Hermes it was

---

91 lac. stat. Groddeck
94 φὰς ἔσσευε Cobet: φασὶν ἔσευε Ω
109 lac. stat. Kuhn

Ἑρμῆς τοι πρώτιστα πυρήϊα πῦρ τ᾽ ἀνέδωκεν.
πολλὰ δὲ κάγκανα κᾶλα κατουδαίωι ἐνὶ βόθρωι
οὖλα λαβὼν ἐπέθηκεν ἐπηετανά· λάμπετο δὲ φλόξ
τηλόσε φῦσαν ἱεῖσα πυρὸς μέγα δαιομένοιο.
115 ὄφρα δὲ πῦρ ἀνέκαιε βίη κλυτοῦ Ἡφαίστοιο,
τόφρα δ᾽ ὑπωροφίας ἕλικας βοῦς εἷλκε θύραζε
δοιὰς ἄγχι πυρός· δύναμις δέ οἱ ἔπλετο πολλή·
ἀμφοτέρας δ᾽ ἐπὶ νῶτα χαμαὶ βάλε φυσιοώσας,
ἐγκλίνων δ᾽ ἐκύλινδε δι᾽ αἰῶνας τετορήσας.
120 ἔργωι δ᾽ ἔργον ὄπαζε ταμὼν κρέα πίονα δημῶι·
ὤπτα δ᾽ ἀμφ᾽ ὀβελοῖσι πεπαρμένα δουρατέοισιν,
σάρκας ὁμοῦ καὶ νῶτα γεράσμια καὶ μέλαν αἷμα
ἐργμένον ἐν χολάδεσσι· τὰ δ᾽ αὐτοῦ κεῖτ᾽ ἐπὶ
        χώρης.
ῥινοὺς δ᾽ ἐξετάνυσσε καταστυφέλωι ἐνὶ πέτρηι,
125 ὡς ἔτι νῦν τὰ μέτασσα πολυχρόνιοι πεφύασιν
δηρὸν δὴ μετὰ ταῦτα καὶ ἄκριτοι. αὐτὰρ ἔπειτα
Ἑρμῆς χαρμόφρων εἰρύσσατο πίονα ἔργα
λείωι ἐπὶ πλαταμῶνι, καὶ ἔσχισε δώδεκα μοίρας
κληροπαλεῖς· τέλεον δὲ γέρας προσέθηκεν ἑκάστηι.
130 ἔνθ᾽ ὁσίης κρεάων ἠράσσατο κύδιμος Ἑρμῆς·
ὀδμὴ γάρ μιν ἔτειρε καὶ ἀθάνατόν περ ἐόντα
ἡδεῖ᾽· ἀλλ᾽ οὐδ᾽ ὣς οἱ ἐπείθετο θυμὸς ἀγήνωρ
καί τε μάλ᾽ ἱμείροντι περᾶν ἱερῆς κατὰ δειρῆς,
ἀλλὰ τὰ μὲν κατέθηκεν ἐς αὔλιον ὑψιμέλαθρον
135 δημὸν καὶ κρέα πολλά, μετήορα δ᾽ αἶψ᾽ ἀνάειρεν,

116 ὑπωροφίας West: ὑποβρυχίας Ω: ἐριβρύχους Barnes

who first delivered up the firesticks and fire. Many dry, close-grained logs he took and laid on the fire in the sunken pit incessantly, and the flame shone far around as it radiated the blast of the blazing fire. While the force of famed Hephaestus was keeping the fire burning up, he dragged two of the curly-horned cows that were under shelter out towards the fire—his strength was great—and threw them both to the ground on their backs, snorting; and leaning against them, he rolled them over after piercing their spinal cords. Following one job with another, he cut up the meat, rich with fat, and roasted it, fixed on wooden spits, the flesh pieces together with the honorific chines and the dark blood in sausages of tripe; the remaining parts lay there on the ground. The hides he spread out on a rugged rock, as even now in after time they remain long-lasting through the ages in a fused mass. Then Hermes happily drew off the rich cooking from the spits onto a smooth slab, and split it into twelve portions determined by lot, and assigned a fixed rank to each one.[26] Whereupon glorious Hermes craved his own due of meat, for the sweet smell tormented him, immortal though he was. Nevertheless his stout heart did not give way to his longing to let it pass down his holy throat; he put it away in the high-roofed steading, the fat and all the meat, and straightway set it up

[26] This foreshadows the Olympic cult of the Twelve Gods. See the Introduction.

---

126 ἄκριτοι West: ἄκριτον Ω   127 χαρμόφρων
Stephanus: χαρμοφέρων Ω (χάρμα φέρων p)
133 περᾶν Barnes: περῆν M, πέρην' Ψ

σῆμα νέης φωρῆς· ἐπὶ δὲ ξύλα κάγκαν᾽ ἀγείρας
οὐλόποδ᾽ οὐλοκάρηνα πυρὸς κατεδάμνατ᾽ ἀϋτμῆι.
αὐτὰρ ἐπεὶ δὴ πάντα κατὰ χρέος ἤνυσε δαίμων,
σάνδαλα μὲν προέηκεν ἐς Ἀλφειὸν βαθυδίνην,
140 ἀνθρακιὴν δ᾽ ἐμάρανε, κόνιν δ᾽ ἀμάθυνε μέλαιναν
παννύχιος· καλὸν δὲ φόως ἐπέλαμπε σελήνης.

    Κυλλήνης δ᾽ αἶψ᾽ αὖτις ἀφίκετο δῖα κάρηνα
ὄρθριος, οὐδέ τίς οἱ δολιχῆς ὁδοῦ ἀντεβόλησεν
οὔτε θεῶν μακάρων οὔτε θνητῶν ἀνθρώπων,
145 οὐδὲ κύνες λελάκοντο. Διὸς δ᾽ ἐριούνιος Ἑρμῆς
δοχμωθεὶς μεγάροιο διὰ κλήϊθρον ἔδυνεν
αὔρηι ὀπωρινῆι ἐναλίγκιος, ἠΰτ᾽ ὀμίχλη,
ἰθύσας δ᾽ ἄντρου ἐξίκετο πίονα νηόν
ἦκα ποσὶ προβιβῶν· οὐ γὰρ κτύπεν ὥς περ ἐπ᾽
    οὔδει·
150 ἐσσυμένως δ᾽ ἄρα λίκνον ἐπώιχετο κύδιμος Ἑρμῆς.
σπάργανον ἀμφ᾽ ὤμοις εἰλυμένος ἠΰτε τέκνον
νήπιον, ἐν παλάμηισι περὶ γνυσὶ λαῖφος ἀθύρων,
κεῖτο, χέλυν ἐρατὴν ἐπ᾽ ἀριστερὰ χειρὸς ἐέργων.
    μητέρα δ᾽ οὐκ ἄρ᾽ ἔληθε θεὰν θεός, εἶπέ τε μῦθον·
155 "τίπτε σύ, ποικιλομῆτα, πόθεν τόδε νυκτὸς ἐν ὥρηι
ἔρχηι, ἀναιδείην ἐπιειμένε; νῦν σε μάλ᾽ οἴω
ἢ τάχ᾽ ἀμήχανα δεσμὰ περὶ πλευρῆισιν ἔχοντα
Λητοΐδου ὑπὸ χερσὶ διὲκ προθύροιο περήσειν,
ἤ σε φέροντα μεταξὺ κατ᾽ ἄγκεα φιλητεύσειν.

    136 φωρῆς Hermann: φωνῆς Ψ (versum om. M)   ἀγείρας
Ilgen: ἀείρας Ψ

high as a token of his recent theft. Gathering dry logs, he consumed it in the heat of the fire, hooves, heads, and all. When the god had finished all he had to do, he threw his sandals into the deep-swirling Alpheios, put out the embers, and levelled the dark dust over them for the rest of the night, while the moon's fair light shone down upon him.

In the early twilight he swiftly returned to Cyllene's noble peaks, and no one met him on the long journey, either blessed god or mortal man, and no dogs barked. Zeus' courser Hermes twisted sideways and slipped in through the latchhole of the mansion like an autumn breeze, in the manner of a mist. Heading straight through the cave he reached the rich sanctum, treading softly, making no noise as on a floor; and speedily glorious Hermes had gone to his cradle. With his swaddling cloth wrapped round his shoulders, he lay like a baby, toying with the sheet round his knees, keeping his lovely lyre on his left hand.

His mother did not fail to notice, the goddess the god, and she said, "What are you up to, you sly thing, where have you been in the nighttime, with shamelessness as your cloak? Now I really think that very soon you'll be going out through that porch with your body bound helplessly at Apollo's hands—or else you'll give him the slip when he's in the middle of carrying you through the glens.

---

152 περὶ γνυσὶ Forssman: περιγνύσι M, περ᾽ ἰγνύσι fx, παρ᾽ ἰγνύσι p
155 τόδε Wolf: τάδε Ω

160 ἔρρε πάλιν· μεγάλην σε πατὴρ ἐφύτευσε μέριμναν
θνητοῖς ἀνθρώποισι καὶ ἀθανάτοισι θεοῖσιν."
    τὴν δ᾽ Ἑρμῆς μύθοισιν ἀμείβετο κερδαλέοισιν·
"μῆτερ ἐμή, τί με ταῦτα δεδίσκεαι ἠΰτε τέκνον
νήπιον, ὃς μάλα παῦρα μετὰ φρεσὶν αἴσυλα οἶδεν,
165 ταρβαλέον, καὶ μητρὸς ὑπαιδείδοικεν ἐνιπάς;
αὐτὰρ ἐγὼ τέχνης ἐπιβήσομαι ἥ τις ἀρίστη,
βουκολέων ἐμὲ καὶ σὲ διαμπερές· οὐδὲ θεοῖσιν
νῶϊ μετ᾽ ἀθανάτοισιν ἀδώρητοι καὶ ἄλιστοι
αὐτοῦ τῇδε μένοντες ἀνεξόμεθ᾽, ὡς σὺ κελεύεις.
170 βέλτερον ἤματα πάντα μετ᾽ ἀθανάτοις ὀαρίζειν
πλούσιον ἀφνειὸν πολυλήϊον ἢ κατὰ δῶμα
ἄντρωι ἐν ἠερόεντι θαασσέμεν· ἀμφὶ δὲ τιμῆς,
κἀγὼ τῆς ὁσίης ἐπιβήσομαι, ἧς περ Ἀπόλλων.
εἰ δέ κε μὴ δώησι πατὴρ ἐμός, ἤτοι ἐγώ γε
175 πειρήσω—δύναμαι—φιλητέων ὄρχαμος εἶναι.
εἰ δέ μ᾽ ἐρευνήσει Λητοῦς ἐρικυδέος υἱός,
ἄλλό τί οἱ καὶ μεῖζον ὀΐομαι ἀντιβολήσειν·
εἶμι γὰρ ἐς Πυθῶνα μέγαν δόμον ἀντιτορήσων,
ἔνθεν ἅλις τρίποδας περικαλλέας ἠδὲ λέβητας
180 πορθήσω καὶ χρυσόν, ἅλις τ᾽ αἴθωνα σίδηρον
καὶ πολλὴν ἐσθῆτα· σὺ δ᾽ ὄψεαι, αἴ κ᾽ ἐθέλῃσθα."
    ὣς οἱ μέν ῥ᾽ ἐπέεσσι πρὸς ἀλλήλους ἀγόρευον
υἱός τ᾽ αἰγιόχοιο Διὸς καὶ πότνια Μαῖα.
    Ἠὼς δ᾽ ἠριγένεια φόως θνητοῖσι φέρουσα
185 ὤρνυτ᾽ ἀπ᾽ Ὠκεανοῖο βαθυρρόου· αὐτὰρ Ἀπόλλων
Ὀγχηστόνδ᾽ ἀφίκανε κιὼν πολυήρατον ἄλσος

Get away back with you! Your father has begotten you to be a great nuisance to mortal men and the immortal gods."

Hermes answered her craftily: "Mother mine, why try to scare me like this, as if I were a baby who knows little of mischief, a timorous one afraid of his mother's scoldings? I am going to embark on the finest of arts, keeping the two of us in clover for ever. We won't put up with staying here and being without offerings or prayers alone of all the immortals, as you would have us do. It's better to spend every day in pleasant chat among the gods, with wealth and riches and substance, than to sit at home in a gloomy cave. As for privilege, I'm going to enter on my rights, the same as Apollo. And if my father doesn't let me, then I shall set out—and I have the means—to be the prince of thieves. And if glorious Leto's son is going to track me down, I reckon I can meet him with something even bigger: I shall go to Pytho to burgle his great house, and from it I'll plunder plenty of beautiful tripods and cauldrons and gold, and plenty of gleaming iron, and lots of vestments—you'll see, if you care to."

Thus they were having words with each other, goat-rider Zeus' son and the lady Maia, when Dawn the early-born emerged from Ocean's deep waters to bring light to mortals. Then Apollo came to Onchestus, to the delightful

---

163 δεδίσκεαι Pierson: τιτύσκεαι Ω
167 βουκολέων Ludwich: βουλεύων Ω
168 ἄλιστοι y: ἄπαστοι ΜΨ
175 δύναμαι δὲ Ω: corr. Chalcondyles

ἁγνὸν ἐρισφαράγου Γαιηόχου· ἔνθα γέροντα
νωχαλὸν ηὗρε δέμοντα πάρεξ ὁδοῦ ἕρκος ἀλωῆς.
τὸν πρότερος προσέφη Λητοῦς ἐρικυδέος υἱός·
190 "ὦ γέρον Ὀγχηστοῖο βατοδρόπε ποιήεντος,
βοῦς ἀπὸ Πιερίης διζήμενος ἐνθάδ' ἱκάνω,
πάσας θηλείας, πάσας κεράεσσιν ἑλικτάς,
ἐξ ἀγέλης· ὁ δὲ ταῦρος ἐβόσκετο μοῦνος ἀπ' ἄλλων
κυάνεος, χαροποὶ δὲ κύνες κατόπισθεν ἕποντο
195 τέσσαρες ἠΰτε φῶτες ὁμόφρονες. οἱ μὲν ἔλειφθεν
οἵ τε κύνες ὅ τε ταῦρος, ὃ δὴ περὶ θαῦμα τέτυκται·
ταὶ δ' ἔβαν ἠελίοιο νέον καταδυομένοιο
ἐκ μαλακοῦ λειμῶνος ἀπὸ γλυκεροῖο νομοῖο.
ταῦτά μοι εἰπέ, γεραιὲ παλαιγενές, εἴ που ὄπωπας
200 ἀνέρα ταῖσδ' ἐπὶ βουσὶ διαπρήσσοντα κέλευθον."
τὸν δ' ὁ γέρων μύθοισιν ἀμειβόμενος προσέειπεν·
"ὦ φίλος, ἀργαλέον μέν, ὅσ' ὀφθαλμοῖσιν ἴδοιτο,
πάντα λέγειν· πολλοὶ γὰρ ὁδὸν πρήσσουσιν ὁδῖται,
τῶν οἱ μὲν κακὰ πολλὰ μεμαότες, οἱ δὲ μάλ' ἐσθλὰ
205 φοιτῶσιν· χαλεπὸν δὲ δαήμεναί ἐστιν ἕκαστον.
αὐτὰρ ἐγὼ πρόπαν ἦμαρ ἐς ἠέλιον καταδύντα
ἔσκαπτον περὶ γουνὸν ἀλωῆς οἰνοπέδοιο·
παῖδα δ' ἔδοξα, φέριστε, σαφὲς δ' οὐκ οἶδα, νοῆσαι,
ὅς τις ὁ παῖς ἅμα βουσὶν ἐϋκραίρῃσιν ὀπήδει
210 νήπιος, εἶχε δὲ ῥάβδον, ἐπιστροφάδην δ' ἐβάδιζεν,
ἐξοπίσω δ' ἀνέεργε, κάρη δ' ἔχον ἀντίον αὐτῶι."
φῆ ῥ' ὁ γέρων· ὁ δὲ θᾶσσον ὁδὸν κίε μῦθον
ἀκούσας.

holy grove of the loud-crashing Earth-rider.[27] There he found a slow-moving old man tilling his vine enclosure just off the road. Glorious Leto's son spoke to him first:

"Old sir, culler of grassy Onchestus' thorns, I have come here searching for some cattle from Pieria, all cows, all with crumpled horns, from a herd. The bull was grazing apart from the rest—sable color—and there were four fierce-eyed dogs following after them, working as a team like humans. But they were left behind, the dogs and the bull, which is an extraordinary thing, while the cows went off soon after sunset, leaving their lush meadow and sweet pasture. Tell me, ancient sir, if you have had any sight of a man on the road with these cows."

The old man answered him: "Friend, it is hard to keep count of everything one's eyes may see. There are many travellers on the road; some of them go with much ill intent, others with much good, and it is difficult to know which is which. But I was digging about my vine slopes all day to sunset, and I thought I saw a boy—but I don't rightly know, sir, what boy it was going behind the strong-horned cows, an infant, with a rod, walking this way and that, and he was driving them backwards, and they had their heads facing him."

So said the old man, and Apollo on hearing his words

[27] Poseidon. For his grove at Onchestos see *Hymn to Apollo* 230.

---

188 νωχαλὸν Hermann: κνώδαλον Ω   δέμοντα (cf. 87) Barnes: νέμοντα Ω
    211 ἔχον Hermann: ἔχεν Ω

οἰωνὸν δ᾽ ἐνόει τανυσίπτερον, αὐτίκα δ᾽ ἔγνω
φιλητὴν γεγαῶτα Διὸς παῖδα Κρονίωνος.
215 ἐσσυμένως δ᾽ ἤϊξεν ἄναξ Διὸς υἱὸς Ἀπόλλων
ἐς Πύλον ἠγαθέην διζήμενος εἰλίποδας βοῦς,
πορφυρέηι νεφέληι κεκαλυμμένος εὐρέας ὤμους·
ἴχνιά τ᾽ εἰσενόησεν Ἑκηβόλος εἶπέ τε μῦθον·
"ὢ πόποι, ἦ μέγα θαῦμα τόδ᾽ ὀφθαλμοῖσιν ὁρῶμαι·
220 ἴχνια μὲν τάδε γ᾽ ἐστὶ βοῶν ὀρθοκραιράων,
ἀλλὰ πάλιν τέτραπται ἐς ἀσφοδελὸν λειμῶνα·
βήματα δ᾽ οὔτ᾽ ἀνδρὸς τάδε γίνεται οὔτε γυναικός
οὔτε λύκων πολιῶν οὔτ᾽ ἄρκτων οὔτε λεόντων
οὔτέ τι κενταύρου λασιαύχενος ἔλπομαι εἶναι,
225 ὅς τις τοῖα πέλωρα βιβᾶι ποσὶ καρπαλίμοισιν.
αἰνὰ μὲν ἔνθεν ὁδοῖο, τὰ δ᾽ αἰνότερ᾽ ἔνθεν ὁδοῖο."
    ὣς εἰπὼν ἤϊξεν ἄναξ Διὸς υἱὸς Ἀπόλλων,
Κυλλήνης δ᾽ ἀφίκανεν ὄρος καταείμενον ὕληι
πέτρης ἐς κευθμῶνα βαθύσκιον, ἔνθά τε νύμφη
230 ἀμβροσίη ἐλόχευσε Διὸς παῖδα Κρονίωνος.
ὀδμὴ δ᾽ ἱμερόεσσα δι᾽ οὔρεος ἠγαθέοιο
κίδνατο, πολλὰ δὲ μῆλα ταναύποδα βόσκετο ποίην.
ἔνθα τότε σπεύδων κατεβήσετο λάϊνον οὐδόν
ἄντρον ἐς ἠερόεν ἑκατηβόλος αὐτὸς Ἀπόλλων.
235 τὸν δ᾽ ὡς οὖν ἐνόησε Διὸς καὶ Μαιάδος υἱός
χωόμενον περὶ βουσὶν ἑκηβόλον Ἀπόλλωνα,
σπάργαν᾽ ἔσω κατέδυνε θυήεντ᾽, ἠΰτε πολλήν
πρέμνων ἀνθρακιὴν ὕλης σποδὸς ἀμφικαλύπτει·
ὣς Ἑρμῆς Ἑκάεργον ἰδὼν ἀνεείλε᾽ ἑ αὐτόν,
240 ἐν δ᾽ ὀλίγωι συνέλασσε κάρη χεῖράς τε πόδας τε

hurried on his way. He observed a spread-winged bird of omen, and at once understood that it was the child of Kronos' son Zeus who had been the thief. Quickly the lord Apollo sped on to holy Pylos in search of his shambling cattle, his broad shoulders wrapped in a crimson cloud. And the Far-shooter noticed the tracks, and said, "Heavens, this is an extraordinary thing that I see. These are certainly the tracks of the high-horned cows, but they are facing back towards the asphodel meadow. And these are footprints of neither man nor woman, nor of grey wolves or bears or lions, nor of a shaggy-maned centaur do I fancy they are, whoever makes such monstrous prints with his swift feet. Strange business one side of the road, and stranger still on the other!"

With these words Zeus' son, lord Apollo, sped on, and came to Cyllene's wooded mountain, to the deep-shadowed cavern in the rock where the divine nymph gave birth to the child of Kronos' son Zeus. An enchanting fragrance pervaded the holy mountain, and numerous long-shanked sheep were grazing the grass. There it was that he then came hurrying, and went down over the stone threshold into the gloomy cave, far-shooting Apollo in person.

When the son of Zeus and Maia saw that it was the far-shooter Apollo angry about his cattle, he burrowed down into his fragrant swaddling cloth; as a mass of log embers is concealed under the wood ash, so Hermes curled himself up on seeing the Far-shooter, and compressed his head and arms and legs into a little space, just like a fresh-

---

239 ἀνεείλε᾽ Postgate: ἀλέεινεν Ω

φῆ ῥα νεόλλουτος προκαλεόμενος ἥδυμον ὕπνον,
ἐγρήσσων ἐτεόν γε· χέλυν <δ᾽> ὑπὸ μασχάληι
εἶχεν.
γνῶ δ᾽ οὐδ᾽ ἠγνοίησε Διὸς καὶ Λητοῦς υἱός
νύμφην τ᾽ οὐρείην περικαλλέα καὶ φίλον υἱόν,
245 παῖδ᾽ ὀλίγον δολίηις εἰλυμένον ἐντροπίηισιν.
παπτήνας δ᾽ ἀνὰ πάντα μυχὸν μεγάλοιο δόμοιο
τρεῖς ἀδύτους ἀνέωιγε λαβὼν κληῖδα φαεινήν
νέκταρος ἐμπλείους ἠδ᾽ ἀμβροσίης ἐρατεινῆς·
πολλὸς δὲ χρυσός τε καὶ ἄργυρος ἔνδον ἔκειτο,
250 πολλὰ δὲ φοινικόεντα καὶ ἄργυφα εἵματα νύμφης,
οἷα θεῶν μακάρων ἱεροὶ δόμοι ἐντὸς ἔχουσιν.
ἔνθ᾽ ἐπεὶ ἐξερέεινε μυχοὺς μεγάλοιο δόμοιο
Λητοΐδης, μύθοισι προσηύδα κύδιμον Ἑρμῆν·
"ὦ παῖ ὃς ἐν λίκνωι κατάκειαι, μήνυέ μοι βοῦς
255 θᾶσσον· ἐπεὶ τάχα νῶϊ διοισόμεθ᾽ οὐ κατὰ κόσμον.
ῥίψω γάρ σε λαβὼν ἐς Τάρταρον ἠερόεντα,
ἐς ζόφον αἰνόμορον καὶ ἀμήχανον· οὐδέ σε μήτηρ
ἐς φάος οὐδὲ πατὴρ ἀναλύσεται, ἀλλ᾽ ὑπὸ γαίηι
ἐρρήσεις ὀλίγοισι μετ᾽ ἀνδράσιν ἡγεμονεύων."
260 τὸν δ᾽ Ἑρμῆς μύθοισιν ἀμείβετο κερδαλέοισιν·
"Λητοΐδη, τίνα τοῦτον ἀπηνέα μῦθον ἔειπες,
καὶ βοῦς ἀγραύλους διζήμενος ἐνθάδ᾽ ἱκάνεις;
οὐκ ἴδον, οὐ πυθόμην, οὐκ ἄλλου μῦθον ἄκουσα,
οὐκ ἂν μηνύσαιμ᾽, οὐκ ἂν μήνυτρον ἀροίμην.
265 οὔ τι βοῶν ἐλατῆρι κραταιῶι φωτὶ ἔοικα.

241 φή ῥα Barnes: δή ῥα Ω: θῆρα νέον λοχάων y

132

bathed baby inviting sweet sleep, though wide awake in reality, keeping his lyre under his armpit. The son of Zeus and Leto did not fail to recognize the beautiful nymph of the mountain and her dear son, the little boy wrapped in his deceitful trickeries. He peered round every cranny of the great house; he took the shining key and opened three closets, full of nectar and lovely ambrosia. There was much gold and silver stored within, and many of the nymph's purple and white garments, such things as the blessed gods' holy houses contain. When Leto's son had investigated the alcoves of the great house, he spoke to glorious Hermes:

"You child lying in your cradle, tell me where my cows are, double quick, otherwise we two shall quarrel in no seemly fashion: I shall take you and hurl you into misty Tartarus, into the dismal Darkness past help. Your mother or father won't release you into the daylight, but you'll go to perdition below the earth, as the leader of human children."[28]

Hermes answered him craftily: "Son of Leto, what do you mean by these harsh words, coming here in search of cattle that dwell in the fields? I haven't seen them, I haven't inquired, I haven't been told. I couldn't tell you where they are, or earn a reward for it. I don't look like a

[28] The idea is that Hermes, condemned to the Underworld as a child, will rule over the human children there.

---

242 ἐγρήσσων Martin, ἐτεόν γε Hermann: ἄγρης εἰνετεόν τε Ω   δ' add. Hermann   256 λαβὼν Ilgen: βαλὼν Ω   265 οὔ τι Hermann: οὔτε Ω

οὐκ ἐμὸν ἔργον τοῦτο, πάρος δέ μοι ἄλλα μέμηλεν·
ὕπνος ἐμοί γε μέμηλε καὶ ἡμετέρης γάλα μητρός
σπάργανά τ᾽ ἀμφ᾽ ὤμοισιν ἔχειν καὶ θερμὰ λοετρά.
μή τις τοῦτο πύθοιτο, πόθεν τόδε νεῖκος ἐτύχθη·
270 καί κεν δὴ μέγα θαῦμα μετ᾽ ἀθανάτοισι γένοιτο,
παῖδα νέον γεγαῶτα διὰ προθύροιο περῆσαι
βουσὶ μετ᾽ ἀγραύλοισι· τὸ δ᾽ ἀπρεπέως ἀγορεύεις.
χθὲς γενόμην, ἁπαλοὶ δὲ πόδες, τρηχεῖα δ᾽ ὕπο
     χθών.
εἰ δ᾽ ἐθέλεις, πατρὸς κεφαλὴν μέγαν ὅρκον ὀμοῦμαι·
275 μὴ μὲν ἐγὼ μήτ᾽ αὐτὸς ὑπίσχομαι αἴτιος εἶναι,
μήτέ τιν᾽ ἄλλον ὄπωπα βοῶν κλοπὸν ὑμετεράων,
αἵ τινες αἱ βόες εἰσί· τὸ δὲ κλέος οἷον ἀκούω."
     ὣς ἄρ᾽ ἔφη, καὶ πυκνὸν ἀπὸ βλεφάρων
          ἀμαρύσσων
ὀφρύσι, ῥιπτάζεσκεν ὁρώμενος ἔνθα καὶ ἔνθα,
280 μάκρ᾽ ἀποσυρίζων, ἄλιον τὸν μῦθον ἀκούων.
τὸν δ᾽ ἁπαλὸν γελάσας προσέφη ἑκάεργος
     Ἀπόλλων·
     "ὦ πέπον ἠπεροπευτὰ δολοφραδές, ἦ σε μάλ᾽ οἴω
πολλάκις ἀντιτορέοντα δόμους εὖ ναιετάοντας
ἔννυχον οὔ χ᾽ ἕνα μοῦνον ἐπ᾽ οὔδει φῶτα καθέσσαι
285 σκευάζοντα κατ᾽ οἶκον ἄτερ ψόφου, οἷ᾽ ἀγορεύεις·
πολλοὺς δ᾽ ἀγραύλους ἀκαχήσεις μηλοβοτῆρας
οὔρεος ἐν βήσσῃς, ὁπόταν κρειῶν ἐρατίζων
ἀντήσῃς ἀγέλῃσι βοῶν καὶ πώεσι μήλων.
ἀλλ᾽ ἄγε, μὴ πύματόν τε καὶ ὕστατον ὕπνον
     ἰαύσῃς,

cattle rustler, a strong man. That isn't my business, I'm more interested in other things: what I'm interested in is sleeping, and my mother's milk, and having wrappings round my shoulders, and warm baths. I hope no one comes to hear what this dispute was about; it would astonish the immortals, the idea of a newborn child coming through the porch with cattle that dwell in the fields. That's nonsense you're talking. I was born yesterday, my feet are tender, and it's rough ground beneath. If you like, I'll swear a big oath, by my father's head: I promise I'm not to blame personally, and I haven't seen anyone else stealing your cows—whatever cows they are, I've only heard talk of them."

So saying, and with many flutterings of his brows and eyelids, he tossed and turned, looking this way and that, whistling away at length, treating Apollo's words as empty. The Far-shooter laughed gently and said:

"My dear sly swindler, by the way you talk, I reckon you will often be burgling prosperous houses by night and leaving more than one man sitting on the floor as you rob his household without a sound; and you'll be vexing many a herdsman who sleeps in the open in the mountain glens, any time you crave meat and come upon their cattle herds and their flocks of sheep. Now then, if you don't want to be put to sleep once and for all, come down from your cradle,

290 ἐκ λίκνου κατάβαινε, μελαίνης νυκτὸς ἑταῖρε.
     τοῦτο γὰρ οὖν καὶ ἔπειτα μετ᾽ ἀθανάτοις γέρας
        ἕξεις·
     ἀρχὸς φιλητέων κεκλήσεαι ἤματα πάντα."
     ὣς ἄρ᾽ ἔφη, καὶ παῖδα λαβὼν φέρε Φοῖβος
        Ἀπόλλων.
     σὺν δ᾽ ἄρα φρασσάμενος τότε δὴ κρατὺς
        Ἀργειφόντης
295 οἰωνὸν προέηκεν ἀειρόμενος μετὰ χερσίν,
     τλήμονα γαστρὸς ἔριθον, ἀτάσθαλον ἀγγελιώτην,
     ἐσσυμένως δὲ μετ᾽ αὐτὸν ἐπέπταρε· τοῖο δ᾽
        Ἀπόλλων
     ἔκλυεν, ἐκ χειρῶν δὲ χαμαὶ βάλε κύδιμον Ἑρμῆν.
     ἕζετο δὲ προπάροιθε καὶ ἐσσύμενός περ ὁδοῖο
300 Ἑρμῆν κερτομέων, καί μιν πρὸς μῦθον ἔειπεν·
        "θάρσει, σπαργανιῶτα, Διὸς καὶ Μαιάδος υἱέ·
     εὑρήσω καὶ ἔπειτα βοῶν ἴφθιμα κάρηνα
     τούτοις οἰωνοῖσι· σὺ δ᾽ αὖθ᾽ ὁδὸν ἡγεμονεύσεις."
     ὣς φάθ᾽· ὁ δ᾽ αὖτ᾽ ἀνόρουσε θοῶς Κυλλήνιος
        Ἑρμῆς
305 σπουδῆι ἰών· ἄμφω δὲ παρ᾽ οὔατα χερσὶν ἐώθει,
     σπάργανον ἀμφ᾽ ὤμοισιν ἐελμένος, εἶπε δὲ μῦθον·
        "πῆι με φέρεις, Ἑκάεργε, θεῶν ζαμενέστατε
        πάντων;
     ἦ με βοῶν ἕνεχ᾽ ὧδε χολούμενος ὀρσολοπεύεις;
     ὦ πόποι, εἴθ᾽ ἀπόλοιτο βοῶν γένος· οὐ γὰρ ἐγώ γε
310 ὑμετέρας ἔκλεψα βόας, οὐδ᾽ ἄλλον ὄπωπα,
     αἵ τινές εἰσι βόες· τὸ δὲ δὴ κλέος οἶον ἀκούω.

you friend of dark night. For in fact you are to have this privilege among the immortals from now on: you shall be known as the prince of thieves for evermore."

So Phoibos Apollo spoke, and picked the child up to carry him. But just then the powerful Argus-slayer made up his mind and, as he was borne aloft in Apollo's arms, he emitted an omen, a menial servant of the belly, an unruly messenger;[29] and after it he promptly sneezed. On hearing that, Apollo dropped glorious Hermes on the ground, squatted down in front of him, eager though he was to be on his way, and bantered with Hermes, saying:

"Don't you worry, swatheling son of Zeus and Maia, I shall yet find my sturdy cattle with these omens, and you will lead the way."

So he spoke; whereupon Cyllenian Hermes quickly jumped up and set off in earnest. He pushed his hands up by his ears, wrapped round the shoulders as he was with the swaddling cloth, and said:

"Which way are you taking me, Far shooter, most irascible of all the gods? Are you harassing me like this because you're angry about your cows? Damn all cows! I haven't stolen your cows, or seen anyone else with them— whatever cows they are, I've only heard talk of them. Put

[29] A fart.

δὸς δὲ δίκην καὶ δέξο παρὰ Ζηνὶ Κρονίωνι."
    αὐτὰρ ἐπεὶ τὰ ἕκαστα διαρρήδην ἐρέεινον
Ἑρμῆς τ' οἰοπόλος καὶ Λητοῦς ἀγλαὸς υἱός,
315 ἀμφὶς θυμὸν ἔχοντες· ὃ μὲν νημερτέα φωνῶν
οὐκ ἀδίκως ἐπὶ βουσὶν ἐλάζυτο κύδιμον Ἑρμῆν,
αὐτὰρ ὃ τέχνῃσίν τε καὶ αἱμυλίοισι λόγοισιν
ἤθελεν ἐξαπατᾶν Κυλλήνιος Ἀργυρότοξον·
αὐτὰρ ἐπεὶ πολύμητις ἐὼν πολυμήχανον ηὗρεν,
320 ἐσσυμένως δήπειτα διὰ ψαμάθοιο βάδιζεν
πρόσθεν, ἀτὰρ κατόπισθε Διὸς καὶ Λητοῦς υἱός.
αἶψα δὲ τέρθρον ἵκοντο θυώδεος Οὐλύμποιο
ἐς πατέρα Κρονίωνα Διὸς περικαλλέα τέκνα·
κεῖθι γὰρ ἀμφοτέροισι δίκης κατέκειτο τάλαντα.
325 εὐωχίη δ' ἔχ' Ὄλυμπον ἀγάννιφον, ἀθάνατοι δέ
ἄφθιτοι ἠγερέθοντο μετὰ χρυσόθρονον Ἠώ.
ἔστησαν δ' Ἑρμῆς τε καὶ ἀργυρότοξος Ἀπόλλων
πρόσθε Διὸς γούνων· ὃ δ' ἀνείρετο φαίδιμον υἱόν
Ζεὺς ὑψιβρεμέτης καί μιν πρὸς μῦθον ἔειπεν·
330 "Φοῖβε, πόθεν ταύτην μενοεικέα ληΐδ' ἐλαύνεις,
παῖδα νέον γεγαῶτα, φυὴν κήρυκος ἔχοντα;
σπουδαῖον τόδε χρῆμα θεῶν μεθ' ὁμήγυριν ἦλθεν."
    τὸν δ' αὖτε προσέειπεν ἄναξ ἑκάεργος Ἀπόλλων·
"ὦ πάτερ, ἦ τάχα μῦθον ἀκούσεαι οὐκ ἀλαπαδνόν,
335 κερτομέων ὡς οἶος ἐγὼ φιλοληΐός εἰμι.
παῖδά τιν' ηὗρον τόνδε διαπρύσιον κεραϊστήν

315 φωνῶν Wolf: φωνὴν Ω
325 εὐωχίη West: εὐμιλίη Μ, εὐμυλίη Ψ

138

the case to trial before Zeus, son of Kronos."

When lone-ranging Hermes and Leto's splendid son had asked all their questions about everything, still in disagreement—the latter, speaking true, was not unjustly apprehending glorious Hermes over the cows, whereas the Cyllenian was hoping to deceive Silverbow with his arts and his wily words—so when he found Apollo as resourceful as he himself was cunning, after that he walked quickly through the sands, leading the way, with the son of Zeus and Leto following. Soon Zeus' handsome children reached the edge of fragrant Olympus, to their father the son of Kronos; there the scales of justice were in place for the two of them. Feasting(?) prevailed on snowy Olympus, and the deathless immortals were assembling after gold-throned Dawn. Hermes and silverbow Apollo took their stand before Zeus' knees. Zeus who thunders on high questioned his resplendent son and addressed him:

"Phoibos, where have you driven this heart-warming prey from, this newborn child with the build of a herald?[30] This is a matter of moment that has come before the gods' assembly."

The far-shooting lord Apollo spoke to him in turn: "Father, you're about to hear a story of no little interest, you who rib me for being uniquely acquisitive. I found this child, a thoroughgoing plunderer type, in the mountains of

---

[30] Hermes was to become the gods' herald.

---

326 μετὰ χρυσόθρονον ἠῶ y: ποτὶ πτύχας Οὐλύμποιο ΜΨ

Κυλλήνης ἐν ὄρεσσι, πολὺν διὰ χῶρον ἀνύσσας,
κέρτομον, οἷον ἐγώ γε θεῶν οὐκ ἄλλον ὄπωπα
οὐδ᾽ ἀνδρῶν, ὁπόσοι λησίμβροτοί εἰσ᾽ ἐπὶ γαῖαν.
340 κλέψας δ᾽ ἐκ λειμῶνος ἐμὰς βοῦς ᾤχετ᾽ ἐλαύνων
ἑσπέριος παρὰ θῖνα πολυφλοίσβοιο θαλάσσης,
εὐθὺ Πύλονδ᾽ ἐλάων· τὰ δ᾽ ἄρ᾽ ἴχνια, δοιὰ πέλωρα,
οἷά τ᾽ ἀγάσσασθαι, καὶ ἀγαυοῦ δαίμονος ἔργα.
τῇσιν μὲν γὰρ βουσὶν ἐς ἀσφοδελὸν λειμῶνα
345 ἀντία βήματ᾽ ἔχουσα κόνις ἀνέφαινε μέλαινα·
αὐτὸς δ᾽ οὔθ᾽ ὁδοῦ ἐκτὸς ἀμήχανος, οὔτ᾽ ἄρα
    ποσσίν
οὔτ᾽ ἄρα χερσὶν ἔβαινε διὰ ψαμαθώδεα χῶρον,
ἀλλ᾽ ἄλλην τινὰ μῆτιν ἔχων διέτριβε κέλευθα
τοῖα πέλωρ᾽, ὡς εἴ τις ἀραιῇσι δρυσὶ βαίνοι.
350 ὄφρα μὲν οὖν ἐδίωκε διὰ ψαμαθώδεα χῶρον,
ῥεῖα μάλ᾽ ἴχνια πάντα διέπρεπεν ἐν κονίῃσιν·
αὐτὰρ ἐπεὶ ψαμάθοιο πολὺν στίβον ἐξεπέρησεν,
ἄφραστος γένετ᾽ ὦκα βοῶν στίβος ἠδὲ καὶ αὐτοῦ
χῶρον ἀνὰ κρατερόν. τὸν δ᾽ ἐφράσατο βροτὸς ἀνήρ
355 ἐς Πύλον εὐθὺς ἐλῶντα βοῶν γένος εὐρυμετώπων.
αὐτὰρ ἐπεὶ δὴ τὰς μὲν ἐν ἡσυχίῃ κατέερξεν
καὶ διαπυρπαλάμησεν ὁδοῦ τὸ μὲν ἔνθα, τὸ δ᾽ ἔνθα,
ἐν λίκνῳ κατέκειτο μελαίνῃ νυκτὶ ἐοικώς
ἄντρῳ ἐν ἠερόεντι κατὰ ζόφον, οὐδέ κεν αὐτόν
360 αἰετὸς ὀξὺ λάων ἐσκέψατο· πολλὰ δὲ χερσίν
αὐγὰς ὠμόργαζε δολοφροσύνην ἀλεγύνων.
αὐτὸς δ᾽ αὐτίκα μῦθον ἀπηλεγέως ἀγόρευεν·
‘οὐκ ἴδον, οὐ πυθόμην, οὐκ ἄλλου μῦθον ἄκουσα,

Cyllene after a long journey: impudent like I've seen no
one else among gods or humans, of all those who are rob-
bers of men on the earth. He stole my cows from the
meadow and drove them off last evening along the shore of
the noisy sea, driving directly towards Pylos. The tracks
were a double monstrosity worthy of amazement, a devil's
doing: for the cows, the dark dust that held their prints
showed them going back towards the asphodel meadow,
while he himself, the impossible fellow, was crossing the
sandy region without either leaving the road, or going on
his feet, or on his hands—he had some other device and
was rubbing such monstrous tracks as if someone were
walking on slender oak trunks. Well, so long as he was
chasing through the sandy region, all the prints stood out
very clearly in the dust, but when he had crossed the long
track of sand, the cows' tracks and his own soon became in-
distinguishable on the rocky terrain. But a mortal man no-
ticed him driving the broad-browed cattle directly towards
Pylos. After he had penned them in quietly and completed
his conjuring act on this side of the road and that, he lay
down in his cradle, invisible as night in the darkness of the
gloomy cave—not even a keen-sighted eagle would have
spotted him—and did a lot of rubbing his eyes to further
his deception. And his own immediate words were quite
forthright: 'I haven't seen them, I haven't inquired, I

---

346 οὔθ᾽ ὁδοῦ West: οὗτος ὅδ᾽ Ω
356 κατέερξε p: κατέρεξε Mfx
361 ὠμόργαζε Ilgen: ὠμάρταζε Ω

οὐδέ κε μηνύσαιμ᾽, οὐδ᾽ ἂν μήνυτρον ἀροίμην.'"

365   ἤτοι ἄρ᾽ ὣς εἰπὼν κατ᾽ ἄρ᾽ ἕζετο Φοῖβος Ἀπόλλων·
Ἑρμῆς δ᾽ ἄλλον μῦθον ἐν ἀθανάτοισιν ἔειπεν,
δείξατο δ᾽ ἐς Κρονίωνα θεῶν σημάντορα πάντων·
"Ζεῦ πάτερ, ἤτοι ἐγώ σοι ἀληθείην ἀγορεύσω·
νημερτής τε γάρ εἰμι καὶ οὐκ οἶδα ψεύδεσθαι.
370   ἦλθεν ἐς ἡμετέρου διζήμενος εἰλίποδας βοῦς
σήμερον ἠελίοιο νέον ἐπιτελλομένοιο,
οὐδὲ θεῶν μακάρων ἄγε μάρτυρας οὐδὲ κατόπτας·
μηνύειν δ᾽ ἐκέλευεν ἀναγκαίης ὕπο πολλῆς,
πολλὰ δέ μ᾽ ἠπείλησε βαλεῖν ἐς Τάρταρον εὐρύν,
375   οὕνεχ᾽ ὃ μὲν τέρεν ἄνθος ἔχει φιλοκυδέος ἥβης,
αὐτὰρ ἐγὼ χθιζὸς γενόμην—τὰ δέ τ᾽ οἶδε καὶ
    αὐτός—
οὔ τι βοῶν ἐλατῆρι κραταιῶι φωτὶ ἐοικώς.
πείθεο, καὶ γὰρ ἐμεῖο πατὴρ φίλος εὔχεαι εἶναι,
ὡς οὐκ οἴκαδ᾽ ἔλασσα βόας, ὡς ὄλβιος εἴην,
380   οὐδ᾽ ὑπὲρ οὐδὸν ἔβην· τὸ δέ τ᾽ ἀτρεκέως ἀγορεύω.
Ἠέλιον δὲ μάλ᾽ αἰδέομαι καὶ δαίμονας ἄλλους,
καὶ σὲ φιλῶ, καὶ τοῦτον ὀπίζομαι· οἶσθα καὶ αὐτός,
ὡς οὐκ αἴτιός εἰμι. μέγαν δ᾽ ἐπιδώσομαι ὅρκον·
οὐ μὰ τάδ᾽ ἀθανάτων εὐκόσμητα προθύραια
385   μή ποτ᾽ ἐγὼ τούτωι τείσω ποτὲ νηλέα φωρήν
καὶ κρατερῶι περ ἐόντι· σὺ δ᾽ ὁπλοτέροισιν ἄρηγε."
ὣς φάτ᾽ ἐπιλλίζων Κυλλήνιος Ἀργειφόντης,
καὶ τὸ σπάργανον εἶχεν ἐπ᾽ ὠλένηι οὐδ᾽ ἀπέβαλλεν.

haven't been told. I couldn't tell you where they are, or earn a reward for it.'"

With these words Phoibos Apollo sat down. Hermes told a different tale among the immortals, gesturing towards Kronos' son, the commander of all the gods:

"Father Zeus, I shall tell you it as it was, for I am truthful and do not know how to tell a lie. He came into our place in search of his shambling cattle today as the sun was just rising. He didn't bring witnesses or observers from the blessed gods, but insisted on disclosure with much duress, and with many threats to throw me into broad Tartarus, because he has the delicate bloom of his glorious prime, while I was born yesterday, as he well knows, and I don't look like a cattle rustler, a strong man. Believe me (since you call yourself my dear father) that I didn't drive his cows home—so may I prosper—or even cross the threshold, and I'm speaking the truth. I am in awe of Helios[31] and the other gods, and I love you, and I respect him. You yourself know I'm not to blame. I'll give you a great oath too: by these finely adorned porches of the gods, I will never ever pay him compensation for that ruthless theft, strong though he is; you must support us younger ones."

So the Cyllenian Argus-slayer spoke, looking sideways, keeping his swaddling cloth on his arm and not letting it

---

31 The Sun god sees everything that is done on earth—by day.

---

380 τὸ δέ τ' Hermann: τόδε δ' Ω
383 ἐπιδώσομαι Barnes: ἐπιδεύομαι M, ἐπιδαίομαι Ψ
385 μή West: καί Ω

Ζεὺς δὲ μέγ᾽ ἐξεγέλασσεν ἰδὼν κακομηδέα παῖδα
390 εὖ καὶ ἐπισταμένως ἀρνεόμενον ἀμφὶ βόεσσιν.
ἀμφοτέρους δ᾽ ἐκέλευσεν ὁμόφρονα θυμὸν ἔχοντας
ζητεύειν, Ἑρμῆν δὲ διάκτορον ἡγεμονεύειν,
καὶ δεῖξαι τὸν χῶρον ἐπ᾽ ἀβλαβίῃσι νόοιο,
ὅππῃ δὴ αὖτ᾽ ἀπέκρυψε βοῶν ἴφθιμα κάρηνα.
395 νεῦσεν δὲ Κρονίδης, ἐπεπείθετο δ᾽ ἀγλαὸς Ἑρμῆς·
ῥηϊδίως γὰρ ἔπειθε Διὸς νόος αἰγιόχοιο.

τὼ δ᾽ ἄμφω σπεύδοντε Διὸς περικαλλέα τέκνα
ἐς Πύλον ἠμαθόεντα ἐπ᾽ Ἀλφειοῦ πόρον ἷξον·
ἀγροὺς δ᾽ ἐξίκοντο καὶ αὔλιον ὑψιμέλαθρον,
400 ἠχοῦ δὴ τὰ χρήματ᾽ ἀτάλλετο νυκτὸς ἐν ὥρῃ.
ἔνθ᾽ Ἑρμῆς μὲν ἔπειτα κιὼν παρὰ λάϊνον ἄντρον
ἐς φάος ἐξήλαυνε βοῶν ἴφθιμα κάρηνα·
Λητοΐδης δ᾽ ἀπάτερθεν ἰδὼν ἐνόησε βοείας
πέτρῃ ἐπ᾽ ἠλιβάτῳ, τάχα δ᾽ ἤρετο κύδιμον Ἑρμῆν·
405 "πῶς ἐδύνω, δολομῆτα, δύω βόε δειροτομῆσαι,
ὧδε νεογνὸς ἐὼν καὶ νήπιος; αὐτὸς ἐγώ γε
θαυμαίνω κατόπισθε τὸ σὸν κράτος· οὐδὲ τί σε χρὴ
μακρὸν ἀέξεσθαι, Κυλλήνιε Μαιάδος υἱέ."

ὣς ἄρ᾽ ἔφη, καὶ χερσὶ περίστρεφε καρτερὰ δεσμά
410 ἄγνου· ταὶ δ᾽ ὑπὸ ποσσὶ κατὰ χθονὸς αἶψα φύοντο
αὐτόθεν ἐμβολάδην ἐστραμμέναι ἀλλήλῃσιν,
ῥεῖά τε καὶ πάσῃσιν ἐπ᾽ ἀγραύλοισι βόεσσιν
Ἑρμέω βουλῇσι κλεψίφρονος· αὐτὰρ Ἀπόλλων
θαύμασεν ἀθρήσας. τότε δὴ κρατὺς Ἀργειφόντης
415 χῶρον ὑποβλήδην ἐσκέψατο πῦρ ἀμαρύσσων,
ἐγκρύψαι μεμαώς· Λητοῦς δ᾽ ἐρικυδέος υἱόν

drop.[32] Zeus laughed out loud when he saw the wicked boy making his fine, expert denials about the cows. He told the two of them to be reconciled and make search, Hermes the go-between to lead the way and without deceit to show the place where he had hidden the sturdy cattle. Kronos' son nodded his head, and bright Hermes acceded, readily persuaded by the purpose of Zeus the goat-rider.

So the two handsome children of Zeus, both in earnest, came to sandy Pylos, to the ford of the Alpheios, and arrived at the fields and high-roofed steading where the stock had been foddered during the night. There Hermes went the length of the rocky cavern and drove the sturdy cattle out into the light. But Apollo, looking away, saw the hides on the rock face, and straightway asked glorious Hermes:

"How were you able to slaughter two cows, trickster, newborn infant that you are? I myself wonder at your strength for the future. You had better not go on growing much longer, Cyllenian son of Maia."

With these words he began to plait strong bonds from osier. But the osiers at once grew into the earth right there beneath his feet, twined into each other like grafts, easily and over all the field-dwelling cattle, by the designs of deceptive Hermes; Apollo was amazed to see it. Then the strong Argus-slayer surveyed the area with his eyes darting fire, intent on hiding it from view. Glorious Leto's son ⟨was

[32] He still had his lyre hidden under it.

---

402 φάος Hermann: φῶς Ω
416 lac. stat. West

. . . .

ῥεῖα μάλ᾽ ἐπρήϋνεν Ἑκηβόλον, ὡς ἔθελ᾽ αὐτός,
καὶ κρατερόν περ ἐόντα· λαβὼν δ᾽ ἐπ᾽ ἀριστερὰ
    χειρός
πλήκτρωι ἐπειρήτιζε κατὰ μέλος· ἡ δ᾽ ὑπὸ χειρός
420 σμερδαλέον κονάβησε. γέλασσε δὲ Φοῖβος
    Ἀπόλλων
γηθήσας, ἐρατὴ δὲ διὰ φρένας ἤλυθ᾽ ἰωή
θεσπεσίης ἐνοπῆς, καί μιν γλυκὺς ἵμερος ᾕρει
θυμὸν ἀκουάζοντα. λύρηι δ᾽ ἐρατὸν κιθαρίζων
στῆ ῥ᾽ ὅ γε θαρσήσας ἐπ᾽ ἀριστερὰ Μαιάδος υἱός
425 Φοίβου Ἀπόλλωνος, τάχα δὲ λιγέως κιθαρίζων
γηρύετ᾽ ἀμβολάδην, ἐρατὴ δέ οἱ ἕσπετο φωνή,
κραίνων ἀθανάτους τε θεοὺς καὶ Γαῖαν ἐρεμνήν,
ὡς τὰ πρῶτα γένοντο καὶ ὡς λάχε μοῖραν ἕκαστος.
Μνημοσύνην μὲν πρῶτα θεῶν ἐγέραιρεν ἀοιδῆι
430 μητέρα Μουσάων, ἡ γὰρ λάχε Μαιάδος υἱόν·
τοὺς δὲ κατὰ πρέσβιν τε καὶ ὡς γεγάασιν ἕκαστος
ἀθανάτους ἐγέραιρε θεοὺς Διὸς ἀγλαὸς υἱός,
πάντ᾽ ἐνέπων κατὰ κόσμον, ὑπωλένιον κιθαρίζων.
τὸν δ᾽ ἔρος ἐν στήθεσσιν ἀμήχανος αἴνυτο θυμόν,
435 καί μιν φωνήσας ἔπεα πτερόεντα προσηύδα·
    "βουφόνε μηχανιῶτα, πονεόμενε δαιτὸς ἑταίρην,
πεντήκοντα βοῶν ἀντάξια ταῦτα μέμηδας·

423 θυμὸν West: θυμῷ Ω
433 ὑπωλένιον (= 510) Barnes: ἐπ- Ω
436 ἑταίρην Matthiae: ἑταῖρε Ω
437 μέμηδας Page: μέμηλας Ω

seized with anger, and he exclaimed, "Oh! You have cap-
tured my cows after all. Now you will have to pay me heavy
compensation if you want to placate me." Then Hermes,
taking out the lyre that he held concealed under his swad-
dling cloth,ˌ[33] easily pacified the Far-shooter for all his
toughness, as he himself desired. Taking it on his left arm,
he tried it out with a plectrum in a tuned scale, and it rang
out impressively under his hand; and Phoibos Apollo
laughed for pleasure, the lovely sound of its wondrous
voice invaded his senses, and sweet longing captivated his
heart as he listened. Playing delightfully on the lyre, the
son of Maia stationed himself unafraid on Phoibos Apollo's
left, and soon, with the lyre's clear accompaniment, he was
striking up his song, and his voice came lovely: he spoke
authoritatively of the immortal gods and of dark Earth,
how they were born originally and how each received his
portion. Remembrance first of the gods he honored in his
song, the mother of the Muses, for she had Maia's son in
her province, and then the rest of the immortal gods Zeus'
splendid son honored according to seniority and affilia-
tion, relating everything in due order, and playing the lyre
that hung from his arm.[34] As for Apollo, helpless longing
seized the spirit in his breast, and he addressed him in
winged words:

"You kill-cow, you ingenious inventor, busy with a din-
ner companion,[35] here you have contrived something of

---

[33] Some lines to this effect have apparently fallen out of the
text; compare 437–438.   [34] The lyre was supported by a strap
attached to the player's left wrist, leaving the fingers free to pluck
or damp the strings, while the right hand wielded the plectrum.

[35] The lyre. Compare 31, 478 ff.

ἡσυχίως καὶ ἔπειτα διακρινέεσθαι ὀίω.
νῦν δ' ἄγε μοι τόδε εἰπέ, πολύτροπε Μαιάδος υἱέ·
440 ἢ σοί γ' ἐκ γενετῆς τάδ' ἅμ' ἕσπετο θαυματὰ ἔργα,
ἦέ τις ἀθανάτων ἠὲ θνητῶν ἀνθρώπων
δῶρον ἀγαυὸν ἔδωκε καὶ ἔφρασε θέσπιν ἀοιδήν;
θαυμασίην γὰρ τήνδε νεήφατον ὄσσαν ἀκούω,
ἣν οὔ πώ ποτέ φημι δαήμεναι οὔτέ τιν' ἀνδρῶν
445 οὔτέ τιν' ἀθανάτων οἳ Ὀλύμπια δώματ' ἔχουσιν,
νόσφι σέθεν, φιλῆτα Διὸς καὶ Μαιάδος υἱέ.
τίς τέχνη, τίς μοῦσα ἀμηχανέων μελεδώνων,
τίς τρίβος; ἀτρεκέως γὰρ ἅμα τρία πάντα πάρεστιν
εὐφροσύνην καὶ ἔρωτα καὶ ἥδυμον ὕπνον ἑλέσθαι.
450 καὶ γὰρ ἐγὼ Μούσῃσιν Ὀλυμπιάδεσσιν ὀπηδός,
τῇσι χοροί τε μέλουσι καὶ ἀγλαὸς οἶμος ἀοιδῆς
καὶ μολπὴ τεθαλυῖα καὶ ἱμερόεις βρόμος αὐλῶν·
ἀλλ' οὔ πώ τί μοι ὧδε μετὰ φρεσὶν ἄλλο μέλησεν,
οἷα νέων θαλίῃς ἐνδέξια ἔργα πέλονται.
455 θαυμάζω, Διὸς υἱέ, τάδ' ὡς ἐρατὸν κιθαρίζεις.
νῦν δ' ἐπεὶ οὖν ὀλίγος περ ἐὼν κλυτὰ μήδεα οἶδας,
ἷζε, πέπον, καὶ μῦθον ἐπαίνει πρεσβυτέροισιν.
νῦν γάρ τοι κλέος ἔσται ἐν ἀθανάτοισι θεοῖσιν
σοί τ' αὐτῷ καὶ μητρί· τὸ δ' ἀτρεκέως ἀγορεύσω·
460 ναὶ μὰ τόδε κρανέϊνον ἀκόντιον, ἦ μὲν ἐγώ σε
κυδρὸν ἐν ἀθανάτοισι καὶ ὄλβιον ἡγεμονεύσω,
δώσω τ' ἀγλαὰ δῶρα καὶ ἐς τέλος οὐκ ἀπατήσω."
τὸν δ' Ἑρμῆς μύθοισιν ἀμείβετο κερδαλέοισιν·

457 μῦθον Ruhnkenius: θυμὸν Ω

matching value to my fifty cows! I think we shall yet achieve a peaceful settlement. But now tell me this, resourceful son of Maia: did these marvellous accomplishments attend you from birth, or did some god or mortal give you this remarkable gift and teach you wondrous singing? For this is a marvellous new-uttered voice I am hearing, that I declare no man and none of the immortals dwelling in Olympus has ever yet known, apart from you, deceitful son of Zeus and Maia. What is the skill, what the art of these baffling diversions, what the method? For truly, this lets one enjoy three boons all together, good cheer, love, and sweet sleep. I too, you know, am a follower of the Olympian Muses, whose concerns are dancing and the splendid course of song, and lively music, and the captivating bray of the shawms. Yet I have never thought of anything else like this—like the passing to the right at young men's feasts.[36] I am amazed, son of Zeus, how beautifully you can play such things on the lyre. Well, seeing that you are so clever, small as you are, pray sit there and acknowledge what your elders say. For now you are going to be renowned among the immortal gods, you and your mother. I'll tell you truly, yes, by this cornel-wood javelin, I guarantee I shall introduce(?) you to the immortals, to enjoy prestige and fortune. I shall give you fine gifts, and never deceive you."

Hermes answered him craftily: "You question me, wise

[36] At the symposium a myrtle branch and/or a lyre was passed round the guests from left to right, and each in turn was expected to sing or improvise a few verses. Our poet represents the practice as already existing in outline and as just waiting for the lyre to be invented for its perfection. Compare 55–56.

"εἰρωτᾷς μ᾽, Ἑκάεργε περιφραδές· αὐτὰρ ἐγώ τοι
465 τέχνης ἡμετέρης ἐπιβήμεναι οὔ τι μεγαίρω.
σήμερον εἰδήσεις· ἐθέλω δέ τοι ἤπιος εἶναι
βουλῆι καὶ μύθοισι, σὺ δὲ φρεσὶ πάντ᾽ εὖ οἶδας.
πρῶτος γάρ, Διὸς υἱέ, μετ᾽ ἀθανάτοισι θαάσσεις,
ἠΰς τε κρατερός τε· φιλεῖ δέ σε μητίετα Ζεύς
470 ἐκ πάσης ὁσίης, ἔπορεν δέ τοι ἀγλαὰ δῶρα·
καὶ τιμὰς σέ γέ φασι δαήμεναι ἐκ Διὸς ὀμφῆς
μαντείας, Ἑκάεργε, Διὸς πάρα θέσφατα πάντα·
τῶν νῦν αὐτὸς ἐγώ σε μάλ᾽ ἀφνειὸν δεδάηκα.
σοὶ δ᾽ αὐτάγρετόν ἐστι δαήμεναι ὅττι μενοινᾷς.
475 ἀλλ᾽ ἐπεὶ οὖν τοι θυμὸς ἐπιθύει κιθαρίζειν,
μέλπεο καὶ κιθάριζε καὶ ἀγλαΐας ἀλέγυνε
δέγμενος ἐξ ἐμέθεν· σὺ δ᾽ ἐμοί, φίλε, κῦδος ὄπαζε.
εὐμόλπει μετὰ χερσὶν ἔχων λιγύφωνον ἑταίρην
καλὰ καὶ εὖ κατὰ κόσμον ἐπισταμένην ἀγορεύειν.
480 εὔκηλός μιν ἔπειτα φέρειν ἐς δαῖτα θάλειαν
καὶ χορὸν ἱμερόεντα καὶ ἐς φιλοκυδέα κῶμον,
εὐφροσύνην νυκτός τε καὶ ἤματος. ὅς τις ἂν αὐτήν
τέχνηι καὶ σοφίηι δεδαημένος ἐξερεείνηι,
φθεγγομένη παντοῖα νόωι χαρίεντα διδάσκει,
485 ῥεῖα συνηθείηισιν ἀθυρομένη μαλακῆισιν,
ἐργασίην φεύγουσα δυήπαθον· ὃς δέ κεν αὐτήν
νῆϊς ἐὼν τὸ πρῶτον ἐπιζαφελῶς ἐρεείνηι,
μὰψ αὔτως κεν ἔπειτα μετήορά τε θρυλίζοι.
σοὶ δ᾽ αὐτάγρετόν ἐστι δαήμεναι ὅττι μενοινᾷς.
490 καί τοι ἐγὼ δώσω ταύτην, Διὸς ἀγλαὲ κοῦρε·
ἡμεῖς δ᾽ αὖτ᾽ ὄρεός τε καὶ ἱπποβότου πεδίοιο

Far-shooter, and I don't mind you embarking on my art.
You shall learn it this very day. I want to be friendly to you
in word and intent: you have a good knowledge of every-
thing, son of Zeus, for you sit in first place among the im-
mortals, noble and powerful, and resourceful Zeus loves
you as is right and proper, and has given you fine gifts. And
they say you have the privilege of prophetic knowledge
from Zeus' utterance, Far-shooter, the complete revela-
tion of Zeus' will; in which I myself have now learned that
you are richly endowed. You can help yourself to the
knowledge you want. But as your heart is set on playing the
lyre, play it, make music, and be festive, accept it from me;
and you, dear friend, give me prestige in turn. Be a fine
musician, fondling this clear-voiced girl friend who knows
how to talk fine and fittingly. Take her confidently to the
banquet and the lovely dance and the bumptious revel, a
source of good cheer day and night. If one questions her
with skill and expertise, she speaks all kinds of lessons
to charm the fancy, easily tickled with tender familiarity,
avoiding tiresome effort. But if a novice questions her
roughly, then she will utter useless, discordant rubbish.
You can help yourself to the knowledge you want. I will
give her to you, splendid son of Zeus, while I for my part,
Far-shooter, will graze the pastures of the mountain and

---

472 μαντείας θ' (vel τ') Ω: corr. Matthiae
473 σε Hermann, μάλ' Evelyn-White: γε παῖδ' Ω
479 ἐπισταμένην Barnes: -μένως Ω
480 μιν Ilgen: μὲν Ω

βουσὶ νομούς, Ἑκάεργε, νομεύσομεν ἀγραύλοισιν.
ἔνθεν ἅλις τέξουσι βόες ταύροισι μιγεῖσαι
μίγδην θηλείας τε καὶ ἄρσενας· οὐδέ τί σε χρή
495 κερδαλέον περ ἐόντα περιζαμενῶς κεχολῶσθαι."
   ὡς εἰπὼν ὤρεξ', ὁ δ' ἐδέξατο Φοῖβος Ἀπόλλων·
Ἑρμῆι δ' ἐγγυάλιξεν ἑκὼν μάστιγα φαεινήν
βουκολίας τ' ἐπέτελλεν· ἔδεκτο δὲ Μαιάδος υἱός
γηθήσας. κίθαριν δὲ λαβὼν ἐπ' ἀριστερὰ χειρός
500 Λητοῦς ἀγλαὸς υἱὸς ἄναξ ἑκάεργος Ἀπόλλων
πλήκτρωι ἐπειρήτιζε κατὰ μέλος, ἡ δ' ὑπὸ νέρθεν
ἱμερόεν κονάβησε, θεὸς δ' ὑπὸ καλὸν ἄεισεν.
   ἔνθα βόας μὲν ἔπειτα ποτὶ ζάθεον λειμῶνα
ἐτραπέτην· αὐτοὶ δὲ Διὸς περικαλλέα τέκνα
505 ἄψορροι πρὸς Ὄλυμπον ἀγάννιφον ἐρρώσαντο
τερπόμενοι φόρμιγγι. χάρη δ' ἄρα μητίετα Ζεύς,
ἄμφω δ' ἐς φιλότητα συνήγαγε· καὶ τὸ μὲν Ἑρμῆς
Λητοΐδην ἐφίλησε διαμπερές, ὡς ἔτι καὶ νῦν,
508a ⟨Λητοΐδης δὲ κασιγνήτου φιλότητος ἀνέγνω⟩
σήματ', ἐπεὶ κίθαριν μὲν Ἑκηβόλωι ἐγγυάλιξεν
510 ἱμερτὴν δεδαώς, ὁ δ' ὑπωλένιον κιθάριζεν,
αὐτὸς δ' αὖθ' ἑτέρης σοφίης ἐκμάσσατο τέχνην·
συρίγγων ἐνοπὴν ποιήσατο τηλόθ' ἀκουστήν.
   καὶ τότε Λητοΐδης Ἑρμῆν πρὸς μῦθον ἔειπεν·
"δείδια, Μαιάδος υἱὲ διάκτορε ποικιλομῆτα,
515 μή μοι ἀνακλέψῃς κίθαριν καὶ καμπύλα τόξα·
τιμὴν γὰρ πὰρ Ζηνὸς ἔχεις ἐπαμοίβιμα ἔργα

497 ἑκὼν Martin: ἔχων Ω   508a e.g. add. West

the horse-nurturing plain with the cattle that dwell in the fields. Then the cows will mate with the bulls and bear calves in plenty, both male and female, so there is no call for you, acquisitive as you are, to be furiously angry."

With these words he held out the lyre, and Phoibos Apollo took it; and he willingly handed Hermes the shining goad and enjoined on him the care of cattle, which Maia's son accepted gladly. Then, taking the lyre on his left arm, Leto's glorious son, the far-shooting lord Apollo, tried it out with a plectrum in a tuned scale, and it rang out enchantingly below, while the god sang beautifully to its accompaniment.

Then they headed the cattle toward their holy meadow, while Zeus' two beautiful children themselves went prancing back to snowy Olympus, entertaining themselves with the lyre. Resourceful Zeus was glad, and reconciled them to friendship: Hermes took to loving Leto's son constantly, as he still does, ‹and Leto's son acknowledged his brother's love› tokens,[37] in that he had handed to the Far-shooter the lovely lyre with which he was expert, for him to play as it hung from his arm, while he himself sought out a different artful skill—he made for himself the panpipes' far-carrying sound.

Then Leto's son said to Hermes, "I am afraid, son of Maia, cunning go-between, that you will steal back my lyre, and my bent bow, as you have this privilege from

[37] Line inserted conjecturally.

θήσειν ἀνθρώποισι κατὰ χθόνα πουλυβότειραν.
ἀλλ᾽ εἴ μοι τλαίης γε θεῶν μέγαν ὅρκον ὀμόσσαι,
ἢ κεφαλῆι νεύσας ἢ ἐπὶ Στυγὸς ὄβριμον ὕδωρ,
520 πάντ᾽ ἂν ἐμῶι θυμῶι κεχαρισμένα καὶ φίλα ἔρδοις."
    καὶ τότε Μαιάδος υἱὸς ὑποσχόμενος κατένευσεν
μή ποτ᾽ ἀποκλέψειν ὅσ᾽ Ἑκηβόλος ἐκτεάτισται,
μηδέ ποτ᾽ ἐμπελάσειν πυκινῶι δόμωι· αὐτὰρ
    Ἀπόλλων
Λητοΐδης κατένευσεν ἐπ᾽ ἀρθμῶι καὶ φιλότητι
525 μή τινα φίλτερον ἄλλον ἐν ἀθανάτοισιν ἔσεσθαι,
μήτε θεὸν μήτ᾽ ἄνδρα Διὸς γόνον· "ἐκ δὲ τέλειον
σύμβολον ἀθανάτων ποιήσομαι †ἠδ᾽ ἅμα πάντων
πιστὸν ἐμῶι θυμῶι καὶ τίμιον. αὐτὰρ ἔπειτα
ὄλβου καὶ πλούτου δώσω περικαλλέα ῥάβδον
530 χρυσείην τριπέτηλον, ἀκήριον ἥ σε φυλάξει,
πάντας ἐπικραίνουσα θε<μ>οὺς ἐπέων τε καὶ ἔργων
τῶν ἀγαθῶν, ὅσα φημὶ δαήμεναι ἐκ Διὸς ὀμφῆς.
μαντείην δέ, φέριστε διοτρεφές, ἣν ἐρεείνεις,
οὔτε σὲ θέσφατόν ἐστι δαήμεναι οὔτε τιν᾽ ἄλλον
535 ἀθανάτων· τὸ γὰρ οἶδε Διὸς νόος, αὐτὰρ ἐγώ γε
πιστωθεὶς κατένευσα καὶ ὤμοσα καρτερὸν ὅρκον,
μή τινα νόσφιν ἐμεῖο θεῶν αἰειγενετάων
ἄλλόν γ᾽ εἴσεσθαι Ζηνὸς πυκινόφρονα βουλήν·
καὶ σύ, κασίγνητε χρυσόρραπι, μή με κέλευε
540 θέσφατα πιφαύσκειν, ὅσα μήδεται εὐρύοπα Ζεύς.
ἀνθρώπων δ᾽ ἄλλον δηλήσομαι, ἄλλον ὀνήσω,
πολλὰ περιτροπέων ἀμεγάρτων φῦλ᾽ ἀνθρώπων·
καὶ μὲν ἐμῆς ὀμφῆς ἀπονήσεται, ὅς τις ἂν ἔλθηι

Zeus, that you will perform property-switchings on men over the nurturing earth.[38] If you could bring yourself to swear the gods' great oath, either by nodding your head, or upon the dread Water of Shuddering, you would be acting entirely after my own heart."

Then Maia's son promised, and confirmed it with a nod, that he would never steal the property that the Far-shooter has, or go near his strong room. And Apollo, Leto's son, agreed in a compact of friendship that he would have no greater friend among the immortals, neither a god nor a man of Zeus' stock; "And I will make it a complete contract from all the immortals,[39] that I will trust and honor in my heart. Moreover, I will give you a beautiful wand of wealth and fortune, made of gold, trefoil; it will keep you safe from harm, fulfilling all the dispositions of good words and events that I claim to know from the utterance of Zeus. But as to the prophetic art, my dear nursling of Zeus, which you ask about, it is not destined that you should know it, nor any other of the immortals. That is known to the mind of Zeus, and I have agreed under pledge, and sworn a powerful oath, that none other of the eternal gods apart from me shall know Zeus' intricate intent; so you, my brother gold-wand, must not ask me to reveal the destinies that wide-sounding Zeus is contriving. As for humans, I shall harm one and profit another as I lead their countless peoples this way and that. He will profit from my utterance who comes

38 In Alcaeus' hymn Hermes did steal Apollo's bow as well as his cattle.

39 Text uncertain.

531 θεμοὺς Ludwich: θεοὺς Ω

φωνῆι τ' ἠδὲ ποτῆισι τεληέντων οἰωνῶν·
545 οὗτος ἐμῆς ὀμφῆς ἀπονήσεται, οὐδ' ἀπατήσω·
ὃς δέ κε μαψιλόγοισι πιθήσας οἰωνοῖσιν
μαντείην ἐθέλησι πάρεκ νόον ἐξερεείνειν
ἡμετέρην, νοέειν δὲ θεῶν πλέον αἰὲν ἐόντων,
φῆμ' ἁλίην ὁδὸν εἶσιν, ἐγὼ δέ κε δῶρα δεχοίμην.
550 ἄλλο δέ τοι ἐρέω, Μαίης ἐρικυδέος υἱέ
καὶ Διὸς αἰγιόχοιο, θεῶν ἐριούνιε δαῖμον·
σεμναὶ γάρ τινές εἰσι κασίγνηται γεγαυῖαι
παρθένοι, ὠκείηισιν ἀγαλλόμεναι πτερύγεσσιν,
τρεῖς· κατὰ δὲ κρατὸς πεπαλαγμέναι ἄλφιτα λευκά
555 οἰκία ναιετάουσιν ὑπὸ πτυχὶ Παρνησσοῖο,
μαντείης ἀπάνευθε διδάσκαλοι, ἣν ἐπὶ βουσίν
παῖς ἔτ' ἐὼν μελέτησα· πατὴρ δ' ἐμὸς οὐκ ἀλέγιζεν.
ἐντεῦθεν δήπειτα ποτώμεναι ἄλλοτε ἄλληι
κηρία βόσκονται καί τε κραίνουσιν ἕκαστα·
560 αἱ δ' ὅτε μὲν θυίωσιν ἐδηδυῖαι μέλι χλωρόν,
προφρονέως ἐθέλουσιν ἀληθείην ἀγορεύειν·
ἢν δ' ἀπονοσφισθῶσι θεῶν ἡδεῖαν ἐδωδήν,
ψεύδονται δήπειτα δι' ἀλλήλων δονέουσαι.
τάς τοι ἔπειτα δίδωμι, σὺ δ' ἀτρεκέως ἐρεείνων

544 τ' ἠδεπότησι Μ: καὶ πτερύγεσσι Ψ
552 σεμναὶ Μ: μοῖραι Ψ: Θριαὶ Hermann
557 ἀλέγιζεν Hermann: ἀλέγυνεν Mfx, ἀλέγεινεν p
558 ἄλλοτε Schneidewin: ἄλλοτ' ἐπ' Ω
563 sic fere y (δενέουσαι: corr. Baumeister): πειρῶνται
δ' ἤπειτα παρὲξ ὁδὸν ἡγεμονεύειν ΜΨ

on the cry or the flights of valid omen birds: that man will profit from my utterance, and I shall not deceive him. But he who puts his trust in omens of vain utterance, and wants to enquire after a prophecy beyond my intention, and to know more than the eternal gods, I declare he will journey for nothing, though I shall take his offerings. I will tell you something else, son of glorious Maia and goat-rider Zeus, courser-deity among the gods:[40] there are certain august maidens, sisters, adorned with swift wings; they are three in number, their heads are dusted with white barley meal, and they dwell down in a hollow of Parnassus. They are sources of separate prophecy, which I practised when still a child tending my cattle, but my father was not interested. From there they go flying now this way, now that, to feed on honeycombs, and make their authoritative pronouncements. When they speed on after consuming the yellow honey, they are favorable and will tell the truth, but if they are turned away from the sweet food of the gods, then they mislead, agitating among themselves. I give them to you for the future; question them accurately for your own

[40] The strange passage which follows seems to conflate (a) a trio of prophetesses on Parnassus known as the Thriai, who produced oracles by casting pebbles, and (b) a rustic form of divination in which honeycombs were put out for swarms of wild bees, and inferences were drawn from the direction in which they flew off. For the Thriai see Jacoby's commentary on Philochorus, *FGrHist* 328 F 195; Frederick Williams, *Callimachus, Hymn to Apollo* (Oxford, 1978), 46 f. Their relevance is disputed by Susan Scheinberg, "The Bee Maidens of the Homeric *Hymn to Hermes*," *HSCP* 83 (1979), 1–28. See also Jennifer Larson, "The Corycian Nymphs and the Bee Maidens of the Homeric Hymn to Hermes," *GRBS* 36 (1995), 341–357.

565 σὴν αὐτοῦ φρένα τέρπε· καὶ εἰ βροτὸν ἄνδρα
       δαείης,
     πολλάκι σῆς ὀμφῆς ἐπακούσεται, αἴ κε τύχησιν.
     ταῦτ᾽ ἔχε, Μαιάδος υἱέ, καὶ ἀγραύλους ἕλικας βοῦς,
     ἵππους τ᾽ ἀμφιπόλευε καὶ ἡμιόνους ταλαεργούς."

       .   .   .   .

     καὶ χαροποῖσι λέουσι καὶ ἀργιόδουσι σύεσσιν
570 καὶ κυσὶ καὶ μήλοισιν, ὅσα τρέφει εὐρεῖα χθών,
     πᾶσι δ᾽ ἐπὶ προβάτοισιν ἀνάσσειν κύδιμον Ἑρμῆν·
     οἶον δ᾽ εἰς Ἀΐδην τετελεσμένον ἄγγελον εἶναι,
     ὅς τ᾽ ἄδοτός περ ἐὼν δώσει γέρας οὐκ ἐλάχιστον.
     οὕτω Μαιάδος υἱὸν ἄναξ ἐφίλησεν Ἀπόλλων
575 παντοίηι φιλότητι, χάριν δ᾽ ἐπέθηκε Κρονίων.
     πᾶσι δ᾽ ὅ γε θνητοῖσι καὶ ἀθανάτοισιν ὁμιλεῖ·
     παῦρα μὲν οὖν ὀνίνησι, τὸ δ᾽ ἄκριτον ἠπεροπεύει
     νύκτα δι᾽ ὀρφναίην φῦλα θνητῶν ἀνθρώπων.
     καὶ σὺ μὲν οὕτω χαῖρε, Διὸς καὶ Μαιάδος υἱέ·
580 αὐτὰρ ἐγὼ καὶ σεῖο καὶ ἄλλης μνήσομ᾽ ἀοιδῆς.

5. ΕΙΣ ΑΦΡΟΔΙΤΗΝ

     Μοῦσά μοι ἔννεπε ἔργα πολυχρύσου Ἀφροδίτης
     Κύπριδος, ἥ τε θεοῖσιν ἐπὶ γλυκὺν ἵμερον ὦρσεν
     καί τ᾽ ἐδαμάσσατο φῦλα καταθνητῶν ἀνθρώπων
     οἰωνούς τε διειπετέας καὶ θηρία πάντα,
5   ἠμὲν ὅσ᾽ ἤπειρος πολλὰ τρέφει ἠδ᾽ ὅσα πόντος·

       568 lac. stat. Wolf

pleasure, and if you teach(?) a mortal man, he will often hearken to your utterance, with luck. Have these things for your own, son of Maia, and the curly-horned, field-dwelling cattle, and concern yourself also with horses and toiling mules."

‹So spoke the son of Leto, the far-shooting lord Apollo. And Zeus confirmed all he had said; and he declared that Hermes should be the herald of the gods, and further that he should rule over animals: bears and grey wolves,›[41] and fierce lions and white-tusked boars, and dogs and sheep, all that the broad earth nourishes; and that glorious Hermes should be lord over all flocks; and that he alone should be empowered as envoy to Hades, who without receiving offerings will yet confer not the smallest of boons.

So the lord Apollo showed his love for the son of Maia in every way, and Kronos' son added his favor. He consorts with all mortals and immortals: rarely he brings them profit, while indiscriminately through the dark night he hoodwinks the peoples of mankind.

So I salute you, son of Zeus and Maia. And I will take heed both for you and for other singing.

5. TO APHRODITE

Muse, tell me of the doings of Aphrodite rich in gold, the Cyprian goddess, who sends sweet longing upon the gods, and overcomes the peoples of mortal kind, and the birds that fly in heaven, and all the numerous creatures that the land and sea foster: all of them are concerned with the

[41] Some lines to this effect have apparently fallen out of the text.

πᾶσιν δ᾽ ἔργα μέμηλεν ἐϋστεφάνου Κυθερείης.
τρισσὰς δ᾽ οὐ δύναται πεπιθεῖν φρένας οὐδ᾽
   ἀπατῆσαι·
κούρην τ᾽ αἰγιόχοιο Διὸς γλαυκῶπιν Ἀθήνην,
οὐ γάρ οἱ εὔαδεν ἔργα πολυχρύσου Ἀφροδίτης,
10 ἀλλ᾽ ἄρα οἱ πόλεμοί τε ἄδον καὶ ἔργον Ἄρηος,
ὑσμῖναί τε μάχαι τε, καὶ ἀγλαὰ ἔργ᾽ ἀλεγύνειν—
πρώτη τέκτονας ἄνδρας ἐπιχθονίους ἐδίδαξεν
ποιῆσαι σατίνα⟨ς τε⟩ καὶ ἅρματα ποικίλα χαλκῶι·
ἢ δέ τε παρθενικὰς ἁπαλόχροας ἐν μεγάροισιν
15 ἀγλαὰ ἔργ᾽ ἐδίδαξεν ἐπὶ φρεσὶ θεῖσα ἑκάστηι—
οὐδέ ποτ᾽ Ἀρτέμιδα χρυσηλάκατον κελαδεινήν
δάμναται ἐν φιλότητι φιλομμειδὴς Ἀφροδίτη·
καὶ γὰρ τῆι ἅδε τόξα καὶ οὔρεσι θῆρας ἐναίρειν
φόρμιγγές τε χοροί τε διαπρύσιοί τ᾽ ὀλολυγαί
20 ἄλσεά τε σκιόεντα δικαίων τε π⟨τ⟩όλις ἀνδρῶν·
οὐδὲ μὲν αἰδοίηι κούρηι ἅδεν ἔργ᾽ Ἀφροδίτης
Ἱστίηι, ἣν πρώτην τέκετο Κρόνος ἀγκυλομήτης,
αὖτις δ᾽ ὁπλοτάτην βουλῆι Διὸς αἰγιόχοιο,
πότνιαν, ἣν ἐμνῶντο Ποσειδάων καὶ Ἀπόλλων·
25 ἢ δὲ μάλ᾽ οὐκ ἔθελεν, ἀλλὰ στερεῶς ἀπέειπεν,
ὤμοσε δὲ μέγαν ὅρκον, ὃ δὴ τετελεσμένος ἐστίν,
ἁψαμένη κεφαλῆς πατρὸς Διὸς αἰγιόχοιο,
παρθένος ἔσσεσθαι πάντ᾽ ἤματα δῖα θεάων.
τῆι δὲ πατὴρ Ζεὺς δῶκε καλὸν γέρας ἀντὶ γάμοιο,
30 καί τε μέσωι οἴκωι κατ᾽ ἄρ᾽ ἕζετο πῖαρ ἑλοῦσα,

13 suppl. Barnes

doings of fair-garlanded Cytherea.

But there are three whose minds she cannot persuade or outwit. There is the daughter of goat-rider Zeus, steely-eyed Athena, for she does not like the doings of Aphrodite rich in gold: she likes wars and the doings of Ares, battles and fights, and fine workmanship—she first taught joiners on earth to make carriages and chariots ornamented with bronze, and she taught fine workmanship to tender-skinned girls in their houses, putting it into each one's mind. Nor is Artemis of the gold shafts and view-halloo ever overcome in love by smile-loving Aphrodite, for she too likes other things, archery and hunting animals in the mountains, lyres, dances, and piercing yells, shady groves, and a community of righteous men. Nor yet do the doings of Aphrodite appeal to the modest maiden Hestia, the first child of crooked-schemer Kronos, and also the youngest through the designs of goat-rider Zeus;[42] lady courted by Poseidon and Apollo, but she was not willing, she firmly refused them, and swore a great oath (which has indeed been kept), touching the head of her father, goat-rider Zeus, that she would be a virgin for all time, the noble goddess. And her father Zeus granted her a fine privilege instead of marriage, and she took fat and seated herself down in mid

[42] According to Hesiod, *Theogony* 459–500, Kronos swallowed his children as they were born, except for Zeus, whom Rhea smuggled away. When Zeus grew up, he forced Kronos to disgorge the swallowed gods, and they reappeared in reverse order, Hestia coming out last.

πᾶσιν δ᾽ ἐν νηοῖσι θεῶν τιμάοχός ἐστιν
καὶ παρὰ πᾶσι βροτοῖσι θεῶν πρέσβειρα τέτυκται.
τάων οὐ δύναται πεπιθεῖν φρένας οὐδ᾽ ἀπατῆσαι·
τῶν δ᾽ ἄλλων οὔ πέρ τι πεφυγμένον ἔστ᾽ Ἀφροδίτην
35 οὔτε θεῶν μακάρων οὔτε θνητῶν ἀνθρώπων.
καί τε πάρεκ Ζηνὸς νόον ἤγαγε τερπικεραύνου,
ὅς τε μέγιστός τ᾽ ἐστὶ μεγίστης τ᾽ ἔμμορε τιμῆς·
καί τε τοῦ εὖτ᾽ ἐθέλοι πυκινὰς φρένας ἐξαπαφοῦσα
ῥηϊδίως συνέμειξε καταθνητῆισι γυναιξίν,
40 Ἥρης ἐκλελαθοῦσα κασιγνήτης ἀλόχου τε,
ἣ μέγα εἶδος ἀρίστη ἐν ἀθανάτηισι θεῆισιν,
κυδίστην δ᾽ ἄρα μιν τέκετο Κρόνος ἀγκυλομήτης
μήτηρ τε Ῥείη· Ζεὺς δ᾽ ἄφθιτα μήδεα εἰδὼς
αἰδοίην ἄλοχον ποιήσατο κέδν᾽ εἰδυῖαν.
45 τῆι δὲ καὶ αὐτῆι Ζεὺς γλυκὺν ἵμερον ἔμβαλε
θυμῶι
ἀνδρὶ καταθνητῶι μιχθήμεναι, ὄφρα τάχιστα
μηδ᾽ αὐτὴ βροτέης εὐνῆς ἀποεργμένη εἴη
καί ποτ᾽ ἐπευξαμένη εἴπηι μετὰ πᾶσι θεοῖσιν
ἡδὺ γελοιήσασα φιλομμειδὴς Ἀφροδίτη,
50 ὥς ῥα θεοὺς συνέμειξε καταθνητῆισι γυναιξίν
καί τε καταθνητοὺς υἱεῖς τέκον ἀθανάτοισιν,
ὥς τε θεὰς ἀνέμειξε καταθνητοῖς ἀνθρώποις.
Ἀγχίσεω δ᾽ ἄρα οἱ γλυκὺν ἵμερον ἔμβαλε θυμῶι,
ὃς τότ᾽ ἐν ἀκροπόλοις ὄρεσιν πολυπίδακος Ἴδης
55 βουκολέεσκεν βοῦς, δέμας ἀθανάτοισιν ἐοικώς.

38 ἐθέλη Μ

house;[43] in all shrines of the gods she enjoys honor, and with all mortals she is senior goddess.

Those are the goddesses whose minds she cannot persuade or outwit. But for the rest, nothing has escaped Aphrodite, either of the blessed gods or of mortal men. She even led astray the mind of Zeus whose sport is the thunderbolt, who is the greatest and has the greatest honor as his portion: even his intricate mind she deceived when she liked, and easily coupled him with mortal women, putting out of his mind Hera his sister and consort, who is much the finest of aspect among the immortal goddesses, the most glorious daughter of crooked-schemer Kronos and her mother Rhea, and Zeus whose counsels do not fade made her his reverend consort, dutiful as she is.

But Zeus cast a sweet longing into Aphrodite's own heart to couple with a mortal man; he wanted to bring it about as soon as possible that not even she was set apart from a mortal bed, to boast among the assembled gods with a merry laugh how she had coupled gods with mortal women, and they had borne mortal sons to immortal fathers, and how she had coupled goddesses with mortal men. So he cast into her heart a sweet longing for Anchises, who at that time tended cattle on the heights of Ida with its many springs, in build like the immortals.

[43] Hestia is the goddess of the hearth fire at the centre of the house, and she receives the fat that drips down when cuts of a sacrificed animal are roasted.

---

54 πολυπίδακος D'Orville: -πιδάκου Ω

τὸν δἤπειτα ἰδοῦσα φιλομμειδὴς Ἀφροδίτη
ἠράσατ᾽, ἐκπάγλως δὲ κατὰ φρένας ἵμερος εἷλεν.
ἐς Κύπρον δ᾽ ἐλθοῦσα θυώδεα νηὸν ἔδυνεν,
ἐς Πάφον· ἔνθα δέ οἱ τέμενος βωμός τε θυώδης·
60 ἔνθ᾽ ἥ γ᾽ εἰσελθοῦσα θύρας ἐπέθηκε φαεινάς,
ἔνθα δέ μιν Χάριτες λοῦσαν καὶ χρῖσαν ἐλαίωι
ἀμβρότωι, οἷα θεοὺς ἐπενήνοθεν αἰὲν ἐόντας,
ἀμβροσίωι ἑ<δ>ανῶι, τό ῥά οἱ τεθυωμένον ἦεν.
ἑσσαμένη δ᾽ εὖ πάντα περὶ χροῒ εἵματα καλά,
65 χρυσῶι κοσμηθεῖσα φιλομμειδὴς Ἀφροδίτη
σεύατ᾽ ἐπὶ Τροίης, προλιποῦσ᾽ εὐώδεα Κύπρον,
ὕψι μετὰ νέφεσιν ῥίμφα πρήσσουσα κέλευθον.
Ἴδην δ᾽ ἵκανεν πολυπίδακα, μητέρα θηρῶν,
βῆ δ᾽ ἰθὺς σταθμοῖο δι᾽ οὔρεος· οἱ δὲ μετ᾽ αὐτήν
70 σαίνοντες πολιοί τε λύκοι χαροποί τε λέοντες
ἄρκτοι παρδάλιές τε θοαὶ προκάδων ἀκόρητοι
ἤισαν· ἡ δ᾽ ὁρόωσα μετὰ φρεσὶ τέρπετο θυμόν,
καὶ τοῖς ἐν στήθεσσι βάλ᾽ ἵμερον, οἱ δ᾽ ἅμα πάντες
σύνδυο κοιμήσαντο κατὰ σκιόεντας ἐναύλους.
75 αὐτὴ δ᾽ ἐς κλισίας εὐποιήτους ἀφίκανεν·
τὸν δ᾽ ηὗρε σταθμοῖσι λελειμμένον οἶον ἀπ᾽ ἄλλων
Ἀγχίσην ἥρωα θεῶν ἄπο κάλλος ἔχοντα·
οἱ δ᾽ ἅμα βουσὶν ἕποντο νομοὺς κάτα ποιήεντας
πάντες, ὁ δὲ σταθμοῖσι λελειμμένος οἶος ἀπ᾽ ἄλλων
80 πωλεῖτ᾽ ἔνθα καὶ ἔνθα, διαπρύσιον κιθαρίζων.
στῆ δ᾽ αὐτοῦ προπάροιθε Διὸς θυγάτηρ Ἀφροδίτη,
παρθένωι ἀδμήτηι μέγεθος καὶ εἶδος ὁμοίη,
μή μιν ταρβήσειεν ἐν ὀφθαλμοῖσι νοήσας.

Thereupon smile-loving Aphrodite fell in love with him at sight, and immoderate longing seized her mind.

Going to Cyprus, to Paphos, she disappeared into her fragrant temple; it is there that she has her precinct and scented altar. There she went in, and closed the gleaming doors, and there the Graces bathed her and rubbed her with olive oil, divine oil, as blooms upon the eternal gods, ambrosial bridal oil that she had ready perfumed. Her body well clad in all her fine garments, adorned with gold, smile-loving Aphrodite left fragrant Cyprus and sped towards Troy, rapidly making her way high among the clouds.

She reached Ida with its many springs, mother of wild creatures, and went straight for the steading across the mountain, while after her went fawning the grey wolves and fierce-eyed lions, bears and swift leopards insatiable for deer. Seeing them, she was glad at heart; in their breasts too she cast longing, and they all lay down in pairs in their shadowy haunts. She herself came to the sturdy huts, and found him left all alone in the steading, the manly Anchises who had his beauty from the gods; the others were all following the cattle over the grassy pastures, while he, left all alone in the steading, was going about this way and that, playing loudly on a lyre. Zeus' daughter Aphrodite stood before him, like an unmarried girl in stature and appearance, so that he should not be afraid when his eyes fell on her. Anchises gazed and took

---

63 ἑδανῶι Clarke: ἑανῶ Ω
66 Κύπρον Ψ: κῆπον Μ

Ἀγχίσης δ' ὁρόων ἐφράζετο θαύμαινέν τε
85 εἶδός τε μέγεθός τε καὶ εἵματα σιγαλόεντα.
πέπλον μὲν γὰρ ἔεστο φαεινότερον πυρὸς αὐγῆς,
εἶχε δ' ἐπιγναμπτὰς ἕλικας κάλυκάς τε φαεινάς,
ὅρμοι δ' ἀμφ' ἁπαλῆι δειρῆι περικαλλέες ἦσαν
καλοὶ χρύσειοι παμποίκιλοι· ὡς δὲ σελήνη
90 στήθεσιν ἀμφ' ἁπαλοῖσιν ἐλάμπετο, θαῦμα ἰδέσθαι.
Ἀγχίσην δ' ἔρος εἷλεν, ἔπος δέ μιν ἀντίον ηὔδα·
"χαῖρε, ἄνασσ', ἥ τις μακάρων τάδε δώμαθ'
     ἱκάνεις,
Ἄρτεμις ἢ Λητὼ ἠὲ χρυσῆ Ἀφροδίτη
ἢ Θέμις ἠϋγενὴς ἠὲ γλαυκῶπις Ἀθήνη
95 ἤ πού τις Χαρίτων δεῦρ' ἤλυθες, αἵ τε θεοῖσιν
πᾶσιν ἑταιρίζουσι καὶ ἀθάνατοι καλέονται,
ἤ τις νυμφάων, αἵ τ' ἄλσεα καλὰ νέμονται,
{ἢ νυμφῶν αἳ καλὸν ὄρος τόδε ναιετάουσιν}
καὶ πηγὰς ποταμῶν καὶ πίσεα ποιήεντα.
100 σοὶ δ' ἐγὼ ἐν σκοπιῆι, περιφαινομένωι ἐνὶ χώρωι,
βωμὸν ποιήσω, ῥέξω δέ τοι ἱερὰ καλὰ
ὥρηισιν πάσηισι· σὺ δ' εὔφρονα θυμὸν ἔχουσα
δός με μετὰ Τρώεσσιν ἀριπρεπέ' ἔμμεναι ἄνδρα,
ποίει δ' εἰσοπίσω θαλερὸν γόνον, αὐτὰρ ἔμ' αὐτόν
105 δηρὸν ἐΰ ζώειν καὶ ὁρᾶν φάος ἠελίοιο
ὄλβιον ἐν λαοῖς καὶ γήραος οὐδὸν ἱκέσθαι."
     τὸν δ' ἠμείβετ' ἔπειτα Διὸς θυγάτηρ Ἀφροδίτη·
"'Ἀγχίση, κύδιστε χαμαιγενέων ἀνθρώπων,
οὔ τίς τοι θεός εἰμι· τί μ' ἀθανάτηισιν ἐΐσκεις;
110 ἀλλὰ καταθνητή τε, γυνὴ δέ με γείνατο μήτηρ.

stock of her, wondering at her appearance, her stature, and her shining garments; for she wore a dress brighter than firelight, and she had twisted bracelets and shining ear buds. Round her tender neck there were beautiful necklaces of gold, most elaborate, and about her tender breasts it shone like the moon, a wonder to behold. Anchises was seized by desire, and he addressed her face to face:

"Hail, Lady, whichever of the blessed ones you are that arrive at this dwelling, Artemis or Leto or golden Aphrodite, high-born Themis or steely-eyed Athena; or perhaps you are one of the Graces come here, who are companions to all the gods and are called immortal; or one of the nymphs, who haunt the fair groves[44] and the waters of rivers and the grassy meads. I will build you an altar on a hilltop, in a conspicuous place, and make goodly sacrifices to you at every due season. Only have a kindly heart, and grant that I may be a man outstanding among the Trojans, and make my future offspring healthy, and myself to live long and well, seeing the light of the sun and enjoying good fortune among the peoples, and to reach the doorstep of old age."

Zeus' daughter Aphrodite answered him: "Anchises, most glorious of earthborn men, I am no goddess—why do you compare me with the immortals?—but a mortal, and the mother who bore me was a woman. My father is the

[44] Here the manuscripts add another line which seems to be a variant: 'or of the nymphs who dwell on this fair mountain.'

---

98 del. Ruhnkenius

Ὀτρεὺς δ᾽ ἐστὶ πατὴρ ὀνομάκλυτος, εἴ που ἀκούεις,
ὃς πάσης Φρυγίης εὐτειχήτοιο ἀνάσσει.
γλῶσσαν δ᾽ ὑμετέρην ⟨τε⟩ καὶ ἡμετέρην σάφα οἶδα·
Τρωιὰς γὰρ μεγάρωι με τροφὸς τρέφεν ἠδὲ διάπρο
115 σμικρὴν παῖδ᾽ ἀτίταλλε φίλης παρὰ μητρὸς
        ἑλοῦσα·
ὡς δή τοι γλῶσσάν γε καὶ ὑμετέρην εὖ οἶδα.
νῦν δέ μ᾽ ἀνήρπαξε χρυσόρραπις Ἀργειφόντης
ἐκ χοροῦ Ἀρτέμιδος χρυσηλακάτου κελαδεινῆς.
πολλαὶ δὲ νύμφαι καὶ παρθένοι ἀλφεσίβοιαι
120 παίζομεν, ἀμφὶ δ᾽ ὅμιλος ἀπείριτος ἐστεφάνωτο·
ἔνθέν μ᾽ ἥρπαξε χρυσόρραπις Ἀργειφόντης,
πολλὰ δ᾽ ἐπ᾽ ἤγαγεν ἔργα καταθνητῶν ἀνθρώπων,
πολλὴν δ᾽ ἄκληρόν τε καὶ ἄκτιτον, ἣν διὰ θῆρες
ὠμοφάγοι φοιτῶσι κατὰ σκιόεντας ἐναύλους,
125 οὐδὲ ποσὶ ψαύειν δόκεον φυσιζόου αἴης·
Ἀγχίσεω δέ με φάσκε παραὶ λέχεσιν καλέεσθαι
κουριδίην ἄλοχον, σοὶ δ᾽ ἀγλαὰ τέκνα τεκεῖσθαι.
αὐτὰρ ἐπεὶ δὴ δεῖξε καὶ ἔφρασεν, ἤτοι ὅ γ᾽ αὖτις
ἀθανάτων μετὰ φῦλ᾽ ἀπέβη κρατὺς Ἀργειφόντης·
130 αὐτὰρ ἐγὼ σ᾽ ἱκόμην, κρατερὴ δέ μοι ἔπλετ᾽
        ἀνάγκη.
ἀλλά σε πρὸς Ζηνὸς γουνάζομαι ἠδὲ τοκήων
ἐσθλῶν· οὐ μὲν γάρ κε κακοὶ τοιόνδε τέκοιεν·
ἀδμήτην μ᾽ ἀγαγὼν καὶ ἀπειρήτην φιλότητος
πατρί τε σῶι δεῖξον καὶ μητέρι κεδν᾽ εἰδυίηι
135 σοῖς τε κασιγνήτοις, οἵ τοι ὁμόθεν γεγάασιν·
οὔ σφιν ἀεικελίη νυὸς ἔσσομαι, ἀλλ᾽ εἰκυῖα.

famed Otreus, if you have perhaps heard of him, who rules over all of well-walled Phrygia.[45] But I know your language as well as ours, because a Trojan nurse nursed me at home and reared me throughout my childhood, taking me over from my dear mother; so I am well acquainted with your language too.[46] But now the gold-wand Argus-slayer has snatched me up from the dance to Artemis of the gold shafts and the view-halloo. There were many of us dancing, brides and marriageable girls, and a vast crowd ringed us about: from there the gold-wand Argus-slayer snatched me, and brought me over much farmland of mortal men, and much ownerless and uncultivated land where ravening beasts roam about their shadowy haunts; I felt that my feet were not touching the grain-growing earth. He told me I should be known as the young wife of Anchises' bed, and bear you splendid children. After showing me the way and pointing you out, the mighty Argus-slayer went off to rejoin the families of the immortals, while I have come to you, forced by necessity. Now I beseech you by Zeus and your noble parents (no humble people would have produced such a child as you): take me, a virgin with no experience of love, and show me to your father and your dutiful mother, and your brothers born of the same stock; I shall not be an unfitting daughter-in-law for them, but a fit one.

[45] Otreus is mentioned in *Iliad* 3.186 as a Phrygian chieftain whom Priam assisted on the occasion of an Amazon invasion.

[46] This is the earliest reference in Greek to bilingualism.

---

113 τε add. Wolf
116 γε Hermann: τε Ω
125 δόκεον La Roche: ἐδόκουν Ω

πέμψαι δ' ἄγγελον ὦκα μετὰ Φρύγας αἰολοπώλους,
εἰπεῖν πατρί τ' ἐμῶι καὶ μητέρι κηδομένηι περ·
οἳ δέ κέ <τοι> χρυσόν τε ἅλις ἐσθῆτά θ' ὑφαντήν
140 πέμψουσιν, σὺ δὲ πολλὰ καὶ ἀγλαὰ δέχθαι ἄποινα.
ταῦτα δὲ ποιήσας δαίνυ γάμον ἱμερόεντα
τίμιον ἀνθρώποισι καὶ ἀθανάτοισι θεοῖσιν."
    ὣς εἰποῦσα θεὰ γλυκὺν ἵμερον ἔμβαλε θυμῶι.
Ἀγχίσην δ' ἔρος εἷλεν, ἔπος τ' ἔφατ' ἔκ τ'
    ὀνόμαζεν·
145 "εἰ μὲν θνητή τ' ἐσσί, γυνὴ δέ σε γείνατο μήτηρ,
Ὀτρεὺς δ' ἐστὶ πατὴρ ὀνομάκλυτος, ὡς ἀγορεύεις,
ἀθανάτου δὲ ἕκητι διακτόρου ἐνθάδ' ἱκάνεις
Ἑρμέω, ἐμὴ δ' ἄλοχος κεκλήσεαι ἤματα πάντα·
οὔ τις ἔπειτα θεῶν οὔτε θνητῶν ἀνθρώπων
150 ἐνθάδε με σχήσει πρὶν σῆι φιλότητι μιγῆναι
αὐτίκα νῦν, οὐδ' εἴ κεν ἑκηβόλος αὐτὸς Ἀπόλλων
τόξου ἄπ' ἀργυρέου προΐηι βέλεα στονόεντα·
βουλοίμην κεν ἔπειτα, γύναι εἰκυῖα θεῆισιν,
σῆς εὐνῆς ἐπιβὰς δῦναι δόμον Ἄϊδος εἴσω."
155   ὣς εἰπὼν λάβε χεῖρα· φιλομμειδὴς δ' Ἀφροδίτη
ἕρπε μεταστρεφθεῖσα, κατ' ὄμματα καλὰ βαλοῦσα,
ἐς λέχος εὔστρωτον, ὅθι περ πάρος ἔσκεν ἄνακτι
χλαίνηισιν μαλακῆις ἐστρωμένον· αὐτὰρ ὕπερθεν
ἄρκτων δέρματ' ἔκειτο βαρυφθόγγων τε λεόντων,
160 τοὺς αὐτὸς κατέπεφνεν ἐν οὔρεσιν ὑψηλοῖσιν.
οἳ δ' ἐπεὶ οὖν λεχέων εὐποιήτων ἐπέβησαν,
κόσμον μέν οἱ πρῶτον ἀπὸ χροὸς εἷλε φαεινόν,

And send a messenger quickly to the Phrygians of the darting steeds, to tell my father and my anxious mother. They will send you gold in plenty and woven cloth, and you must accept the many fine dowry gifts. When you have done that, hold a delightful wedding-feast that will impress men and immortal gods."

With these words the goddess cast sweet longing into his heart. Anchises was seized by desire, and he spoke and addressed her: "If you are a mortal, and the mother who bore you was a woman, and your father is the famed Otreus, as you say, and you have come here by the will of the immortal go-between Hermes, and you are to be known as my wife for ever, then no god or mortal man is going to hold me back from making love to you right now, not even if far-shooting Apollo himself discharges baleful arrows from his silver bow: I should choose in that case, O woman like a goddess, after once mounting your bed, to go down into the house of Hades."

With these words he took her hand, and smile-loving Aphrodite, casting her lovely eyes down, turned and moved to the well-bedecked bed, where the lord kept it spread with soft blankets, on top of which lay skins of bears and roaring lions that he himself had killed in the high mountains. When they had mounted the sturdy bed, he first removed the shining adornment from her body, the

---

139 κέ τοι . . . τε Matthiae: κε . . . τε M: τε . . . κεν Ψ

πόρπας τε γναμπτάς θ' ἕλικας κάλυκάς τε καὶ
  ὅρμους,
λῦσε δέ οἱ ζώνην, ἰδὲ εἵματα σιγαλόεντα
165 ἔκδυε καὶ κατέθηκεν ἐπὶ θρόνου ἀργυροήλου
Ἀγχίσης· ὁ δ' ἔπειτα θεῶν ἰότητι καὶ αἴσηι
ἀθανάτηι παρέλεκτο θεᾶι βροτός, οὐ σάφα εἰδώς.

  ἦμος δ' ἂψ εἰς αὖλιν ἀποκλίνουσι νομῆες
βοῦς τε καὶ ἴφια μῆλα νομῶν ἐξ ἀνθεμοέντων,
170 τῆμος ἄρ' Ἀγχίσηι μὲν ἐπὶ γλυκὺν ὕπνον ἔχευεν
νήδυμον, αὐτὴ δὲ χροῒ ἔννυτο εἵματα καλά.
ἑσσαμένη δ' εὖ πάντα περὶ χροῒ δῖα θεάων
ἔστη ἄρα κλισίηι εὐποιήτου ⟨δὲ⟩ μελάθρου
κῦρε κάρη, κάλλος δὲ παρειάων ἀπέλαμπεν
175 ἄμβροτον, οἷόν τ' ἐστὶν ἐϋστεφάνου Κυθερείης·
ἐξ ὕπνου τ' ἀνέγειρεν, ἔπος τ' ἔφατ' ἔκ τ' ὀνόμαζεν·

  "ὄρσεο, Δαρδανίδη· τί νυ νήγρετον ὕπνον ἰαύεις;
καὶ φράσαι, εἴ τοι ὁμοίη ἐγὼν ἰνδάλλομαι εἶναι,
οἵην δή με τὸ πρῶτον ἐν ὀφθαλμοῖσι νόησας."

180   ὣς φάθ'· ὁ δ' ἐξ ὕπνοιο μάλ' ἐμμαπέως
  ὑπάκουσεν.
ὡς δὲ ἴδεν δειρήν τε καὶ ὄμματα κάλ' Ἀφροδίτης,
τάρβησέν τε καὶ ὄσσε παρακλιδὸν ἔτραπεν ἄλληι,
ἂψ δ' αὖτις χλαίνηι ἐκαλύψατο καλὰ πρόσωπα.
καί μιν λισσόμενος ἔπεα πτερόεντα προσηύδα·

185   "αὐτίκα σ' ὡς τὰ πρῶτα, θεά, ἴδον ὀφθαλμοῖσιν,
ἔγνων ὡς θεὸς ἦσθα· σὺ δ' οὐ νημερτὲς ἔειπες.
ἀλλά σε πρὸς Ζηνὸς γουνάζομαι αἰγιόχοιο,
μή με ζῶντ' ἀμενηνὸν ἐν ἀνθρώποισιν ἐάσηις

pins and twisted bracelets and ear buds and necklaces; he
undid her girdle, and divested her of her gleaming gar-
ments and laid them on a silver-riveted chair. And then
Anchises by divine will and destiny lay with the immortal
goddess, the mortal, not knowing the truth of it.

At the hour when herdsmen turn their cattle and fat
sheep back to the steading from the flowery pastures, then
she poured a sweet, peaceful sleep upon Anchises, while
she dressed herself in her fine garments. Her body well
clad in them all, the noble goddess stood in the hut—her
head reached to the sturdy rafter, while from her cheeks
shone a divine beauty, such as belongs to fair-garlanded
Cytherea—and roused him from sleep, and spoke and ad-
dressed him:

"Be up, descendant of Dardanus—why do you slumber
in unbroken sleep?—and mark whether I look to you like I
did when you first set eyes on me."

So she spoke, and he responded promptly from out
of his sleep. But when he saw the neck and lovely eyes
of Aphrodite, he was afraid, and averted his gaze, and
covered his handsome face up again in the blanket, and
begged her with winged words:

"As soon as I first saw you, goddess, I realized you were
a deity, but you did not tell the truth. Now I beseech you by
Zeus the goat-rider, do not leave me to dwell among man-

---

173 εὐποιήτου δὲ Ruhnkenius: -τοιο Ω
175 ἰοστεφάνου M
183 ἐκαλύψατο West: τ' ἐκαλ- (vel τε καλ-) Ω

ναίειν, ἀλλ᾽ ἐλέαιρ᾽· ἐπεὶ οὐ βιοθάλμιος ἀνήρ
190 γίνεται, ὅς τε θεαῖς εὐνάζεται ἀθανάτηισιν."
　　τὸν δ᾽ ἠμείβετ᾽ ἔπειτα Διὸς θυγάτηρ Ἀφροδίτη·
"Ἀγχίση, κύδιστε καταθνητῶν ἀνθρώπων,
θάρσει, μηδέ τι σῆισι μετὰ φρεσὶ δείδιθι λίην·
οὐ γάρ τοί τι δέος παθέειν κακὸν ἐξ ἐμέθεν γε
195 οὐδ᾽ ἄλλων μακάρων, ἐπεὶ ἦ φίλος ἐσσὶ θεοῖσιν.
σοὶ δ᾽ ἔσται φίλος υἱός, ὃς ἐν Τρώεσσιν ἀνάξει
καὶ παῖδες παίδεσσι διαμπερὲς ἐκγεγάοντες·
τῶι δὲ καὶ Αἰνείας ὄνομ᾽ ἔσσεται, οὕνεκά μ᾽ αἰνόν
ἔσχεν ἄχος, ἕνεκα βροτοῦ ἀνέρος ἔμπεσον εὐνῆι.
200 ἀγχίθεοι δὲ μάλιστα καταθνητῶν ἀνθρώπων
αἰεὶ ἀφ᾽ ὑμετέρης γενεῆς εἶδός τε φυήν τε·
ἤτοι μὲν ξανθὸν Γανυμήδεα μητίετα Ζεύς
ἥρπασεν ὃν διὰ κάλλος, ἵν᾽ ἀθανάτοισι μετείη
καί τε Διὸς κατὰ δῶμα θεοῖς ἐπιοινοχοέυοι,
205 θαῦμα ἰδεῖν, πάντεσσι τετιμένος ἀθανάτοισιν,
χρυσέου ἐκ κρητῆρος ἀφύσσων νέκταρ ἐρυθρόν.
Τρῶα δὲ πένθος ἄλαστον ἔχε φρένας, οὐδέ τι ἤιδει
ὅππηι οἱ φίλον υἱὸν ἀνήρπασε θέσπις ἄελλα·
τὸν δἤπειτα γόασκε διαμπερὲς ἤματα πάντα.
210 καί μιν Ζεὺς ἐλέησε, δίδου δέ οἱ υἷος ἄποινα,
ἵππους ἀρσίποδας, τοί τ᾽ ἀθανάτους φορέουσιν·
τούς οἱ δῶρον ἔδωκεν ἔχειν, εἶπέν τε ἕκαστα
Ζηνὸς ἐφημοσύνηισι διάκτορος Ἀργειφόντης,
ὡς ἔοι ἀθάνατος καὶ ἀγήρως ἶσα θεοῖσιν.
215 αὐτὰρ ἐπεὶ δὴ Ζηνὸς ὅ γ᾽ ἔκλυεν ἀγγελιάων,

kind as a living invalid, but be merciful; for a man does not enjoy vital vigor who goes to bed with immortal goddesses."

Zeus' daughter Aphrodite answered him: "Anchises, most glorious of mortal men, be of good courage, and let your heart not be too afraid. You need have no fear of suffering any harm from me or the other blessed ones, for you are dear to the gods indeed. You are to have a dear son who will rule among the Trojans, as will the children born to his children continually; his name shall be Aeneas (*Aineias*), because an *ainon akhos* (terrible sorrow) took me, that I fell into a mortal man's bed. Of all humankind, those close to the gods in appearance and stature always come especially from your family. Flaxen-haired Ganymede was seized by resourceful Zeus because of his beauty, so that he should be among the immortals and serve drink to the gods in Zeus' house, a wonder to see, esteemed by all the immortals as he draws the red nectar from the golden bowl. As for Tros,[47] nagging grief possessed his heart; he did not know which way the miraculous whirlwind had snatched up his dear son, and he went on lamenting him day after day. Zeus took pity on him, and to compensate for his son he gave him prancing horses, of the breed that carry the immortals: those he gave him to keep, and on Zeus' instructions the go-between, the Argus-slayer, explained everything, how Ganymede was immortal and unaging just like the gods. When he heard Zeus' message, he stopped

[47] Legendary ancestor of the Trojans (*Troes*).

---

197 ἐκγεγάοντες Baumeister: -ονται Ω

οὐκέτ᾽ ἔπειτα γόασκε, γεγήθει δὲ φρένας ἔνδον,
γηθόσυνος δ᾽ ἵπποισιν ἀελλοπόδεσσιν ὀχεῖτο.
ὣς δ᾽ αὖ Τιθωνὸν χρυσόθρονος ἥρπασεν Ἠώς
ὑμετέρης γενεῆς, ἐπιείκελον ἀθανάτοισιν·
220 βῆ δ᾽ ἴμεν αἰτήσουσα κελαινεφέα Κρονίωνα
ἀθάνατόν τ᾽ εἶναι καὶ ζώειν ἤματα πάντα·
τῆι δὲ Ζεὺς ἐπένευσε καὶ ἐκρήηνεν ἐέλδωρ·
νηπίη, οὐδ᾽ ἐνόησε μετὰ φρεσὶ πότνια Ἠώς
ἥβην αἰτῆσαι ξῦσαί τ᾽ ἄπο γῆρας ὀλοιόν.
225 τὸν δ᾽ ἤτοι εἵως μὲν ἔχεν πολυήρατος ἥβη,
Ἠοῖ τερπόμενος χρυσοθρόνωι ἠριγενείηι
ναῖε παρ᾽ Ὠκεανοῖο ῥοῆς ἐπὶ πείρασι γαίης·
αὐτὰρ ἐπεὶ πρῶται πολιαὶ κατέχυντο ἔθειραι
καλῆς ἐκ κεφαλῆς εὐηγενέος τε γενείου,
230 τοῦ δ᾽ ἤτοι εὐνῆς μὲν ἀπείχετο πότνια Ἠώς,
αὐτὸν δ᾽ αὖτ᾽ ἀτίταλλεν ἐνὶ μεγάροισιν ἔχουσα
σίτωι τ᾽ ἀμβροσίηι τε καὶ εἵματα καλὰ διδοῦσα.
ἀλλ᾽ ὅτε δὴ πάμπαν στυγερὸν κατὰ γῆρας ἔπειγεν,
οὐδέ τι κινῆσαι μελέων δύνατ᾽ οὐδ᾽ ἀναεῖραι,
235 ἥδε δέ οἱ κατὰ θυμὸν ἀρίστη φαίνετο βουλή·
ἐν θαλάμωι κατέθηκε, θύρας δ᾽ ἐπέθηκε φαεινάς.
τοῦ δ᾽ ἤτοι φωνὴ ῥέει ἄσπετος, οὐδέ τι κῖκυς
ἔσθ᾽ οἵη πάρος ἔσκεν ἐνὶ γναμπτοῖσι μέλεσσιν.
    "οὐκ ἂν ἐγώ γε σὲ τοῖον ἐν ἀθανάτοισιν ἑλοίμην
240 ἀθάνατόν τ᾽ εἶναι καὶ ζώειν ἤματα πάντα·
ἀλλ᾽ εἰ μὲν τοιοῦτος ἐὼν εἶδός τε δέμας τε
ζώοις ἡμέτερός τε πόσις κεκλημένος εἴης,

lamenting, and was glad in his heart, and in gladness he took to riding with the storm-footed horses. So again Tithonus was seized by golden-throned Dawn from your family, a man like the immortals. She went to ask the dark-cloud son of Kronos for him to be immortal and live for ever, and Zeus assented and fulfilled her wish—foolish lady Dawn, she did not think to ask for youth for him, and the stripping away of baneful old age. So long as lovely youth possessed him, he took his delight in Dawn of the golden throne, the early-born, and dwelt by the waters of Ocean at the ends of the earth; but when the first scattering of grey hairs came forth from his handsome head and his noble chin, the lady Dawn stayed away from his bed, but kept him in her mansion and nurtured him with food and ambrosia, and gave him fine clothing. And when repulsive old age pressed fully upon him, and he could not move or lift any of his limbs, this is what she decided was the best course: she laid him away in a chamber, and shut its shining doors. His voice still runs on unceasing, but there is none of the strength that there used to be in his bent limbs.[48]

"I would not choose for you to be like that among the gods, to be immortal and live for ever. If you could go on living as you are now in appearance and build, and be known as my husband, sorrow would not then enfold my

[48] This account seems to hint at the myth, first attested in Hellanicus (fr. 140 Fowler), that Tithonus became a cicada. Cicadas begin to be noisy around dawn.

---

237 ῥέει Wolf: ῥεῖ Ω

οὐκ ἂν ἔπειτά μ' ἄχος πυκινὰς φρένας
    ἀμφικαλύπτοι.
  νῦν δὲ σὲ μὲν τάχα γῆρας ὁμοίιον ἀμφικαλύψει
245 νηλειές, τό τ' ἔπειτα παρίσταται ἀνθρώποισιν,
  οὐλόμενον καματηρόν, ὅ τε στυγέουσι θεοί περ,
  αὐτὰρ ἐμοὶ μέγ' ὄνειδος ἐν ἀθανάτοισι θεοῖσιν
  ἔσσεται ἤματα πάντα διαμπερὲς εἵνεκα σεῖο,
  οἳ πρὶν ἐμοὺς ὀάρους καὶ μήτιας, αἷς ποτε πάντας
250 ἀθανάτους συνέμειξα καταθνητῆισι γυναιξίν,
  τάρβεσκον· πάντας γὰρ ἐμὸν δάμνασκε νόημα·
  νῦν δὲ δὴ οὐκέτι μοι στόμα χείσεται ἐξονομῆναι
  τοῦτο μετ' ἀθανάτοισιν, ἐπεὶ μάλα πολλὸν ἀάσθην,
  σχέτλιον, οὐκ ὀνομαστόν, ἀπεπλάγχθην δὲ νόοιο,
255 παῖδα δ' ὑπὸ ζώνηι ἐθέμην βροτῶι εὐνηθεῖσα.
    "τὸν μὲν ἐπὴν δὴ πρῶτον ἴδηι φάος ἠελίοιο,
  νύμφαι μιν θρέψουσιν ὀρεσκῶιοι βαθύκολποι,
  αἳ τόδε ναιετάουσιν ὄρος μέγα τε ζάθεόν τε·
  αἵ ῥ' οὔτε θνητοῖς οὔτ' ἀθανάτοισιν ἕπονται.
260 δηρὸν μὲν ζώουσι καὶ ἄμβροτον εἶδαρ ἔδουσιν,
  καί τε μετ' ἀθανάτοισι καλὸν χορὸν ἐρρώσαντο,
  τῆισι δὲ Σειληνοί τε καὶ εὔσκοπος Ἀργειφόντης
  μίσγοντ' ἐν φιλότητι μυχῶι σπείων ἐροέντων.
  τῆισι δ' ἅμ' ἢ ἐλάται ἠὲ δρύες ὑψικάρηνοι
265 γεινομένηισιν ἔφυσαν ἐπὶ χθονὶ βωτιανείρηι·
  καλαὶ τηλεθάουσαι ἐν οὔρεσιν ὑψηλοῖσιν
  ἑστᾶσ' ἠλίβατοι, τεμένη δέ ἑ κικλήσκουσιν
  ἀθανάτων· τὰς δ' οὔ τι βροτοὶ κείρουσι σιδήρωι.
  ἀλλ' ὅτε κεν δὴ μοῖρα παρεστήκηι θανάτοιο,

subtle mind. But as it is, you will soon be enfolded by hostile, merciless old age, which attends men in the time to come, accursed, wearisome, abhorred by the gods; while I shall suffer great reproach among the gods evermore on your account. Formerly they used to be afraid of my whisperings and wiles, with which at one time or another I have coupled all the immortals with mortal women, for my will would overcome them all. But now my mouth will no longer open wide enough to mention this among the immortals, since I have been led very far astray, awfully and unutterably, gone out of my mind, and got a child under my girdle after going to bed with a mortal.

"As for him, once he sees the sunlight, he will be nursed by the deep-bosomed, mountain-couching nymphs who dwell on this great and holy mountain, who belong with neither mortals nor gods. They have long lives, and eat divine food, and step the fair dance with the immortals; Sileni and the keen-sighted Argus-slayer unite in love with them in the recesses of lovely caves. As they are born, fir trees or tall oaks come forth on the earth that feeds mankind: fine and healthy they stand towering in the high mountains, and people call them precincts of the gods, and mortals do not cut them with the axe. But when their fated

---

252 στόμα χείσεται Martin: στοναχήσεται Ω
254 ὀνομαστόν Martin: ὀνόατον Ω

270 ἀζάνεται μὲν πρῶτον ἐπὶ χθονὶ δένδρεα καλά,
φλοιὸς δ᾽ ἀμφιπεριφθινύθει, πίπτουσι δ᾽ ἄπ᾽ ὄζοι,
τῶν δέ θ᾽ ὁμοῦ ψυχὴ λείπει φάος ἠελίοιο.
    "αἳ μὲν ἐμὸν θρέψουσι παρὰ σφίσιν υἱὸν ἔχουσαι·
τὸν μὲν ἐπὴν δὴ πρῶτον ἕληι πολυήρατος ἥβη,
275 ἄξουσίν τοι δεῦρο θεαὶ δείξουσί τε παῖδα.
σοὶ δ᾽ ἐγώ, ὄφρα <κε> ταῦτα μετὰ φρεσὶ πάντα
    διέλθω,
ἐς πέμπτον ἔτος αὖτις ἐλεύσομαι υἱὸν ἄγουσα.
τὸν μὲν ἐπὴν δὴ πρῶτον ἴδηις θάλος ὀφθαλμοῖσιν,
γηθήσεις ὁρόων· μάλα γὰρ θεοείκελος ἔσται·
280 ἄξεις δ᾽ αὐτίκα μιν ποτὶ Ἴλιον ἠνεμόεσσαν.
ἢν δέ τις εἴρηταί σε καταθνητῶν ἀνθρώπων,
ἥ τις σοὶ φίλον υἱὸν ὑπὸ ζώνηι θέτο μήτηρ,
τῶι δὲ σὺ μυθεῖσθαι μεμνημένος ὥς σε κελεύω·
φάσθαι τοι νύμφης καλυκώπιδος ἔκγονον εἶναι,
285 αἳ τόδε ναιετάουσιν ὄρος καταειμένον ὕληι.
εἰ δέ κεν ἐξείπηις καὶ ἐπεύξεαι ἄφρονι θυμῶι
ἐν φιλότητι μιγῆναι ἐϋστεφάνωι Κυθερείηι,
Ζεύς σε χολωσάμενος βαλέει ψολόεντι κεραυνῶι.
εἴρηταί τοι πάντα· σὺ δὲ φρεσὶ σῆισι νοήσας
290 ἴσχεο, μηδ᾽ ὀνόμαινε, θεῶν δ᾽ ἐποπίζεο μῆνιν."
    ὣς εἰποῦσ᾽ ἤϊξε πρὸς οὐρανὸν ἠνεμόεντα.

272 θ᾽ Hermann: χ᾽ Ω
274–5 del. Matthiae
276 <κε> ταῦτα Barnes: τ<οι> αὖ τὰ Kamerbeek   δαήηις
Schneidewin   280 μιν Hermann: νιν Ψ, νῦν Μ
284 φάσθαι Matthiae: φασίν Ω

death is at hand, first the fair trees wither where they stand, their bark decays about them, their branches fall off, and simultaneously the nymphs' souls depart from the sunlight.

"They will keep my son among them and nurse him.[49] As soon as the lovely prime of youth possesses him, the goddesses will bring him here to you and show you your son. As soon as you set eyes on your scion, you will rejoice as you look on him, for he will be quite godlike. You will take him straight away to windy Ilios. If anyone asks you who was the mother that got your dear son under her girdle, be sure to answer him as I tell you: say he is the child of a nymph with eyes like buds, one of those who dwell on this forest-clad mountain. But if you speak out and foolishly boast of having united in love with fair-garlanded Cytherea, Zeus will be angry and will strike you with a smoking bolt.[50] There, I have told you everything. Take note of it, restrain yourself from mentioning me, and have regard for the gods' wrath."

With these words she sped away to the winds of heaven.

[49] Two alternate versions of the next sentence are transmitted. The second—"And I (to go over all this in my mind) will come to you again in the fifth year from now, bringing your son."—is the better, though the phrase translated as 'to go over all this in my mind' is difficult and perhaps corrupt.

[50] According to some later sources this happened: Sophocles, *Laocoon* fr. 373.2; Virgil, *Aeneid* 2.649 with Servius' commentary; Hyginus, *Fab.* 94.

χαῖρε, θεά, Κύπροιο ἐϋκτιμένης μεδέουσα·
σέο δ' ἐγὼ ἀρξάμενος μεταβήσομαι ἄλλον ἐς
ὕμνον.

6. ΕΙΣ ΑΦΡΟΔΙΤΗΝ

Αἰδοίην χρυσοστέφανον καλὴν Ἀφροδίτην
ᾄσομαι, ἣ πάσης Κύπρου κρήδεμνα λέλογχεν
εἰναλίης, ὅθι μιν Ζεφύρου μένος ὑγρὸν ἀέντος
ἤνεικεν κατὰ κῦμα πολυφλοίσβοιο θαλάσσης
5 ἀφρῶι ἔνι μαλακῶι· τὴν δὲ χρυσάμπυκες Ὧραι
δέξαντ' ἀσπασίως, περὶ δ' ἄμβροτα εἵματα ἕσσαν,
κρατὶ δ' ἔπ' ἀθανάτωι στεφάνην εὔτυκτον ἔθηκαν
καλὴν χρυσείην, ἐν δὲ τρητοῖσι λοβοῖσιν
ἄνθεμ' ὀρειχάλκου χρυσοῖό τε τιμήεντος,
10 δειρῆι δ' ἀμφ' ἁπαλῆι καὶ στήθεσιν ἀργυφέοισιν
ὅρμοισι χρυσέοισιν ἐκόσμεον, οἷσί περ αὐταὶ
Ὧραι κοσμείσθην χρυσάμπυκες, ὁππότ' ἴοιεν
ἐς χορὸν ἱμερόεντα θεῶν καὶ δώματα πατρός.
αὐτὰρ ἐπεὶ δὴ πάντα περὶ χροῒ κόσμον ἔθηκαν,
15 ἦγον ἐς ἀθανάτους· οἳ δ' ἠσπάζοντο ἰδόντες
χερσί τ' ἐδεξιόωντο· καὶ ἠρήσαντο ἕκαστος
εἶναι κουριδίην ἄλοχον καὶ οἴκαδ' ἄγεσθαι,
εἶδος θαυμάζοντες ἰοστεφάνου Κυθερείης.
χαῖρ' ἑλικοβλέφαρε, γλυκυμείλιχε, δὸς δ' ἐν
ἀγῶνι
20 νίκην τῶιδε φέρεσθαι, ἐμὴν δ' ἔντυνον ἀοιδήν.
αὐτὰρ ἐγὼ καὶ σεῖο καὶ ἄλλης μνήσομ' ἀοιδῆς.

5. TO APHRODITE

I salute you, goddess, queen of well-cultivated Cyprus.
After beginning from you, I will pass over to another song.

6. TO APHRODITE

Of the reverend, gold-crowned, lovely Aphrodite I will
sing, who has been assigned the citadels of all Cyprus that
is in the sea. That is where the wet-blowing westerly's force
brought her across the swell of the noisy main, in soft
foam;[51] and the Horai with headbands of gold received her
gladly, and clothed her in divine clothing. On her immortal
head they put a finely wrought diadem, a beautiful gold
one, and in her pierced ear lobes flowers of orichalc and
precious gold. About her tender throat and her white
breast they decked her in golden necklaces, the ones that
the gold-crowned Horai themselves would be decked with
whenever they went to the gods' lovely dance at their
father's house. When they had put all the finery about her
body, they led her to the immortals, who welcomed her on
sight and took her hand in greeting; and each of them
prayed to take her home as his wedded wife, as they
admired the beauty of violet-crowned Cytherea.

I salute you, sweet-and-gentle one of curling lashes:
grant me victory in this competition, and order my singing.
And I will take heed both for you and for other singing.

---

[51] Hesiod, *Theogony* 188–200, relates that when Kronos cut
off his father Ouranos' genitals and threw them in the sea, foam
formed round them, and in it Aphrodite was born. It floated first
to Cythera and then to Cyprus, where she emerged. Hence she
is called Cytherea, Cyprian, and because of the foam (*aphros*)
Aphrodite.

7. ΕΙΣ ΔΙΟΝΥΣΟΝ

Ἀμφὶ Διώνυσον Σεμέλης ἐρικυδέος υἱόν
μνήσομαι, ὡς ἐφάνη παρὰ θῖν' ἁλὸς ἀτρυγέτοιο
ἀκτῆι ἔπι προβλῆτι, νεηνίηι ἀνδρὶ ἐοικώς
πρωθήβηι· καλαὶ δὲ περισσείοντο ἔθειραι
5 κυάνεαι, φᾶρος δὲ περὶ στιβαροῖς ἔχεν ὤμοις
πορφύρεον. τάχα δ' ἄνδρες ἐϋσσέλμου ἀπὸ νηός
ληϊσταὶ προγένοντο θοῶς ἐπὶ οἴνοπα πόντον,
Τυρσηνοί· τοὺς δ' ἦγε κακὸς μόρος. οἱ δὲ ἰδόντες
νεῦσαν ἐς ἀλλήλους, τάχα δ' ἔκθορον· αἶψα δ' ἑλόντες
10 εἶσαν ἐπὶ σφετέρης νηός, κεχαρημένοι ἦτορ·
υἱὸν γάρ μιν ἔφαντο διοτρεφέων βασιλήων
εἶναι. καὶ δεσμοῖς ἔθελον δεῖν ἀργαλέοισιν·
τὸν δ' οὐκ ἴσχανε δεσμά, λύγοι δ' ἀπὸ τηλόσ' ἔπιπτον
χειρῶν ἠδὲ ποδῶν, ὁ δὲ μειδιάων ἐκάθητο
15 ὄμμασι κυανέοισι. κυβερνήτης δὲ νοήσας
αὐτίκα οἷς ἑτάροισιν ἐκέκλετο φώνησέν τε·
"δαιμόνιοι, τίνα τόνδε θεῶν δεσμεύεθ' ἑλόντες,
καρτερόν; οὐδὲ φέρειν δύναταί μιν νηῦς εὐεργής.
ἦ γὰρ Ζεὺς ὅδε γ' ἐστὶν ἢ ἀργυρότοξος Ἀπόλλων
20 ἠὲ Ποσειδάων, ἐπεὶ οὐ θνητοῖσι βροτοῖσιν
εἴκελος, ἀλλὰ θεοῖς οἳ Ὀλύμπια δώματ' ἔχουσιν.
ἀλλ' ἄγετ' αὐτὸν ἀφῶμεν ἐπ' ἠπείροιο μελαίνης
αὐτίκα, μηδ' ἐπὶ χεῖρας ἰάλλετε, μή τι χολωθεὶς
ὄρσηι ἀργαλέους τ' ἀνέμους καὶ λαίλαπα πολλήν."

7. TO DIONYSUS

Of Dionysus, glorious Semele's son, I will make remembrance: how he appeared by the shore of the barren sea, on a jutting headland, in the likeness of a youth in first manhood; the fine sable locks waved about him, and he had a cloak of crimson about his strong shoulders. Suddenly men from a galley came speeding over the wine-faced sea, freebooters from Tuscany, led on by an ill doom. When they saw him, they nodded to one another, and at once leapt out, seized him, and set him aboard their ship, exulting, for they reckoned he was the son of a princely line fostered by Zeus. And they meant to bind him in grievous bonds; but the bonds would not contain him, the osiers fell clear away from his hands and feet, while he sat there smiling with his dark eyes. When the helmsman saw it, he at once cried out to his comrades:

"Madmen, which of the gods is this that you would bind prisoner?—a mighty one, our sturdy ship cannot support him. This is either Zeus, or silverbow Apollo, or Poseidon; he is not like mortal men, but the gods who dwell on Olympus. Come on, let's put him ashore straight away on the dark land. Don't lay hands on him, or he may be angered and raise fierce winds and tempest!"

---

13 λύγοι Chalcondyles: λυδοὶ Ψ, ληδοὶ M

25   ὣς φάτο· τὸν δ' ἀρχὸς στυγερῶι ἠνίπαπε μύθωι·
"δαιμόνι᾽, οὖρον ὅρα, ἅμα δ' ἱστίον ἕλκεο νηός
σύμπανθ᾽ ὅπλα λαβών· ὅδε δ' αὖτ' ἄνδρεσσι
    μελήσει.
ἔλπομαι ἢ Αἴγυπτον ἀφίξεται ἢ ὅ γε Κύπρον
ἢ ἐς Ὑπερβορέους ἢ ἑκαστέρω· ἐς δὲ τελευτήν
30   ἔκ ποτ' ἐρεῖ αὐτοῦ τε φίλους καὶ κτήματα πάντα
οὕς τε κασιγνήτους, ἐπεὶ ἡμῖν ἔμβαλε δαίμων."
    ὣς εἰπὼν ἱστόν τε καὶ ἱστίον ἕλκετο νηός·
ἔμπνευσεν δ' ἄνεμος μέσον ἱστίον, ἀμφὶ δ' ἄρ'
    ὅπλα
κατ-άννυσαν. τάχα δέ σφιν ἐφαίνετο θαυματὰ ἔργα·
35   οἶνος μὲν πρώτιστα θοὴν ἀνὰ νῆα μέλαιναν
ἡδύποτος κελάρυξ' εὐώδης, ὤρνυτο δ' ὀδμή
ἀμβροσίη· ναύτας δὲ τάφος λάβε πάντας ἰδόντας·
αὐτίκα δ' ἀκρότατον παρὰ ἱστίον ἐξετανύσθη
ἄμπελος ἔνθα καὶ ἔνθα, κατεκρημνῶντο δὲ πολλοί
40   βότρυες· ἀμφ' ἱστὸν δὲ μέλας εἰλίσσετο κισσός
ἄνθεσι τηλεθάων, χαρίεις δ' ἐπὶ καρπὸς ὀρώρει·
πάντες δὲ σκαλμοὶ στεφάνους ἔχον. οἳ δὲ ἰδόντες
νῆ᾽ ἤδη τότ' ἔπειτα κυβερνήτην ἐκέλευον
γῆι πελάαν. ὃ δ' ἄρα σφι λέων γένετ' ἔνδοθι νηός
45   δεινὸς ἐπ' ἀκροτάτης, μέγα δ' ἔβραχεν· ἐν δ' ἄρα
    μέσσηι
ἄρκτον ἐποίησεν λασιαύχενα, σήματα φαίνων·
ἂν δ' ἔστη μεμαυῖα, λέων δ' ἐπὶ σέλματος ἄκρου
δεινὸν ὑπόδρα ἰδών· οἳ δ' ἐς πρύμνην ἐφόβηθεν,
ἀμφὶ κυβερνήτην δὲ σαόφρονα θυμὸν ἔχοντα

7. TO DIONYSUS

So he spoke, but the captain rebuked him harshly: "Madman, you watch the wind; help me hoist the sail, catch all the sheets together. Leave this fellow for men to worry about. I fancy he will get to Egypt, or Cyprus, or the Hyperboreans, or beyond, and in the end he'll speak out and tell us his kinsmen and their possessions and who his brothers are, seeing that fortune has thrown him among us."

With these words he turned to hoist the mast and sail. The wind blew full into the sail, and they tightened the sheets at the sides. But suddenly they began to see miraculous apparitions. First of all, wine gushed out over the dark swift ship, sweet-tasting and fragrant, and there rose a smell ambrosial, and the sailors were all seized with astonishment as they saw it. Then along the top of the sail there spread a vine in both directions, hung with many grape clusters. About the mast dark ivy was winding, all flowering, and pretty berries were out on it; and all the tholes were decorated with garlands. When they saw this, then they did start calling on the helmsman to take the ship to land. But the god became a lion in the ship, a terrible lion in the bows, and he roared loud; and amidships he made a shaggy-maned bear, to signal his power. Up it reared in fury, while the lion at the top of the deck stood glaring fearsomely. They fled to the stern, and about the prudent-hearted helmsman they halted in terror. Without

---

37 τάφος Ψ: φόβος Μy
43 νῆ᾽ ἤδη Hermann: μὴ δ᾽ ἤδη Μ, μὴ δήδειν Ψ
45–47 damn. Sparshott

50 ἔσταν ἄρ' ἐκπληγέντες. ὁ δ' ἐξαπίνης ἐπορούσας
    ἀρχὸν ἔλ'· οἱ δὲ θύραζε κακὸν μόρον ἐξαλύοντες
    πάντες ὁμῶς πήδησαν, ἐπεὶ ἴδον, εἰς ἅλα δῖαν,
    δελφῖνες δ' ἐγένοντο. κυβερνήτην δ' ἐλεήσας
    ἔσχεθε καί μιν ἔθηκε πανόλβιον, εἶπέ τε μῦθον·
55   "θάρσει, †δῖ' ἑκάτωρ†, τῶμῶι κεχαρισμένε θυμῶι·
    εἰμὶ δ' ἐγὼ Διόνυσος ἐρίβρομος, ὃν τέκε μήτηρ
    Καδμηὶς Σεμέλη Διὸς ἐν φιλότητι μιγεῖσα."
    χαῖρε, τέκος Σεμέλης εὐώπιδος· οὐδέ πηι ἔστιν
    σεῖό γε ληθόμενον γλυκερὴν κοσμῆσαι ἀοιδήν.

{8. ΕΙΣ ΑΡΕΑ

Ἄρες ὑπερμενέτα, βρισάρματε, χρυσεοπήληξ,
ὀβριμόθυμε, φέρασπι, πολισσόε, χαλκοκορυστά,
καρτερόχειρ, ἀμόγητε, δορισθενές, ἔρκος Ὀλύμπου,
Νίκης εὐπολέμοιο πάτερ, συναρωγὲ Θέμιστος,
5 ἀντιβίοισι τύραννε, δικαιοτάτων ἀγὲ φωτῶν,
ἠνορέης σκηπτοῦχε, πυραυγέα κύκλον ἑλίσσων
αἰθέρος ἑπταπόροις ἐνὶ τείρεσιν, ἔνθά σε πῶλοι
ζαφλεγέες τριτάτης ὑπὲρ ἄντυγος αἰὲν ἔχουσιν·
κλῦθι, βροτῶν ἐπίκουρε, δοτὴρ εὐθαρσέος ἥβης,
10 πρηΰ καταστίλβων σέλας ὑψόθεν ἐς βιότητα
ἡμετέρην καὶ κάρτος ἀρήϊον, ὥς κε δυναίμην
σεύασθαι κακότητα πικρὴν ἀπ' ἐμεῖο καρήνου

---

52 Text obscure.

warning the lion sprang forward and seized the captain. The others all leapt out into the sea when they saw it, to avoid an ill doom, and they turned into dolphins. But as for the helmsman, the god took pity on him and held him back, and gave him the highest blessings, saying:

"Be not afraid, good mariner(?),[52] lief to my heart. I am Dionysus the mighty roarer, born to Cadmus' daughter Semele in union of love with Zeus."

I salute you, child of fair Semele; there is no way to adorn sweet singing while heedless of you.

{8. TO ARES[53]

Ares haughty in spirit, heavy on chariot, golden-helmed; grim-hearted, shieldbearer, city-savior, bronze-armored; tough of arm, untiring, spear-strong, bulwark of Olympus; father of Victory in the good fight, ally of Law; oppressor of the rebellious, leader of the righteous; sceptred king of manliness, as you wheel your fiery circle among the seven coursing lights of the ether, where your flaming steeds ever keep you up on the third orbit:[54] hearken, helper of mankind, giver of brave young manhood, and gleam down your kindly flare from on high into my life, and martial strength, so that I might chase bitter wickedness away from my

[53] This hymn is a late intruder in the Homeric collection, to be attributed to the fifth-century Neoplatonist Proclus. See the Introduction.

[54] Ares is identified as the red planet Mars. In the ancient view Mars was the third of the seven 'planets', counting inwards from the outer firmament. The orbits of Jupiter and Saturn lay beyond his, while those of Mercury, Venus, the Sun, and the Moon were closer to the earth.

καὶ ψυχῆς ἀπατηλὸν ὑπογνάμψαι φρεσὶν ὁρμήν
θυμοῦ τ᾽ αὖ μένος ὀξὺ κατισχέμεν, ὅς μ᾽ ἐρέθησιν
15 φυλόπιδος κρυερῆς ἐπιβαινέμεν· ἀλλὰ σὺ θάρσος
δός, μάκαρ, εἰρήνης τε μένειν ἐν ἀπήμοσι θεσμοῖς,
δυσμενέων προφυγόντα μόθον κῆράς τε βιαίους.}

9. ΕΙΣ ΑΡΤΕΜΙΝ

Ἄρτεμιν ὕμνει, Μοῦσα, κασιγνήτην Ἑκάτοιο,
παρθένον ἰοχέαιραν, ὁμότροφον Ἀπόλλωνος,
ἥ θ᾽ ἵππους ἄρσασα βαθυσχοίνοιο Μέλητος
ῥίμφα διὰ Σμύρνης παγχρύσεον ἅρμα διώκει
5 ἐς Κλάρον ἀμπελόεσσαν, ὅθ᾽ ἀργυρότοξος Ἀπόλλων
ἧσται μιμνάζων ἑκατηβόλον Ἰοχέαιραν.
    καὶ σὺ μὲν οὕτω χαῖρε θεαί θ᾽ ἅμα πᾶσαι ἀοιδῆι·
αὐτὰρ ἐγὼ σέ τε πρῶτα καὶ ἐκ σέθεν ἄρχομ᾽
    ἀείδειν.
{σέο δ᾽ ἐγὼ ἀρξάμενος μεταβήσομαι ἄλλον ἐς
    ὕμνον.}

9 secl. Ilgen

10. ΕΙΣ ΑΦΡΟΔΙΤΗΝ

Κυπρογενῆ Κυθέρειαν ἀείσομαι, ἥ τε βροτοῖσιν
μείλιχα δῶρα δίδωσιν· ἐφ᾽ ἱμερτῶι δὲ προσώπωι
αἰεὶ μειδιάει, καὶ ἐφ᾽ ἱμερτὸν θέει ἄνθος.
    χαῖρε, θεά, Σαλαμῖνος ἐϋκτιμένης μεδέουσα

8. TO ARES

head, deflect the soul-deceiving impulse in my thoughts, and restrain the sharp force of appetite that provokes me to embark on chill conflict. Blessed one, grant me courage to abide by the innocuous principles of peace, escaping battle with my enemies and the perils of violence.}

9. TO ARTEMIS

Sing, Muse, of Artemis, sister of the Far-shooter, the virgin profuse of arrows, fellow nursling of Apollo; who after watering her horses at the reedy Meles[55] drives her chariot all of gold swiftly through Smyrna to vine-terraced Claros, where silverbow Apollo sits awaiting the far-shooting one, the profuse of arrows.[56]

So I salute you, and all goddesses, in my song; of you and from you first I sing.

10. TO APHRODITE

Of Cyprus-born Cytherea I will sing, who gives mortals honeyed gifts. On her lovely face she is always smiling, and a lovely bloom runs over it.

I salute you, goddess, queen of well-cultivated Sala-

[55] A river close to Smyrna.

[56] Two alternatives of the next sentence are transmitted. The other reads: "And beginning from you, I will pass over to another song."

5 καὶ πάσης Κύπρου· δὸς δ' ἱμερόεσσαν ἀοιδήν.
   αὐτὰρ ἐγὼ καὶ σεῖο καὶ ἄλλης μνήσομ' ἀοιδῆς.

11. ΕΙΣ ΑΘΗΝΑΝ

Παλλάδ' Ἀθηναίην ἐρυσίπτολιν ἄρχομ' ἀείδειν,
δεινήν, ἧι σὺν Ἄρηϊ μέλει πολεμήϊα ἔργα
περθόμεναί τε πόληες ἀϋτή τε πτόλεμοί τε,
καί τ' ἐρρύσατο λαὸν ἰόντά τε νισόμενόν τε.
5   χαῖρε, θεά, δὸς δ' ἄμμι τύχην εὐδαιμονίην τε.

12. ΕΙΣ ΗΡΑΝ

Ἥρην ἀείδω χρυσόθρονον, ἣν τέκε Ῥείη,
ἀθανάτων βασίλειαν, ὑπείροχον εἶδος ἔχουσαν,
Ζηνὸς ἐριγδούποιο κασιγνήτην ἄλοχόν τε
κυδρήν, ἣν πάντες μάκαρες κατὰ μακρὸν Ὄλυμπον
5 ἁζόμενοι τίουσιν ὁμῶς Διὶ τερπικεραύνωι.

2 ἀθανάτων Matthiae: ἀθανάτην Ω

13. ΕΙΣ ΔΗΜΗΤΡΑΝ

Δήμητρ' ἠΰκομον σεμνὴν θεὸν ἄρχομ' ἀείδειν,
αὐτὴν καὶ κούρην περικαλλέα Περσεφόνειαν.
   χαῖρε, θεά, καὶ τήνδε σάου πόλιν, ἄρχε δ' ἀοιδῆς.

mis[57] and of all Cyprus: grant me beautiful singing. And I will take heed both for you and for other singing.

11. TO ATHENA

Of Pallas Athena the city-savior first I sing, dread goddess, who with Ares attends to the works of war, the sacking of towns, shouting and fighting, and keeps the army safe as it goes out and returns.

I salute you, goddess: grant us success and prosperity!

12. TO HERA

Of Hera I sing, the golden-throned, whom Rhea bore to be queen of the immortals, of supreme beauty, sister and wife of Zeus the loud-booming; glorious one, whom all of the blessed ones on long Olympus revere and honor no less than Zeus whose sport is the thunderbolt.

13. TO DEMETER

Of Demeter the lovely-haired, the august goddess first I sing, of her and her daughter, beautiful Persephone.

I salute you, goddess: keep this city safe, and give my song its beginning.

[57] Not the island but the town in Cyprus.

14. ΕΙΣ ΜΗΤΕΡΑ ΘΕΩΝ

Μητέρα μοι πάντων τε θεῶν πάντων τ' ἀνθρώπων
ὕμνει, Μοῦσα λίγεια, Διὸς θύγατερ μεγάλοιο,
ἧι κροτάλων τυπάνων τ' ἰαχὴ σύν τε βρόμος αὐλῶν
εὔαδεν ἠδὲ λύκων κλαγγὴ χαροπῶν τε λεόντων
5   οὔρεά τ' ἠχήεντα καὶ ὑλήεντες ἔναυλοι.
    καὶ σὺ μὲν οὕτω χαῖρε θεαί θ' ἅμα πᾶσαι ἀοιδῆι.

2 θυγάτηρ Ω

15. ΕΙΣ ΗΡΑΚΛΕΑ ΛΕΟΝΤΟΘΥΜΟΝ

Ἡρακλέα Διὸς υἱὸν ἀείσομαι, ὃν μέγ' ἄριστον
γείνατ' ἐπιχθονίων Θήβηις ἔνι καλλιχόροισιν
Ἀλκμήνη μιχθεῖσα κελαινεφέϊ Κρονίωνι·
ὃς πρὶν μὲν κατὰ γαῖαν ἀθέσφατον ἠδὲ θάλασσαν
5   πλαζόμενος πομπῆισιν ὑπ' Εὐρυσθῆος ἄνακτος
πολλὰ μὲν αὐτὸς ἔρεξεν ἀτάσθαλα, πολλὰ δ'
    ἀνέτλη·
νῦν δ' ἤδη κατὰ καλὸν ἕδος νιφόεντος Ὀλύμπου
ναίει τερπόμενος καὶ ἔχει καλλίσφυρον Ἥβην.
    χαῖρε, ἄναξ Διὸς υἱέ· δίδου δ' ἀρετήν τε καὶ
    ὄλβον.

14. TO THE MOTHER OF THE GODS

Celebrate, clear-voiced Muse, daughter of great Zeus, the Mother of all gods and all mankind, whose pleasure is the din of cymbal-clappers and tambours and the bray of the shawms, the howling of wolves and fierce lions, the echoing mountains and wooded valleys.

So I salute you, and all goddesses, in my song.

15. TO HERACLES THE LIONHEART

Of Heracles the son of Zeus I will sing, far the finest of men on earth, born in Thebes of the beautiful dances to Alcmena in union with the dark-cloud son of Kronos. Formerly he roamed the vastness of land and sea at the behest of King Eurystheus, causing much suffering himself and enduring much; but now in the fair abode of snowy Olympus he lives in pleasure and has fair-ankled Hebe as his wife.

I salute you, lord, son of Zeus: grant me status and fortune.

16. ΕΙΣ ΑΣΚΛΗΠΙΟΝ

Ἰητῆρα νόσων Ἀσκληπιὸν ἄρχομ' ἀείδειν,
υἱὸν Ἀπόλλωνος, τὸν ἐγείνατο δῖα Κορωνὶς
Δωτίωι ἐν πεδίωι, κούρη Φλεγύου βασιλῆος,
χάρμα μέγ' ἀνθρώποισι, κακῶν θελκτῆρ' ὀδυνάων.
5 καὶ σὺ μὲν οὕτω χαῖρε, ἄναξ· λίτομαι δέ σ'
   ἀοιδῆι.

17. ΕΙΣ ΔΙΟΣΚΟΥΡΟΥΣ

Κάστορα καὶ Πολυδεύκε' ἀείσεο, Μοῦσα λίγεια,
Τυνδαρίδας, οἳ Ζηνὸς Ὀλυμπίου ἐξεγένοντο·
τοὺς ὑπὸ Τηϋγέτου κορυφῆις τέκε πότνια Λήδη
λάθρηι ὑποδμηθεῖσα κελαινεφέϊ Κρονίωνι.
5 χαίρετε Τυνδαρίδαι, ταχέων ἐπιβήτορες ἵππων.

18. ΕΙΣ ΕΡΜΗΝ

Ἑρμῆν ἀείδω Κυλλήνιον Ἀργειφόντην,
Κυλλήνης μεδέοντα καὶ Ἀρκαδίης πολυμήλου,
ἄγγελον ἀθανάτων ἐριούνιον, ὃν τέκε Μαῖα
Ἄτλαντος θυγάτηρ Διὸς ἐν φιλότητι μιγεῖσα
5 αἰδοίη· μακάρων δὲ θεῶν ἀλέεινεν ὅμιλον
ἄντρωι ναιετάουσα παλισκίωι, ἔνθα Κρονίων
νύμφηι ἐϋπλοκάμωι μισγέσκετο νυκτὸς ἀμολγῶι,
εὖτε κατὰ γλυκὺς ὕπνος ἔχοι λευκώλενον Ἥρην,

16. TO ASCLEPIUS

Of Asclepius the healer of sicknesses first I sing, son of Apollo, born in the Dotian Plain to the lady Coronis, daughter of king Phlegyas, a great joy to mankind, the soother of horrid pains.

So I salute you, lord; I supplicate you with my song.

17. TO THE DIOSCURI

Of Castor and Polydeuces you shall sing, clear-voiced Muse, of the Tyndarids, born of Olympian Zeus; below the peaks of Taygetus the mistress Leda bore them after secretly surrendering to the dark-cloud son of Kronos.

I salute you, Tyndarids, riders of swift steeds.

18. TO HERMES

Of Hermes I sing, the Cyllenian Argus-slayer, the lord of Cyllene and Arcadia rich in flocks, the immortals' coursing messenger, whom Maia bore, the daughter of Atlas, in shared intimacy with Zeus; modest one, who shunned the company of the blessed gods, dwelling in a cave's shadow. There the son of Kronos used to unite with the nymph of lovely tresses in the depth of the night, so long as sweet sleep held white-armed Hera fast, and neither immortal

197

λάνθανε δ᾽ ἀθανάτους τε θεοὺς θνητούς τ᾽
ἀνθρώπους.
10 {καὶ σὺ μὲν οὕτω χαῖρε, Διὸς καὶ Μαιάδος υἱέ·
σέο δ᾽ ἐγὼ ἀρξάμενος μεταβήσομαι ἄλλον ἐς
ὕμνον.}
χαῖρ᾽, Ἑρμῆ χαριδῶτα διάκτορε, δῶτορ ἐάων.

10–11 secl. West: 12 (secl. Ilgen) om. Π3

19. ΕΙΣ ΠΑΝΑ

Ἀμφί μοι Ἑρμείαο φίλον γόνον ἔννεπε, Μοῦσα,
αἰγοπόδην δικέρωτα φιλόκροτον, ὅς τ᾽ ἀνὰ πίση
δενδρήεντ᾽ ἄμυδις φοιτᾷ χορο‹γ›ηθέσι νύμφαις,
αἵ τε κατ᾽ αἰγίλιπος πέτρης στείβουσι κάρηνα
5 Πᾶν᾽ ἀνακεκλόμεναι, νόμιον θεὸν ἀγλαέθειρον
αὐχμήενθ᾽, ὃς πάντα λόφον νιφόεντα λέλογχεν
καὶ κορυφὰς ὀρέων καὶ πετρήεντα κέλευθα.
φοιτᾷ δ᾽ ἔνθα καὶ ἔνθα διὰ ῥωπήϊα πυκνά,
ἄλλοτε μὲν ῥείθροισιν ἐφελκόμενος μαλακοῖσιν,
10 ἄλλοτε δ᾽ αὖ πέτρῃσιν ἐν ἠλιβάτοισι διοιχνεῖ,
ἀκροτάτην κορυφὴν μηλοσκόπον εἰσαναβαίνων.
πολλάκι δ᾽ ἀργινόεντα διέδραμεν οὔρεα μακρά,
πολλάκι δ᾽ ἐν κνημοῖσι διήλασε θῆρας ἐναίρων,
ὀξέα δερκόμενος· ποτὶ δ᾽ ἕσπερον ἔκλαγεν οἶος
15 ἄγρης ἐξανιών, δονάκων ὕπο μοῦσαν ἀθύρων
νήδυμον· οὐκ ἂν τόν γε παραδράμοι ἐν μελέεσσιν
ὄρνις, ἥ τ᾽ ἔαρος πολυανθέος ἐν πετάλοισιν

gods nor mortal men knew of it.[58]

So I salute you, son of Zeus and Maia. After beginning from you, I will pass over to another song.

19. TO PAN

About Hermes' dear child tell me, Muse, the goat-footed, two-horned rowdy, who roams about the wooded fields together with the dance-merry nymphs: along the precipitous crag they tread the summits, calling on Pan, god of the pastures with splendor of rough hair, who has been assigned every snowy hill, the mountain peaks, and the rocky tracks. This way and that he roams through the thick brush, sometimes drawn to the gentle streams, sometimes again passing among the towering crags as he climbs up to the highest peak to survey the flocks; often he runs through the long white mountains, and often he drives the wild creatures through the glens, killing them, keen-sighted. Towards evening his solitary sound is heard as he returns from the hunt, playing sweet music from his reed pipes; his melodies would not be surpassed by that bird that in

---

[58] Two alternatives of the next sentence are transmitted. The other reads: "I salute you, Hermes bestower of favor, go-between, giver of blessings."

---

3 χορογηθέσι Schmidt: χοροήθεσι Ψ

12 ἀργινόεντα Martin: αἰγι- Ψ

14 ποτὶ δ᾿ ἕσπερον Baumeister, οἶος Hermann: τότε (vel τοτὲ) δ᾿ ἕσπερος ἔκλαγεν οἶον Ψ

15 ἄγρης Pierson: ἄκρης Ψ

θρῆνον ἐπιπροχέουσα χέει μελίγηρυν ἀοιδήν.
σὺν δέ σφιν τότε νύμφαι ὀρεστιάδες λιγύμολποι
20 φοιτῶσαι πύκα ποσσὶν ἐπὶ κρήνηι μελανύδρωι
μέλπονται—κορυφὴν δὲ περιστένει οὔρεος ἠχώ·
δαίμων δ' ἔνθα καὶ ἔνθα χορῶν, τοτὲ ⟨δ'⟩ ἐς μέσον
    ἕρπων
πυκνὰ ποσὶν διέπει, λαῖφος δ' ἐπὶ νῶτα δαφοινόν
λυγκὸς ἔχει, λιγυρῆισιν ἀγαλλόμενος φρένα
    μολπαῖς—
25 ἐν μαλακῶι λειμῶνι, τόθι κρόκος ἠδ' ὑάκινθος
εὐώδης θαλέθων καταμίσγεται ἄκριτα ποίηι.
ὑμνέουσιν δὲ θεοὺς μάκαρας καὶ μακρὸν Ὄλυμπον·
οἷόν θ' Ἑρμείην ἐριούνιον ἔξοχον ἄλλων
ἔννεπον, ὡς ὅ γ' ἅπασι θεοῖς θοὸς ἄγγελός ἐστιν,
30 καί ῥ' ὅ γ' ἐς Ἀρκαδίην πολυπίδακα, μητέρα
    μήλων,
ἐξίκετ'· ἔνθα δέ οἱ τέμενος Κυλληνίου ἐστίν.
ἔνθ' ὅ γε καὶ θεὸς ὢν ψαφαρότριχα μῆλ' ἐνόμευεν
ἀνδρὶ πάρα θνητῶι· θάλε γὰρ πόθος ὑγρὸς ἐπελθών
νύμφηι ἐϋπλοκάμωι Δρύοπος φιλότητι μιγῆναι.
35 ἐκ δ' ἐτέλεσσε γάμον θαλερόν, τέκε δ' ἐν
    μεγάροισιν
Ἑρμείηι φίλον υἱὸν ἄφαρ τερατωπὸν ἰδέσθαι,
αἰγοπόδην δικέρωτα πολύκροτον ἡδυγέλωτα.
φεῦγε δ' ἀναΐξασα, λίπεν δ' ἄρα παῖδα τιθήνη·
δεῖσε γάρ, ὡς ἴδεν ὄψιν ἀμείλιχον ἠϋγένειον.
40 τὸν δ' αἶψ' Ἑρμείας ἐριούνιος ἐς χέρα θῆκεν
δεξάμενος, χαῖρεν δὲ νόωι περιώσια δαίμων·

flowery spring among the leaves pours forth her lament in honey-voiced song.[59]

With him then the clear-singing mountain nymphs, tripping nimbly by a dark spring, dance and sing; the echo moans round the mountaintop, while the god, moving from side to side of the dance rings, or again in the middle, cuts a nimble caper, a brown lynx hide over his back, delighting in the silvery singing—all in a soft meadow, where crocus and fragrant hyacinth spring up inextricably mingled with the grass. They celebrate the blessed gods and long Olympus; and they tell of one god above all, Hermes the courser, how he is the swift messenger for all the gods, and how he came to Arcadia with its many springs, the mother of flocks; it is there that he has his precinct as Cyllenian Hermes. There, though a god, he pastured dirt-crusted flocks beside a mortal man, because a surging desire had come upon him to unite in love with Dryops' lovely-tressed girl. He accomplished the fruitful coupling; and she bore Hermes a dear son in the house, at once a prodigy to behold, goat-footed, two-horned rowdy, merry laugher. She jumped up and ran away, nurse abandoning child, for she was frightened when she saw his unprepossessing face with its full beard. But Hermes the courser quickly took him and laid him in his arm, and the god's

[59] The nightingale.

---

20 πύκα Barnes: πυκνὰ Ψ
22 δ' add. Buttmann
26 ποίηι Hermann: ποίην Ψ
37 αἰγιπόδην Ψ; cf. 2
38 ἀναΐξασα, λίπεν Martin: ἀναΐξας λεῖπεν Ψ

ῥίμφα δ' ἐς ἀθανάτων ἕδρας κίε παῖδα καλύψας
δέρμασιν ἐν πυκινοῖσιν ὀρεσκώιοιο λαγωοῦ·
πὰρ δὲ Ζηνὶ καθῖζε καὶ ἄλλοις ἀθανάτοισιν,
45 δεῖξε δὲ κοῦρον ἑόν· πάντες δ' ἄρα θυμὸν ἔτερφθεν
ἀθάνατοι, περίαλλα δ' ὁ Βάκχειος Διόνυσος·
Πᾶνα δέ μιν καλέεσκον, ὅτι φρένα πᾶσιν ἔτερψεν.
    καὶ σὺ μὲν οὕτω χαῖρε, ἄναξ, ἵλαμαι δέ σ'
        ἀοιδῆι·
αὐτὰρ ἐγὼ καὶ σεῖο καὶ ἄλλης μνήσομ' ἀοιδῆς.

20. ΕΙΣ ΗΦΑΙΣΤΟΝ

Ἥφαιστον κλυτόμητιν ἀείσεο, Μοῦσα λίγεια,
ὃς μετ' Ἀθηναίης γλαυκώπιδος ἀγλαὰ ἔργα
ἀνθρώπους ἐδίδαξεν ἐπὶ χθονός, οἳ τὸ πάρος περ
ἄντροις ναιετάασκον ἐν οὔρεσιν ἠύτε θῆρες.
5 νῦν δὲ δι' Ἥφαιστον κλυτοτέχνην ἔργα δαέντες
ῥηϊδίως αἰῶνα τελεσφόρον εἰς ἐνιαυτόν
εὔκηλοι διάγουσιν ἐνὶ σφετέροισι δόμοισιν.
    ἀλλ' ἵληθ', Ἥφαιστε· δίδου δ' ἀρετήν τε καὶ
        ὄλβον.

21. ΕΙΣ ΑΠΟΛΛΩΝΑ

Φοῖβε, σὲ μὲν καὶ κύκνος ὑπὸ πτερύγων λίγ' ἀείδει
ὄχθηι ἐπιθρώισκων ποταμὸν πάρα δινήεντα
Πηνειόν· σὲ δ' ἀοιδὸς ἔχων φόρμιγγα λίγειαν
ἡδυεπὴς πρῶτόν τε καὶ ὕστατον αἰὲν ἀείδει.

mind was exceedingly glad. He went rapidly to the abodes of the immortals, wrapping the child closely in skins of mountain hare, and sat down beside Zeus and the other gods and displayed his son. All the immortals were delighted, especially Bacchic Dionysus; and they took to calling him Pan, because he delighted them all (*pantes*).

So I salute you, lord; I seek your favor with my song. And I will take heed both for you and for other singing.

20. TO HEPHAESTUS

Of Hephaestus famous for contrivance you shall sing, clear-voiced Muse, of him who with steely-eyed Athena has taught splendid crafts to mankind on earth, that previously used to live in caves in the mountains like animals. But now that they have learned crafts through Hephaestus the famously skilled, they pass their lives at ease in their own houses the whole year through.

So be favorable, Hephaestus: grant me status and fortune.

21. TO APOLLO

Phoibos, of you the swan too sings in clear tone from its wings as it alights on the bank beside the eddying river Peneios; and of you the bard with his clear-toned lyre and sweet verse ever sings in first place and last.

---

45 ἔτερφθεν Stephanus: -φθον Ψ
20.1 ἀείσεο Buttmann: ἀείδεο Ψ

5   καὶ σὺ μὲν οὕτω χαῖρε, ἄναξ· ἵλαμαι δέ σ'
    ἀοιδῆι.

22. ΕΙΣ ΠΟΣΕΙΔΩΝΑ

Ἀμφὶ Ποσειδάωνα, μέγαν θεόν, ἄρχομ' ἀείδειν,
γαίης κινητῆρα καὶ ἀτρυγέτοιο θαλάσσης,
πόντιον, ὅς θ' Ἑλικῶνα καὶ εὐρείας ἔχει Αἰγάς.
διχθά τοι, Ἐννοσίγαιε, θεοὶ τιμὴν ἐδάσαντο,
5   ἵππων τε δμητῆρ' ἔμεναι σωτῆρά τε νηῶν.
    χαῖρε, Ποσείδαον γαιήοχε κυανοχαῖτα,
    καί, μάκαρ, εὐμενὲς ἦτορ ἔχων πλώουσιν ἄρηγε.

23. ΕΙΣ ΔΙΑ

Ζῆνα θεῶν τὸν ἄριστον ἀείσομαι ἠδὲ μέγιστον,
εὐρύοπα κρείοντα τελεσφόρον, ὅς τε Θέμι‹σ›τι
ἐγκλιδὸν ἑζομένηι πυκινοὺς ὀάρους ὀαρίζει.
    ἵληθ', εὐρύοπα Κρονίδη κύδιστε μέγιστε.

24. ΕΙΣ ΕΣΤΙΑΝ

Ἑστίη, ἥ τε ἄνακτος Ἀπόλλωνος ἑκάτοιο
Πυθοῖ ἐν ἠγαθέηι ἱερὸν δόμον ἀμφιπολεύεις,
αἰεὶ σῶν πλοκάμων ἀπολείβεται ὑγρὸν ἔλαιον.
ἔρχεο τόνδ' ἀνὰ οἶκον †ἐπέρχεο θυμὸν ἔχουσα

21. TO APOLLO

So I salute you, lord, and seek your favor with my singing.

22. TO POSEIDON

About Poseidon the great god first I sing, mover of the earth and the barren sea, marine god, who possesses Helicon and broad Aegae. In two parts, Earth-shaker, the gods assigned you your privilege: to be a tamer of horses, and savior of ships.

I salute you, Poseidon, earth-rider, sable-hair. Keep your heart well disposed, blessed one, and assist those at sea.

23. TO ZEUS

Of Zeus, best and greatest of the gods, I will sing, the wide-sounding ruler, the one that brings to fulfilment, who consults closely with Themis as she sits leaning against him.

Be favorable, wide-sounding son of Kronos, greatest and most glorious.

24. TO HESTIA

Hestia, you that tend the far-shooting lord Apollo's sacred house at holy Pytho, from your locks the oozing oil ever drips down. Come to this house in kindly(?) heart, to-

---

22.1 μέγαν θεόν Hermann: θεὸν μέγαν Ψ
23.2 θέμιτι Ψ: corr. Barnes
23.4 ἔν’ ἔρχεο Tucker: ἐΰφρονα Barnes

5 σὺν Διὶ μητιόεντι· χάριν δ' ἄμ' ὄπασσον ἀοιδῆι.

25. ΕΙΣ ΜΟΥΣΑΣ ΚΑΙ ΑΠΟΛΛΩΝΑ

Μουσάων ἄρχωμαι Ἀπόλλωνός τε Διός τε·
ἐκ γὰρ Μουσάων καὶ ἑκηβόλου Ἀπόλλωνος
ἄνδρες ἀοιδοὶ ἔασιν ἐπὶ χθονὶ καὶ κιθαρισταί,
ἐκ δὲ Διὸς βασιλῆες· ὃ δ' ὄλβιος, ὅν τινα Μοῦσαι
5 φίλωνται· γλυκερή οἱ ἀπὸ στόματος ῥέει αὐδή.
    χαίρετε, τέκνα Διός, καὶ ἐμὴν τιμήσατ' ἀοιδήν·
αὐτὰρ ἐγὼν ὑμέων τε καὶ ἄλλης μνήσομ' ἀοιδῆς.

26. ΕΙΣ ΔΙΟΝΥΣΟΝ

Κισσοκόμην Διόνυσον ἐρίβρομον ἄρχομ' ἀείδειν,
Ζηνὸς καὶ Σεμέλης ἐρικυδέος ἀγλαὸν υἱόν,
ὃν τρέφον ἠΰκομοι νύμφαι παρὰ πατρὸς ἄνακτος
δεξάμεναι κόλποισι καὶ ἐνδυκέως ἀτίταλλον
5 Νύσης ἐν γυάλοις· ὃ δ' ἀέξετο πατρὸς ἔκητι
ἄντρωι ἐν εὐώδει μεταρίθμιος ἀθανάτοισιν.
αὐτὰρ ἐπεὶ δὴ τόν γε θεαὶ πολύυμνον ἔθρεψαν,
δὴ τότε φοιτίζεσκε καθ' ὑλήεντας ἐναύλους,
κισσῶι καὶ δάφνηι πεπυκασμένος· αἱ δ' ἄμ' ἕποντο
10 νύμφαι, ὃ δ' ἐξηγεῖτο· βρόμος δ' ἔχεν ἄσπετον
    ὕλην.
    καὶ σὺ μὲν οὕτω χαῖρε, πολυστάφυλ' ὦ Διόνυσε·
δὸς δ' ἡμᾶς χαίροντας ἐς ὥρας αὖτις ἱκέσθαι,
ἐκ δ' αὖθ' ὡράων εἰς τοὺς πολλοὺς ἐνιαυτούς.

gether with Zeus the resourceful, and bestow beauty on my singing.

25. TO THE MUSES AND APOLLO

From the Muses let me begin, and Apollo and Zeus. For from the Muses and far-shooting Apollo men are singers and lyre-players on earth, and from Zeus they are kings. He is fortunate whom the Muses love: the voice flows sweet from his lips.

I salute you, children of Zeus; honor my singing. And I will take heed both for you and for other singing.

26. TO DIONYSUS

Of ivy-haired Dionysus the mighty roarer first I sing, Zeus' and glorious Semele's splendid son, whom the lovely-haired nymphs took to their bosoms from his divine father and reared and fostered attentively in Nysa's glens; and he grew according to his father's design in the fragrant cave, numbered among the immortals. After the goddesses had raised him, god of much song, he took to going about the wooded valleys, wreathed with ivy and bay; the nymphs would follow along as he led, and the noise of the revel pervaded the boundless woodland.

So I salute you, Dionysus of the abundant grape clusters: grant that we may come again in happiness at the due time, and time after time for many a year.

26.7 τόν γε Gemoll: τόνδε Ψ

27. ΕΙΣ ΑΡΤΕΜΙΝ

Ἄρτεμιν ἀείδω χρυσηλάκατον κελαδεινήν,
παρθένον αἰδοίην ἐλαφηβόλον ἰοχέαιραν,
αὐτοκασιγνήτην χρυσαόρου Ἀπόλλωνος,
ἣ κατ᾽ ὄρη σκιόεντα καὶ ἄκριας ἠνεμοέσσας
5 ἄγρηι τερπομένη παγχρύσεα τόξα τιταίνει,
πέμπουσα στονόεντα βέλη· τρομέει δὲ κάρηνα
ὑψηλῶν ὀρέων, ἰαχεῖ δ᾽ ἔπι δάσκιος ὕλη
δεινὸν ὑπὸ κλαγγῆς θηρῶν, φρίσσει δέ τε γαῖα
πόντός τ᾽ ἰχθυόεις· ἣ δ᾽ ἄλκιμον ἦτορ ἔχουσα
10 πάντηι ἐπιστρέφεται θηρῶν ὀλέκουσα γενέθλην.
αὐτὰρ ἐπὴν τερφθῆι θηροσκόπος Ἰοχέαιρα,
εὐφρήνηι δὲ νόον, χαλάσασ᾽ εὐκαμπέα τόξα
ἔρχεται ἐς μέγα δῶμα κασιγνήτοιο φίλοιο
Φοίβου Ἀπόλλωνος, Δελφῶν ἐς πίονα δῆμον,
15 Μουσῶν καὶ Χαρίτων καλὸν χορὸν ἀρτυνέουσα.
ἔνθα κατακρεμάσασα παλίντονα τόξα καὶ ἰοὺς
ἡγεῖται, χαρίεντα περὶ χροῒ κόσμον ἔχουσα,
ἐξάρχουσα χορούς· αἱ δ᾽ ἀμβροσίην ὄπ᾽ ἰεῖσαι
ὑμνέουσιν Λητὼ καλλίσφυρον, ὡς τέκε παῖδας
20 ἀθανάτων βουλῆι τε καὶ ἔργμασιν ἔξοχ᾽ ἀρίστους.
χαίρετε, τέκνα Διὸς καὶ Λητοῦς ἠϋκόμοιο·
αὐτὰρ ἐγὼν ὑμέων ⟨τε⟩ καὶ ἄλλης μνήσομ᾽ ἀοιδῆς.

22 τε add. Barnes

27. TO ARTEMIS

I sing of Artemis of the gold shafts and the view-halloo, the modest virgin, the deer-shooter profuse of arrows, own sister to Apollo of the golden sword; of her who in the shadowed mountains and windy heights takes her pleasure in the hunt, and draws her golden bow to discharge grievous arrows. And the peaks of the high mountains tremble, the deep-shaded wood resounds fearsomely from the animals' howling, and the earth shudders, and the fishy sea; but she with dauntless heart turns every way, killing the animals' brood.

When the animal-watcher goddess profuse of arrows has had her pleasure and cheered her spirits, she unstrings her bent bow and goes to the great house of her dear brother Phoibos Apollo, to Delphi's rich community, to organize the Muses' and Graces' fair dance. There she hangs up her bent-back bow and her arrows and goes before, her body beautifully adorned, leading the dances, while they with divine voices celebrate fair-ankled Leto, how she bore children outstanding among the immortals both in counsel and action.

I salute you, children of Zeus and lovely-haired Leto. And I will take heed both for you and for other singing.

28. ΕΙΣ ΑΘΗΝΑΝ

Παλλάδ᾽ Ἀθηναίην, κυδρὴν θεόν, ἄρχομ᾽ ἀείδειν,
γλαυκῶπιν πολύμητιν ἀμείλιχον ἦτορ ἔχουσαν,
παρθένον αἰδοίην ἐρυσίπτολιν ἀλκήεσσαν
Τριτογενῆ, τὴν αὐτὸς ἐγείνατο μητίετα Ζεύς
5 σεμνῆς ἐκ κεφαλῆς, πολεμήϊα τεύχε᾽ ἔχουσαν
χρύσεα παμφανόωντα· σέβας δ᾽ ἔχε πάντας
    ὁρῶντας
ἀθανάτους· ἡ δὲ πρόσθεν Διὸς αἰγιόχοιο
ἐσσυμένως ὤρουσεν ἀπ᾽ ἀθανάτοιο καρήνου
σείσασ᾽ ὀξὺν ἄκοντα· μέγας δ᾽ ἐλελίζετ᾽ Ὄλυμπος
10 δεινὸν ὑπὸ βρίμης Γλαυκώπιδος, ἀμφὶ δὲ γαῖα
σμερδαλέον ἰάχησεν, ἐκινήθη δ᾽ ἄρα πόντος
κύμασι πορφυρέοισι κυκώμενος, ἔσχετο δ᾽ ἅλμη
ἐξαπίνης· στῆσεν δ᾽ Ὑπερίονος ἀγλαὸς υἱός
ἵππους ὠκύποδας δηρὸν χρόνον, εἰσότε κούρη
15 εἵλετ᾽ ἀπ᾽ ἀθανάτων ὤμων θεοείκελα τεύχη
Παλλὰς Ἀθηναίη· γήθησε δὲ μητίετα Ζεύς.
    καὶ σὺ μὲν οὕτω χαῖρε, Διὸς τέκος αἰγιόχοιο·
αὐτὰρ ἐγὼ καὶ σεῖο καὶ ἄλλης μνήσομ᾽ ἀοιδῆς.

29. ΕΙΣ ΕΣΤΙΑΝ

Ἱστίη, ἣ πάντων ἐν δώμασιν ὑψηλοῖσιν
ἀθανάτων τε θεῶν χαμαὶ ἐρχομένων τ᾽ ἀνθρώπων
ἕδρην ἀΐδιον ἔλαχες πρεσβηΐδα τιμήν,
καλὸν ἔχουσα γέρας καὶ τιμήν· οὐ γὰρ ἄτερ σοῦ

28. TO ATHENA

Of Pallas Athena, glorious goddess, first I sing, the steely-eyed, resourceful one with implacable heart, the reverend virgin, city-savior, doughty one, Tritogeneia, to whom wise Zeus himself gave birth out of his august head, in battle armor of shining gold: all the immortals watched in awe, as before Zeus the goat-rider she sprang quickly down from his immortal head with a brandish of her sharp javelin. A fearsome tremor went through great Olympus from the power of the Steely-eyed one, the earth resounded terribly round about, and the sea heaved in a confusion of swirling waves. But suddenly the main was held in check, and Hyperion's splendid son[60] halted his swift-footed steeds for a long time, until the maiden, Pallas Athena, took off the godlike armor from her immortal shoulders, and wise Zeus rejoiced.

So I salute you, child of goat-rider Zeus. And I will take heed both for you and for other singing.

29. TO HESTIA

Hestia, you that in the high dwellings of all, both immortal gods and men who walk on earth, have been assigned an everlasting seat as the privilege of seniority, and enjoy a fine honor and privilege, for mortals have no feasts without

[60] Helios, the Sun.

---

10 ὑπὸ βρίμης Ilgen: ὑπ' ὀβρίμης Ψ
12 δ' Chalcondyles: θ' Ψ
29.1 Ἱστίη Wolf: ἑστίη Ψ

5 εἰλαπίναι θνητοῖσιν, ἵν' οὐ πρώτηι πυμάτηι τε
 Ἱστίηι ἀρχόμενος σπένδει μελιηδέα οἶνον·
 καὶ σύ μοι, Ἀργειφόντα, Διὸς καὶ Μαιάδος υἱέ,
8 ἄγγελε τῶν μακάρων, χρυσόρραπι, δῶτορ ἐάων,
10 ἵλαος ὢν ἐπάρηγε σὺν αἰδοίηι τε φίληι τε
11 Ἱστίηι· ἀμφότεροι γὰρ ἐπιχθονίων ἀνθρώπων
9 ναίετε δώματα καλά, φίλα φρεσὶν ἀλλήλοισιν
12 εἰδότες, ἔρματα καλά, νόωι θ' ἕσπεσθε καὶ ἥβηι.
 χαῖρε, Κρόνου θύγατερ, σύ τε καὶ χρυσόρραπις
  Ἑρμῆς·
 αὐτὰρ ἐγὼν ὑμέων τε καὶ ἄλλης μνήσομ' ἀοιδῆς.

30. ΕΙΣ ΓΗΝ ΜΗΤΕΡΑ ΠΑΝΤΩΝ

Γαῖαν παμμήτειραν ἀείσομαι, ἠϋθέμεθλον,
πρεσβίστην, ἣ φέρβει ἐπὶ χθονὶ πάνθ' ὁπόσ' ἐστίν,
ἠμὲν ὅσα χθόνα δῖαν ἐπέρχεται ἠδ' ὅσα πόντον
ἠδ' ὅσα πωτῶνται· τὰ δὲ φέρβεται ἐκ σέθεν ὄλβου.
5 ἐκ σέο δ' εὔπαιδές τε καὶ εὔκαρποι τελέθουσιν,
πότνια, σεῦ δ' ἔχεται δοῦναι βίον ἠδ' ἀφελέσθαι
θνητοῖς ἀνθρώποισιν· ὃ δ' ὄλβιος, ὅν κε σὺ θυμῶι
πρόφρων τιμήσηις, τῶι τ' ἄφθονα πάντα πάρεστιν·
βρίθει μέν σφιν ἄρουρα φερέσβιος, ἠδὲ κατ'
  ἀγρούς
10 κτήνεσιν εὐθηνεῖ, οἶκος δ' ἐμπίμπλαται ἐσθλῶν·
αὐτοὶ δ' εὐνομίηισι πόλιν κάτα καλλιγύναικα
κοιρανέουσ', ὄλβος δὲ πολὺς καὶ πλοῦτος ὀπηδεῖ·
παῖδες δ' εὐφροσύνηι νεοθηλέι κυδιόωσιν,

you where the libation-pourer does not begin by offering honey-sweet wine to Hestia in first place and last: and you, Argus-slayer, son of Zeus and Maia, messenger of the blessed ones, gold-wand, giver of blessings, be favorable and assist together with Hestia whom you love and revere. For both of you dwell in the fine houses of men on earth, in friendship towards each other, fine supports (of the house), and you attend intelligence and youth.

I salute you, daughter of Kronos, and you too, gold-wand Hermes. And I will take heed both for you and for other singing.

30. TO EARTH MOTHER OF ALL

Of Earth the universal mother I will sing, the firmly-grounded, the eldest, who nourishes everything there is on the land, both all that moves on the holy land and in the sea and all that flies: they are nourished from your bounty. From you they become fertile in children and in crops, mistress, and it depends on you to give livelihood or take it away from mortal men. He is fortunate whom your heart favors and privileges, and everything is his in abundance. His plowland is weighed down with its vital produce, in the fields he is prosperous with livestock, and his house is filled with commodities. Such men are lords in communities where law and order prevail and the women are fair, and much fortune and wealth attends them; their sons exult in youthful vigor and good cheer, and their girls in flower-

---

29.9 post 11 transp. Martin
29.12 ἔρματα West: ἔργματα Ψ

παρθενικαί τε χοροῖς φερεσανθέσιν εὔφρονι θυμῶι
15 παίζουσ‹α›ι χαίρουσι κατ' ἄνθεα μαλ‹θ›ακὰ ποίης,
οὕς κε σὺ τιμήσηις, σεμνὴ θεά, ἄφθονε δαῖμον.
χαῖρε, θεῶν μήτηρ, ἄλοχ' Οὐρανοῦ ἀστερόεντος,
πρόφρων δ' ἀντ' ὠιδῆς βίοτον θυμήρε' ὄπαζε·
αὐτὰρ ἐγὼ καὶ σεῖο καὶ ἄλλης μνήσομ' ἀοιδῆς.

14 φερεσανθέσιν Ernesti: περεσ- ƒx, παρ' εὐ- p

31. ΕΙΣ ΗΛΙΟΝ

Ἥλιον ὑμνεῖν αὖτε Διὸς τέκος ἄρχεο Μοῦσα
Καλλιόπη, φαέθοντα, τὸν Εὐρυφάεσσα βοῶπις
γείνατο Γαίης παιδὶ καὶ Οὐρανοῦ ἀστερόεντος·
γῆμε γὰρ Εὐρυφάεσσαν ἀγακλειτὴν Ὑπερίων
5 αὐτοκασιγνήτην, ἥ οἱ τέκε κάλλιμα τέκνα,
Ἠῶ τε ῥοδόπηχυν ἐϋπλόκαμόν τε Σελήνην
Ἠέλιόν τ' ἀκάμαντ' ἐπιείκελον ἀθανάτοισιν,
ὃς φαίνει θνητοῖσι καὶ ἀθανάτοισι θεοῖσιν
ἵπποις ἐμβεβαώς· σμερδνὸν δ' ὅ γε δέρκεται ὄσσοις
10 χρυσέης ἐκ κόρυθος, λαμπραὶ δ' ἀκτῖνες ἀπ' αὐτοῦ
αἰγλῆεν στίλβουσι, παρὰ κροτάφων τε ἔθειραι
λαμπραὶ ἀπὸ κρατὸς χαρίεν κατέχουσι πρόσωπον
τηλαυγές· καλὸν δὲ περὶ χροῒ λάμπεται ἔσθος
λεπτουργὲς πνοιῆι ἀνέμων. ὑπὸ δ' ἄρσενες ἵπποι
14a ‹ἀΐσσουσ', ὄφρ' ἂν μέσον οὐρανὸν αὐτὸν ἵκωνται·›

11 ἔθειραι Pierson: παρειαὶ Ψ
14a lac. stat. Hermann, suppl. Allen–Halliday

decked dances delight to frolic happily through the soft
meadow flowers—so it is with those whom you privilege,
august goddess, bounteous deity.

I salute you, mother of the gods, consort of starry
Heaven: be favorable, and grant comfortable livelihood in
return for my singing. And I will take heed both for you
and for other singing.

31. TO HELIOS

Of Helios again begin your song, daughter of Zeus, Muse
Calliope: the shining one, whom mild-eyed Euryphaessa[61]
bore to the son of Earth and starry Heaven. For Hyperion
married the famed Euryphaessa, his own sister, who bore
him fine children: rose-armed Eos (Dawn), lovely-tressed
Selene (Moon), and tireless Helios (Sun), who is in the
gods' likeness. He shines for mortals and immortals,
mounted on his chariot; his eyes gaze fearsomely out of his
golden helm, the bright rays from him gleam brilliant, and
from beside his temples the bright hair of his head en-
closes his beautiful face that beams afar, while about his
body glows his fair garment, fine-woven by the blowing
winds. Below him his stallions ‹speed on till they reach the

---

[61] Euryphaessa, "Shining Far and Wide," appears only here as
the name of the Titan whom Hesiod and others call Theia.

15 ἔνθ' ἄρ' ὅ γε στήσας χρυσόζυγον ἅρμα καὶ ἵππους
15a θεσπεσι<   .   .   .   .
ἑσπέρι>ος πέμπησι δι' οὐρανοῦ Ὠκεανόνδε.
    χαῖρε, ἄναξ, πρόφρων δὲ βίον θυμήρε' ὄπαζε·
ἐκ σέο δ' ἀρξάμενος κλήσω μερόπων γένος ἀνδρῶν
ἡμιθέων, ὧν ἔργα θεοὶ θνητοῖσιν ἔδειξαν.

15a lac. stat. Allen–Sikes: 16 ἑσπέριος Ruhnkenius, θεσπέ-
σιος Ψ: ut supra West

32. ΕΙΣ ΣΕΛΗΝΗΝ

Μήνην εὐειδῆ τανυσίπτερον ἔσπετε Μοῦσαι,
ἡδυεπεῖς κοῦραι Κρονίδεω Διός, ἵστορες ὠιδῆς·
ἧς ἄπο αἴγλη γαῖαν ἑλίσσεται οὐρανόδεικτος
κρατὸς ἄπ' ἀθανάτοιο, πολὺς δ' ὑπὸ κόσμος ὄρωρεν
5 αἴγλης λαμπούσης· στίλβει δ<έ τ>' ἀλάμπετος ἀήρ
χρυσέου ἄπο στεφάνου, ἀκτῖνες δ' ἐνδιάονται,
εὖτ' ἂν ἀπ' Ὠκεανοῖο λοεσσαμένη χρόα καλόν,
εἵματα ἑσσαμένη τηλαυγέα, δῖα Σελήνη
ζευξαμένη πώλους ἐριαύχενας αἰγλήεντας
10 ἐσσυμένως προτέρωσ' ἐλάσηι καλλίτριχας ἵππους
ἑσπερίη διχόμηνος, ὅτε πλήθει μέγας ὄγμος,
λαμπρόταταί τ' αὐγαὶ τότ' ἀεξομένης τελέθωσιν
οὐρανόθεν· τέκμωρ δὲ βροτοῖς καὶ σῆμα τέτυκται.
    τῆι ῥά ποτε Κρονίδης ἐμίγη φιλότητι καὶ εὐνῆι·
15 ἣ δ' ὑποκυσαμένη Πανδίην γείνατο κούρην

very mid-point of heaven>;[62] there he halts his horses and gold-yoked car, and a wondrous < . . . until> at evening he guides them through the sky towards Ocean's stream.

I salute you, lord: be favorable, and grant comfortable livelihood. After beginning from you, I will celebrate the brood of mortal heroes, whose deeds the gods have disclosed to mankind.

32. TO SELENE

Tell of the fair, spread-winged Moon, O Muses, sweet-versing daughters of Kronos' son Zeus, expert in song: of her whose brightness displayed in heaven encircles the earth from her immortal head, and a rich beauty emerges where the brightness shines. The unlit air gleams from her golden circlet, and her rays disport themselves in it, when from Ocean's stream, where she has bathed her fair body and put on her far-beaming raiment, the lady Selene yokes her proud-necked, shining colts and speedily drives those fair-maned steeds onwards on the evening of full moon, when the great orbit is complete, and with her waxing her rays then shine from heaven at their brightest; it is a marker and a sign for mankind.

With her the son of Kronos once united in the bed of love; and she conceived, and bore the maiden Pandia,[63]

[62] Line supplied by conjecture. Another line has evidently fallen out after "wondrous."

[63] See Introduction.

---

1 εὐειδῆ Bothe: ἀείδειν Ψ: ἀϊδίην Sikes
5 δέ τ' Barnes: δ' Ψ   15 Πανδίην Hermann: πανδείην Ψ

ἐκπρεπὲς εἶδος ἔχουσαν ἐν ἀθανάτοισι θεοῖσιν.
χαῖρε, ἄνασσα, θεὰ λευκώλενε δῖα Σελήνη,
πρόφρον, ἐϋπλόκαμος· σέο δ' ἀρχόμενος κλέα
    φωτῶν
ἄισομαι ἡμιθέων, ὧν κλείουσ' ἔργματ' ἀοιδοί
20 Μουσάων θεράποντες ἀπὸ στομάτων ἐροέντων.

33. ΕΙΣ ΔΙΟΣΚΟΤΡΟΥΣ

Ἀμφὶ Διὸς κούρους ἑλικώπιδες ἔσπετε Μοῦσαι,
Τυνδαρίδας, Λήδης καλλισφύρου ἀγλαὰ τέκνα,
Κάστορά θ' ἱππόδαμον καὶ ἀμώμητον Πολυδεύκεα,
τοὺς ὑπὸ Ταϋγέτου κορυφῆι ὄρεος μεγάλοιο
5   μιχθεῖσ' ἐν φιλότητι κελαινεφέϊ Κρονίωνι
σωτῆρας τέκε παῖδας ἐπιχθονίων ἀνθρώπων
ὠκυπόρων τε νεῶν, ὅτε τε σπέρχωσιν ἄελλαι
χειμέριαι κατὰ πόντον ἀμείλιχον· οἱ δ' ἀπὸ νηῶν
εὐχόμενοι καλέουσι Διὸς κούρους μεγάλοιο
10 ἄρνεσσιν λευκοῖσιν, ἐπ' ἀκρωτήρια βάντες
πρύμνης· τὴν δ' ἄνεμός τε μέγας καὶ κῦμα
    θαλάσσης
θῆκαν ὑποβρυχίην. οἱ δ' ἐξαπίνης ἐφάνησαν
ξουθῆισι πτερύγεσσι δι' αἰθέρος ἀΐξαντες,
αὐτίκα δ' ἀργαλέων ἀνέμων κατέπαυσαν ἀέλλας,
15 κύματα δ' ἐστόρεσαν λευκῆς ἁλὸς ἐν πελάγεσσιν,
σήματα καλά, πόνου <ἀπονό>σφισιν· οἱ δὲ ἰδόντες
γήθησαν, παύσαντο δ' ὀϊζυροῖο πόνοιο.

32. TO SELENE

whose beauty is outstanding among the immortals.

I salute you, Mistress, goddess of white arms, lady Selene, propitious, lovely-tressed. Beginning from you, I will sing of famous tales of heroes, whose deeds are celebrated by singers, the Muses' servants, from their enchanting mouths.

33. TO THE DIOSCURI

Tell about the Sons of Zeus, O curly-eyed Muses—the Tyndarids, fair-ankled Leda's splendid children, Castor the horse-tamer and faultless Polydeuces, whom below the peaks of the great mountain Taygetus, after uniting in love with the dark-cloud son of Kronos, she bore to be saviors of mankind on earth and of swift-faring ships, when winter tempests race over the implacable sea, and the men from their ships invoke the Sons of great Zeus in prayer, with (sacrifice of) white lambs, going onto the stern deck, and the strong wind and sea swell overwhelm the ship: suddenly they appear, speeding through the air on tawny wings, and at once they make the fierce squalls cease, and lay the waves amid the flats of a clear sea—fair portents, and release from travail; the sailors rejoice at the sight, and their misery and stress are ended.

---

16 σήματα καλά, πόνου ἀπονόσφισιν Bury: ναύταις σήματα καλὰ πόνου σφίσιν Ψ

χαίρετε, Τυνδαρίδαι, ταχέων ἐπιβήτορες ἵππων·
αὐτὰρ ἐγὼν ὑμέων ⟨τε⟩ καὶ ἄλλης μνήσομ᾽ ἀοιδῆς.

19 τε add. Barnes

FRAGMENTUM

Ael. Dion. α 76, "ἀλλὰ ἄναξ"

ἀρχὴ ἐξοδίου κιθαρωιδικοῦ, ὥσπερ κωμικοῦ μὲν ἤδε …
ῥαψωιδοῦ δὲ αὕτη·

νῦν δὲ θεοὶ μάκαρες τῶν ἐσθλῶν ἄφθονοι ἔστε.

33. TO THE DIOSCURI

I salute you, Tyndarids, riders on swift steeds. And I will take heed both for you and for other singing.

HYMN FRAGMENT

Aelius Dionysius, *Attic Lexicon*

"So, lord": the beginning of a citharode's envoi, just as this is of a comic poet's: . . . and this of a rhapsode's:

But now, blessed gods, be unstinting of blessings.[64]

---

[64] Apparently a line from the closing section of a Hymn not included in the "Homeric" collection.

HOMERIC APOCRYPHA

INTRODUCTION

Plato (*Phaedrus* 252b) quotes two lines that he says the Homeridai recite ἐκ τῶν ἀποθέτων ἐπῶν, "from their stored-away verses." Whether or not the existence of such a Reserve is to be taken seriously, I have seen fit to paraphrase Plato's expression as "from their Apocrypha," and to use this as a term of convenience to cover a group of non-serious or burlesque poems that were current in or after the classical period under Homer's name.

The pseudo-Herodotean Life (24) gives a list of "fun poems" (παίγνια) that Homer composed for the boys whom he taught at Bolissos in Chios: the *Cercopes*, the *Battle of Frogs*, the *Battle of Starlings*, the *Heptapaktike* (?), the *Epikichlides*, "and all the others." Most of these will be discussed below. One title, *Heptapaktike*, is enigmatic, being transmitted in a different meaningless form in each of the sources, unless the latest of all, Tzetzes, has the correct version with his *Hepta ep'aktion*, "Seven against the Headland," or "Seven against Actium." In this case it was some sort of parody of the story of the Seven against Thebes. But an equally plausible reading is *Heptapektos Aix*, "the Seven-times-shorn Goat" (Toup, after Leo Allatius). The lexica, in an entry probably going back to Seleucus, explain *heptapekt(i)os* as meaning "with abundant hair." If this referred to the poem, the inference would be that it was current by the first century BC.[1]

Margites

The oldest of the "fun poems," perhaps, was a comic narrative poem entitled, after its central character, *Margites*; his name means something like "Impetuous." He apparently rushed into many undertakings without having the requisite knowledge or understanding, for he was an exceptionally ignorant and naive man. Naturally he got himself into a series of ridiculous situations. The sources refer especially to the matter of his wedding, which was initially unsatisfactory because he knew nothing about sex and had to be coaxed by means of a stratagem into doing what was required.

There are more allusions and general references to Margites, whose name became proverbial for a simpleton, than actual quotations from the poem. Our knowledge of it has, however, been somewhat extended by the publication of three papyrus fragments from Oxyrhynchus which can with some probability be ascribed to it. One of them (fr. 7) contains remnants of an otherwise unattested episode involving a nocturnal misadventure with a narrow-necked

---

[1] In the *Suda* the corrupt Ἠθιέπακτος is followed by ἤτοι Ἴαμβοι, apparently indicating *Iamboi* as an alternative title of the poem. This would imply, not necessarily that its meter was iambic, but rather that it was of a scurrilous or invective nature. The *Suda*'s list of work attributed to Homer also includes a new item, *Epithalamia*. Tzetzes too speaks of "bridal hymns." We can make nothing of this.

chamber pot, from which Margites is unable to extricate his penis. This may have been simply because he had an abnormally large one (something that the Greeks considered gross and comical),[2] or because he was in a state of sexual excitement, in which case this may have been part of the narrative of the wedding night (or the night when the marriage was eventually consummated). In the second papyrus (fr. 8) someone says "and examine my . . .": this is perhaps connected with the bride's device of presenting her vulva to Margites as a wound that needed his attention. The third papyrus (fr. 9) apparently refers to the successful consummation, achieved in an atmosphere of festivity. This perhaps formed the conclusion of the poem. Many comedies end with a wedding.

The dialect is Ionic, as we should expect of a poem ascribed to Homer. The metre is unusual: an irregular alternation of hexameters with iambic trimeters. Parallels occur in one of the earliest vase epigrams (*CEG* 454, "Nestor's cup," around 730 BC) and in a fragment of Xenophanes of Colophon (B 14 Diels = West).

The Xenophanes parallel is interesting, because the *Margites* itself has an association with Colophon. According to the *Contest of Homer and Hesiod* (2) there was a place at Colophon where the locals claimed that Homer had started his poetic career and composed the *Margites* as his first work. A fragment from the poem, probably its opening (fr. 1), speaks of an old bard coming to Colophon with his lyre in his hands. It seems likely that he was represented as the narrator of the following tale, whether or not

[2] K. J. Dover, *Greek Homosexuality* (London, 1978), 125–128.

the author intended him to be identified as Homer. It is a reasonable inference that the poem did come from Colophon.

As to its date of composition, it cannot be later than the mid fifth century if, as stated by the Aristotelian commentator Eustratius, Cratinus alluded to the work.[3] The late sixth century would be a plausible time for its production; if the meter reminds us of Xenophanes, the farcical events and scatological humor remind us of Hipponax, both Ionian poets of that era. In Hipponax too we find hexameters used for comic purpose (epic parody, frs. 128–129a West) and the occasional hexameter line or half-line amid iambics (frs. 23 and 35).

If the *Margites* dates from that period, when Homer had recently begun to be celebrated as the greatest of the old bards, whose wanderings from city to city could be documented from the poems he left in them, the probability is that he was from the start represented as the author, and that the "old, godly singer" of the introductory lines was meant to be understood as Homer. His authorship was apparently accepted by the pseudo-Plato of the second *Alcibiades*, Aristotle, Zeno, and Callimachus. Later writers often express reserve, using phrases such as "the *Margites* attributed to Homer," or they deny his author-

---

[3] See the Testimonia. He also says it was mentioned by Archilochus, but that may be a distorted allusion to the fact that the same verse about the fox and the hedgehog was found both in Archilochus and in the *Margites* (fr. 5). The author may have borrowed it from Archilochus. Another explanation of Eustratius' remark is that his "Archilochus and Cratinus" is an error for "Cratinus in his comedy *Archilochoi*."

ship outright. The assertion of Hesychius of Miletus that the *Margites* and *Battle of Frogs and Mice* were both the work of the Carian Pigres, the brother of Queen Artemisia, is without historical value, though frequently grasped at by scholars eager to have a named author. It may be an invention of Ptolemy Hephaestion.[4]

Cercopes

This poem dealt with an amusing incident in Heracles' career, one of several episodes in which he rid the land of brigands or other nuisances who plagued the local population. The Cercopes, literally "Dick-faces," were a pair of rascally brothers who tormented people with their tricks. Different versions locate them in different parts of Greece; Herodotus (7.216) knew a place associated with them near Thermopylae. Their mother warned them that they were in danger of encountering a "black-ass." They may have thought she meant the fierce variety of eagle that was so called.[5] But their black-ass turned out to be Heracles, as they discovered when he captured them and hung them upside down from a pole which he carried on his shoulder, so that they had a good view of his hairy nether parts. The scene is depicted on vases from the early sixth century on.[6]

[4] Otto Crusius, *Philologus* 54 (1895), 734 ff.; 58 (1899), 577 ff.; Rudolf Peppmüller, *Berliner Philologische Wochenschrift* (1897), 513 ff.

[5] Compare Archilochus, fr. 178.

[6] See further Timothy Gantz, *Early Greek Myth* (Baltimore and London, 1993), 441 f.

Epikichlides

Another work attributed to Homer by the late classical period was a poem of amorous character, apparently addressed to a boy or boys; pseudo-Herodotus implies that these were the sons of the Chian who employed Homer at Bolissos. So much we gather from the scanty testimonia. The curious title *Epikichlides* was explained by Menaechmus of Sicyon from *kichlai* "thrushes," which he alleged that the boys gave Homer as a token of their appreciation. More likely it is to be connected with the verb *kichlizein*, to snigger or giggle. The poet may have addressed *Epikichlides Mousai*, Sniggering Muses.

To this poem I have conjecturally assigned the fragment quoted by Plato from the Homeric "Apocrypha," as it concerns the Love god and appears to be of a somewhat facetious nature.

Animal and Bird Epics

The *Battle of Frogs and Mice* (*Batrachomyomachia*) is a later composition. It contains echoes of Callimachus and Moschus, there is no mention of its existence before the first century AD, and Wackernagel showed that on linguistic grounds it can hardly be pre-Augustan. The riddling description of the crabs in lines 294–298 seems to stand in a close relationship with an epigram by Statilius Flaccus, who perhaps wrote under Augustus.[7] However, this amus-

---

[7] Jacob Wackernagel, *Sprachliche Untersuchungen zu Homer* (Göttingen, 1916), 188–196; Statilius Flaccus, *Anth. Pal.* 6.196 (3802 ff. Gow–Page, *The Garland of Philip*). No allusion to the

ing epyllion, in which a short-lived conflict between pondside creatures is treated in the epic style, has a remarkable prehistory going back long before the *Iliad* and *Odyssey*.

In Egypt there was an ancient tradition, extending well into the third millennium, of pictures, probably associated with stories, in which animals of all kinds were humorously shown engaging in human activities. Among them there emerge certain well-defined themes, some of which can be illustrated from Aesopic fables and others from modern African folktales. They presumably correspond to animal tales that were current in oral tradition. From the fourteenth century BC to the seventh or eighth century AD there are representations of a war between cats and mice. They correspond to tales that survive in modern Egypt and have left traces also in Arabic and Persian sources.[8]

Although the Greeks knew cats from the fifth century BC, it was the weasel that they thought of as the mouse's standard enemy. In Ptolemaic times the Egyptian motif of the War of the Cats and Mice was adapted in a Greek poem

poem is to be seen in Archelaus of Priene's famous relief "the Apotheosis of Homer" (about 125 BC), which originally showed two mice nibbling a papyrus roll at Homer's feet (not a frog and a mouse, as erroneously restored in the eighteenth century). See *HSCP* 73 (1968), 123 n. 35.

8 Emma Brunner-Traut, "Der Katzenmäuserkrieg im Alten und Neuen Orient," *Zeitschrift der Deutschen Morgenländischen Gesellschaft* 104 (1954), 347–351; "Ägyptische Tiermärchen," *Zeitschrift für ägyptische Sprache und Altertumskunde* 80 (1955), 12–32; *Altägyptische Märchen* (Düsseldorf and Köln, 1963), 59.

in epic style on a battle between the mice and a weasel or weasels. Before a fragment of this work was discovered on papyrus in 1983, its existence had been surmised. There is an Aesopic fable on the subject (165 Perry; Babrius 31), and Phaedrus in retailing it (4.6) mentions that it was a story depicted in all the taverns. The poet of the *Battle of Frogs and Mice* alludes at line 128 to a previous occasion when the mice had killed a weasel and skinned it for shield hides.

The papyrus containing *The Battle of the Weasel and the Mice* is dated to the second or first century BC. The main fragment comprises one relatively well preserved column of 31 lines and the lower part of a second, with a few letters from line-beginnings in the upper part. There are also a few unplaced scraps. The tenth line of the second column of the main piece is marked with the stichometric sign Δ, meaning "line 400," indicating that eleven columns of the roll are lost before the preserved text. But they must have contained other matter, for what we have is evidently the beginning of the story of the mice and the weasel. An over-bold mouse named Trixos ("Squeakos") is killed by the weasel, and this is what provokes the first gathering of the mouse army. The comparative material would lead us to suppose that the mice gained at least a temporary victory. Whether more weasels became involved later in the narrative, it is impossible to say.

There is no evidence that this poem was put under Homer's name; it is included in the present volume because it makes a natural companion to the *Battle of Frogs and Mice*, and because it has hitherto been accessible only in the pages of a periodical. Several other animal and bird epics, however, did become attributed to Homer, probably in jest at first, though the ascription imposed on the more dull-witted. Pseudo-Herodotus (24) mentions a *Battle of Starlings*, and Hesychius of Miletus lists a *Battle of Spiders* and a *Battle of Cranes*.[9]

These have vanished. But one such poem, the *Battle of Frogs and Mice*, achieved unique success. Martial and Statius accepted it as the Homeric counterpart to the Virgilian *Culex*, the light-hearted prelude to the epic poet's more serious work.[10] It is noticed in the pseudo-Herodotean *Life* and some of the others. A fragment of it is found in a second-century papyrus to be published in volume 68 of *The Oxyrhynchus Papyri*.

The author took his starting point from another Aesopic fable (384 Perry), according to which a mouse made friends with a frog and entertained him to a meal. The frog returned the invitation and led the way to his pool. As the mouse could not swim, the frog tied his foot to his own, and dived. The mouse felt himself drowning and cried out, "I shall have my revenge on you even when I am dead." The prophecy was fulfilled, for as the dead mouse lay floating on the surface of the water, a raven flew down and carried it off, with the frog still tied to it.

The poet begins his narrative in the manner of the fable: "A mouse one day . . . ." But he gives the story a differ-

[9] This last perhaps never existed: it could derive from Strabo's reference to "the Homeric crane-battle of the Pygmies" (2.1.9), which alludes to *Iliad* 3.3–7. There is, however, another reference in the *Life of Aesop* (recension G, 14), where Aesop's appearance is likened to "a trumpeter in the Battle of the Cranes."

[10] Martial, *Epigrams* 14.183–186; Statius, prefatory epistle to *Silvae* 1.

ent turn. Instead of the dead mouse and the live frog being carried off by a bird, a second mouse on the bank takes the news of what has happened back to the other mice. Here the model of the older poem about the mice and the weasel makes its influence felt. The mice make preparations for war; so do the frogs. Zeus calls the gods to assembly to debate the situation. They decide not to involve themselves. Zeus thunders, and the battle goes forward. After a ferocious struggle the mice are on the point of victory. Zeus takes pity on the suffering frogs and, after failing to persuade Athena or Ares to intervene, hurls a thunderbolt. But the mice fight on. Finally Zeus sends in a battalion of crabs. These bite the feet and tails of the mice, who retire in disorderly haste.

As already in the *Battle of the Weasel and the Mice*, the individual creatures are given meaningful names appropriate to their species. The mice have theirs in two cases from their domestic habits (Troglodytes "Creephole," Knaison "Scratchaway"), but mostly from their propensity for stealing human food: Embasichytros "Paddlepot," Kroustophagos[11] "Pastrygobble," Leichenor "Lickhart," Leichomyle "Lickmill," Leichopinax "Lickplatter," Meridarpax "Filchpiece," Psicharpax "Filchcrumbe," Pternoglyphos "Hamgraver," Pternotroktes "Hamchamper," Sitophagos "Graingobble," Troxartes "Champbread," Tyroglyphos "Cheesegraver," Tyrophagos "Cheesegobble." Of the frogs, some are named for their noisiness or other ostentation: Physignathos "Puffjawe," Hypsiboas "Loudhaylor," Kraugasides "MacCroak"; others from their liking for moist surroundings: Borborokoites "Sludge-

---

[11] Emended from the obscure Koustophagos.

couch," Hygraios[12] "Dampfred," Hydromedousa "Water-queen, Aquareine," Peleus and Peleion "Mudfred," "MacMudd" (with a play on the Homeric Peleus and Peleion "son of Peleus"); others again from plants in the kitchen garden where frogs are to be found lurking: Kalaminthios "Catmint," Krambobates "Mountcabbage," Okimides "MacBasil," Origanion "Origano," Pras(s)eios and Pras(s)aios "Leekhart, Leekhold," and Seutlaios "Mangelwurzel."

The poet is able and inventive, although his work has suffered badly in the transmission. Once at war, his frogs and mice conduct themselves with due gravity, following the general procedures of Homeric battle, though the poet does not limit himself to Homeric cliché. The humor of the piece derives partly from the solemn epic treatment of the little creatures with their diminutive arms and armour made from snail shells, bean pods, and so on; partly from the gods' engagement with the conflict, their fear of being hurt if they join in on the ground, the final failure even of Zeus' thunderbolt to halt the mice in their triumphant on-slaught. The highlight is Athena's speech in 178–196, with her account of the vexations caused her by both mice and frogs; here we are in sight of the Second Sophistic and Lucian's view of the Olympian world in his *Dialogues of the Gods*.

The text displays a number of incoherencies (more in some editions than in others). Most of them can be put down to the vagaries of the manuscript tradition, of which more below. But there is a real problem about the reap-

---

[12] Emended from the obscure Litraios.

pearance of certain mice or frogs after they have been killed. Psicharpax-Filchcrumbe, the mouse whose drowning is the cause of the war, apparently plays a part in the combat at 234 ff. Troglodytes-Creephole is fatally hit at 213, but recurs in the better manuscripts at 247, though others give Sitophagos-Graingobble. Prasseios-Leekhart is slain at 236, but a frog with an almost identical name appears at 252. In the last two cases we can avoid contradiction by accepting the variant form of the name, but the case of Psicharpax is recalcitrant. An oversight by the poet is unlikely in view of the importance of the original Psicharpax to the plot. Are we to take the second one as a homonym, or is the poet parodying the notorious instance in the *Iliad* where the Paphlagonian leader Pylaemenes, killed at 5.576–579, reappears alive (to the perplexity of ancient commentators) at 13.658?

To conclude, a summary account must be given of the poem's transmission. We have seen that by the time of Domitian, at latest, it was in general currency under the name of Homer. During the next few centuries it enjoyed no special popularity. The second-century papyrus fragment mentioned above is the only one so far found, and there are few literary allusions to the work.

That changed in the Byzantine period. From about 800 onwards there appear a whole series of quotations and allusions.[13] The poem was adopted as a school text, to make a short and entertaining introduction to Homer. Because of this there is a large number of manuscripts, often

[13] Hansjörg Wölke, *Untersuchungen zur Batrachomyomachie*, 33–43.

furnished with explanatory glosses and scholia, none of which go back to antiquity. The oldest extant manuscript (Z = Oxon. Barocc. 50) dates from around 925, and there are four more from the eleventh and twelfth centuries.

Normally we should expect such relatively early copies of a classical poem to provide a well-founded text. In the case of the *Battle of Frogs and Mice*, however, the Byzantines felt an unusual licence and impulse to rewrite and expand. The scribe of Z seems already to have known divergent forms of the text, and he is prepared to emend it on his own initiative where he finds a difficulty. When we take in the later manuscripts, the amount of variation is bewildering. Some contain lines and passages that are absent from others; the same lines may appear in a different order; names of frogs or mice are replaced by completely different ones; a frog who slays a mouse in some copies is slain by him in others; what is part of the narrative in these appears as a speech by a mouse in those.

The root of the trouble appears to have been a particular rewriting that took place sometime in or before the eleventh century, best represented by the so-called Florentine family of manuscripts (*l*).[14] The person responsible added new lines and passages here and there—many of them seriously unmetrical—sometimes in place of existing verses. He altered names and details of the action so as to produce a more regular alternation of mouse and frog successes.

Apart from Z, the best manuscripts are those of the *a*

[14] This consists of L = Laur. 32.3 (eleventh–twelfth century); J = Ambr. I 4 sup. (AD 1276); F = Vat. gr. 915 (before 1311). J is inclined to introduce further alterations.

family.[15] Sometimes, however, the better reading is preserved in the interpolated *l* family. Z sometimes agrees with *l*, but more often with *a*; at other times it is isolated, for good or ill. The many dozens of later manuscripts are characterized by various degrees of compromise between the two extremes represented by *a* and *l*, and they have little of value to offer beyond the occasional good conjecture.

By judicious choice among the readings of Z, *a*, and *l*, and a principled rejection of the extra verses in *l*, one may arrive at a text considerably more promising in appearance than seemed likely to emerge from the initial vista of chaos. But it still falls some way short of the presumed original; there remain some interpolated lines, some lines apparently out of place, and some defects of sense or metre, all of which call for active intervention on the editor's part. In the battle narrative, between lines 247 and 270, there is such a lack of coherence that it seems necessary to suppose the Byzantine tradition to have been dependent on a damaged archetype with verses missing at several points.

[15] This consists of P and Q = Par. suppl. gr. 690 and 663 (both eleventh century); Y = Heidelberg, Palat. 45 (AD 1202); T = Par. gr. 2723 (thirteenth century).

SIGLA AND BIBLIOGRAPHY

Margites

Allen, T. W. *Homeri Opera*, v. Oxford Classical Texts, 1912, pp. 152–159.

West, Martin L. *Iambi et Elegi Graeci*, ii, ed. altera. Oxford, 1992, pp. 69–77.

Battle of the Weasel and The Mice

Schibli, H. S. "Fragments of a Weasel and Mouse War." *ZPE* 53 (1983): 1–25.

Battle of Frogs and Mice

Manuscript Sigla

Z   Oxford, Barocci Gr. 50 (tenth century)

a   Family consisting of: P and Q = Paris, Supplément grec 690 and 663 (both eleventh century); Y = Heidelberg, Palatinus 45 (AD 1202); T = Paris. gr. 2723 (thirteenth century)

l   Florentine family, consisting of: L = Florence, Laurentianus 32.3 (eleventh–twelfth century); J = Milan, Ambrosianus I 4 sup. (AD 1276); F = Vaticanus gr. 915 (before 1311)

S   Escorial, Ω I 12 (eleventh–twelfth century)

INTRODUCTION

Editions, Commentaries
(see also under Homeric Hymns)

Ludwich, Arthur. *Die homerische Batrachomyomachia des Karers Pigres*. Leipzig, 1896.

Allen, T. W. *Homeri Opera*, v (as above), pp. 161–183.

Ahlborn, Helmut. *Pseudo-Homer. Der Froschmäuserkrieg. Theodoros Prodromos. Der Katzenmäuserkrieg.* Berlin, 1968.

Glei, Reinhold. *Die Batrachomyomachie. Synoptische Edition und Kommentar*. Frankfurt, 1984.

Fusillo, Massimo. *La Battaglia delle rane e dei topi. Batrachomyomachia*. Milan, 1988.

Other Studies

Ahlborn, Helmut. *Untersuchungen zur pseudo-homerischen Batrachomyomachie*. Diss. Göttingen, 1959.

Morenz, Siegfried. "Ägyptische Tierkriege und die Batrachomyomachie," in *Neue Beiträge zur klassischen Altertumswissenschaft* (Festschrift Bernhard Schweitzer). Stuttgart, 1954, pp. 87–94.

Wölke, Hansjörg. *Untersuchungen zur Batrachomyomachie*. Meisenheim, 1978.

ΜΑΡΓΙΤΗΣ

TESTIMONIA

Arist. *Poet.* 1448b24

διεσπάσθη δὲ κατὰ τὰ οἰκεῖα ἤθη ἡ ποίησις· οἱ μὲν γὰρ σεμνότεροι τὰς καλὰς ἐμιμοῦντο πράξεις καὶ τὰς τῶν τοιούτων, οἱ δὲ εὐτελέστεροι τὰς τῶν φαύλων, πρῶτον ψόγους ποιοῦντες, ὥσπερ ἕτεροι ὕμνους καὶ ἐγκώμια. τῶν μὲν οὖν πρὸ Ὁμήρου οὐδενὸς ἔχομεν εἰπεῖν τοιοῦτον ποίημα, εἰκὸς δὲ εἶναι πολλούς, ἀπὸ δὲ Ὁμήρου ἀρξαμένοις ἔστιν, οἷον ἐκείνου ὁ Μαργίτης καὶ τὰ τοιαῦτα. . . . ὥσπερ δὲ καὶ τὰ σπουδαῖα μάλιστα ποιητὴς Ὅμηρος ἦν (μόνος γὰρ οὐχ ὅτι εὖ ἀλλὰ καὶ μιμήσεις δραματικὰς ἐποίησεν), οὕτως καὶ τὸ τῆς κωμῳδίας σχῆμα πρῶτος ὑπέδειξεν, οὐ ψόγον ἀλλὰ τὸ γελοῖον δραματοποιήσας· ὁ γὰρ Μαργίτης ἀνάλο-γον ἔχει, ὥσπερ Ἰλιὰς καὶ ἡ Ὀδύσσεια πρὸς τὰς τραγῳδίας, οὕτω καὶ οὗτος πρὸς τὰς κωμῳδίας.

Hephaestion, *Isagoge* 4 (p. 59.21 Consbruch)

μετρικὰ δὲ ἄτακτα . . . οἷός ἐστιν ὁ Μαργίτης ὁ εἰς Ὅμηρον ἀναφερόμενος, ἐν ὧι παρέσπαρται τοῖς ἔπε-σιν ἰαμβικά, καὶ ταῦτα οὐ κατ᾽ ἴσον σύστημα.

MARGITES

Aristotle, *Poetics*

Poetry divided according to the (poets') native characters: the more dignified poets represented noble actions and those of noble people, while the more vulgar represented those of the low class, initially by composing derogatory pieces, just as another group composed hymns and encomia. Of poets before Homer we cannot name any author of such a poem, though many probably existed; but from Homer onwards we can, for example his *Margites* and the like.... And just as Homer above all was the poet of serious subjects—for he alone, besides composing well, composed dramatic representations—so too he was the first to reveal the outlines of comedy, by dramatization that was not derogatory but humorous. For the *Margites* stands in a similar relation to comedies as the *Iliad* and *Odyssey* do to tragedies.

Hephaestion, *Introduction to Metre*

Unregulated metres ... such as the *Margites* attributed to Homer, in which there are iambic lines scattered among the hexameters, and on no regular system.

Cf. eund. *De poem.* 3.4 (p. 65.10 C.); schol. ad loc. (p. 168.13);
Aphthonius, *Gramm. Lat.* vi.68.9, 79.8, 133.30.

Dio Prus. 53.4 (ii.110.24 Arnim)

γέγραφε δὲ καὶ Ζήνων ὁ φιλόσοφος (*SVF* i.63.6) εἴς τε
τὴν Ἰλιάδα καὶ τὴν Ὀδύσσειαν, καὶ περὶ τοῦ Μαργί-
του δέ· δοκεῖ γὰρ καὶ τοῦτο τὸ ποίημα ὑπὸ Ὁμήρου
γεγονέναι νεωτέρου καὶ ἀποπειρωμένου τῆς αὑτοῦ
φύσεως πρὸς ποίησιν.

Certamen Hom. et Hes. 2

Κολοφώνιοι δὲ καὶ τόπον δεικνύουσιν ἐν ὧι φασιν
αὐτὸν γράμματα διδάσκοντα τῆς ποιήσεως ἄρξασθαι
καὶ ποιῆσαι πρῶτον τὸν Μαργίτην.

Eustratius in Arist. *Eth. Nic.* 6.7 (*CAG* xx.320.36)

παράγει δὲ εἰς μαρτυρίαν τοῦ εἶναι τὸν ὅλως σοφὸν
ἕτερον παρὰ τόν τινα σοφὸν καί τινα ποίησιν Μαργί-
την ὀνομαζομένην Ὁμήρου. μνημονεύει δὲ αὐτῆς οὐ
μόνον αὐτὸς Ἀριστοτέλης ἐν τῶι πρώτωι περὶ ποιητι-
κῆς (v. supra), ἀλλὰ καὶ Ἀρχίλοχος (fr. 303 W., cf. 201)
καὶ Κρατῖνος (fr. 368 K.–A.) καὶ Καλλίμαχος ἐν τοῖς
Ἐπιγράμμασι (fr. 397 Pf.), καὶ μαρτυροῦσιν εἶναι
Ὁμήρου τὸ ποίημα.

Dio of Prusa, *On Homer*

The philosopher Zeno too has written on the *Iliad* and *Odyssey*, and also about the *Margites*, for this poem too is thought to have been produced by Homer when he was young and trying out his gift for poetry.

The Contest of Homer and Hesiod

The Colophonians even point to a spot where they say Homer, as a teacher of reading and writing, started his poetic career and composed the *Margites* as his first work.

Eustratius, commentary on Aristotle's *Nicomachean Ethics*

As evidence of the difference between being clever absolutely and clever at particular things, he cites a poem of Homer called *Margites*. It is mentioned not only by Aristotle himself in Book 1 of the *Poetics*, but also by Archilochus, Cratinus, and Callimachus in his *Epigrams*, and they attest that it is by Homer.

Harpocr. M 6

Αἰσχίνης ἐν τῶι κατὰ Κτησιφῶντος (Or. 3.160)· "ἐπωνυμίαν δ᾿ Ἀλεξάνδρωι Μαργίτην ἔθετο." καὶ Μαρσύας ἐν ε᾿ τῶν περὶ Ἀλεξάνδρου (FGrHist 135 F 3) ἱστορεῖ, λέγων Μαργίτην ὑπὸ Δημοσθένους καλεῖσθαι τὸν Ἀλέξανδρον. ἐκάλουν δὲ τοὺς ἀνοήτους οὕτω διὰ τὸν εἰς Ὅμηρον ἀναφερόμενον Μαργίτην, ὅπερ ποίημα Καλλίμαχος θαυμάζειν ἔοικεν.

Schol. Ar. Av. 914

ἐπεπίστευτο δὲ καὶ ὁ Μαργίτης τοῦ Ὁμήρου εἶναι, ἐν ὧι εἴρηται· (fr. 1.2).

Schol. Dion. Thr. i.471.35 Hilgard

πολλὰ γὰρ νοθευόμενά ἐστιν, ὡς ἡ Σοφοκλέους Ἀντιγόνη, λέγεται γὰρ εἶναι Ἰοφῶντος τοῦ Σοφοκλέους υἱοῦ· Ὁμήρου τὰ Κυπριακὰ καὶ ὁ Μαργίτης· Ἀράτου τὰ Θυτικὰ καὶ τὰ περὶ ὀρνέων· Ἡσιόδου ἡ Ἀσπίς.

Suda π 1551 (iv.127.24 Adler)

Πίγρης, Κὰρ ἀπὸ Ἁλικαρνασοῦ, ἀδελφὸς Ἀρτεμισίας τῆς ἐν τοῖς πολέμοις διαφανοῦς, Μαυσώλου γυναικός . . . ἔγραψε καὶ τὸν εἰς Ὅμηρον ἀναφερόμενον Μαργίτην καὶ Βατραχομυομαχίαν.

See also references in the Lives of Homer edited in this volume: ps.-Plutarch 1.5; Proclus (end); Anon. III.

Harpocration, *Lexicon to the Orators*

Margites: mentioned by Aeschines, *Against Ctesiphon*, "and he gave Alexander the nickname Margites." And Marsyas in Book 5 of his Alexander history records it, saying that Alexander was called Margites by Demosthenes. They gave this name to foolish people because of the *Margites* attributed to Homer, a poem which Callimachus seems to admire.

Scholiast on Aristophanes, *Birds*

The *Margites* too was believed to be by Homer, in which it is said: (fr. 1.2).

Scholiast on Dionysius of Thrace

For many works are spurious, such as Sophocles' *Antigone* (said to be by Sophocles' son Iophon), Homer's *Cypria* and *Margites*, Aratus' *Thytika* and the poem on birds, Hesiod's *Shield*.

Suda (from Hesychius of Miletus)

Pigres, a Carian from Halicarnassus, brother of Artemisia the famous warrior, the wife of Mausolus[1] . . . He also wrote the *Margites* attributed to Homer and the *Battle of Frogs and Mice*.

---

[1] This confuses two Artemisias: the warrior queen of the early fifth century known from Herodotus, and the sister and wife of Mausolus in the mid fourth century.

FRAGMENTA

1 Anon. P. Fackelmann 6 fr. a 17–21 + 26–27 (ZPE 34
[1979], 16); Atil. Fort., *Gramm. Lat.* vi.286.2; fr. Berol.,
ib. 633; line 2 also sch. Ar. *Av.* 914

ἦλθέ τις ἐς Κολοφῶνα γέρων καὶ θεῖος ἀοιδός,
Μουσάων θεράπων καὶ ἑκηβόλου Ἀπόλλωνος,
φίληις ἔχων ἐν χερσὶν εὔφθογγον λύρην.

3 φιλαις pap.: φιαις fr. Berol.: φιλην Atil.

2 Arist. *Eth. Nic.* 1141a12 (– σοφόν); Clem. *Strom.*
1.25.1; (οὔτε σκαπτῆρα – ἀροτῆρα) Dio Prus. 7.116
(i.211.8 Arnim)

τὸν δ᾽ οὔτ᾽ ἀρ σκαπτῆρα θεοὶ θέσαν οὔτ᾽ ἀροτῆρα
οὔτ᾽ ἄλλως τι σοφόν· πάσης δ᾽ ἡμάρτανε τέχνης.

3 Ps.-Plato, *Alcib. II* 147b

πόλλ᾽ ἠπίστατο ἔργα, κακῶς δ᾽ ἠπίστατο πάντα.

4 Dio Prus. 67.4 (ii.170.18 Arnim)

⟨οὐ⟩ πολύ γ᾽ ἂν εἴη τοῦ Μαργίτου σοφώτερος ἀγνο-
οῦντος ὅτι χρὴ γήμαντα χρῆσθαι τῆι γυναικί.

Hesych. μ 267 (supplemented from Cyril's *Lexicon*)

Μαργε⟨ί⟩της· μωρός τις ἦν, μὴ εἰδὼς μίξιν γυναικός. καὶ
⟨ἡ⟩ γυνὴ προτρέπεται αὐτόν, ˏεἰποῦσα σκορπίον αὐτὴν

FRAGMENTS

1 Papyrus Fackelmann 6; Atilius Fortunatianus, *Art of Meter*; scholiast on Aristophanes, *Birds*

There came to Colophon an old, godly singer, a servant of the Muses and of far-shooting Apollo, with his true-sounding lyre in his hands.

2 Aristotle, *Nicomachean Ethics*; Clement, *Miscellanies*; Dio of Prusa, *Euboicus*

The gods had made him neither a digger nor a plowman, nor skilled in any other way: he fell short at every craft.

3 Pseudo-Plato, *Alcibiades II*

He knew a lot of things, but he knew them all badly.[2]

4 Dio of Prusa, *On Reputation II*

He would not be much smarter than Margites, who did not know what you have to do with a wife when you have got married.

Hesychius, *Lexicon*

Margites: he was an idiot who did not know about copulation. His wife encouraged him by saying that a scorpion had bitten

---

[2] This verse perhaps followed immediately after fr. 2.

δῆξαι καὶ ὑπὸ τῆς ὀχείας ⟨δεῖν⟩ θεραπευθῆναι﹐.

Eust. in *Od.* 1669.48

οὕτως ἔγνωμεν καὶ τὸν ἄφρονα Μαργίτην . . . ὃν ὁ
ποιήσας τὸν ἐπιγραφόμενον Ὁμήρου Μαργίτην ὑποτίθ-
εται εὐπόρων μὲν εἰς ὑπερβολὴν γονέων φῦναι, γήμαντα
δὲ μὴ συμπεσεῖν τῆι νύμφηι ἕως ἀναπεισθεῖσα ἐκείνη
⟨ὑπὸ τῆς μητρὸς⟩ τετραυματίσθαι τὰ κάτω ἐσκήψατο,
φάρμακόν τε μηδὲν ὠφελήσειν ἔφη πλὴν εἰ τὸ ἀνδρεῖον
αἰδοῖον ἐκεῖ ἐφαρμοσθείη· καὶ οὕτω θεραπείας χάριν
ἐκεῖνος ἐπλησίασεν.

cf. sch. Luc. *Philops.* p. 162.7 Rabe.

5 Zenob. vulg. 5.68

πόλλ᾽ οἶδ᾽ ἀλώπηξ, ἀλλ᾽ ἐχῖνος ἓν μέγα.

μέμνηται ταύτης Ἀρχίλοχος ἐν ἐπωιδῆι (Archil. fr. 201)·
γράφει δὲ καὶ Ὅμηρος τὸν στίχον.

Cited without attribution by Plut. *Sollert. anim.* 971e and various
scholia, lexica, and paroemiographers.

6 Theodorus Metochita, *Miscellanea* p. 510 Müller–
Kiessling

καὶ ξυμβαίνει πολλάκις δυσπραγήματα, καὶ βιωτέον ἂν
εἴη, εἰ καὶ ὅλως εἴη, κατὰ τὸν Ὁμήρου Μαργίτην, μηδὲν
πονοῦντα μηδενὸς ἐπαΐοντα.

her and that she had to be healed by means of intercourse.

Eustathius, commentary on *Odyssey* 10.552

In the same way we have heard of the foolish Margites . . . whom the author of the *Margites* that bears Homer's name represents as having been born to exceedingly affluent parents, but when he married he did not fall upon his bride until she, at her mother's instigation, pretended to have suffered a wound in her lower parts, and said that no remedy would be of any help except for a male member being fitted to the place: so it was that he made love to her, for therapeutic purposes.

5 Zenobius, *Proverbs*

The fox knows many tricks, but the hedgehog knows one big one.

Archilochus mentions this proverb in an Epode. Homer too writes the line.

6 Theodorus Metochita, *Miscellanies*

And misfortunes often occur, so that it would be best to live (if at all) like Homer's Margites, doing nothing and knowing nothing.

7 P. Oxy. 2309

$$\kappa]\acute{\upsilon}\sigma\tau\iota\nu[, \ \chi]\epsilon\iota\rho\grave{\iota} \ \delta\grave{\epsilon} \ \mu\alpha\kappa\rho\hat{\eta}\iota$$
$$] \ \tau\epsilon\acute{\upsilon}\chi\epsilon\alpha, \ [\kappa]\alpha\acute{\iota} \ \dot{\rho}\alpha \ \check{\epsilon}\lambda\alpha\sigma\sigma\epsilon$$
$$\delta\upsilon o\hat{\iota}\sigma\iota \ \delta' \ \acute{\epsilon}\nu \ \pi]\acute{o}\nu o\iota[\sigma\iota]\nu \ \epsilon\check{\iota}\chi\epsilon\tauo$$
$$]\nu\cdot \ \acute{\epsilon}\nu \ \delta\grave{\epsilon} \ [\tau]\hat{\eta}\iota \ \acute{\alpha}\mu\acute{\iota}\delta\iota$$
5
$$] \ \acute{\epsilon}\xi\epsilon\lambda\epsilon\hat{\iota}\nu \ \delta' \ \acute{\alpha}\mu\acute{\eta}\chi\alpha\nu o\nu$$
$$\kappa]\alpha\acute{\iota} \ \dot{\rho}' \ \acute{\epsilon}\nu\acute{\omega}\mu\epsilon\iota\xi\epsilon\nu \ \tau\alpha\chi\acute{\upsilon}$$
$$] \ \kappa[\alpha\iota\nu]\grave{\eta}\nu \ \acute{\epsilon}\phi\rho\acute{\alpha}\sigma\sigma\alpha\tauo \ \mu\hat{\eta}\tau\iota[\nu\cdot$$
$$\acute{\alpha}\nu\acute{o}\rho o\upsilon\sigma\epsilon] \ \lambda\iota\pi\grave{\omega}\nu \ \check{\alpha}\pi o \ \delta\acute{\epsilon}\mu\nu\iota\alpha \ [\theta\epsilon\rho\mu\acute{\alpha}$$
$$\check{\omega}\epsilon\iota\xi\epsilon] \ \theta\acute{\upsilon}\rho\alpha\varsigma, \ \acute{\epsilon}\kappa \ \delta' \ \check{\epsilon}\delta\rho\alpha\mu\epsilon\nu \ \check{\epsilon}\xi\omega$$
10
$$]\omega\nu \ \delta\iota\grave{\alpha} \ \nu\acute{\upsilon}\kappa\tau\alpha \ \mu\acute{\epsilon}\lambda\alpha[\iota\nu\alpha\nu$$
$$]\upsilon\sigma\epsilon\iota\epsilon \ \delta\grave{\epsilon} \ \chi\epsilon\hat{\iota}\rho\alpha[\![\varsigma]\!]$$
$$\delta\iota]\grave{\alpha} \ \nu\acute{\upsilon}\kappa\tau\alpha \ \mu\acute{\epsilon}\lambda\alpha\iota\nu[\alpha\nu$$
$$]\mu\epsilon\nu \ o\grave{\upsilon}\delta\grave{\epsilon} \ \phi\alpha\nu\acute{\iota}o[\nu$$
$$] \ \delta\acute{\upsilon}\sigma\tau\eta\nu o\nu \ \kappa\acute{\alpha}\rho[\eta$$
15
$$]\epsilon\delta\acute{o}\kappa\epsilon\epsilon\nu \ \lambda\acute{\iota}\theta[$$
$$]\omega\iota \ \kappa\alpha\grave{\iota} \ \chi\epsilon\iota\rho\grave{\iota} \ \pi\alpha\chi[\epsilon\acute{\iota}\eta\iota$$
$$\lambda\acute{\epsilon}\pi\tau' \ \check{\epsilon}]\theta\eta\kappa\epsilon\nu \ \check{o}\sigma\tau\rho\alpha[\kappa\alpha$$

(fragments of four more lines)

8 θερμά suppl. Latte, cetera Lobel, West

8 P. Oxy. 3963

1 α]ὐτίκ' ἀνέδραμ[ε, 2]ωι πεφοβημέν[, 3]συνοικέτεω, 4 ἐ]ξαλευμένη, 6]τά τ' ἐμὰ σκοπεῦ, 7]ους δόμους, 8 (ἀνα)κ]εκαλυμ‹μ›ένη· 9]φάσγανον

7 Oxyrhynchus papyrus (first century BC or AD)[3]

. . . bl]adder, and with hand outstretched [he set his dick to] the pot, and thrust [it in. Then in two] pinches he was caught . . . while in the chamber pot . . . and it was impossible to get it out . . . and he very soon pissed into it . . . He thought of a new stratagem . . . [He jumped up,] leaving the [warm] bed . . . [opened] the doors and ran out . . . through the dark night . . . and . . . his hand . . . through the dark night . . . and no torch [he had] . . . unlucky he[ad] . . . thought it was a stone . . . and with his stout hand . . . [sma]shed the pot [on it . . .

8 Oxyrhynchus papyrus (second century)

. . . at once ran up . . . afraid . . . the fellow domestic's . . . she avoiding . . . ". . . and examine my . . ." . . . house . . . her (un)veiled . . . sword . . .

---

[3] On the content of this and the following fragments see the Introduction.

HOMERIC APOCRYPHA

9 P. Oxy. 3964

1].ων γὰρ [ο]ὐδὲ μηδενηισι ποικίλ[, 2]. εὖτ᾽ Ἑλένην
ἰδών, 3]νεν ἄλσεσι, 4]σσ᾽ Ἀφροδίτης, 5 παρθέ]νους
ὁμήλικας, 6]ηισιν εὐπινέως, 11]νέον γαμ[ον] βρ[α-
χ]εῖ, 12–13]ς, ὡς ὅθ᾽ Ἡρακλ[ῆ]ς | [Ἥβηι καλλικόμωι
ῥοδοπήχεϊ πρ]ῶτον ἐμίχ[θ]η, 14]λεμμα[..]σ[..] ποσί,
15] ὑπὸ πηκτίδος· 17 ἁ]ρπ[α]λέον, 18 κα]κῶν [ὕπ]ο·

5, 13 suppl. West

ΚΕΡΚΩΠΕΣ

TESTIMONIA

Ps.-Herod. *Vita Homeri* 24

καὶ τοὺς Κέρκωπας καὶ Βατραχομαχίαν ... καὶ τἄλλα
πάντα ὅσα παίγνιά ἐστιν Ὁμήρου ἐνταῦθα ἐποίησε
παρὰ τῶι Χίωι ἐν Βολισσῶι.

Proclus, *Vita Homeri* 9

οἱ μέντοι γε ἀρχαῖοι καὶ τὸν Κύκλον ἀναφέρουσιν εἰς
αὐτόν· προστιθέασι δέ τινες αὐτῶι καὶ παίγνιά τινα·
Μαργίτην ... Κέρκωπας, κτλ.

FRAGMENTUM

Harpocr. K 42

ἐν τοῖς εἰς Ὅμηρον ἀναφερομένοις Κέρκωψιν δηλοῦται
ὡς ἐξαπατητῆρές τε ἦσαν καὶ ψεῦσται οἱ Κέρκωπες.

252

MARGITES

9 Oxyrhynchus papyrus (second century)

. . . [like Paris] when he saw Helen and . . . in the groves . . .
of Aphrodite . . . [mai]dens of like age . . . cleanly . . . his
new marr[iage in a sho]rt [time he consummated man-
fully,] as when Heracles first made love [to lovely-haired,
rose-armed Hebe] . . . with feet . . . to the accompaniment
of a harp . . . g[la]d . . . fr[om his troub]les . . .

CERCOPES

TESTIMONIA

Pseudo-Herodotus, *Life of Homer*

And the *Cercopes*, the *Battle of Frogs*, . . . and the rest of
Homer's fun poems, he composed there in the Chian's
house at Bolissos.

Proclus, *Life of Homer*

But the ancients also ascribe the *Cycle* to him, and some
people add certain fun poems too: the *Margites* . . . the
Cercopes, etc.

FRAGMENT

Harpocration, *Lexicon to the Orators*

In the *Cercopes* attributed to Homer it is stated that the
Cercopes were "deceivers" and "liars."

253

Suda κ 1406

φασὶ τοὺς Κέρκωπας γενέσθαι

ψεύστας, ἠπεροπῆας, ἀμήχανά τ᾽ ἔργα δαέντας,
ἐξαπατητῆρας· πολλὴν δ᾽ ἐπὶ γαῖαν ἰόντες
ἀνθρώπους ἀπάτασκον ἀλώμενοι ἤματα πάντα.

1 ἔργα δαέντας Lobeck: ἔργ᾽ ἐάσαντας codd.

ΕΠΙΚΙΧΛΙΔΕΣ

TESTIMONIA

Ath. 65a

ὅτι τὸ εἰς Ὅμηρον ἀναφερόμενον ἐπύλλιον, ἐπιγραφό-
μενον δὲ Ἐπικιχλίδες, ἔτυχε ταύτης τῆς προσηγορίας
διὰ τὸ τὸν Ὅμηρον ᾄδοντα αὐτὸ τοῖς παισὶ κίχλας
δῶρον λαμβάνειν, ἱστορεῖ Μέναιχμος ἐν τῶι περὶ
τεχνιτῶν (FGrHist 131 F 3).

Id. 639a

Κλέαρχος δὲ ἐν δευτέρωι Ἐρωτικῶν (fr. 33 Wehrli) τὰ
ἐρωτικά φησιν ᾄσματα καὶ τὰ Λοκρικὰ καλούμενα
οὐδὲν τῶν Σαπφοῦς καὶ Ἀνακρέοντος διαφέρειν. ἔτι δὲ
τὰ Ἀρχιλόχου καὶ τῶν Ὁμήρου Ἐπικιχλίδων τὰ πολ-
λὰ διὰ τῆς ἐμμέτρου ποιήσεως τούτων ἔχεταί τινος
τῶν παθῶν.

EPIKICHLIDES

The *Suda*

They say that the Cercopes were

liars, tricksters, schooled in mischief, deceivers; they used
to travel far abroad and trick people, always roaming.

EPIKICHLIDES

TESTIMONIA

Athenaeus, *Scholars at Dinner*

The little hexameter poem attributed to Homer and en-
titled *Epikichlides* got this name because when Homer
recited it to the boys he was rewarded with thrushes
(*kichlai*); so Menaechmus[4] records in his work *On Per-
forming Artists*.

Athenaeus, *Scholars at Dinner*

Clearchus in book two of his *Erotic Questions* says that the
love songs and the so-called Locrian songs are no different
from those of Sappho and Anacreon. And Archilochus'
pieces and most of Homer's *Epikichlides*, in the realm of
verse, also have to do with these emotions.

[4] A Sicyonian writer of the third century BC.

Ps.-Herod. *Vita Homeri* 24

καὶ τοὺς Κέρκωπας καὶ Βατραχομαχίαν καὶ Ψαρομα-
χίην καὶ Ἑπτἀπακτικὴν καὶ Ἐπικιχλίδας καὶ τἄλλα
πάντα ὅσα παίγνιά ἐστιν Ὁμήρου ἐνταῦθα ἐποίησε
παρὰ τῶι Χίωι ἐν Βολισσῶι.

Hesychius Milesius, *Vita Homeri* 6

ἀναφέρεται δὲ εἰς αὐτὸν καὶ ἄλλα τινὰ ποιήματα·
Ἀμαζονία, Ἰλιὰς Μικρά, Νόστοι, Ἐπικιχλίδες, κτλ.

FRAGMENTUM?

Plato *Phaedr.* 252b

λέγουσι δὲ οἶμαί τινες Ὁμηριδῶν ἐκ τῶν ἀποθέτων ἐπῶν
δύο ἔπη εἰς τὸν Ἔρωτα, ὧν τὸ ἕτερον ὑβριστικὸν πάνυ
καὶ οὐ σφόδρα τι ἔμμετρον· ὑμνοῦσι δὲ ὧδε·

τὸν δ᾽ ἤτοι θνητοὶ μὲν Ἔρωτα καλοῦσι ποτηνόν,
ἀθάνατοι δὲ Πτέρωτα διὰ πτεροφύτορ᾽ ἀνάγκην.

EPIKICHLIDES

Pseudo-Herodotus, *Life of Homer*

And the *Cercopes*, the *Battle of Frogs*, the *Battle of Starlings*, the *Heptapaktike*, the *Epikichlides*, and the rest of Homer's fun poems, he composed there in the Chian's house at Bolissos.

Hesychius of Miletus, *Index of Famous Authors*

Certain other poems are also attributed to him (Homer): the *Amazonia*, the *Little Iliad*, the *Returns*, the *Epikichlides*, etc.

FRAGMENT?

Plato, *Phaedrus*

And I believe some of the Homeridai recite from their Apocrypha[5] two verses about Eros, one of which is quite outrageous and not particularly metrical—this is how they hymn him:

And mortals call him Eros the flighty, while the immortals call him Pteros, because he makes one grow wings (*ptera*).[6]

---

[5] Literally "the stored-away verses." I attribute the fragment to the *Epikichlides* conjecturally on account of its content.

[6] Compare Anacreon, *PMG* 378; Alexis, fr. 20 Kassel–Austin.

ΓΑΛΕΟΜΥΟΜΑΧΙΑ

P. Mich. inv. 6946, ed. H. S. Schibli, *ZPE* 53 (1983), 1–25

Μοῦσά μοι ἔννεπ]ε νεῖκο[ς] ὅπως [πολέμ]ου
 [κρυ]όεν[τ]ος
ἦλθε μύεσσ', οἳ] δ' ἀντὶ γαλῆς ἔστη[σαν ἀολλεῖς
[..]αι[..].[...].επ[..]ωι προμάχιζε ετ[..]ιδε
 Τρῖξος.
χορ]δῆς ἀρ[π]ακτὴ[ρ γ]ένετ' ἐμ μυέ[σ]σιν
 ἄριστος·
5 ἀ]λλ' οὔ μιν πάλιν αὖτις ἐδέξατο πατρὶς ἄρουρα·
πρῶτον γάρ μιν ἑλοῦσα γαλῆ μέσσον διέβρυξεν.
 τοῦ δὲ καὶ ἀμφιδρυφὴς ἄλοχος οἴκωι
  ἐλέλειπτο,
τρ]ωγλαίωι {ἐν} θαλάμωι, φρεσὶν αἱμύλα πόλλ'
  εἰδυῖα,
Κνι]σέωνος θ[υ]γάτη[ρ]· καὶ ἐλίσσετο πολλάκι
 Τρῖξον·
10 "μῦ]ς μῆν[α]ντα γαλῆς, ἀλλ' ἐμ μύεσσι γεγώνει."
.....(.)] δ' ἄγγελ[ος] ἦλθε θέ[ω]ν ποσὶ
  καρπαλίμοισι
Ἀρ]π[αγίδ]ης, ὃς ἔν[α]ιε Μυ..[....]ν ἐνὶ δήμωι,
καί [μι]ν φωνήσας ἔπεα πτερ[όε]ντα προσηύ[δα·
"τέθ]νηκεν δὴ Τρῖξο[ς] ἀμύμω[ν ἐ]ν πολέμοισιν."
15 ἣ δ' ὀξὺ] στενάχουσα παρειάς τ' ἀ[μφί] τε
  χαίτας

258

THE BATTLE OF THE WEASEL
AND THE MICE

Michigan papyrus (second–first century BC)

[Tell me, Muse,] of how the contention of chilling war [came upon the mice, and they made a un]ited stand against a weasel . . . fought in the front . . . Squeakos. He was the finest filcher of [tri]pe among the mice, but his native soil did not receive him back again; for he was the first that the weasel seized and crunched through the middle.

His grieving wife was left at home[7] in their [h]oley chamber, that creature of much cunning, the daughter of [Grav]yon; and often she used to beseech Squeakos, "[As a mou]se, speak aloud among mice, not in front of a weasel." [. . .] came running on swift feet to bring the news, the so[n of Filcher], who dwelt in the parish of the My. . .ans,[8] and he addressed her in winged words: "Noble Squeakos has [d]ied in battle."

She, [shrilly] lamenting, [began to tear at] her cheeks

[7] Parody of *Iliad* 2.700 on the widow of Protesilaos, the first Greek to be killed in the Trojan War.

[8] Perhaps a heroic community such as "Mycenaeans" (compare 51), or perhaps a comic name based on "Mouse."

Suppl. Burkert, Schibli, West
7 αλοχωι pap.   οἴκοι Schibli
8]ωγιαιωι pap.

δρύπτετο, κ]αὶ ṿ ͎.[.] πόσιν ἀφ[ραίνουσα
προσηύδα·
".[......]δε ἔπη ζεύγνν κλ[..] ̣ροṇα μο[υ]σαν
ων[.......(.)]ειρε χαλινοὺς εἰς φ[ρέ]νας ἁμάς."
    οἳ μ[έν νυ]ṇ δαίννντο θεοὶ κατὰ [μα]κρὸν
    Ὄλυμπον·
20 ἀ]λλ' ὅ [γ'] ἐπὶ τρασιὴν [ἔκι]εν Κυλλή[ν]ιος
    Ἑρμῆς
τ]ῶν [εὖ β]ρ̣ιθ̣ομ[έ]νων, κạ[..] ̣τ[..]ων ἐξεγένọντο
......(.)... ἀγρ[ο]ῦ σταφυ[λ...] ̣ατ[.]ς ἀνὰ
    πάντ[α]ς
ἀμπελε]ῶṇα λιπόντ[ες, ἐπε]ὶ θεοῦ αἶ[σ]α συνῆγεν
πάντας] ἐπὶ στρατιάν. [το]ὺ̣ς δ' εἴσιδεν αἶψα
    κιόṇ[τας
25 ἀγχίνοο]ς γαλέη, καὶ ἑ[ῶι] προσελέξατο θυμῶι·
"ὤ μοι ἐγώ,] τί ποτ' ἆρ[α] μṹ[ες σ]νṿέλεχθεν
    ἀολλεῖς;
δειμαίν]ῳ, μή ποṿ πολ[έμ]ου μέγα νεῖκος ἀέξηι
Ἄρης β]αι[ομ]όροισι μυσὶν [καὶ ἐμ]οὶ περὶ νίκης.
ἀλκῆς] δ[ὴ] καὶ ἔγωγε νέ[ης] ἐμπίπ[λα]μαι ἦτορ
30 .....] ̣χ ̣[.]μενης φοι ̣[..]ληṃε[
....]θα[.] εἰσῆλθε, μέγ[αν] δ̣' ὑπὸ π[νθ]μέν'
    ἐλαίης

(From lines 32–50 only a few letters survive.)

51 ο]ἳ̣ Σπάρτην ἐνέμοντο Πύλου θ' ἱ̣[ερ]ὸν
    πτολ[ίεθρον·

and her hair ro[und ab]out, and, ins[ane with grief, . . . ad-dressed] her husband:

". . . harness words . . . bridle upon my wits."

The gods meanwhile were feasting on long Olympus; but Cyllenian Hermes [wen]t onto the cheese rack, one of the [well l]aden ones, and . . . they came out . . . of the field . . . [grape clu]sters . . . over all the . . ., leaving the [vineya]rd, for divine destiny was bringing them [all] to-gether for the march to battle. They were quickly seen as they went forth by the [clever] weasel, and it spoke to its heart:

"[O alas,] why have the mi[ce] all gathered together? [I am afraid that Ares] may perhaps be fomenting a great battle contention for victory between the b[rief-d]oomed mice and m[yself]. Well, I too find my heart filled with ne[w valor . . ."

. . . it went into the . . ., and [concealed itself] under a large olive trunk . . .

. . . .

. . . those who dwelt in Sparta and Pylos' h[ol]y city; for

---

27 μητου pap.

οὔτε γὰρ εἰς πλίνθους οὔτ᾽ εἰς ὀρ[ο]φὴ[ν]
   ἀν[έβαινον,
ἀλλ᾽ ἐν ἀρουραίοις πεδίοις ἐνέμοντ̣[ο κ]ᾳ̣ὶ̣ ὕ[λαις.
οὗτοι ἄρ᾽ ἠγερέθοντο γαλῆ[ς] ἐ̣ς̣ φύλο[πι]ν̣
   αἰ[νήν.
55   τοῖσι δὲ καὶ μετέειπε Μυ[λ]εύς, ὃς [π]ᾶ̣σι
     δ[ίκαζεν·
ἦν γάρ τ᾽ οὐδὲ πόδεσ‹σ›ιν ἔτ̣᾽ ἄρτιος, ἀλλὰ
   ν̣ο̣ή[μων,
τοῖσι δ᾽ ἐνέπρεπε πᾶσι, παλαι̣ά̣ τ̣ε̣ π̣[ολλά τε
   εἰδώς·
ὅ σφ[ι]ν̣ ἔϋ φρονέων ἀγορήσατο κ̣α̣ὶ [μετέειπεν·
"ἦ δὴ ἐγὼ τάδ[ε π]ά̣ν̣τ̣α, μύες, π̣ᾳ̣[ρὰ πατρὸς
   ἄκουσα
60   ἡμετέρου· κ̣εῖν[ο]ς δ̣[. . . .]λακ[

ΒΑΤΡΑΧΟΜΥΟΜΑΧΙΑ

TESTIMONIA

Mart. *Epigr.* 14.183, *Homeri Batrachomachia*

Perlege Maeonio cantatas carmine ranas,
   et frontem nugis soluere disce meis.

Stat. praef. ad *Silv.* 1

Sed et Culicem legimus et Batrachomachiam etiam ag-
noscimus, nec quisquam est inlustrium poetarum qui non

they did not [seek their homes] among bricks or roofed building, but lived in the farm fields and the w[oodland]. These it was, then, that assembled for the fierce war of the weasel.[9]

Among them spoke Mi[ll]er, who [used to judge] all their d[isputes: he was no longer sound of foot, but he was int[elligent], and stood out among them all for his long and w[ide experience]. He addressed them with kind counsel and [spoke among them]:

"All about this matter, O mice, I [learned fr]om my [father]. He . . . "[10]

THE BATTLE OF FROGS AND MICE

TESTIMONIA

Martial, *Epigrams,* "Homer's Battle of Frogs"

Read the tale of the frogs as poetically narrated in Maeonian song and learn to smile at my trifles.

Statius, Preface to the *Siluae*

But we read the (Virgilian) *Culex,* and we acknowledge the *Battle of Frogs* too; there is none of the famous poets who

---

[9] The preceding lines parodied the Homeric Catalogue of Ships.

[10] Presumably what this wise elder had from his father was either a prophecy relating to the present conflict (compare *Odyssey* 8.564 ff., 13.172 ff.) or the memory of an older battle with a weasel that held useful lessons.

---

59 ἤ(ι)δη . . . ἀκούσας Burkert, Merkelbach

aliquid operibus suis stilo remissiore praeluserit.

Ps.-Herod. *Vita Homeri* 24

καὶ τοὺς Κέρκωπας καὶ Βατραχομαχίαν καὶ Ψαρομα-
χίην καὶ Ἐπταπακτικὴν καὶ Ἐπικιχλίδας καὶ τἆλλα
πάντα ὅσα παίγνιά ἐστιν Ὁμήρου ἐνταῦθα ἐποίησε
παρὰ τῶι Χίωι ἐν Βολισσῶι.

Ps.-Plut. *Vita Homeri* 1.5

ἔγραψε δὲ ποιήματα δύο, Ἰλιάδα καὶ Ὀδύσσειαν· ὡς
δέ τινες, οὐκ ἀληθῶς λέγοντες, γυμνασίας καὶ παιδιᾶς
ἕνεκα καὶ Βατραχομυομαχίαν προσθεὶς καὶ Μαργί-
την.

See also other references in the Lives of Homer edited in this
volume: Proclus (9); Hesychius (6); also *Suda* π 1551 (above,
Testimonia to *Margites*).

TEXT

Ἀρχόμενος πρώτης σελίδος χορὸν ἐξ Ἑλικῶνος
ἐλθεῖν εἰς ἐμὸν ἦτορ ἐπεύχομαι εἵνεκ' ἀοιδῆς,
ἣν νέον ἐν δέλτοισιν ἐμοῖς ἐπὶ γούνασι θῆκα,
δῆριν ἀπειρεσίην, πολεμόκλονον ἔργον Ἄρηος,
5   εὐχόμενος μερόπεσσιν ἐς οὔατα πᾶσι βαλέσθαι,
πῶς μύες ἐν βατράχοισιν ἀριστεύσαντες ἔβησαν,
γηγενέων ἀνδρῶν μιμούμενοι ἔργα Γιγάντων,
ὡς λόγος ἐν θνητοῖσιν ἔην· τοίην δ' ἔχεν ἀρχήν.

has not prefaced his works with something in a lighter style.

Pseudo-Herodotus, *Life of Homer*

And the *Cercopes,* the *Battle of Frogs,* the *Battle of Starlings,* the *Heptapaktike,* the *Epikichlides,* and the rest of Homer's fun poems, he composed there in the Chian's house at Bolissos.

Pseudo-Plutarch, *Life of Homer*

He wrote two poems, the *Iliad* and the *Odyssey*; and as some say—incorrectly—he added the *Battle of Frogs and Mice* and *Margites* by way of exercise and light relief.

TEXT

As I begin on my first column, I pray for the chorus from Helicon[11] to come into my heart for the song that I have just set down in tablets on my knees,[12] bidding to bring that boundless conflict, the war-rousing work of Ares, to the ears of all mortals: how the mice went triumphant among the frogs, emulating the deeds of those earthborn men, the Giants, as the tale was told among men. And this is how it began.

[11] The Muses.
[12] An echo of Callimachus' prologue to the *Aetia*, fr. 1.21.

---

1 πρώτης σελίδος Z: πρῶτον Μουσῶν *al*

μῦς ποτε διψαλέος, γαλέης κίνδυνον ἀλύξας
10 πλησίον, ἐν λίμνηι λίχνον προσέθηκε γένειον,
ὕδατι τερπόμενος μελιηδέϊ· τὸν δὲ κατεῖδεν
λιμνόχαρις πολύφημος, ἔπος δ' ἐφθέγξατο τοῖον·
"ξεῖνε, τίς εἶ; πόθεν ἦλθες ἐπ' ἠιόνα; τίς δέ σ'
ὁ φύσας;
πάντα δ' ἀλήθευσον, μὴ ψευδόμενόν σε νοήσω.
15 εἰ γάρ σε γνοίην φίλον ἄξιον, ἐς δόμον ἄξω,
δῶρα δέ τοι δώσω ξεινήϊα πολλὰ καὶ ἐσθλά.
εἰμὶ δ' ἐγὼ βασιλεὺς Φυσίγναθος, ὃς κατὰ
λίμνην
τιμῶμαι βατράχων ἡγούμενος ἤματα πάντα·
καί με πατὴρ Πηλεὺς ἀνεθρέψατο, Ὑδρομεδούσηι
20 μιχθεὶς ἐν φιλότητι παρ' ὄχθας Ἠριδανοῖο.
21 καὶ σὲ δ' ὁρῶ καλόν τε καὶ ἄλκιμον ἔξοχον
ἄλλων."
24 τὸν δ' αὖ Ψιχάρπαξ ἀπαμείβετο φώνησέν τε·
25 "τίπτε γένος τοὐμὸν ζητεῖς; τὸ δὲ δῆλον ἅπασιν.
27 Ψιχάρπαξ μὲν ἐγὼ κικλήσκομαι· εἰμὶ δὲ κοῦρος
Τρωξάρταο πατρὸς μεγαλήτορος· ἡ δέ νυ μήτηρ
Λειχομύλη, θυγάτηρ Πτερνοτρώκτου βασιλῆος.
30 γείνατο δ' ἐν Καλύβηι με καὶ ἐξεθρέψατο
βρωτοῖς,
σύκοις καὶ καρύοις καὶ ἐδέσμασι παντοδαποῖσιν.
πῶς δὲ φίλον ποιῆι με, τὸν εἰς φύσιν οὐδὲν
ὁμοῖον;
σοὶ μὲν γὰρ βίος ἐστὶν ἐν ὕδασιν· αὐτὰρ ἐμοί γε

A mouse one day, thirsty after escaping the close danger of a weasel, set his greedy mouth to a pool, delighting in the honey-sweet water. A pooljoy of much renown saw him, and made utterance thus:

"Who are you, stranger? Whence come you to the strand? Who is he that begot you? Tell me everything truly, and let me not find you lying; for if I should judge you a worthy friend, I will take you to my home and give you many fine guest-gifts. I am king Puffjawe, who am honored across the pool as leader of the frogs for ever; the father who raised me was Mudfred,[13] who united in love with Aquareine by the banks of Eridanos. You too I perceive to be one outstanding for nobility and valor."

Filchcrumbe answered him and said: "Why do you inquire into my family? It is no secret: I am called Filchcrumbe, and I am the son of a heroic father, Champbread, while my mother is Lickmill, daughter of king Hamchamper. She bore me in Cottage,[14] and raised me on foodstuffs, figs, walnuts, eatables of every sort. But how can you make me your friend, who am quite unlike you in nature? You live in the waters, whereas my way is to eat

[13] The heroic name Peleus is here used with a play on the unrelated word *pelos* "mud."

[14] *Kalybe* "cottage", a typical habitat for mice, is here made into the name of a city, echoing the Homeric Alybe.

20 Ἠριδανοῖο *a*Z: ὠκεανοῖο *l*
22–23 interpolatio in *l*
26 interpolatio in JF

ὅσσα παρ' ἀνθρώποις τρώγειν ἔθος· οὔ τί με
λήθει
35 ἄρτος δισκοπάνιστος ἀπ' εὐκύκλου κανέοιο,
οὐδὲ πλακοῦς τανύπεπλος ἔχων πολὺ
σησαμότυρον,
οὐ τόμος ἐκ πτέρνης, οὐχ ἥπατα λευκοχίτωνα,
οὐ τυρὸς νεόπηκτος ἀπὸ γλυκεροῖο γάλακτος,
οὐ χρηστὸν μελίτωμα, τὸ καὶ μάκαρες
ποθέουσιν,
40 οὐδ' ὅσα πρὸς θοίνας μερόπων τεύχουσι
μάγειροι
κοσμοῦντες χύτρας ἀρτύμασι παντοδαποῖσιν.
53 οὐ τρώγω ῥαφάνους, οὐ κράμβας, οὐ κολοκύντας,
οὐδὲ πράσοις χλωροῖς ἐπιβόσκομαι, οὐδὲ
σελίνοις·
55 ταῦτα γὰρ ὑμέτερ' ἐστὶν ἐδέσματα τῶν κατὰ
λίμνην."
πρὸς τάδε μειδήσας Φυσίγναθος ἀντίον ηὔδα·
"ξεῖνε, λίην αὐχεῖς ἐπὶ γαστέρι· ἔστι καὶ ἡμῖν
πολλὰ γὰρ ἐν λίμνηι καὶ ἐπὶ χθονὶ θαύματ'
ἰδέσθαι.
ἀμφίβιον γὰρ ἔδωκε νομὴν βατράχοισι Κρονίων,
60 σκιρτῆσαι κατὰ γαῖαν, ἐν ὕδασι σῶμα καλύψαι.
62 εἰ δ' ἐθέλεις καὶ ταῦτα δαήμεναι, εὐχερές ἐστιν·
βαῖνέ μοι ἐν νώτοισι, κράτει δέ με μή ποτ'
ὀλίσθηις,
ὅππως γηθόσυνος τὸν ἐμὸν δόμον εἰσαφίκηαι."

whatever men do: I never miss the double-milled bread from the circular basket, or the bun well coated with sesame and cheese, or the slice of ham, or the liver white-dressed with tripe, or the cheese new-set from sweet milk, or the good honeycake that even the blessed gods crave, or whatever cooks prepare for mortal feasts, decking their dishes with condiments of every sort. I eat no radishes, no cabbages, no marrows, nor do I feed on green leeks or celery: these are the foods of you pool-dwellers."

Puffjawe smiled at this and replied: "Stranger, you make too much of your stomach. We too have many wonderful things to see, in the pool and on land. For the son of Kronos has given frogs an amphibious life, to hop on land, to hide in the waters. If you care to learn about it, it is easily done. Climb on my back, and hold on to me in case you slip off, so that you may come in gladness to my home."

42–52 interpolatio in *l*
61 interpolatio in *a*Z

65   ὣς ἄρ᾽ ἔφη, καὶ νῶτ᾽ ἐδίδου· ὁ δ᾽ ἔβαινε
   τάχιστα,
  χεῖρας ἔχων ἁπαλοῖο κατ᾽ αὐχένος ἅμματι
   κούφωι.

78   οὐχ οὕτω νώτοισιν ἐβάστασε φόρτον ἔρωτος
  ταῦρος, ὅτ᾽ Εὐρώπην διὰ κύματος ἦγ᾽ ἐπὶ
   Κρήτην,
  ὡς μῦν ὑψώσας ἐπινώτιον ἦγεν ἐς οἶκον
81   βάτραχος ἁπλώσας ὠχρὸν δέμας ὕδατι λευκῶι.

67   καὶ τὸ πρῶτον ἔχαιρεν, ὅτ᾽ ἔβλεπε γείτονας
   ὅρμους,
  νήξει τερπόμενος Φυσιγνάθου· ἀλλ᾽ ὅτε δή ῥα
  κύμασι πορφυρέοισιν ἐκλύζετο, πολλὰ δακρύων
70   ἄχρηστον μετάνοιαν ἐμέμφετο, τίλλε δὲ χαίτας,
  καὶ πόδας ἔσφιγγεν κατὰ γαστέρος, ἐν δέ οἱ
   ἦτορ
  πάλλετ᾽ ἀηθείηι, καὶ ἐπὶ χθόνα βούλεθ᾽ ἱκέσθαι·
  δεινὰ δ᾽ ὑπεστονάχιζε φόβου κρυόεντος ἀνάγκηι.
  {οὐρὴν πρῶτ᾽ ἔπλωσεν ἐφ᾽ ὕδασιν ἠΰτε κώπην
75   σύρων, εὐχόμενός τε θεοῖς ἐπὶ γαῖαν ἱκέσθαι·
  ὕδασι πορφυρέοισι δ᾽ ἐκλύζετο, πολλὰ δ᾽
   ἐβώστρει.}

82   ὕδρος δ᾽ ἐξαπίνης ἀνεφαίνετο, πικρὸν ὅραμα
  ἀμφοτέροις, ὀρθὸν δ᾽ ὑπὲρ ὕδατος εἶχε τράχηλον.
  τοῦτον ἰδὼν κατέδυ Φυσίγναθος, οὔ τι νοήσας
85   οἷον ἑταῖρον ἔμελλεν ἀπολλύμενον καταλείπειν·
  δῦ δὲ βάθος λίμνης καὶ ἀλεύατο κῆρα μέλαιναν.
  κεῖνος δ᾽ ὡς ἀφέθη, πέσεν ὕπτιος εὐθὺς ἐφ᾽ ὕδωρ·

With these words he offered his back, and the mouse at once climbed on, clasping his paws lightly round the soft neck. It was not like this that the bull carried his love burden on his back, when he carried Europa through the waves to Crete,[15] not as when the frog raised the mouse on his back and set off to take him home, extending his yellow body on the clear water. At first the mouse enjoyed it, while he could see the landing places nearby, and delighted in Puffjawe's swimming. But when he began to be washed by turbulent waves, with many a tear he cursed his unavailing change of heart, tore his hair, and clenched his feet on the frog's belly; his heart throbbed at the unfamiliar situation, he wanted to make land, and he groaned horribly in the compulsion of icy fear. {At first he sailed trailing his tail on the water like a steering oar, and praying to the gods to make land, but he was being washed by turbulent waves, and uttered many a shout.}

Suddenly a water snake appeared—an unwelcome sight for both of them—rearing its neck erect above the water. Seeing it, Puffjawe dived, not realizing what a comrade he would be leaving behind to perish; he dived to the depths of the pool and so avoided a dark fate. The mouse, cast off, fell backwards straight into the water, {and

[15] The poet alludes to the narrative of Moschus' famous epyllion *Europa*.

78–81 post 66 trai. Ludwich

80 ὑψώσας Althaus: ἁπλώσας codd.

81 ἁπλώσας *a*Z: ὑψώσας *l*   74–76 del. Draheim

74 ἔπλωσεν West: ἔπλασεν, ἤπλωσεν, sim., codd.

77 interpolatio in *a*Z

271

{καὶ χεῖρας ἔσφιγγε καὶ ὀλλύμενος κατέτριζε·}
πολλάκι μὲν κατέδυνεν ὑφ᾽ ὕδατι, πολλάκι δ᾽
    αὖτε
90   λακτίζων ἀνέδυνε· μόρον δ᾽ οὐκ ἦν ὑπαλύξαι·
δευόμεναι δὲ τρίχες πλεῖον βάρος εἷλκον ἐπ᾽
    αὐτῶι.
ὕδασι δ᾽ ὀλλύμενος τοίους ἐφθέγξατο μύθους·
    "οὐ λήσεις γε θεούς, Φυσίγναθε, ταῦτα
    ποιήσας,
ναυηγὸν ῥίψας ἀπὸ σώματος ὡς ἀπὸ πέτρης.
95   οὐκ ἄν μου κατὰ γαῖαν ἀμείνων ἦσθα, κάκιστε,
παγκρατίωι τε πάληι τε καὶ εἰς δρόμον· ἀλλὰ
    πλανήσας
εἰς ὕδωρ μ᾽ ἔρριψας. ἔχει θεὸς ἔκδικον ὄμμα·
ποινὴν αὖ τείσεις σὺ μυῶν στρατῶι, οὐδ᾽
    ὑπαλύξεις."
ὣς εἰπὼν ἀπέπνευσεν ἐν ὕδασι. τὸν δὲ
    κατεῖδεν
100 Λειχοπίναξ, ὄχθηισιν ἐφεζόμενος μαλακῆισιν·
δεινὸν δ᾽ ἐξολόλυξε, δραμὼν δ᾽ ἤγγειλε μύεσσιν·
ὡς δ᾽ ἔμαθον τὴν μοῖραν, ἔδυ χόλος αἰνὸς
    ἅπαντας.
καὶ τότε κηρύκεσσιν ἑοῖς ἐκέλευον ὑπ᾽ ὄρθρον
κηρύσσειν ἀγορὴν ἐς δώματα Τρωξάρταο,
105 πατρὸς δυστήνου Ψιχάρπαγος, ὃς κατὰ λίμνην
ὕπτιος ἐξήπλωτο νεκρὸν δέμας, οὐδὲ παρ᾽ ὄχθας
ἦν ἤδη τλήμων, μέσσωι δ᾽ ἐπενήχετο πόντωι.
ὡς δ᾽ ἦλθον σπεύδοντες ἅμ᾽ ἠοῖ, πρῶτος ἀνέστη

clenched his paws, and squeaked as he perished}. Several times he sank into the water, and several times he surfaced again, kicking, but he could not avoid his doom, and his wet fur weighed him down even more. As he perished in the waters he uttered these words:

"You will not escape the gods' notice, Puffjawe, in doing this, casting me shipwrecked from your body as from a rock. You would not have got the better of me on land, you villain, in the pankration, in wrestling, in running, but you led me astray and cast me into the water. God has an avenging eye: you will pay the penalty to the mouse army, and not escape."

With these words he expired in the waters. But he was seen by Lickplatter, who was sitting on the grassy banks. With a fearful shriek, he ran to tell the mice. When they heard what had befallen, they were all filled with anger. Then they instructed their heralds to summon an assembly at first light at the house of Champbread, the father of the unfortunate Filchcrumbe, whose dead body was stretched out belly-up in the pool; no more was the poor creature to be found on the banks, but floating out at sea. When they came hastening at dawn, Champbread was the first to rise,

---

88 del. Althaus

89 ὑφ' rec.: ἐφ' codd. (ἐν J)

98 ποινὴν αὖ τίσεις σὺ Barnes: ποινὴν σὺ τίσεις l, τοῖς τίσουσί σε a, ⟦τοῖς τίσουσι⟧ Z

Τρωξάρτης ἐπὶ παιδὶ χολούμενος, εἶπέ τε μῦθον·

110   "ὦ φίλοι, εἰ καὶ μοῦνος ἐγὼ κακὰ πολλὰ
πέπονθα

ἐκ βατράχων, ἡ πεῖρα κακὴ πάντεσσι τέτυκται.

εἰμὶ δὲ νῦν ἐλεεινός, ἐπεὶ τρεῖς παῖδας ὄλεσσα·

καὶ τὸν μὲν πρῶτόν γε κατέκτανεν ἁρπάξασα

ἐχθίστη γαλέη, τρώγλης ἔκτοσθεν ἑλοῦσα,

115 τὸν δ᾽ ἄλλον πάλιν ἄνδρες ἀπηνέες ἐς μόρον
εἷλξαν

καινοτέραις τέχναις, ξύλινον δόλον ἐξευρόντες,

ἣν παγίδα κλείουσι, μυῶν ὀλέτειραν ἐοῦσαν·

ὃς δ᾽ ἔτ᾽ ἔην ἀγαπητὸς ἐμοὶ καὶ μητέρι κεδνῇ,

τοῦτον ἀπέπνιξεν βάτραχος κακὸς ἐς βυθὸν
ἄιξας.

120 ἀλλ᾽ ἄγεθ᾽ ὁπλίζεσθε καὶ ἐξέλθωμεν ἐπ᾽ αὐτούς."

122   ταῦτ᾽ εἰπὼν ἀνέπεισε καθοπλίζεσθαι ἅπαντας.

124 κνημῖδας μὲν πρῶτον ἐφήρμοσαν, εἰς δύο μοίρας

125 ῥήξαντες κυάμους χλωρούς, εὖ δ᾽ ἀσκήσαντες,

οὓς αὐτοὶ διὰ νυκτὸς ἐπιστάντες κατέτρωξαν.

θώρηκας δ᾽ εἶχον καλαμορραφέων ἀπὸ βυρσῶν,

οὓς γαλέην δείραντες ἐπισταμένως ἐποίησαν.

ἀσπὶς δ᾽ ἦν λύχνου τὸ μεσόμφαλον· ἡ δέ νυ
λόγχη

130 εὐμήκης βελόνη, παγχάλκεον ἔργον Ἄρηος·

ἡ δὲ κόρυς τὸ λέπυρον ἐπὶ κροτάφοις ἐρεβίνθου.

    οὕτω μὲν μύες ἦσαν ἐν ὅπλοις· ὡς δ᾽ ἐνόησαν

βάτραχοι, ἐξανέδυσαν ἀφ᾽ ὕδατος, εἰς δ᾽ ἕνα
χῶρον

angered about his son, and spoke thus:

"Friends, even though I alone have suffered grievous wrong from the frogs, this is a foretaste of evil for us all. I am now pitiable indeed, as I have lost three sons. The first was seized and killed by a most hateful weasel who caught him outside our hole; the second was lured to his doom with newfangled arts by cruel men who invented a wooden trap that they call a deadfall, being a destroyer of mice;[16] and the one that still remained, beloved by me and his good mother, has been drowned by an evil frog darting into the depths. So come, arm yourselves, and let us go forth against them."

With these words he persuaded them all to arm themselves. First they fitted on greaves, breaking in half and fashioning well the green bean pods that they had set upon and gnawed during the night. They had corslets from straw-sewn hides that they had made skilfully after skinning a weasel. Their shield was the bossed lid of a lamp; their spear a long needle, bronze work of the War god; and the helmet on their heads the husk of a chickpea.

So the mice were in arms; and when the frogs saw it, they came up out of the water and gathered in one place

[16] Another echo of Callimachus' *Aetia*: fr. 177.16–17.

---

117 κλείουσι Ludwich: καλέουσι codd.

118 ὃς δ᾽ ἔτ᾽ ἔην West: (ὁ) τρίτος (δ᾽) ἦν codd.

121 , 123 interpolationes in *l*   124 ἐφήρμοσαν εἰς δύο μηροὺς Z*l* (μοίρας Barnes): περὶ κνήμησιν ἔθεντο *a*

127 καλαμορραφέων Herwerden: καλαμοστεφέων *a*, καλῶν εὐτρεφέων *l* (-τραφ- Z in ras.)

132 ἐν ὅπλοις Barnes: ἔνοπλοι codd.

ἐλθόντες βουλὴν ξύναγον πολέμοιο κακοῖο.
135 σκεπτομένων δ' αὐτῶν πόθεν ἡ στάσις ἢ τίς ὁ
μῦθος,
κῆρυξ ἐγγύθεν ἦλθε φέρων ῥάβδον μετὰ χερσίν,
Τυρογλύφου υἱὸς μεγαλήτορος Ἐμβασίχυτρος,
ἀγγέλλων πολέμοιο κακὴν φάτιν, εἶπέ τε τοῖα·
"ὦ βάτραχοι, μύες ὕμμιν ἀπειλήσαντες
ἔπεμψαν
140 εἰπεῖν ὁπλίζεσθαι ἐπὶ πτόλεμόν τε μάχην τε.
εἶδον γὰρ καθ' ὕδωρ Ψιχάρπαγα, τόν περ
ἔπεφνεν
ὑμέτερος βασιλεὺς Φυσίγναθος. ἀλλὰ μάχεσθε,
οἵ τινες ἐν βατράχοισιν ἀριστῆες γεγάατε."
ὣς εἰπὼν ἀπέφηνε· λόγος δ' εἰς οὔατα πάντων
145 εἰσελθὼν ἐτάραξε φρένας βατράχων ἀγερώχων.
μεμφομένων δ' αὐτῶν Φυσίγναθος εἶπεν
ἀναστάς·
"ὦ φίλοι, οὐκ ἔκτεινον ἐγὼ μῦν, οὐδὲ κατεῖδον
ὀλλύμενον· πάντως δ' ἐπνίγη παίζων παρὰ
λίμνην,
νήξεις τὰς βατράχων μιμούμενος· οἱ δὲ κάκιστοι
150 νῦν ἐμὲ μέμφονται τὸν ἀναίτιον. ἀλλ' ἄγε
βουλήν
ζητήσωμεν, ὅπως δολίους μύας ἐξολέσωμεν.
τοιγὰρ ἐγὼν ἐρέω, ὥς μοι δοκεῖ εἶναι ἄριστα·
σώματα κοσμήσαντες ἐν ὅπλοις στῶμεν ἄπαντες
ἄκροις πὰρ χείλεσσιν, ὅπου κατάκρημνος ὁ
χῶρος·

for a council of woeful war. As they were enquiring what was the source of dissension, or what the word was, a herald approached bearing a rod in his hands, the son of the hero Cheesegraver, Paddlepot, bringing the woeful declaration of war, and he said:

"O frogs, the mice challenge you and send me to tell you to arm yourselves for battle. For they have seen Filch-crumbe in the water, whom your king Puffjawe has slain. So prepare to fight, whichever of you are the champions among the frogs."

So he made his declaration; and his words entered the ears of all the doughty frogs and disturbed their spirits. As they criticized him, Puffjawe arose and said:

"Friends, I did not kill the mouse or see him perish. He surely drowned while fooling about at the poolside, trying to swim like the frogs. And now the villains are blaming me, who am innocent. Well then, let us look for a plan to destroy these crafty mice. I will tell you what seems best to me. Let us all array ourselves in armor and take our stand on the edge of the bank, where the ground is precipitous,

---

141 τόν Brandt: ὄν codd.

155 ἡνίκα δ᾽ ὁρμηθέντες ἐφ᾽ ἡμέας ἐξέλθωσιν,
δραξάμενοι κορύθων, ὅς τις σχεδὸν ἀντίος ἔλθῃ,
ἐς λίμνην αὐτοὺς σὺν ἐκείνωι εὐθὺ βάλωμεν.
οὕτω γὰρ πνίξαντες ἐν ὕδασι τοὺς ἀκολύμβους
στήσομεν εὐθύμως τὸ μυοκτόνον ὧδε τρόπαιον."

160 ὣς εἰπὼν συνέπεισε καθοπλίζεσθαι ἅπαντας.
φύλλοις μὲν μαλαχῶν ἀμφὶ κνήμας ἐκάλυψαν,
θώρηκας δ᾽ εἶχον καλοὺς χλοερῶν ἀπὸ σεύτλων,
φύλλα δὲ τῶν κραμβῶν εἰς ἀσπίδας εὖ ἤσκησαν,
ἔγχος δ᾽ ὀξύσχοινος ἑκάστωι μακρὸς ἀρήρει,

165 καὶ κόρυθες κοχλιῶν λεπτῶν ἐκάλυπτε κάρηνα.
φραξάμενοι δ᾽ ἔστησαν ἐπ᾽ ὄχθῃς ὑψηλῇσιν
σείοντες λόγχας, θυμοῦ δ᾽ ἔμπληντο ἕκαστος.

Ζεὺς δὲ θεοὺς καλέσας εἰς οὐρανὸν ἀστερόεντα
καὶ πολέμου πληθὺν δείξας κρατερούς τε μαχητάς

170 πολλοὺς καὶ μεγάλους ἠδ᾽ ἔγχεα μακρὰ φέροντας,
οἷος Κενταύρων στρατὸς ἔρχεται ἠὲ Γιγάντων,
ἡδὺ γελῶν ἐρέεινε, τίνες βατράχοισιν ἀρωγοί
ἢ μυσὶν ἀθανάτων, καὶ Ἀθηναίην προσέειπεν·
"ὦ θύγατερ, μυσὶν ἦ ῥ᾽ ἀπαλεξήσουσα
πορεύσῃι;

175 καὶ γὰρ σοῦ κατὰ νηὸν ἀεὶ σκιρτῶσιν ἅπαντες
κνίσῃι τερπόμενοι καὶ ἐδέσμασι παντοδαποῖσιν."

161 ἀμφὶ κνήμας Ludwich (ἀμφὶ δὲ κν. rec.): κνήμας ἀμφ-
codd.
162 καλῶν χλοερῶν aZ (καλοὺς West): χλωρῶν πλατέων l

and when they come out and attack us, let us seize by the helmet whoever comes up close and throw them straight into the pool to join Filchcrumbe. So we shall drown those nonswimmers in the waters, and in good heart we will set up here the trophy to commemorate the killing of the mice."

With these words he persuaded them all to arm themselves. They covered their shanks in mallow leaves; they had fine corslets from green mangelwurzels; they fashioned cabbage leaves well into shields; each had a long needle-rush held firm for a spear; and helmets from thin snail shells protected their heads. On guard, they took their stand upon the high banks, brandishing their spears, and each one full of spirit.

Zeus called the gods to the starry heaven, and pointing out the massing for battle and the hardy warriors, big and numerous and carrying long spears, much as the Centaurs' or the Giants' army goes forth, he laughed amiably and asked which of the immortals were aiding the frogs or the mice, and he addressed Athena:

"Daughter, are you going to go to defend the mice? They are always skipping about your temple, enjoying the savor of the sacrifical meat and the eatables of every sort."

ὡς ἄρ᾽ ἔφη Κρονίδης· τὸν δὲ προσέειπεν Ἀθήνη·
"ὦ πάτερ, οὐκ ἄν πώ ποτ᾽ ἐγὼ μυσὶ τειρομένοισιν
ἐλθοίμην ἐπαρωγός, ἐπεὶ κακὰ πολλά μ᾽ ἔοργαν
180 στέμματα βλάπτοντες καὶ λύχνους εἵνεκ᾽ ἐλαίου.
τοῦτο δέ μοι λίην ἔδακε φρένας, οἷον ἔρεξαν·
πέπλον μου κατέτρωξαν, ὃν ἐξύφηνα καμοῦσα
ἐκ ῥοδάνης λεπτῆς καὶ στήμονα μακρὸν ἔνησα,
καὶ τρώγλας ἐτέλεσσαν· ὁ δ᾽ ἠπητής μοι ἐπέστη,
185 καὶ πράσσει με τόκον· τό γε ῥίγιον ἀθανάτοισιν·
χρησαμένη γὰρ ἔνησα, καὶ οὐκ ἔχω ἀνταποδοῦναι.
ἀλλ᾽ οὐδ᾽ ὣς βατράχοισιν ἀρηγέμεν οὐκ ἐθελήσω·
εἰσὶ γὰρ οὐδ᾽ αὐτοὶ φρένας ἔμπεδοι, ἀλλά με
      πρώιην
ἐκ πολέμου ἀνιοῦσαν, ἐπεὶ λίην ἐκοπώθην,
190 ὕπνου δευομένην οὐκ εἴασαν θορυβοῦντες
οὐδ᾽ ὀλίγον καταμῦσαι· ἐγὼ δ᾽ ἄυπνος κατεκείμην
τὴν κεφαλὴν ἀλγοῦσα, ἕως ἐβόησεν ἀλέκτωρ.
ἀλλ᾽ ἄγε παυσώμεσθα, θεοί, τούτοισιν ἀρήγειν,
μή κέ τις ὑμείων τρωθῆι βέλει ὀξυόεντι·
195 εἰσὶ γὰρ ἀγχέμαχοι, εἰ καὶ θεὸς ἀντίον ἔλθοι·
πάντες δ᾽ οὐρανόθεν τερπώμεθα δῆριν ὁρῶντες."
ὣς ἄρ᾽ ἔφη· τῆι δ᾽ αὖτ᾽ ἐπεπείθοντο θεοὶ ἄλλοι.
   πάντες δ᾽ αὖτ᾽ εἰσῆλθον ἀολλέες εἰς ἕνα χῶρον·
καὶ τότε κώνωπες μεγάλας σάλπιγγας ἔχοντες

So said the son of Kronos, but Athena answered him: "Father, I would never go to aid the mice in their distress; they have done me much harm, damaging my garlands and my lamps on account of the oil.[17] And I was particularly stung by this that they did: they chewed up my robe that I wove with much effort from a fine woof, and I had spun a long warp for it, and they made holes; and the sempster is at my door extorting interest payments—a horrid thing for immortals to put up with—because I borrowed for my spinning, and I can't pay it back. Even so, I won't be wanting to help the frogs, for they're not sensible creatures either. The other day when I came back from battle, worn out and needing to sleep, they wouldn't let me close my eyes even for a little with their racket; I lay there sleepless with an aching head till the cock crowed. So, gods, let's forget about aiding these creatures, in case one of you gets wounded by a sharp missile: they are close fighters, even if a god should come against them. Let's all just enjoy watching the battle from heaven." So she spoke, and the other gods went along with her advice.

All the combatants came in together to one place, and then mosquitoes with big trumpets sounded the signal for

[17] A further echo of Callimachus' *Aetia*: fr. 177.22.

200 δεινὸν ἐσάλπιγξαν πολέμου κτύπον· οὐρανόθεν δέ
Ζεὺς Κρονίδης βρόντησε, τέρας πολέμοιο κακοῖο.
πρῶτος δ' Ὑψιβόας Λειχήνορα οὔτασε δουρί
ἑσταότ' ἐν προμάχοις κατὰ γαστέρα ἐς μέσον
ἧπαρ·
κὰδ δ' ἔπεσε πρηνής, ἁπαλὰς δ' ἐκόνισεν ἐθείρας.
206 Τρωγλοδύτης δὲ μετ' αὐτὸν ἀκόντισε
Πηλείωνος,
πῆξεν δ' ἐν στέρνωι στιβαρὸν δόρυ· τὸν δὲ
πεσόντα
εἷλε μέλας θάνατος, ψυχὴ δ' ἐκ σώματος ἔπτη·
Σευτλαῖον δ' ἄρ' ἔπεφνε βαλὼν κέαρ
Ἐμβασίχυτρος.
214 Ὠκιμίδην δ' ἄχος εἷλε, καὶ ἤλασεν ὀξέϊ σχοίνωι
213 Τρωγλοδύτην ἁπαλοῖο δι' αὐχένος, ἤριπε δ' εὐθύς·
215 οὐδ' ἐξέσπασεν ἔγχος, ἐναντίβιον δ' ἐνόησεν
218 Κρουστοφάγον φεύγοντα· βαθείαις δ' ἔμπεσεν
ὄχθαις,
ἀλλ' οὐδ' ὣς ἀπέληγεν ἐν ὕδασιν· ἤλασε δ' αὐτόν.
220 κάππεσε δ', οὐδ' ἀνένευσεν, ἐβάπτετο δ' αἵματι
λίμνη
πορφυρέωι· αὐτὸς δὲ παρ' ἠιόν' ἐξετανύσθη.
†χορδῇσιν λιπαρῇσί τ' ἐπορνυμένου λαγόνεσσιν†

the dread battle clash, while from heaven Zeus the son of Kronos thundered as a portent of woeful war.

First Loudhaylor hit Lickhart with his spear as he stood in the front line, getting him in the belly, right in the liver, and he fell headlong, defiling his gentle whiskers in the dust.

After him, Creephole aimed a lance at MacMudd, and fixed his stout spear in his chest: he fell, the darkness of death seized him, and his soul flew forth from his body. And Mangelwurzel was hit in the heart and killed by Paddlepot.

MacBasil was seized by grief, and with his sharp reed he struck Creephole through his tender neck, and he collapsed at once. He had not pulled his spear out again, when he saw Pastrygobble running towards him in flight: he had fallen down the steep banks, but he kept going even in the water. He struck him, and he fell down, he did not swim up again, and the pool was tinged with his crimson blood, while his body was stretched out on the strand. †As he rushed at the guts and the sleek flanks.†[18] And Cheese-

---

[18] This line, if genuine, is clearly out of place.

---

205 interpolatio in *l*
210–212 interpolatio in *l*
214–213 hoc ordine *a*(Z); 214 om. *l*
215 ἐναντίβιον West: ἐναντίον ὡς codd.
216–217 interpolatio in *l*
218 Κρουστοφάγον West: Κουστο- *a*Z: Κραμβο- *l*
220 οὐδ' Barnes: οὐκ codd.
222 huius loci alienus; deest in *l*

Τυροφάγον δ᾽ αὐτῇσιν ἐπ᾽ ὄχθῃς ἐξενάριξεν.
   Πτερνογλύφον δὲ ἰδὼν Καλαμίνθιος εἰς φόβον
      ἦλθεν,
225 ἤλατο δ᾽ ἐς λίμνην φεύγων, τὴν ἀσπίδα ῥίψας.
   Ὑγραῖον δ᾽ ἀρ᾽ ἔπεφνεν ἀμύμων Ἐμβασίχυτρος,
228 χερμαδίωι πλήξας κατὰ βρέγματος· ἐγκέφαλος δέ
   ἐκ ῥινῶν ἔσταξε, παλάσσετο δ᾽ αἵματι γαῖα.
230   Λειχοπίνακα δ᾽ ἔπεφνεν ἀμύμων
      Βορβοροκοίτης,
   ἔγχει ἐπαΐξας· τὸν δὲ σκότος ὄσσε κάλυψεν·
   Πρασσεῖος δ᾽ ἐσιδὼν ποδὸς εἵλκυσε νεκρὸν ἐόντα,
   ἐν λίμνηι δ᾽ ἀπέπνιξε κρατήσας χειρὶ τένοντα.
    Ψιχάρπαξ δ᾽ ἤμυν᾽ ἑτάρου πέρι τεθνειῶτος,
235 καὶ βάλε Πρασσεῖον μήπω γαίης ἐπιβάντα·
   πίπτε δέ οἱ πρόσθεν, ψυχὴ δ᾽ Ἀϊδόσδε βεβήκει.
   Κραμβοβάτης δ᾽ ἐσιδὼν πηλοῦ δράκα ῥῖψεν ἐπ᾽
      αὐτόν,
   καὶ τὸ μέτωπον ἔχρισε καὶ ἐξετύφλου παρὰ μικρόν·
   θυμώθη δ᾽ ἄρα κεῖνος, ἑλὼν δ᾽ ἄρα χειρὶ παχείηι
240 κείμενον ἐν δαπέδωι λίθον ὄβριμον, ἄχθος
      ἀρούρης,
   τῶι βάλε Κραμβοβάτην ὑπὸ γούνατα· πᾶσα δ᾽
      ἐκλάσθη
   κνήμη δεξιτερή, πέσε δ᾽ ὕπτιος ἐν κονίηισιν.

gobble he slew on the bank itself.

On seeing Hamgraver, Catmint became afraid, and leapt into the pool in flight, throwing down his shield, while Dampfred was slain by the worthy Paddlepot, who hit him on the pate with a boulder; his brain ran out through his nostrils, and the earth was spattered with blood.

Lickplatter was slain by the worthy Sludgecouch, who charged at him with his spear, and darkness covered his eyes. Leekhold on seeing this dragged the dead mouse away by the foot and drowned him in the pool, holding on to his ankle.

Filchcrumbe came to the defence of his dead comrade, and hit Leekhold before he had got back on land: he fell before him, and his soul departed to Hades. Mountcabbage on seeing this hurled a handful of mud at him, which smeared his forehead and nearly blinded him. He was enraged, and taking in his stout hand a formidable stone that was lying on the ground, a burden on the soil, he hit Mountcabbage with it below the knee; his whole right shank was smashed, and he fell on his back in the dust.

---

226 Ὑγραῖον West: Λιτραῖον fere aZ (λιμν- T): Ὑδρόχαρις l in 227, qui est 226 in l refictus

234 ἑτάρου πέρι τεθνειῶτος Z: ἑτάρων . . . -ώτων al

239 θυμώθη recc.: ουνώθη L, μουνώθη JF: ὠργίσθη Z, ὀργισθεὶς a

Κραυγασίδης δ' ἤμυνε καὶ ἰθὺς βαῖνεν ἐπ'
αὐτόν,
τύψε δέ μιν μέσσην κατὰ γαστέρα· πᾶς δέ οἱ
εἴσω
245 ὀξύσχοινος ἔδυνε, χαμαὶ δ' ἔκχυντο ἅπαντα
ἔγκατ' ἐφελκομένωι ὑπὸ δούρατι χειρὶ παχείηι.
Σιτοφάγος δ' ὡς εἶδεν ἐπ' ὄχθηισιν ποταμοῖο,

.   .   .   .

250 Τρωξάρτης δ' ἔβαλεν Φυσίγναθον ἐς ποδὸς
ἄκρον·
ἔσχατος ἐκ λίμνης ἀνεδύσετο, {τείρετο δ' αἰνῶς}

.   .   .   .

248 σκάζων ἐκ πολέμου ἀνεχάζετο, τείρετο δ' αἰνῶς·
249 ἤλατο δ' <αἶψ'> ἐς τάφρον, ὅπως φύγοι αἰπὺν
ὄλεθρον.

.   .   .   .

252 Πρασσαῖος δ' ὡς εἶδεν ἔθ' ἡμίπνοον προπεσόντα,
ἦλθε διὰ προμάχων καὶ ἀκόντισεν ὀξύσχοινον,
οὐδ' ἔρρηξε σάκος, σχέτο δ' αὐτοῦ δουρὸς
ἀκωκή.
255 τοῦ δ' ἔβαλε τρυφάλειαν ἀμύμονα τετραλέπυρον
δῖος Ὀριγανίων, μιμούμενος αὐτὸν Ἄρηα,
ὃς μόνος ἐν βατράχοισιν ἀρίστευεν καθ' ὅμιλον.

.   .   .   .

ὥρμησαν δ' ἄρ' ἐπ' αὐτόν· ὁ δ' ὡς ἴδεν, οὐχ
ὑπέμεινεν
ἥρωας κρατερούς, ἀλλ' ἔνδυ βένθεσι λίμνης.

MacCroak came to the defence and went straight for him. He struck him square in the belly: his needle reed went right inside, and all his entrails dropped out on the ground as he withdrew the spear with his stout hand. When Graingobble saw this on the river bank, . . .[19]

Champbread hit Puffjawe on the tip of his foot: he was the last to come up out of the pool . . . He withdrew limping from the battle, in sore distress, and leapt into the ditch to escape sheer destruction. . . . When Leekhart saw him still advancing half alive, he came through the front line and hurled his needle-reed, but did not break his shield; the spearpoint was held there. But his good four-husk helmet was struck by noble Origano, emulating the very War god; he alone among the frogs was triumphing amid the throng . . . And they went for him. When he saw them, he did not stand against the doughty heroes, but dived into the depths of the pool.

---

[19] The following passage is incoherent at several points and seems to be lacunose.

---

243 ἰθὺς Stadtmüller: αὖθις codd.

244 μιν Wolf: οἱ codd.

247–252 lacunas stat. Ludwich; 250 post 247 trai. Stadtmüller; ut supra West

247 Σιτοφάγος LF: Τρωγλοδύτης aZ: Πρασσοφάγος J

252 ἡμίπνοον Draheim: -πνουν codd.

255 τοῦ δ' recc.: οὐδ' vett.   τετραλέπυρον West: καὶ τετράχυτρον codd. (καὶ om. recc.)

post 257 lac. stat. West

258 ὥρμησαν recc.: -σεν vett.

259 ἔνδυ Weissenfels: ἔδυ fere codd. (ἔνδυνεν Q)

260   ἦν δέ τις ἐν μυσὶν Μεριδάρπαξ, ἔξοχος ἄλλων,
    Κναίσωνος φίλος υἱὸς ἀμύμονος ἀρτεπιβούλου,
    ⟨ὃς . . . . .⟩
    οἴκαδ' ἰών, πολέμου δὲ μετασχεῖν παῖδ' ἐκέλευεν·
264   οὗτος ἀναρπάξαι βατράχων γενεὴν ἐπαπείλει,
263   ἀγχοῦ δ' ἑστήκει μενεαίνων ἶφι μάχεσθαι.
265   καὶ ῥήξας καρύοιο μέσην ῥάχιν εἰς δύο μοίρας
    φράγδην ἀμφοτέροισι κενώμασι χεῖρας ἔθηκεν.

    . . . . . .

    οἱ δὲ τάχος δείσαντες ἔβαν πάντες κατὰ λίμνην.
270   καὶ τότ' ἀπολλυμένους βατράχους ᾤκτιρε
      Κρονίων,
    κινήσας δὲ κάρη τοίην ἐφθέγξατο φωνήν·
    "ὦ πόποι, ἦ μέγα ἔργον ἐν ὀφθαλμοῖσιν ὁρῶμαι·
    {οὐ μικρόν με πλήσσει Μεριδάρπαξ, ὃς κατὰ
      λίμνην}
    Ἅρπαξ ἐν βατράχοισιν ἀμείβεται· ἀλλὰ τάχιστα
275   Παλλάδα πέμψωμεν πολεμόκλονον, ἢ καὶ Ἄρηα,
    οἵ μιν ἐπισχήσουσι μάχης κρατερόν περ ἐόντα."
    ὣς ἄρ' ἔφη Κρονίδης· Ἥρη δ' ἀπαμείβετο
      μύθοι·
    "οὔτ' ἄρ' Ἀθηναίης, Κρονίδη, σθένος οὔτε Ἄρηος
    ἰσχύσει βατράχοισιν ἀμυνέμεν αἰπὺν ὄλεθρον.
280   ἀλλ' ἄγε πάντες ἴωμεν ἀρηγόνες· ἢ τὸ σὸν ὅπλον
    κινείσθω· οὕτω γὰρ ἁλώσεται ὅς τις ἄριστος,
    ὥς ποτε καὶ Καπανῆα κατέκτανες, ὄβριμον ἄνδρα,

There was among the mice one Filchpiece, outstanding above the rest, the dear son of worthy Scratchaway, targeter of bread, who . . . as he went off home, but urged his son to take part in the fighting. He was threatening he would take the frog race by storm, and he stood nearby, eager to fight stoutly. Breaking a walnut along its central ridge into two halves, he put his paws into both cavities for protection[20] . . . They quickly became afraid and all went into the pool.

Then the son of Kronos pitied the frogs in their plight, and shaking his head he voiced this utterance: "Oh, I see a great exploit before my eyes: Filcher is crossing over among the frogs. Quick, let us send Pallas the battle-rouser, or even Ares, to stop him fighting, doughty though he is."

So said the son of Kronos. But Hera responded: "Neither Athena's strength, O son of Kronos, nor Ares' will suffice to defend the frogs from sheer destruction. No, let us all go to their aid. Or let your weapon[21] be set in motion, for so the greatest warrior will be taken, even as once you killed the formidable Capaneus, and great Enceladus and

[20] It seems that in what followed he used the half-shells as powerful knuckledusters, causing havoc among the frogs and putting them to flight.   [21] The thunderbolt.

---

261 lac. stat. Ludwich
264–263 hoc ordine Z, 263–264 a; 264–268 om. l
263 $\epsilon(i)\sigma\tau\acute{\eta}\kappa\epsilon\iota$ recc.: $\acute{\epsilon}\sigma\tau\eta\kappa\epsilon\nu$ vett.
post 266 lac. stat. West
273 del. Allen   268–9 v. post 291
277 Ἥρη Baumeister: ἄρης codd.

καὶ μέγαν Ἐγκέλαδόν τε καὶ ἄγρια φῦλα
　Γιγάντων."

285　ὡς ἄρ' ἔφη· Κρονίδης δὲ λαβὼν ἀργῆτα
　κεραυνόν
{πρῶτα μὲν ἐβρόντησε, μέγαν δ' ἐλέλιξεν
　Ὄλυμπον,}

288　ἦκ' ἐπιδινήσας, ὁ δ' ἄρ' ἔπτατο χειρὸς ἄνακτος.
πάντας μέν ῥ' ἐφόβησε βαλὼν βατράχους τε
　μύας τε·

290　ἀλλ' οὐδ' ὣς ἀπέληγε μυῶν στρατός, ἀλλ' ἔτι
　μᾶλλον
ἵετο πορθήσειν βατράχων γένος αἰχμητάων.

268　καί νύ κεν ἐξετέλεσσαν, ἐπεὶ μέγα οἱ σθένος ἦεν,
269　εἰ μὴ ἄρ' ὀξὺ νόησε πατὴρ ἀνδρῶν τε θεῶν τε,
292　{εἰ μὴ ἀπ' Οὐλύμπου βατράχους ἐλέησε Κρονίων,}
ὅς ῥα φθειρομένοισιν ἀρωγοὺς αὐτὸς ἔπεμψεν.
ἦλθον δ' ἐξαίφνης νωτάκμονες, ἀγκυλοχῆλαι,
295　λοξοβάται, στρεβλοί, ψαλιδόστομοι,
　ὀστρακόδερμοι,
ὀστοφυεῖς, πλατύνωτοι, ἀποστίλβοντες ἐν ὤμοις,
βλαισοί, χειροτένοντες, ἀπὸ στέρνων ὁρόωντες,
ὀκτάποδες, δικέραιοι, ἀτειρέες, οἵ τε καλεῦνται
καρκίνοι· οἵ ῥα μυῶν οὐρὰς στομάτεσσιν ἔκοπτον

283 Ἐγκέλαδόν τε Barnes: (ἐγ)κελάδοντα codd.
284 nullus est

the wild tribe of Giants."[22]

So she spoke; and Zeus, taking up the bright bolt, {first thundered, and made great Olympus quake,} discharged it with a whirl, and it flew from the lord's hand. His throw frightened all of them, frogs and mice alike. But not even then did the mouse army give up: it strove yet harder to destroy the race of the warrior frogs. And they would have done it, for great was their strength, if the father of gods and men had not thought quickly and sent aid on his own initiative to the frogs as they perished. And there came of a sudden creatures with backs hard as anvils, bent of claw, walking aslant, squinting, scissor-mouthed, shell-skinned, bony-natured, flat-backed, gleaming-shouldered, bandy-legged, with tendons for hands, peering from their chests, eight-legged, twin-feelered, unwearying: those known as crabs. They snapped at the mice's tails and their hands and

---

[22] Capaneus was one of the Seven who attacked Thebes. He boasted that not even Zeus' thunderbolt would stop him; but it did. Enceladus was one of the Giants who fought against the gods and were defeated

---

285 βαλὼν ἀργῆτα κεραυνὸν Z (λαβὼν Ludwich): ἔβαλε ψολόεντι κεραυνῷ aJ, -εντα κεραυνὸν LF

286 del. Kühn, 287 interpolatio in F^m S

289 βατράχους τε μύας τε Chalcondyles: ἐπὶ τοὺς δέ τε μύας codd.

268–269 huc trai. West deleto 292

268 οἱ σθένος recc.: ὡς θεὸν fere vett.

294 ἀγκυλοχῆλαι recc.: -χεῖλαι vett.

298 δικέραιοι Clarke: δικάρηνοι codd.   ἀτειρέες Nauck: ἀχειρέες codd. (ἀχειλέες Y)   τε West: δὲ codd.

300 ἠδὲ πόδας καὶ χεῖρας· ἀνεγνάμπτοντο δὲ λόγχαι.
τοὺς καὶ ὑπέδδεισαν πάντες μύες, οὐδ' ἔτ'
   ἔμειναν,
ἐς δὲ φυγὴν ἐτράποντο. ἐδύετο δ' ἥλιος ἤδη,
καὶ πολέμου τελετὴ μονοήμερος ἐξετελέσθη.

feet; their spears were bent back. The mice all took fright at them, stood their ground no longer, but turned to flight. By now the sun was setting, and so the one-day war ceremony was concluded.

LIVES OF HOMER

INTRODUCTION

The ten texts edited in this section all date from the Roman or the early Byzantine period. They are:

1. The work commonly known as *The Contest of Homer and Hesiod* or *Certamen*.

2. Pseudo-Herodotus, *On Homer's Origins, Date, and Life*.

3, 4. The biographical sections from the two treatises which make up pseudo-Plutarch, *On the Life and Poetry of Homer*.

5. Proclus' *Life of Homer*.

6. That portion of the *Suda* entry on Homer which comes from Hesychius Illustris' *Index of Famous Authors*.

7–9. Three anonymous Lives from medieval manuscripts of Homer or Homeric scholia: the so-called Vita Romana (= Vita VI Allen) and Vitae Scorialenses (= Vitae IV and V Allen).[1]

10. Some nonbiographical material that appears following the Vita Romana.

---

[1] Allen's curiously incomplete numbering system is a relic of that adopted by Westermann in his Βιογράφοι. The titles Vita Romana, Vita Scorialensis, introduced by Wilamowitz, identify the anonymous Lives by reference to the location of the oldest manuscript in which each is contained.

The first two items in the list are free-standing literary compositions. Number 6 is an encyclopedia entry. The rest are of an introductory nature, designed to provide a starting point for those about to read Homer or further critical work about Homer. Although conventionally called "Lives" of Homer, they are in fact assemblages of material practically confined to the following topics: his parentage and place of birth, for which various different opinions are cited; his change of name from Melesigenes to Homer; his date, again as variously estimated by different authorities; the story of his death; a list of the works composed by him or wrongly ascribed to him. There is very little else about the events of his life. Only the *Certamen* and pseudo-Herodotus offer anything like a continuous biographical narrative.

Let us now consider each of these texts in turn in somewhat more detail.

1. The Contest of Homer and Hesiod

This work survives in a single fourteenth-century manuscript (Laur. 56.1), where it bears the cumbrous but accurate title *On Homer and Hesiod and their Lineage and Contest*. It begins with a brief discussion of the origins of the two poets, and then launches into an extended account of their fabled contest at the funeral games for Amphidamas at Chalcis, in which Homer acquitted himself supremely well in the public's opinion, but the judge, Panedes, awarded the victory to Hesiod on the ground that the poet who promoted the peaceful works of agriculture was to be preferred to the one who told of battle and slaughter. The remainder of the work relates what happened to the poets subsequently and how each met his death in fulfilment of an oracle.

In its present form the *Certamen* dates from the reign of Antoninus Pius, as appears from the reference in §3 to his predecessor Hadrian. But much of it, including the account of the actual contest, was taken over from the *Mouseion* of the sophist Alcidamas, written in the first half of the fourth century BC. This was argued by Friedrich Nietzsche in 1870, on the grounds that two of the verses in §7 are quoted by Stobaeus as from that work, and that the *Certamen* itself cites it for the death of Hesiod at a point where an alternative version is given (§14). Nietzsche's hypothesis was confirmed, firstly by a papyrus of the third century BC (P. Lit. Lond. 191), which contains a portion of the contest narrative differing only trivially from that in the *Certamen*, and secondly by another of the second or third century AD (P. Michigan inv. 2754), which has the end of a narrative closely resembling the end of the *Certamen*, followed by an epilogue and the subscription Ἀλκι]δάμαντος περὶ Ὁμήρου, "Alcidamas, *On Homer*." This presumably marked the conclusion of one section of the *Mouseion*, which then went on to speak of other poets.[2]

Alcidamas' narrative included, besides the contest, the oracles warning the two poets of where they would die, and the story of their deaths. It may also have included

[2] The Michigan papyrus was first edited by J. G. Winter, *TAPA* 56 (1925), 120–129. For discussion of its relationship to the *Mouseion* see G. S. Kirk, *CQ* 44 (1950), 149–167; E. R. Dodds, *CQ* 2 (1952), 187–188; Ernst Vogt, *Rh. Mus.* 102 (1959), 208–211; M. L. West, *CQ* 17 (1967), 434–438; G. L. Koniaris, *HSCP* 75 (1971), 107–129.

Homer's composition of the epitaph for Midas and his dedication at Delphi of the silver cup which he received in fee (*Certamen* 15). The Antonine compiler (for he was no more than a compiler) added material from other sources, in particular from one or more Lives of Homer. §§2–4 are similar in character to the shorter Lives, listing different opinions about Homer's birthplace, parentage, and chronology, and naming a variety of authorities. §§15–18 are more like the pseudo-Herodotean Life, with its account of Homer's travels from town to town, his production of particular epics at different places, and his improvisation of occasional verses in certain particular situations.

The story of the contest with Hesiod was based on Hesiod's own mention of a victory that he won in a poetic competition at the funeral games for Amphidamas in Chalcis (*Works and Days* 650–659). It is ignored in the other Lives (except that Proclus dismisses it), and it may have been Alcidamas' invention. However, some of the verses exchanged in the contest were already current in the fifth century,[3] and literary treatment of a contest between poets or seers was by no means a new idea. Aristophanes had set Aeschylus and Euripides against each other in the *Frogs*, and the *Melampodia* ascribed to Hesiod had related a contest at Claros between the seers Calchas and Mopsus (fr. 278). The Peripatetic writer Phaenias (fr. 33 Wehrli) mentioned a contest between Lesches and Arctinus, the two main poets associated with the Epic Cycle.

It is a curious feature of Alcidamas' contest that it consists almost entirely of tests set by Hesiod to Homer, who

[3] See the notes to the translation.

passes them with ease, demonstrating the ready wit and improvisatory ability that Alcidamas valued in oratory.[4] Hesiod himself is not put to the test, and indeed anyone else might have taken his place as questioner. It is only when each poet is asked to recite the finest piece of his poetry that their abilities can be weighed against one another, and it is on this basis that Hesiod, as the poet of peace, is suddenly declared to have won. Alcidamas was here making a typically sophistic point about judging art by its benefit to society.

The earlier questions put to Homer fall into three series. The first (§7) are of the type, what is the best thing for men, or what the loveliest, and Homer answers with old verses, in the second case taken from the *Odyssey*. The second series (§§8–10) consists of puzzles: demands difficult to fulfil, and apparently nonsensical lines that have to be made sense of by a suitable continuation. Again Alcidamas seems to be using preexisting material. The third series, however (§11), may be of his own composition, as the questions and answers are of a distinctly modern, sophistic character.

2. *The Pseudo-Herodotean Life*

This most extensive of the Lives announces itself as a work of Herodotus of Halicarnassus, and it is written in an imitation of Herodotus' dialect and style. There is no possibility of its being a genuine work of Herodotus. Apart from anything else, it dates Homer some 250 years earlier than the

---

[4] See his extant essay *On those who write written speeches.*

historian did,[5] and it mentions the *Battle of Frogs and Mice*, which we have seen to be a very late composition. The Life was probably written sometime between about 50 and 150 AD; when Tatian (*Oration to the Greeks* 31, around 160 AD) names Herodotus among those who have written about Homer's poetry, origins, and date, he presumably has this work in view and not the real Herodotus' casual remarks on the subject. Affectation of Ionic dialect was not uncommon in the second century, as in Arrian's *Indica*, some works of Lucian, and Aretaeus. As possible authors of our work the medical writer Hermogenes of Smyrna and the historian Cephalion of Gergithos have been suggested on plausible grounds,[6] but no certainty is possible.

As he pretends to be Herodotus, the author cannot name other writers he has used. He can only (in the Herodotean manner) use such expressions as "the Ithacans say . . . But I say . . . and the Colophonians agree with me" (§7). Another Herodotean feature is his down-to-earth rationalism. Homer—or Melesigenes, as he is originally called—is not descended from Orpheus, or born of the river Meles, as in some versions, but beside it; his mother Cretheis is not a nymph, but an ordinary girl made pregnant by an unidentified man. The poet does not die because he cannot solve the fisherboys' riddle, "as some

---

[5] See the note at the end of the translation.

[6] Ioannes Schmidt, *De Herodotea quae fertur vita Homeri*, ii (Halle, 1876), 218; T. W. Allen, *Homer, The Origins and the Transmission* (Oxford, 1924), 17–18. Both lived in the first half of the second century.

think," he dies of a malady that came upon him shortly before he encountered the boys.

Whereas the other Lives regularly set out the conflicting claims concerning Homer's birthplace and parentage, this one constructs a harmonizing narrative. Homer is conceived in Cyme, born at Smyrna, becomes blind at Colophon, returns to Cyme to acquire the name Homer (for it is the Cymaeans who call the blind *homēroi*), composes most of his poetry at Chios, and dies on Ios. He visits many other places in the course of his life. He goes on voyages with the shipowner Mentes: this accounts for his knowledge of Ithaca and the western Mediterranean as displayed in the *Odyssey*. In Ionia he calls at Neonteichos, Phocaea, Erythrae, and Samos, all somehow associated with poems said to have been his. He plans a journey to Athens: it was in preparation for this, the author explains, that he inserted certain passages in praise of Athens into the *Iliad* and *Odyssey*.

The prominence given in the Homeric poems to certain untraditional characters is likewise explained by pseudo-Herodotus (§26) from the poet's life. The Mentes and Mentor of the *Odyssey* commemorate Homer's shipowner companion and a friend of his. The bard Phemios commemorates Homer's teacher and adoptive father of that name. The highly commended leather worker Tychios who made Ajax's great shield (*Iliad* 7.220) commemorates a Tychios who took the poet in at Neonteichos.

The list of poems attributed to Homer in this work is rather a strange one. The *Iliad* and *Odyssey* are clearly treated as the major ones. Of the Cyclic epics, only the *Little Iliad* is mentioned (§16); the old story that he gave the *Cypria* to the Cypriot Stasinus as his daughter's dowry is implicitly denied in §25, where we read that one of his two daughters never married and the other married a Chian.[7] The other epic poems mentioned are *Amphiaraus' Expedition to Thebes* (§9, presumably part of the *Thebaid*) and a *Phocais* (§16, otherwise unknown). Besides them there are the *Hymns* (§9), the collection of "fun pieces" (παίγνια) listed in §24 (where the *Margites* is lacking, but several out-of-the-way titles appear), and some seventeen short occasional poems which Homer improvises in response to various situations that arise in the course of his life.

These occasional poems, the so-called Homeric *Epigrams*, appear distributed through the narrative, much of which is constructed to support them. Most of them are known only from pseudo-Herodotus, though a few are found also in other sources, including a couple in the *Certamen*. Two are quoted with individual titles: *The Kiln* (*Epigram* 14)[8] and the *Eiresione* (*Epigram* 15). The *Eiresione* was a traditional poem recited by Samian children as they went round the houses on a certain day each year, carrying a swallow and asking for gifts of food; it is akin to the Rhodian Swallow Song (*PMG* 848) and the more literary *Koronistai* of Phoenix of Colophon.[9] Of the

---

[7] Likewise excluded are Homer's friendship with Creophylus of Samos (although the poet spends some time on that island) and his gift to him of the *Capture of Oichalia*.

[8] This had the alternative title *The Potters*, and according to Pollux 10.85 some people ascribed it to Hesiod (= Hes. fr. 302 M.–W.).

[9] Similar customs are well attested in modern Greece and other parts of Europe. See Albert Dieterich, *Sommertag* (*Archiv für Religionswissenschaft* 8, 1905, Beiheft 82–117) = *Kleine*

remaining *Epigrams*, one is the famous epitaph for Midas, sometimes ascribed to Cleobulus of Lindos (Simonides, *PMG* 581; Diogenes Laertius 1.89); others are appeals to men or gods, or brief gnomic utterances.

It is generally agreed that these little poems must all be quite old, from the sixth or fifth century BC. But most of them only make sense in the context of the narrative frame that explains the circumstances in which they were composed. The inference is that some such narrative of Homer's life, incorporating the *Epigrams*, existed from the classical period and served as a basis for pseudo-Herodotus' work. Wilamowitz was tempted by the idea that a biography by Heraclides Ponticus was involved; but he preferred to assume that the story was transmitted from an earlier time by some sort of Ionian popular tradition, as an anonymous "Volksbuch." Jacoby more realistically saw it as a sophistic creation, similar in style to Alcidamas' story of the contest with Hesiod.[10]

There is a parallel situation with the life of Aesop.[11] When he first appears in literature, in the second half of the fifth century, Aesop is already more than an inventor of fables: there is something like a coherent legend about his

Schriften (Leipzig and Berlin, 1911), 324–352; Samuel Baud-Bovy, *Byzantina-Metabyzantina* 1 (1946), 23–32; Iona and Peter Opie, *The Lore and Language of Schoolchildren* (Oxford, 1959), 288–289; Otto Schönberger, *Griechische Heischelieder* (Meisenheim, 1980).

[10] Wilamowitz, *Die Ilias und Homer*, 417, 437–439; Jacoby, "Homerisches I," *Hermes* 68 (1933), 10–12 = *Kleine philologische Schriften* i (Berlin, 1961), 11–13.

[11] M. L. West in *La Fable* (*Entretiens sur l'antiquité classique* 30, Vandœuvres and Genève, 1984), 116–126.

life, and certain fables are associated with particular occasions when he used them for his own ends. The legend is centered on Samos; and Homer's sojourn on Samos occupies an important part of the pseudo-Herodotean Life. The Samian historian Euagon, who apparently wrote both about Aesop and about Homer, may have been somehow involved in the codification of the legends.

3, 4. The Pseudo-Plutarchean Lives

The two books *On the Life and Poetry of Homer* which come down to us under the name of Plutarch are in fact two independent works. The first, in a mere eight chapters, is intended as a preface to the *Iliad*. By way of a biographical introduction the author sets out, more fully than is usual in the Lives, two alternative accounts of Homer's origins: one from Ephorus, which makes him of Cymaean stock, and one from Aristotle, which has him conceived on Ios and which goes on to tell the story of his death. In both versions his actual birth takes place at Smyrna beside the Meles. The author then mentions the Colophonian claim, quoting the epigram on a statuary group at Colophon, and caps it with a literary epigram which dismisses the whole controversy about Homer's citizenship and acclaims him as a son of the Muse, of heavenly descent. There follow brief notes on his dating and on the works to be acknowledged as his. In three further chapters omitted in the present edition the author explains the origins of the Trojan War, the scope of the *Iliad*, and the poet's reason for beginning in the ninth year.

The second treatise is much more extended (218 chapters). It is a disquisition on Homer's poetry, its educative value, its meter, its dialect mixture, its use of archaisms, tropes and figures, its stylistic variety, subject matter, cosmology, theology, ethics, and its archetypal status for philosophy, rhetoric, politics, morality, strategy, medicine, and other arts, all illustrated with numerous quotations from the *Iliad* and *Odyssey*. The latest commentator on the work has argued that while it cannot, as it stands, be regarded as a work of Plutarch, it may draw to a considerable extent on Plutarch's lost *Homeric Studies*, and date from no later than the end of the second century.[12] For the present volume only the short biographical section at the beginning has been taken. It cannot really be called a Life; it is no more than a succinct survey of different opinions on Homer's citizenship, parentage, and date. §2 is closely related to §1 of the third Anonymous Life.

5. Proclus' Life

Proclus included a Life of Homer in that part of the *Chrestomathy* which dealt with the principal epic poets. It is omitted in Photius' summary of the *Chrestomathy* (*Bibliotheca* cod. 239, p. 319a19 Bekker), but appears in over a dozen manuscripts of the *Iliad*, including Venetus A. Besides the conventional review of conflicting opinions on Homer's parentage and date, the story of his death, and the list of his works and reputed works (§§2–5, 7, 9), Proclus adds some remarks ridiculing the belief that he was blind and the tale that he contested unsuccessfully against

[12] Michael Hillgruber, *Die pseudoplutarchische Schrift De Homero* (Stuttgart and Leipzig, 1994–1999), i. 1–5, 74–76.

Hesiod (§6), and some inferences concerning his longevity, wide experience of travel, and affluence (§8).

Proclus' aphorism, "those who have stated that he was blind seem to me to be mentally blind themselves," is paralleled earlier in Velleius Paterculus (1.5.3), "anyone who thinks he was born blind is lacking all his senses." Both this and the denial that Homer and Hesiod were cousins may derive from an older historian opposed to Ephorus, such as Timaeus. A number of agreements between Velleius and Timaeus were noted by Rohde.[13]

The paragraph on chronology (§ 7) is taken almost verbatim from pseudo-Plutarch II 3.

6. *The Hesychian Life*

The tenth-century encyclopedia known as the *Suda* contains a lengthy article on Homer, reproduced in full by Allen in his Oxford Text. Only the first part (as far as line 55 Allen) is of independent value; the rest consists of excerpts from Athenaeus (8e–9c) and the Herodotean Life. The first part comes from the usual source of the biographical articles in the *Suda*: an epitome of the *Index of Famous Authors* by Hesychius of Miletus (Hesychius Illustris), a sixth-century writer not to be confused with the somewhat earlier lexicographer Hesychius.

The plan and scope of this Life are thoroughly conventional, but it contains some unique information. It distinguishes itself from the rest by the lateness of some of the authors cited (Castricius, Charax, Porphyry) and by its in-

[13] *Kleine Schriften* i (Tübingen and Leipzig, 1901), 86 n.1.

comparably long list of local origins proposed for Homer, twenty in number.

7–10. The Anonymous Lives. Appendix Romana

Anon. I (the Vita Romana) forms part of the introductory material in cod. gr. 6 in the Biblioteca Nazionale in Rome, which is the oldest manuscript of the so-called D scholia, dating from the ninth century. It is followed by an explanation of Aristarchus' critical signs and by some other scholarly notes of great interest, which I have printed at the end of the Lives under the heading "Appendix Romana." The Life follows the usual plan, but it cites a number of Hellenistic and earlier sources not reported elsewhere, and includes a rare version of how Homer became blind.

Anon. II and III are transmitted in some twenty manuscripts of the *Iliad*, the earliest being the eleventh-century Escorial codex Ω.1.12 (509), which has given them the appellation of Vitae Scorialenses. The first is very cursory and contains practically nothing individual; after the first paragraph it reads like an abridgment of the second. The second is of greater interest. Its initial section, as noted above, closely parallels the second pseudo-Plutarch. It adduces evidence against the view (Crates') that Homer lived only a few decades after the Trojan War. It denies, on literary-critical grounds, his authorship of any other poems than the *Iliad* and *Odyssey*, even the *Hymns*. It purveys the doctrine that the epics were not collected and put in order until Pisistratus, and quotes in support an epigram displayed on an Athenian statue of the tyrant. It also has a mention of Homer's travels, and specifically of his stay in Ithaca, presumably after the Herodotean Life.

The Earlier Biographical Tradition

Tatian's list of writers who inquired into "Homer's poetry and his origins and date" begins with Theagenes of Rhegium, said to have flourished in the time of Cambyses.[14] So far as we know from other sources, Theagenes' interest was in allegorical interpretation of Homer, and it may not have extended to biographical matters. However, the topics regularly treated in the Lives—Homer's parentage and place of birth, his change of name from Melesigenes, his date, the manner of his death, and the authenticity of the works ascribed to him—were certainly all matters of discussion as early as the fifth century BC, if not the late sixth. Heraclitus already knew the story of the poet's defeat by the boys' riddle. Simonides, Pindar, and Bacchylides acknowledged the claims of various cities (Smyrna, Chios, Ios) to have been Homer's home. Pindar also knew the story of his giving the *Cypria* as his daughter's dowry to Stasinus, which presupposes a dispute over which poet was the author of that epic. Herodotus gives his opinions on the authenticity of the *Cypria* and *Epigoni*, and also on the date of Homer and Hesiod, clearly taking a stand against an alternative view.[15] A string of other fifth-century writers are cited in the Lives in connection with Homer's origins: Pherecydes of Athens, Hellanicus of Lesbos, Damastes of Sigeum, Euagon of Samos, Gorgias of Leontini, Hippias of Elis, Stesimbrotus of Thasos, Antimachus of Colophon.

[14] Tatian, *Oration to the Greeks* 31.
[15] Heraclitus DK 22 B 56; Simonides eleg. 19.1; Pindar, frs. 264 (cf. 204), 265; Bacchylides, fr. 48; Herodotus 2.53, 117; 4.32.

The initial impression may be that it is a case of *quot homines, tot sententiae*. Yet certain claims seem to have become so firmly established at an early date that variant views had to compromise with them. Thus, whether Homer is represented as a Cymaean, a Smyrnaean, or an Ietan by birth, it is agreed that he lived and worked on Chios (where he is never said to have been born).[16] Again, while Ephorus had Homer conceived at Cyme, and the Ietans reported by Aristotle had him conceived on Ios, in both accounts the pregnant mother came to Smyrna and gave birth to the poet beside the river Meles. The Smyrnaean claim was evidently prior and could not be gainsaid. In the Pisistratus epigram quoted in the second and third Anonymous Lives, Homer is claimed as an Athenian, but on the ground that Smyrna was an Athenian foundation.

This claim of Smyrna's depended on Homer's birth beside the river or (according to Euagon and others) actually from the river. But the connection of Homer with the Meles was only made in order to account for the name Melesigenes which he was held originally to have borne. In fact, as has long been recognized, Melesigenes is a normal type of man's name meaning "caring about his clan," and it had nothing to do with the Meles. This undermines the claim that the poet was born at Smyrna, leaving only the premise, which was evidently uncontested, that "Homer" was a secondary name given to a poet called Melesigenes.

---

[16] Note that already in the *Hymn to Apollo* (172) the blind poet who is to be understood as Homer is not said to be a native Chian (Χῖος δὲ γένος, it might have been) but to *live* on Chios. Compare Erwin Rohde, *Kleine Schriften* i. 9 n.2.

The other points on which the tradition was agreed are
that he was active on Chios and died on Ios.

We should not succumb to the temptation to look here
for historical information about the poet of the *Iliad*. The
figure of Homer was a creation of the sixth-century
Homeridai, a professional organization of bards who at-
tributed their traditional poetry to their fictitious eponym
and imagined that there had earlier been a clan of his
descendants.[17] These Homeridai were the primary source
of stories about Homer's life.[18] As they themselves were
based on Chios, it was inferred that that was where Homer
had lived. Certain poems current under the names of other
poets were appropriated for Homer by means of such sto-
ries as that he gave the *Cypria* to Stasinus and the *Capture
of Oichalia* to Creophylus, or that the *Little Iliad* and
Phocais were stolen from him by Thestorides. The story
that his original name was Melesigenes is best understood
in the same way, as a device for making Homer the author
of poetry that had been known as Melesigenes', whoever
Melesigenes may have been.[19]

It is hard to say on what ground Ios made its claim,
which none disputed, to be the place where Homer died.
Perhaps there were some Homeridai there who practised
a hero cult of their supposed ancestor and set up a memo-
rial to which they could bring him offerings, and this be-
came his tomb. The tale of the fisherboys' riddle remained
canonical, but its connection with the poet's death was sub-

[17] Acusilaus fr. 2, Hellanicus fr. 20 Fowler; Strabo 14.1.35;
Certamen 2; schol. Pind. *Nem.* 2.1c, e.

[18] Plato, *Republic* 599e; Isocrates 10.65.

[19] Wilamowitz, *Die Ilias und Homer*, 370 f.

ject to various rationalizations. In the original version it was a sufficient cause of death for a singer or seer to be worsted in a riddle challenge, as in the Hesiodic story of Calchas and Mopsus, or in the myth of the Sphinx at Thebes. But later narrators were not content with this. They explain that Homer died of depression at his failure (ps.-Plut. I, Anon. III), or that in his chagrin he starved himself to death (Anon. II), or that he suffered a fatal fall through slipping on some mud (Alcidamas/*Certamen*) or tripping over a stone (Proclus), or that he succumbed to a preexisting illness (ps.-Herodotus).

Secondary claims about his origins proliferated in the fifth and earlier fourth centuries. Hellanicus made Homer a cousin of Hesiod, and both of them descendants of Orpheus, in a factitious genealogy going back to Atlas. As Hesiod's father was known to come from Cyme (*Works and Days* 636), Hellanicus probably represented Homer too as of Cymaean stock. Hippias did so, at any rate, and this was taken up gladly by the Cymaean Ephorus, who adopted Hellanicus' stemma with modifications. Damastes and Gorgias preferred to make Homer descend from Musaeus. The Colophonian poet Antimachus made him a Colophonian, probably appealing to the Colophonian associations of the *Margites*.[20]

In the Hellenistic period things went further. One Callicles made Homer originate from Salamis in Cyprus, like his supposed son-in-law Stasinus.[21] Philochorus made

[20] See *Certamen* 2, and the introduction to the *Margites* in this volume.

[21] *FGrHist* 754 F 13; Jacoby, *RE* x.1635. An epigram probably by Alcaeus of Messene (22 Gow–Page) protests at the suggestion.

him an Argive, no doubt because of the prominence of "Argeioi" in the epics.[22] The notion that he was an Athenian appears with Aristarchus and his pupil Dionysius Thrax, but they were probably not the first.[23] More fanciful writers made him an Ithacan, the son of Telemachus and of Nestor's daughter Polycaste, or an Egyptian, or a Roman.[24] Epigrammatists wrote that "seven cities" claimed to be Homer's home, without altogether agreeing on which seven.[25] Hesychius Illustris, as noted above, was able to enumerate twenty.

Opinions on when Homer lived also varied widely.[26] The oldest belief, as promulgated by the Homeridai and probably by Hellanicus, may have been that he lived at the time of the Trojan War and was thus able to tell of it from personal knowledge. This was perhaps the view against which Herodotus (2.53) was reacting when he stated his opinion that Hesiod and Homer lived "four hundred years before me, and not more." Most historians and chron-

[22] Herodotus 5.67.1; *Certamen* 17; pseudo-Herodotus 28; Philochorus, *FGrHist* 328 F 209 with Jacoby's commentary.

[23] See Jacoby on *FGrHist* 328 F 209 (n.11).

[24] Polycaste gives Telemachus a bath at *Odyssey* 3.464, and is already married to him in the pseudo-Hesiodic *Catalogue* (fr. 221). A version of the Egyptian story is ascribed to one Alexander of Paphos, who may be the same as Alexander of Myndus (Eustathius, *Odyssey* 1713.17, printed by Allen, 253; G. E. V. Gigante, *Vite di Omero*, 66–67, 148). Rome: Aristodemus of Nysa, cited in Anon. I.

[25] *Anth. Pal.* 16.297, 298.

[26] See Felix Jacoby, *Apollodors Chronik* (Berlin, 1902), 98–107; *Das Marmor Parium* (Berlin, 1904), 152–157; his commentary on Philochorus, *FGrHist* 328 F 210–211.

ographers put Homer somewhere between these dates. The major epochs of Greek mythical history, after the Trojan War, were the Return of the Heraclids, which Eratosthenes and Apollodorus put at eighty years after the war, and the Ionian migration, which they put at sixty years after that. Homer was sometimes dated in relation to these events, on the ground that he showed no knowledge of one or both of them. Those who accepted that he was born at Smyrna could not put him earlier than the date when they believed that city to have been founded. Pseudo-Herodotus connects him directly with that event. Others dated him on the basis of his legendary meeting with the Spartan lawgiver Lycurgus, who could be fixed in relation to the Spartan king list; this encounter, however, plays no part in the *Lives*.

The chronological sections in the *Lives* depend on Peripatetic or later authorities. The earliest cited by name are: for relative dates, Aristotle (ps.-Plutarch I 3: synchronism with the Ionian migration) and Heraclides Ponticus (Anon. I 4: Homer older than Hesiod); and for absolute dates, Eratosthenes, Crates, Aristarchus, Apollodorus, and (in Hesychius) Porphyry.

SELECT BIBLIOGRAPHY

The Contest of Homer and Hesiod

Editions, Commentaries

Nietzsche, Friedrich, in *Acta Societatis Philologae Lipsiensis* I(1) (1871), pp. 1–23.

Rzach, Alois. *Hesiodi Carmina*. Leipzig, 1902, pp. 433–450.

Allen, Thomas W. *Homeri Opera*, v. Oxford Classical Texts, 1912, pp. 218–238.

von Wilamowitz-Moellendorff, Ulrich. *Vitae Homeri et Hesiodi*. Berlin, 1916, pp. 34–47.

Colonna, Aristide. *Hesiodi Opera et Dies*. Milan, 1059, pp. 71–86.

Avezzù, Guido. *Alcidamante. Orazioni e frammenti*. Rome, 1982, pp. 38–51, 86–90.

Other Studies

Heldmann, Konrad. *Die Niederlage Homers im Dichterwettstreit mit Hesiod* (*Hypomnemata*, 75). Göttingen, 1982.

Koniaris, G. L. "Michigan Papyrus 2754 and the Certamen," *HSCP* 75 (1971), 107–129.

Nietzsche, Friedrich. "Die Florentinische Traktat über Homer und Hesiod, ihr Geschlecht und ihren Wettkampf," *Rh. Mus.* 25 (1870), 528–540; 28 (1873), 211–249.

Richardson, Nicholas J. "The Contest of Homer and Hesiod and Alcidamas' Mouseion," *CQ* 31 (1981), 1–10.

West, M. L. "The Contest of Homer and Hesiod," *CQ* 17 (1967), 433–450.

von Wilamowitz-Moellendorff, Ulrich. *Die Ilias und Homer.* Berlin, 1916, pp. 396–413.

Lives

Editions

Westermann, Anton. Βιογράφοι. *Vitarum Scriptores Graeci Minores*, Braunschweig, 1845, pp. 1–45.

Allen, Thomas W. *Homeri Opera*, v (as above), pp. 184–268.

von Wilamowitz-Moellendorff, Ulrich. *Vitae Homeri et Hesiodi.* Berlin, 1916.

Gigante, G. E. V. *Vite di Omero.* Naples, 1996.

Other Studies

Allen, Thomas W. *Homer, The Origins and the Transmission.* Oxford, 1924, pp. 11–41.

Jacoby, Felix. "Homerisches I: Der Bios und die Person," *Hermes* 68 (1933), 1–50 = *Kleine philologische Schriften* i (Berlin, 1961), 1–53.

Lefkowitz, Mary. *The Lives of the Greek Poets.* London, 1983, pp. 12–24.

Markwald, Georg. *Die homerischen Epigramme.* Meisenheim, 1986.

Raddatz, Georg. "Homeros," in *RE* viii (1913), 2188–2213.

Schadewaldt, Wolfgang. *Legende von Homer, dem fahr-
enden Sänger.* Leipzig, 1942.
von Wilamowitz-Moellendorff, Ulrich. *Die Ilias und
Homer.* Berlin, 1916, pp. 413–439.

Appendix Romana

Montanari, Franco. *Studi di filologia omerica antica*, i.
Pisa, 1979, pp. 43–75.

ΠΕΡΙ ΟΜΗΡΟΥ ΚΑΙ ΗΣΙΟΔΟΥ
ΚΑΙ ΤΟΥ ΓΕΝΟΥΣ ΚΑΙ
ΑΓΩΝΟΣ ΑΥΤΩΝ

1 Ὅμηρον καὶ Ἡσίοδον τοὺς θειοτάτους ποιητὰς πάν-
τες ἄνθρωποι πολίτας ἰδίους εὔχονται λέγεσθαι. ἀλλ᾽
Ἡσίοδος μὲν τὴν ἰδίαν ὀνομάσας πατρίδα πάντας τῆς
φιλονικίας ἀπήλλαξεν εἰπὼν (Op.639) ὡς ὁ πατὴρ
αὐτοῦ

εἴσατο δ᾽ ἄγχ᾽ Ἑλικῶνος ὀϊζυρῆι ἐνὶ κώμηι,
Ἄσκρηι, χεῖμα κακῆι, θέρει ἀργαλέηι, οὐδέ ποτ᾽
ἐσθλῆι.

2 Ὅμηρον δὲ πᾶσαι ὡς εἰπεῖν αἱ πόλεις καὶ οἱ ἔποικοι
αὐτῶν παρ᾽ ἑαυτοῖς γεγενῆσθαι λέγουσιν. καὶ πρῶτοί
γε Σμυρναῖοι Μέλητος ὄντα τοῦ παρ᾽ αὐτοῖς ποταμοῦ
καὶ Κρηθηΐδος νύμφης κεκλῆσθαί φασι πρότερον
Μελησιγένη, ὕστερον μέντοι τυφλωθέντα Ὅμηρον
μετονομασθῆναι διὰ τὴν παρ᾽ αὐτοῖς ἐπὶ τῶν τοιούτων
συνήθη προσηγορίαν. Χῖοι δὲ πάλιν τεκμήρια φέρου-
σιν ἴδιον εἶναι πολίτην, λέγοντες καὶ περισώιζεσθαί
τινας ἐκ τοῦ γένους αὐτοῦ παρ᾽ αὐτοῖς Ὁμηρίδας
καλουμένους. Κολοφώνιοι δὲ καὶ τόπον δεικνύουσιν,

1. THE CONTEST OF
HOMER AND HESIOD

Homer and Hesiod are the most inspired of poets, and all mankind would like to have them reckoned as their own fellow-citizens. Hesiod at least, by naming his own homeland, precluded any rivalry: he said that his father

> settled near Helicon in a miserable village,
> Ascra, bad in winter, foul in summer, good at no time.

With Homer, on the other hand, practically all cities and their inhabitants claim that he was born among them. First of all, the Smyrnaeans say that he was the son of their local river Meles and of a nymph Cretheis, and that he was formerly called Melesigenes,[1] but later, after becoming blind, was renamed Homer, from the ordinary term applied to that condition among them.[2] The Chians, again, produce evidence that he was a citizen of theirs, saying that some of his descendants actually survive among them, known as Homeridai. And the Colophonians even point to a spot

---

[1] Understood as "Meles-born."

[2] According to Ephorus (*FGrHist* 70 F 1), *homēros* was an Aeolic word meaning "blind."

ἐν ὧι φασιν αὐτὸν γράμματα διδάσκοντα τῆς ποιή-
σεως ἄρξασθαι καὶ ποιῆσαι πρῶτον τὸν Μαργίτην.

3   περὶ δὲ τῶν γονέων αὐτοῦ πάλιν πολλὴ διαφωνία
παρὰ πᾶσίν ἐστιν. Ἑλλάνικος μὲν γὰρ (fr. 5 Fowler)
καὶ Κλεάνθης (Neanthes 84 F 40) Μαίονα λέγουσιν,
Εὐγαίων δὲ (Euagon fr. 2 Fowler) Μέλητα, Καλλικλῆς
δὲ (758 F 13) <Δ>μασαγόραν,¹ Δημόκριτος² δὲ ὁ Τροι-
ζήνιος (Demetrius *Supp. Hell.* 378) Δαήμονα³ ἔμπορον,
ἔνιοι δὲ Θαμύραν, Αἰγύπτιοι δὲ Μενέμαχον ἱερογραμ-
ματέα, εἰσὶ δὲ οἳ Τηλέμαχον τὸν Ὀδυσσέως· μητέρα
δὲ οἱ μὲν Μῆτιν, οἱ δὲ Κρηθηΐδα, οἱ δὲ Θεμίστην,⁴ οἱ
δὲ Ὑρνηθώ,⁵ ἔνιοι δὲ Ἰθακησίαν τινὰ ὑπὸ Φοινίκων
ἀπεμποληθεῖσαν, οἱ δὲ Καλλιόπην τὴν Μοῦσαν, τινὲς
δὲ Πολυκάστην τὴν Νέστορος.

ἐκαλεῖτο δὲ Μέλης, ὡς δέ τινές φασι Μελησιγένης,
ὡς δὲ ἔνιοι Ἄλτης.⁶ ὀνομασθῆναι <δὲ> αὐτόν φασί
τινες Ὅμηρον διὰ τὸ τὸν πατέρα αὐτοῦ ὅμηρον δοθῆ-
ναι ὑπὸ Κυπρίων Πέρσαις· οἱ δὲ διὰ τὴν πήρωσιν τῶν
ὀμμάτων· παρὰ γὰρ τοῖς Αἰολεῦσιν οὕτως οἱ πηροὶ
καλοῦνται.

ὅπερ δὲ ἀκηκόαμεν ἐπὶ τοῦ θειοτάτου αὐτοκράτορος
Ἀδ<ρ>ιανοῦ εἰρημένον ὑπὸ τῆς Πυθίας περὶ Ὁμήρου,
ἐκθησόμεθα. τοῦ γὰρ βασιλέως πυθομένου πόθεν

---

¹ μασαγόραν cod.: Δμασαγ- Barnes ex Eust. *Od.* 1713.18:
Δημαγ- Alcaeus epigr. 22 Gow–Page.
² Δημοκρίνης vit. Rom.   ³ Ἀλήμονα vit. Rom.
⁴ Θεμιστώ Barnes e Paus. 10.24.3.
⁵ Ὑρνηθώ Westermann: εὐγνηθώ cod.

where they say Homer, as a teacher of reading and writing, started his poetic career and composed the *Margites* as his first work.

As to his parents there is again much disagreement in all the sources. For Hellanicus and Cleanthes[3] say (his father) was Maion, Eugaion says Meles, Callicles Dmasagoras, Democritus of Troezen[4] a merchant Daëmon, some say Thamyras, the Egyptians say a temple scribe Menemachus, and there are those who say it was Telemachus the son of Odysseus. As for his mother, some say Metis, some Cretheis, some Themiste, some Hyrnetho, some an Ithacan woman sold abroad by Phoenicians, some the Muse Calliope, and some Nestor's daughter Polycaste.

He was called Meles, or as some say, Melesigenes, or as others say, Altes. And some say he was named Homer because his father was given by the Cyprians to the Persians as a hostage (*homēros*); others say it was because of his ocular handicap, as among the Aeolians the handicapped are so called.

But we will set forth what we have heard stated about Homer by the Pythia in the time of the most godly emperor Hadrian. When he enquired where Homer came

[3] Perhaps an error for Neanthes (of Cyzicus). In what follows, the compiler has made a list of couples into separate lists of fathers and mothers.

[4] Perhaps an error for Demetrius of Troezen, a poet of the Augustan period.

---

[6] Ἄλτης Welcker (Athenocles ap. sch. *Il.* 22.51): αὐλητὴν cod.

Ὅμηρος καὶ τίνος, ἀπεφοίβασε δι' ἑξαμέτρου τόνδε
τὸν τρόπον·

ἄγνωστόν μ' ἔρεαι γενεὴν καὶ πατρίδα γαῖαν
ἀμβροσίου Σειρῆνος. ἔδος δ' Ἰθακήσιός ἐστιν,
Τηλέμαχος δὲ πατὴρ καὶ Νεστορέη Πολυκάστη[7]
μήτηρ, ἥ μιν ἔτικτε βροτῶν πέρι[8] πάνσοφον
   ἄνδρα.

οἷς μάλιστα δεῖ πιστεύειν διά τε τὸν πυθόμενον καὶ
τὸν ἀποκρινάμενον, ἄλλως τε οὕτως τοῦ ποιητοῦ μεγα-
λοφυῶς τὸν προπάτορα διὰ τῶν ἐπῶν δεδοξακότος.

4   ἔνιοι μὲν οὖν αὐτὸν προγενέστερον Ἡσιόδου φασὶν
εἶναι, τινὲς δὲ νεώτερον καὶ συγγενῆ. γενεαλογοῦσι δὲ
οὕτως· Ἀπόλλωνός φασι καὶ Θοώσης τῆς Ποσειδῶνος
γενέσθαι Λίνον, Λίνου δὲ Πίερον, Πιέρου δὲ καὶ νύμ-
φης Μεθώνης Οἴαγρον, Οἰάγρου δὲ καὶ Καλλιόπης
Ὀρφέα, Ὀρφέως δὲ Ὄρτην, ‹τοῦ δὲ Εὐκλέα,›[9] τοῦ δὲ
Ἁρμονίδην,[10] τοῦ δὲ Φιλοτέρπην, τοῦ δὲ Εὔφημον, τοῦ
δὲ Ἐπιφράδην, τοῦ δὲ Μελάνωπον, τούτου δὲ Δῖον καὶ
Ἀπέλλαιον· Δίου δὲ καὶ Πυκιμήδης τῆς Ἀπόλλωνος
θυγατρὸς Ἡσίοδον καὶ Πέρσην, Ἀπελλαίου[11] δὲ Μαί-
ονα, Μαίονος δὲ θυγατρὸς καὶ Μέλητος τοῦ ποταμοῦ
Ὅμηρον.

5   τινὲς δὲ συνακμάσαι φασὶν αὐτούς, ὥστε καὶ ἀγω-
νίσασθαι ὁμόσε ‹γενομένους›[12] ἐν Αὐλίδι τῆς Βοι-

----

[7] Πολυκάστη (ut supra) Nietzsche: ἐπικάστη cod.
[8] πέρι West: πολυ cod.   [9] ‹ › add. Goettling ex *Suda*.

from and whose son he was, she made her inspired utter-
ance in hexameters as follows:

> You ask me the unknown lineage and fatherland
> of an immortal Siren. As to his home, he is an
>   Ithacan;
> Telemachus was his father, and Nestor's daughter
>   Polycaste
> his mother who bore him, a man outstanding for his
>   all-round expertise.

We should treat these statements as the most trustworthy,
given the identity of the enquirer and the responder, not
to mention the fact that the poet has so magnificently
glorified his paternal grandfather in his poetry.

Now some say that he was older than Hesiod, others
that he was younger, and related to him. This is the geneal-
ogy they give: from Apollo and Thoösa, daughter of Posei-
don, they say Linus was born, from Linus Pierus, from
Pierus and the nymph Methone Oeagrus, from Oeagrus
and Calliope Orpheus, from Orpheus Ortes, ⟨from him
Eucles,⟩ from him Harmonides, from him Philoterpes,
from him Euphemus, from him Epiphrades, from him
Melanopus, and from him Dios and Apellaios; from Dios
and Apollo's daughter Pykimede, Hesiod and Perses; from
Apellaios Maion, and from a daughter of Maion and the
river Meles, Homer.

Some, however, say that they flourished at the same
time, so as actually to compete with each other after

---

10 ἁρμονίδην cod: Ἰδμον- Proclus, *Suda*.
11 Ἀπελλαίου Sittl: πέρσου cod.
12 ⟨ ⟩ add. Busse.

ωτίας. ποιήσαντα γὰρ τὸν Μαργίτην Ὅμηρον περι-
έρχεσθαι κατὰ πόλιν ῥαψῳδοῦντα, ἐλθόντα δὲ καὶ εἰς
Δελφοὺς περὶ τῆς πατρίδος αὐτοῦ πυνθάνεσθαι τίς
εἴη, τὴν δὲ Πυθίαν εἰπεῖν·

ἔστιν Ἴος νῆσος μητρὸς πατρίς, ἥ σε θανόντα
δέξεται· ἀλλὰ νέων παίδων αἴνιγμα φύλαξαι.

τὸν δὲ ἀκούσαντα περιίστασθαι μὲν τὴν εἰς Ἴον
6 ἄφιξιν, διατρίβειν δὲ περὶ τὴν ἐκεῖ χώραν. | κατὰ δὲ
τὸν αὐτὸν χρόνον Γανύκτωρ ἐπιτάφιον τοῦ πατρὸς
Ἀμφιδάμαντος βασιλέως Εὐβοίας ἐπιτελῶν πάντας
τοὺς ἐπισήμους ἄνδρας οὐ μόνον ῥώμῃ καὶ τάχει
ἀλλὰ καὶ σοφίαι ἐπὶ τὸν ἀγῶνα μεγάλαις δωρεαῖς
τιμῶν συνεκάλεσεν. καὶ οὗτοι οὖν ἐκ τύχης, ὥς φασι,
συμβαλόντες ἀλλήλοις ἦλθον εἰς τὴν Χαλκίδα. τοῦ δὲ
ἀγῶνος ἄλλοι τέ τινες τῶν ἐπισήμων Χαλκιδέων ἐκα-
θέζοντο κριταὶ καὶ μετ' αὐτῶν Πανήδης, ἀδελφὸς ὢν
τοῦ τετελευτηκότος. ἀμφοτέρων δὲ τῶν ποιητῶν θαυ-
μαστῶς ἀγωνισαμένων νικῆσαί φασι τὸν Ἡσίοδον
τὸν τρόπον τοῦτον· προελθόντα γὰρ εἰς τὸ μέσον
πυνθάνεσθαι τοῦ Ὁμήρου καθ' ἓν ἕκαστον, τὸν δὲ
7 Ὅμηρον ἀποκρίνασθαι. | φησὶν οὖν Ἡσίοδος·

υἱὲ Μέλητος Ὅμηρε, θεῶν ἄπο μήδεα εἰδώς,
εἴπ' ἄγε μοι πάμπρωτα, τί φέρτατόν ἐστι
βροτοῖσιν;

Ὅμηρος·

meeting up at Aulis in Boeotia. For after composing the
Margites, they say, Homer went round from town to town
reciting, and on coming to Delphi he enquired what his
native land was; and the Pythia said:

> There is an island Ios, your mother's home, which on
> your death
> will receive you. Only beware the young boys' riddle.

After hearing this, they say, he avoided going on to Ios, and
remained in those parts. Around the same time Ganyctor
was organizing the funeral of his father Amphidamas, a
king in Euboea, and he invited to the contest all the men
who were noted not only for strength and speed at run-
ning, but also for intellectual accomplishments, honoring
them with sizeable gifts. So these two also, having met up
by chance, as they say, went to Chalcis. At the contest,
among other Chalcidian notables who were sitting as
judges, there was Panedes, a brother of the deceased. And
after both poets had put up wonderful performances, they
say that Hesiod was the winner, in the following manner.
He came forward onto the floor and set Homer a series of
questions, to which Homer responded. So Hesiod said:

> Son of Meles, Homer, with your wisdom from the
> gods,
> come, tell me first of all, what is the best thing for
> mortals?

Homer:

ἀρχὴν μὲν μὴ φῦναι ἐπιχθονίοισιν ἄριστον,
φύντα δ' ὅπως ὤκιστα πύλας Ἀΐδαο περῆσαι.

Ἡσίοδος τὸ δεύτερον·

εἴπ' ἄγε μοι καὶ τοῦτο, θεοῖς ἐπιείκελ' Ὅμηρε,
τί θνητοῖς κάλλιστον ὀίεαι ἐν φρεσὶν εἶναι;

ὁ δέ (Od. 9.6–11)·

ὁππότ' ἂν εὐφροσύνη μὲν ἔχηι κάτα δῆμον
    ἅπαντα,
δαιτυμόνες δ' ἀνὰ δώματ' ἀκουάζωνται ἀοιδοῦ
ἥμενοι ἑξείης, παρὰ δὲ πλήθωσι τράπεζαι
σίτου καὶ κρειῶν, μέθυ δ' ἐκ κρητῆρος ἀφύσσων
οἰνοχόος φορέησι καὶ ἐγχείηι δεπάεσσιν·
τοῦτό τί μοι κάλλιστον ἐνὶ φρεσὶν εἴδεται εἶναι.

8 ῥηθέντων δὲ τούτων τῶν ἐπῶν, οὕτως σφοδρῶς φασι
θαυμασθῆναι τοὺς στίχους ὑπὸ τῶν Ἑλλήνων ὥστε
χρυσοῦς αὐτοὺς προσαγορευθῆναι, καὶ ἔτι καὶ νῦν ἐν
ταῖς κοιναῖς θυσίαις πρὸ τῶν δείπνων καὶ σπονδῶν
προκατεύχεσθαι πάντας.

ὁ δὲ Ἡσίοδος, ἀχθεσθεὶς ἐπὶ τῆι Ὁμήρου εὐ-
ημερίαι, ἐπὶ τὴν τῶν ἀπόρων ὥρμησεν ἐπερώτησιν,
καί φησι τούσδε τοὺς στίχους·

1. THE CONTEST

Not to be born in the first place is best for men on
   earth,
or if born, to pass through Hades' gates as fast as
   possible.[5]

Hesiod again:

Come, tell me this too, godlike Homer:
what do you consider to be the finest thing for
   mortals?

He replied:

When good cheer prevails thoughout the people,
and banqueters in the hall are listening to a bard,
sitting in line, and beside them the tables are laden
with bread and meat; and drawing wine from the
   bowl
the wine waiter brings it round and pours it in the
   cups—
this sort of thing is what seems to me the finest.

When these verses were spoken, they say the lines were so
intensely admired by the Greeks that they were dubbed
"golden," and even today everyone invokes them at public
sacrifices before the feasting and libations.

But Hesiod, vexed at Homer's success, turned to asking
conundrums, and spoke these lines:

[5] Stobaeus 4.52.22 quotes these lines as from Alcidamas'
Mouseion. They are found, with added pentameters, as lines 425–
428 of the Theognidea. For the sentiment see also Bacchylides
5.160; Euripides, fr. 285.1–2; Sophocles, *Oedipus at Colonus*
1224–1227; Alexis, fr. 145.14–16 K.–A.

Μοῦσ' ἄγε μοι, τά τ' ἐόντα τά τ' ἐσσόμενα πρό
   τ' ἐόντα,
τῶν μὲν μηδὲν ἄειδε, σὺ δ' ἄλλης μνῆσαι ἀοιδῆς.

ὁ δὲ Ὅμηρος βουλόμενος ἀκολούθως τὸ ἄπορον λῦ-
σαί φησιν·

  οὐδέ ποτ' ἀμφὶ Διὸς τύμβωι καναχήποδες ἵπποι
  ἄρματα συντρίψουσιν ἐρίζοντες περὶ νίκης.

9   καλῶς δὲ καὶ ἐν τούτοις ἀπαντήσαντος, ἐπὶ τὰς
ἀμφιβόλους γνώμας ὥρμησεν ὁ Ἡσίοδος, καὶ πλείο-
νας στίχους λέγων ἠξίου καθ' ἕνα ἕκαστον συμφώνως
ἀποκρίνασθαι τὸν Ὅμηρον. ἔστιν οὖν ὁ μὲν πρῶτος
Ἡσιόδου, ὁ δὲ ἑξῆς Ὁμήρου, ἐνίοτε δὲ καὶ διὰ δύο
στίχων τὴν ἐπερώτησιν ποιουμένου τοῦ Ἡσιόδου·

  δεῖπνον ἔπειθ' εἵλοντο βοῶν κρέα καὐχένας
    ἵππων
—ἔκλυον ἱδρώοντας, ἐπεὶ πολέμοιο κορέσθην.

  καὶ Φρύγες, οἳ πάντων ἀνδρῶν ἐπὶ νηυσὶν
    ἄριστοι
—ἀνδράσι ληϊστῆρσιν ἐπ' ἀκτῆς δόρπα πένεσθαι.[13]

13 δόρπα πένεσθαι Wilamowitz: δόρπον ἑλέσθαι cod.

1. THE CONTEST

Come now, Muse, of things that are and will be and
    were aforetime—
sing nothing of those, but take heed for other singing.

Homer, looking for a logical solution to the problem, said:

Never shall clattering steeds about the tomb of Zeus
smash chariots as they contend for victory.[6]

As he had countered well in this challenge too, Hesiod
turned to ambivalent propositions: he spoke a number of
lines, and required Homer to supply a harmonious contin-
uation for each one in turn. So the first line in each case
is Hesiod's, and the following one Homer's, except that
sometimes Hesiod uses two lines for his question:[7]

Then they dined on beef and the horses' necks—
They cleansed of sweat, having had their fill of
    fighting.[8]

And the Phrygians, who of all men on shipboard are
    the finest—[9]
At preparing supper on shore for a pirate crew.

---

[6] Plutarch, *Symposium of the Seven Sages* 154a, gives a version
of this exchange in which the problem is set by the cyclic poet
Lesches and it is Hesiod who solves it, thus winning the contest.

[7] The author has not fully understood the riddles he is using.
Some of them are double riddles, in which the responder, in solv-
ing the problem, at the same time sets a new one for the first
speaker.

[8] These two lines appear in a slightly different form in Aris-
tophanes, *Peace* 1282–1283.

[9] This is a paradox because to the Greeks the Phrygians were a
byword for cowardice.

χερσὶ βαλὼν ἰοὺς ἀνόμων κατὰ φῦλα Γιγάντων
—Ἡρακλέης ἀπέλυσεν ἀπ' ὤμων καμπύλα τόξα.[14]

οὗτος ἀνὴρ ἀνδρός τ' ἀγαθοῦ καὶ ἀνάλκιδός
 ἐστιν
—μητρός, ἐπεὶ πόλεμος χαλεπὸς πάσηισι γυναιξίν.

οὔτ' ἄρ σοί γε πατὴρ ἐμίγη καὶ πότνια μήτηρ
—†σῶμα, τό γ' ἐσπείραντο† διὰ χρυσῆν
 Ἀφροδίτην.

αὐτὰρ ἐπεὶ δμήθη γάμωι Ἄρτεμις ἰοχέαιρα
—Καλλιστὼ κατέπεφνεν ἀπ' ἀργυρέοιο βιοῖ<ο>.

ὣς οἱ μὲν δαίνυντο πανήμεροι, οὐδὲν ἔχοντες
—οἴκοθεν, ἀλλὰ παρεῖχεν ἄναξ ἀνδρῶν
 Ἀγαμέμνων.

δεῖπνον δειπνήσαντες ἐνὶ σποδῶι αἰθαλοέσσηι
—σύλλεγον ὀστέα λευκὰ Διὸς κατατεθνειῶτος
—παιδὸς ὑπερθύμου Σαρπηδόνος ἀντιθέοιο.

ἡμεῖς δ' ἂμ πεδίον Σιμοούντιον †ἥμενοι οὕτως†
—ἴομεν ἐκ νηῶν ὁδὸν ἀμφ' ὤμοισιν ἔχοντες
—φάσγανα κωπήεντα καὶ αἰγανέας δολιχαύλους.

δὴ τότ' ἀριστῆ<ες> κοῦροι χείρεσσι θαλάσσης

[14] Hos duos versus hoc ordine Nietzsche: inverso cod. ἰοὺς
Nietzsche, ἀνόμων Wilamowitz: ἰοῖσιν ὄλλων cod.

1. THE CONTEST

After shooting arrows at the lawless Giants with his
  hands—
Heracles undid from his shoulders his bent bow.

This man's father is brave, and a coward—
His mother, as fighting is a hard challenge for all
  women.

Nor with you did your father and lady mother make
  love—
†the body which†[10] they sowed through golden
  Aphrodite.

And as she had surrendered to sex, Artemis profuse
  of arrows—[11]
Slew Callisto with a shot from her silver bow.

So they feasted throughout the day with no food—
Of their own; it was provided by Agamemnon, lord of
  men.

After making their feast among the sooty ashes—
They collected the white bones of the dead one,
  Zeus'—
Proud son, the godlike Sarpedon.

We over the plain of Simois †sitting thus†—
Stepped out from the ships our path slung round our
  shoulders—
Our hilted swords and long-socketed javelins.

Then forsooth the heroic youths with hands from the
  sea—

10 Unintelligible.   11 Artemis was an eternal virgin.

—ἄσμενοι ἐσσυμένως τε ἀπείρυσαν ὠκύαλον ναῦν.

Κολχίδ᾽ ἔπειτ᾽ ἤγοντο[15] καὶ Αἰήτην βασιλῆα
—φεῦγον, ἐπεὶ γίνωσκον ἀνέστιον ἠδ᾽ ἀθέμιστον.

αὐτὰρ ἐπεὶ σπεῖσάν τε καὶ ἔκπιον οἶδμα
    θαλάσσης
—ποντοπορεῖν ἤμελλον ἐϋσσέλμων ἐπὶ νηῶν.

τοῖσιν δ᾽ Ἀτρείδης μεγάλ᾽ εὔχετο πᾶσιν ὀλέσθαι
—μηδέ ποτ᾽ ἐν πόντωι, καὶ φωνήσας ἔπος ηὔδα·
ἐσθίετ᾽ ὦ ξεῖνοι, καὶ πίνετε· μηδέ τις ὕμων
οἴκαδε νοστήσειε φίλην ἐς πατρίδα γαῖαν
—πημανθείς, ἀλλ᾽ αὖθις ἀπήμονες οἴκαδ᾽ ἵκοισθε.

10   πρὸς πάντα δὲ τοῦ Ὁμήρου καλῶς ἀπαντήσαντος
πάλιν φησὶν ὁ Ἡσίοδος·

τοῦτό τι δή μοι μοῦνον ἐειρομένωι κατάλεξον·
πόσσοι ἅμ᾽ Ἀτρείδηισιν ἐς Ἴλιον ἦλθον Ἀχαιοί;

ὁ δὲ διὰ λογιστικοῦ προβλήματος ἀποκρίνεται οὕτως·

πεντήκοντ᾽ ἦσαν πυρὸς ἐσχάραι, ἐν δὲ ἑκάστηι
πεντήκοντ᾽ ὀβελοί, περὶ δὲ κρέα πεντήκοντα·
τρὶς δὲ τριηκόσιοι περὶ ἓν κρέας ἦσαν Ἀχαιοί.

{τοῦτο δὲ εὑρίσκεται πλῆθος ἄπιστον· τῶν γὰρ ἐσχα-
ρῶν οὐσῶν πεντήκοντα, ὀβελίσκοι γίνονται πεντακό-

15 ἤγοντο Wilamowitz: ἵκοντο cod.

Gladly and swift hauled up the speedy ship.

The Colchian maid[12] then they bore away, and king
  Aietes—
They fled, for they saw he was inhospitable and
  uncivilized.

But when they had made libation and drunk up the
  sea swell—
They prepared to sail in their well-benched ships.

The son of Atreus prayed loud for them all, that they
  should perish—
At sea never, and he spoke this utterance:
"Eat, my guests, and drink, and may none of you
return home to his dear homeland—
Harmed, but may you all arrive home in safety."

As Homer had countered everything satisfactorily,
Hesiod tried again:

Just tell me this one little thing that I ask:
how many Achaeans went to Troy with the sons of
  Atreus?

He answered by means of an arithmetical problem:

There were fifty fire-hearths, and in each one
fifty spits, with fifty pieces of meat on them,
and thrice three hundred Achaeans round one piece
  of meat.

{This works out as an incredible quantity, for if there are 50
hearths, the spits come out at 2,500, and the meat pieces at

12 Medea.

σιοι καὶ χιλιάδες β′, κρεῶν δὲ δεκαδύο μυριάδες ‹καὶ
χιλιάδες› ε′, †ὕῦ† . . .}[16]

11   κατὰ πάντα δὴ τοῦ Ὁμήρου ὑπερτεροῦντος, φθο-
νῶν ὁ Ἡσίοδος ἄρχεται πάλιν·

> υἱὲ Μέλητος Ὅμηρ᾽, εἴ περ τιμῶσί σε Μοῦσαι,
> ὡς λόγος, ὑψίστοι‹ο› Διὸς μεγάλοιο θύγατρες,
> λέξον μέτρωι[17] ἐναρμόζων, ὅ τι δὴ θνητοῖσιν
> κάλλιστόν ‹τε› καὶ ἔχθιστον· ‹πο›θέω γὰρ
>   ἀκοῦσαι.

ὁ δέ φησι·

> Ἡσίοδ᾽ ἔκγονε Δίου, ἑκόντά με ταῦτα κελεύεις
> εἰπεῖν· αὐτὰρ ἐγὼ μάλα τοι πρόφρων ἀγορεύσω.
> κάλλιστον μὲν τῶν ἀγαθῶν ἔσται μέτρον εἶναι
> αὐτὸν ἑαυτῶι, τῶν δὲ κακῶν ἔχθιστον ἁπάντων.
> ἄλλο δὲ πᾶν ὅ τι σῶι θυμῶι φίλον ἐστὶν ἐρώτα.

> πῶς ἂν ἄριστ᾽ οἰκοῖντο πόλεις καὶ ἐν ἤθεσι
>   ποίοις;
> —εἰ μὴ κερδαίνειν ἀπὸ τῶν αἰσχρῶν ἐθέλοιεν,
> οἱ δ᾽ ἀγαθοὶ τιμῶντο, δίκη δ᾽ ἀδίκοισιν ἐπείη.

> εὔχεσθαι δὲ θεοῖσι τί[18] πάντων ἐστὶν ἄμεινον;
> —εὔνουν †εἶναι ἑαυτῶι†[19] χρόνον ἐς τὸν ἅπαντα.

---

[16] καὶ χιλιάδες ε′ Boissonade: ͵εὖ cod. Interpolationem
notavit West.   [17] μέτρωι Barnes: μέτρον cod.
[18] θεοῖσι τί Rohde: θεοῖς ὅτι cod.
[19] E.g. εὔνουν θυμὸν ἔχειν ἀστοῖς.

125,000, so the number of men would be 112,500,000.}[13]

As Homer was keeping the upper hand throughout, Hesiod in frustration began again:

> Son of Meles, Homer, if the Muses esteem you
> as is said, those daughters of Zeus the highest and
>   greatest,
> say—fitting it into metre—what it is for mortals
> that is finest and what worst; I am eager to hear.

He said:

> Hesiod, offspring of Dios, I am willing to say
> what you bid me; I will tell you very gladly.
> The finest thing is to be the measure of good
> for oneself, and the worst of all, to be so of evil.
> Now ask me anything else you fancy.

> How would cities best be run, and by what
>   standards?
> —If they were prepared to abstain from immoral
>   profiteering,
> and the men of quality were esteemed, and
>   wrongdoers punished.

> And what is the best thing to pray to the gods for?
> —That they be well-disposed to the city evermore.[14]

---

[13] This looks like a Byzantine annotation, originally written in a margin; hence the Greek is damaged at the end.

[14] Text uncertain.

ἐν δ᾽ ἐλαχίστωι ἄριστον ἔχεις[20] ὅ τι φύεται
  εἰπεῖν;
—ὡς μὲν ἐμῆι γνώμηι, φρένες ἐσθλαὶ στήθεσιν[21]
  ἀνδρῶν.

ἡ δὲ δικαιοσύνη τε καὶ ἀνδρείη δύναται τί;
—κοινὰς ὠφελίας ἰδίοις μόχθοισι πορίζειν.

τῆς σοφίης δὲ τί τέκμαρ ἐπ᾽ ἀνθρώποισι
  πέφυκεν;
—γινώσκειν τὰ παρόντ᾽ ὀρθῶς, καιρῶι δ᾽ ἅμ᾽
  ἕπεσθαι.

πιστεῦσαι δὲ βροτοῖς ποῖον χρέος ἄξιόν ἐστιν;
—οἷς αὐτὸς κίνδυνος ἐπὶ[22] πραχθεῖσιν ἕπεται.

ἡ δ᾽ εὐδαιμονίη τί ποτ᾽ ἀνθρώποισι καλεῖται;
—λυπηθέντ᾽ ἐλάχιστα θανεῖν ἡσθέντά <τε>
  πλεῖστα.

12   ῥηθέντων δὲ καὶ τούτων, οἱ μὲν Ἕλληνες πάντες
τὸν Ὅμηρον ἐκέλευον στεφανοῦν· ὁ δὲ βασιλεὺς
Πανήδης ἐκέλευσεν ἕκαστον τὸ κάλλιστον ἐκ τῶν
ἰδίων ποιημάτων εἰπεῖν. Ἡσίοδος οὖν ἔφη πρῶτος
(Op. 383–392)·

Πληϊάδων Ἀτλαγενέων ἐπιτελλομενάων
ἄρχεσθ᾽ ἀμητοῦ, ἀρότοιό τε δυσομενάων·
αἱ δή τοι νύκτας τε καὶ ἤματα τεσσαράκοντα
κεκρύφαται, αὖθις δὲ περιπλομένου ἐνιαυτοῦ

1. THE CONTEST

And can you say what best thing grows in smallest
    space?
—In my opinion, good sense in the human breast.

And what does righteousness and manliness mean?
—Providing public benefit through private strain.

And what is wisdom's birthmark upon men?
—Judging situations correctly, and seizing the moment.

And what circumstances merit putting trust in
    people?
—When they are equally at risk from the outcome.

And what is it that humans call happiness?
—Minimum pain and maximum pleasure before you
    die.

When these dicta too had been spoken, the Greeks
all called for Homer to be garlanded as victor. But King
Panedes told each poet to recite the finest passage from his
own compositions. So Hesiod said first:

When the Pleiades born of Atlas rise before the sun,
begin the reaping; the plowing, when they set.
They for forty nights and days
are hidden, and again as the year goes round

---

20 ἔχειν σ᾿ cod.: corr. Hutchinson.
21 στήθεσιν West: σώμασιν cod. (cf. Stob. 3.3.45).
22 ἐπὶ Stephanus: ἔτι cod.

φαίνονται τὰ πρῶτα χαρασσομένοιο σιδήρου.
οὗτός τοι πεδίων πέλεται νόμος, οἵ τε θαλάσσης
ἐγγύθι ναιετάουσ᾽, οἵ τ᾽ ἄγκεα βησσήεντα
πόντου κυμαίνοντος ἀπόπροθι πίονα χῶρον
ναίουσιν· γυμνὸν σπείρειν, γυμνὸν δὲ βοωτεῖν,
γυμνούς τ᾽ ἀμάειν, ὅτ᾽ ἂν ὥρια πάντα πέλωνται.

μεθ᾽ ὃν Ὅμηρος (Il. 13.126–33 + 339–344)·

ἀμφὶ δ᾽ ἄρ᾽ Αἴαντας δοιοὺς ἵσταντο φάλαγγες
καρτεραί, ἃς οὔτ᾽ ἄν κεν Ἄρης ὀνόσαιτο μετελθὼν
οὔτέ κ᾽ Ἀθηναίη λαοσσόος· οἱ γὰρ ἄριστοι
κρινθέντες Τρῶάς τε καὶ Ἕκτορα δῖον ἔμιμνον,
φράξαντες δόρυ δουρί, σάκος σάκεϊ προθελύμνωι·
ἀσπὶς ἄρ᾽ ἀσπίδ᾽ ἔρειδε, κόρυς κόρυν, ἀνέρα δ᾽
    ἀνήρ,
ψαῦον δ᾽ ἱππόκομοι κόρυθες λαμπροῖσι φάλοισιν
νευόντων· ὡς πυκνοὶ ἐφέστασαν ἀλλήλοισιν.
ἔφριξεν δὲ μάχη φθεισίμβροτος ἐγχείηισιν
μακραῖς, ἃς εἶχον ταμεσίχροας· ὄσσε δ᾽ ἄμερδεν
αὐγὴ χαλκείη κορύθων ἄπο λαμπομενάων
θωρήκων τε νεοσμήκτων σακέων τε φαεινῶν,
ἐρχομένων ἄμυδις. μάλα κεν θρασυκάρδιος εἴη,
ὃς τότε γηθήσειεν ἰδὼν πόνον οὐδ᾽ ἀκάχοιτο.

13   θαυμάσαντες δὲ καὶ ἐν τούτωι τὸν Ὅμηρον οἱ
Ἕλληνες ἐπήινουν, ὡς παρὰ τὸ προσῆκον γεγονότων

they first appear at the time of iron-sharpening.
This is the rule of the land, both for those who live
near the sea, and for those who live in the winding
    glens
far from the swelling sea, a rich terrain:
naked sow and naked drive the oxen,
and naked reap, when all is in good season.

Then came Homer:

About the two Ajaxes the battle lines stood strong
that neither would Ares have faulted had he come
    there
nor Athena driver of armies; for the finest
picked men were awaiting the Trojans and lordly
    Hector,
hedging lance with lance, shield with shield
    overlapping;
targe pressed on targe, helm on helm, man on man,
and the horsehair plumes touched on the bright
    crests
as they nodded, so close they stood to one another.
The murderous battle bristled with long spears
that they held to slice the skin; eyes were dazzled
with the glint of the bronze from the shining helmets,
the fresh-polished corslets, and the bright shields
as the armies clashed. It would have been a bold-
    hearted man
who felt joy at sight of that toil and not dismay.

Once again the Greeks were struck with admiration
for Homer, praising the way the verses transcended the

τῶν ἐπῶν, καὶ ἐκέλευον διδόναι τὴν νίκην. ὁ δὲ βασι-
λεὺς τὸν Ἡσίοδον ἐστεφάνωσεν, εἰπὼν δίκαιον εἶναι
τὸν ἐπὶ γεωργίαν καὶ εἰρήνην προκαλούμενον νικᾶν,
οὐ τὸν πολέμους καὶ σφαγὰς διεξιόντα. τῆς μὲν οὖν
νίκης οὕτως φασὶ τυχεῖν τὸν Ἡσίοδον, καὶ λαβόντα
τρίποδα χαλκοῦν ἀναθεῖναι ταῖς Μούσαις ἐπιγρά-
ψαντα·

ὁ Ἡσίοδος Μούσαις Ἑλικωνίσι τόνδ᾽ ἀνέθηκεν,
ὕμνωι νικήσας ἐν Χαλκίδι θεῖον Ὅμηρον.

τοῦ δὲ ἀγῶνος διαλυθέντος διέπλευσεν ὁ Ἡσίοδος
εἰς Δελφοὺς χρησόμενος καὶ τῆς νίκης ἀπαρχὰς τῶι
θεῶι ἀναθήσων. προσερχομένου δὲ αὐτοῦ τῶι ναῶι
ἔνθεον γενομένην τὴν προφῆτίν φασιν εἰπεῖν·

ὄλβιος οὗτος ἀνὴρ ὃς ἐμὸν δόμον ἀμφιπολεύει,
Ἡσίοδος Μούσηισι τετιμένος ἀθανάτηισιν·
τοῦ δ᾽ ἤτοι κλέος ἔσται, ὅσην τ᾽ ἐπικίδναται ἠώς.
ἀλλὰ Διὸς πεφύλαξο Νεμείου κάλλιμον ἄλσος·
κεῖθι δέ τοι θανάτοιο τέλος πεπρωμένον ἐστίν.

14 ὁ δὲ Ἡσίοδος ἀκούσας τοῦ χρησμοῦ τῆς Πελοπον-
νήσου μὲν ἀνεχώρει, νομίσας τὴν ἐκεῖ Νεμέαν τὸν
θεὸν λέγειν, εἰς δὲ Οἰνόην τῆς Λοκρίδος ἐλθὼν κατα-
λύει παρ᾽ Ἀμφιφάνει καὶ Γανύκτορι τοῖς Φηγέως
παισίν, ἀγνοήσας τὸ μαντεῖον· ὁ γὰρ τόπος οὗτος
ἅπας ἐκαλεῖτο Διὸς Νεμείου ἱερόν. διατριβῆς δὲ αὐτῶι
πλείονος γενομένης ἐν τοῖς Οἰνοεῦσιν, ὑπονοήσαντες
οἱ νεανίσκοι τὴν ἀδελφὴν αὐτῶν μοιχεύειν τὸν Ἡσί-

merely fitting, and they called for him to be awarded the victory. The king, however, garlanded Hesiod, saying that it was right for the poet who encouraged people towards agriculture and peace to win, not the one who rehearsed battle and carnage. So that is how they say Hesiod got his victory, and that he received a bronze tripod and dedicated it the Muses with this inscription:

> Hesiod dedicated this to the Muses of Helicon,
> having defeated in song at Chalcis the godly Homer.

When the games broke up, Hesiod sailed across to Delphi to consult the oracle and to dedicate a tithe of his victory to Apollo. As he approached the temple, they say the prophetess became possessed, and declared:

> This is a fortunate man who attends my house:
> Hesiod, esteemed by the immortal Muses;
> his fame shall be known as far as the daylight
> spreads.
> Only beware Nemean Zeus' fair grove,
> for there your mortal terminus is destined.

After hearing this oracle, Hesiod withdrew further away from the Peloponnese, thinking that the god meant the Nemea there, and he went to Oinoe in Locris, where he lodged with Amphiphanes and Ganyctor, the sons of Phegeus, not recognizing the reference of the prophecy, for that whole region was called sacred to Nemean Zeus. When he had stayed for some time among the people of Oinoe, the young men came to suspect that Hesiod was

οδον ἀποκτείναντες εἰς τὸ μεταξὺ τῆς Εὐβοίας καὶ τῆς
Λοκρίδος πέλαγος κατεπόντισαν. τοῦ δὲ νεκροῦ τρι-
ταίου πρὸς τὴν γῆν ὑπὸ δελφίνων προσενεχθέντος,
ἑορτῆς τινος ἐπιχωρίου παρ' αὐτοῖς οὔσης Ῥίου
ἁγνείας,[23] πάντες ἐπὶ τὸν αἰγιαλὸν ἔδραμον, καὶ τὸ
σῶμα γνωρίσαντες ἐκεῖνο μὲν πενθήσαντες ἔθαψαν,
τοὺς δὲ φονεῖς ἀνεζήτουν. οἳ δέ, φοβηθέντες τὴν τῶν
πολιτῶν ὀργήν, κατασπάσαντες ἁλιευτικὸν σκάφος
διέπλευσαν εἰς Κρήτην· οὓς κατὰ μέσον τὸν πλοῦν ὁ
Ζεὺς κεραυνώσας κατεπόντωσεν, ὥς φησιν Ἀλκιδά-
μας ἐν Μουσείωι. Ἐρατοσθένης δέ φησιν ἐν Ἡσιό-
δωι[24] (fr. 17 Powell) Κτίμενον καὶ Ἄντιφον τοὺς
Γανύκτορος, ἐπὶ τῆι προειρημένηι αἰτίαι ἀνελόντας
⟨τὸν ποιητήν⟩,[25] σφαγιασθῆναι θεοῖς ξενίοις ὑπ' Εὐ-
ρυκλέους τοῦ μάντεως· τὴν μέντοι παρθένον τὴν
ἀδελφὴν τῶν προειρημένων μετὰ τὴν φθορὰν ἑαυτὴν
ἀναρτῆσαι· φθαρῆναι δὲ ὑπό τινος ξένου συνόδου τοῦ
Ἡσιόδου Δημώδους ὄνομα, ὃν καὶ αὐτὸν ἀναιρεθῆναι
ὑπὸ τῶν αὐτῶν φησιν. ὕστερον δὲ Ὀρχομένιοι κατὰ
χρησμὸν μετενέγκαντες αὐτὸν παρ' αὐτοῖς ἔθαψαν,
καὶ ἐπέγραψαν ἐπὶ τῶι τάφωι·

Ἄσκρη μὲν πατρὶς πολυλήϊος, ἀλλὰ θανόντος
ὀστέα πληξίππων γῆ Μινυῶν κατέχει

23 Ῥίου ἁγνείας Nietzsche ex Plut. *Mor.* 162e: ἀριαδνειας
cod.
24 Ἡσιόδωι Göttling: ἐνηπόδω cod.
25 ⟨ ⟩ add. West.

fornicating with their sister, and they killed him by drowning him in the sea between Locris and Euboea.[15] His corpse was brought to land by dolphins two days later while a certain local festival was in progress, the Purification of Rhion. Everyone ran to the shore and, recognizing the body, mourned him and gave him burial, and began to seek his murderers. They, fearing their fellow citizens' wrath, pulled a fishing boat down and sailed off towards Crete. In mid voyage Zeus cast a thunderbolt and drowned them, as Alcidamas says in his *Museum*. Eratosthenes in his *Hesiod*, however, says that Ganyctor's sons Ktimenos and Antiphos killed ⟨the poet⟩ for the reason aforesaid, and were slaughtered in sacrifice to the Gods of Hospitality by the seer Eurycles; and that the girl, their sister, hanged herself following her defloration, which had been done by a foreigner travelling with Hesiod, Demodes by name; and he says that this man too was killed by the same pair. Subsequently the Orchomenians transported Hesiod's body on the basis of an oracle and buried it in their territory, inscribing on the tombstone:

Ascra, the rich cornland, was my home, but my dead bones
the horse-goading Minyans' country holds:

[15] The compiler has wrongly taken the Locris of the story to be the eastern Locris. It is clear from all other versions that it was Ozolian Locris. Oinoe was the later name of the place that appears in Thucydides 3.95.3 as Oineon; see W. A. Oldfather, *RE* xvii. 2192.

Ἡσιόδου, τοῦ πλεῖστον ἐν ἀνθρώποις κλέος
ἐστίν
ἀνδρῶν κρινομένων ἐν βασάνωι σοφίης.

15 καὶ περὶ μὲν Ἡσιόδου τοσαῦτα. ὁ δὲ Ὅμηρος
ἀποτυχὼν τῆς νίκης περιερχόμενος ἔλεγε τὰ ποιή-
ματα, πρῶτον μὲν τὴν Θηβαΐδα, ἔπη ͵ζ, ἧς ἡ ἀρχή
(fr. 1)·

Ἄργος ἄειδε, θεά, πολυδίψιον, ἔνθεν ἄνακτες·

εἶτα Ἐπιγόνους,²⁶ ἔπη ͵ζ, ὧν ἡ ἀρχή (fr. 1)·

νῦν αὖθ᾽ ὁπλοτέρων ἀνδρῶν ἀρχώμεθα, Μοῦσαι.

φᾶσι γάρ τινες καὶ ταῦτα Ὁμήρου εἶναι. ἀκούσαντες
δὲ τῶν ἐπῶν οἱ Μίδου τοῦ βασιλέως παῖδες Ξάνθος
καὶ Γόργος παρακαλοῦσιν αὐτὸν ἐπίγραμμα ποιῆσαι
ἐπὶ τοῦ τάφου τοῦ πατρὸς αὐτῶν, ἐφ᾽ οὗ ἦν παρθένος
χαλκῆ τὸν Μίδου θάνατον οἰκτιζομένη. καὶ ποιεῖ οὕ-
τως (Epigr. 3)·

χαλκῆ παρθένος εἰμί, Μίδου δ᾽ ἐπὶ σήματος
ἧμαι.
ἔστ᾽ ἂν ὕδωρ τε νάηι καὶ δένδρεα μακρὰ τεθήληι
καὶ ποταμοὶ πλήθωσι, περικλύζηι δὲ θάλασσα,
ἠέλιος δ᾽ ἀνιὼν φαίνηι λαμπρά τε σελήνη,
αὐτοῦ τῆιδε μένουσα πολυκλαύτωι ἐπὶ τύμβωι
σημανέω παριοῦσι, Μίδης ὅτι τῆιδε τέθαπται.

mine, Hesiod's, whose fame is greatest in the world
  when men are tested by the touchstone of art.

So much for Hesiod. Homer, after his defeat in the contest, went about reciting his poems: firstly the *Thebaid* (7,000 lines), which begins

Sing, goddess, of thirsty Argos, from where the lords,

and then the *Epigoni* (7,000 lines), which begins

But now, Muses, let us begin on the younger men.

(For some say that this too is Homer's work.) When King Midas' sons Xanthos and Gorgos heard his poetry, they invited him to compose an inscription on their father's tomb, which was surmounted by a bronze figure of a girl lamenting Midas' death. He composed this:

A bronze girl am I, and I sit on Midas' monument.
So long as water flows, and trees grow tall,
and rivers fill, and the sea surges round coasts,
and the sun rises and shines, and the bright moon,
I shall remain here on this tear-stained tomb
to tell wayfarers that Midas is buried here.

---

26 ἐπειγομένου cod.: corr. Barnes.

λαβὼν δὲ παρ' αὐτῶν φιάλην ἀργυρᾶν ἀνατίθησιν ἐν
Δελφοῖς τῶι Ἀπόλλωνι, ἐπιγράψας·

Φοῖβε ἄναξ, δῶρόν τοι Ὅμηρος καλὸν ἔδωκα
σῆισιν ἐπιφροσύναις· σὺ δέ μοι κλέος αἰὲν
ὀπάζοις.

16   μετὰ δὲ ταῦτα ποιεῖ τὴν Ὀδύσσειαν ἔπη Μ,β,
πεποιηκὼς ἤδη τὴν Ἰλιάδα ἐπῶν Μ,εφ'.[27] παραγενό-
μενον δὲ ἐκεῖθεν εἰς Ἀθήνας αὐτὸν ξενισθῆναί φασι
παρὰ Μέδοντι τῶι βασιλεῖ τῶν Ἀθηναίων. ἐν δὲ τῶι
βουλευτηρίωι ψύχους ὄντος καὶ πυρὸς καιομένου σχε-
διάσαι λέγεται τούσδε τοὺς στίχους (Epigr. 13)·

ἀνδρὸς μὲν στέφανος[28] παῖδες, πύργοι δὲ
πόληος,
ἵπποι δ' αὖ πεδίου κόσμος, νῆες δὲ θαλάσσης,
λαὸς δ' εἰν ἀγορῆισι καθήμενος εἰσοράασθαι·
αἰθομένου δὲ πυρὸς γεραρώτερος οἶκος ἰδέσθαι
ἤματι χειμερίωι, ὁπότ' ἂν νείφησι Κρονίων.

17   ἐκεῖθεν δὲ παραγενόμενος εἰς Κόρινθον ἐρραψώιδει
τὰ ποιήματα. τιμηθεὶς δὲ μεγάλως παραγίνεται εἰς
Ἄργος, καὶ λέγει ἐκ τῆς Ἰλιάδος (2.559–568ab) τὰ ἔπη
τάδε·

οἳ δ' Ἄργός τ' εἶχον Τίρυνθά τε τειχιόεσσαν
Ἑρμιόνην τ' Ἀσίνην τε, βαθὺν κατὰ κόλπον
ἐχούσας,
Τροιζῆν' Ἠϊόνας τε καὶ ἀμπελόεντ' Ἐπίδαυρον

They gave him a silver cup, which he dedicated to Apollo at Delphi with the inscription:

> Lord Phoibos, this fair gift I, Homer, give you
> for your thoughtfulness. May you ever grant me
> fame.

After this he composed the *Odyssey* (12,000 lines), having already composed the *Iliad* (15,500 lines). They say he went on from there to Athens, where he was the guest of Medon, the Athenian king. And in the council chamber, the weather being cold and a fire burning, he is said to have improvised these lines:

> A man's crown is his sons, a city's its walls;
> horses adorn the plain, and ships the sea,
> and the people that sits in the gathering to behold;[16]
> but a burning fire makes the house a prouder sight
> on a winter's day, when Kronos' son sends snow.

From there he arrived in Corinth, and recited his poems. Receiving much honor there, he arrived in Argos, and spoke these verses from the *Iliad*:

> And those who held Argos and Tiryns with its walls,
> and Hermione and Asine, that command a deep gulf,
> Troezen and Eïones and vine-growing Epidaurus

---

[16] This line is a democratic adaptation of two lines in the version of the pseudo-Herodotean Life, 31.

---

[27] M,β . . . M,εφ′ Nietzsche: μβφ . . . με cod.
[28] στέφανος vit. Hdt.: στέφανοι cod.

νῆσόν τ᾽ Αἴγιναν Μάσητά τε κοῦροι Ἀχαιῶν,
τῶν αὖθ᾽ ἡγεμόνευε βοὴν ἀγαθὸς Διομήδης
Τυδείδης, οὗ πατρὸς ἔχων μένος Οἰνείδαο,
καὶ Σθένελος, Καπανῆος ἀγακλειτοῦ φίλος υἱός·
τοῖσι δ᾽ ἅμ᾽ Εὐρύπυλος τρίτατος κίεν ἰσόθεος
   φώς,
Μηκιστέως υἱὸς Ταλαϊονίδαο ἄνακτος.
ἐκ πάντων δ᾽ ἡγεῖτο βοὴν ἀγαθὸς Διομήδης·
τοῖσι δ᾽ ἅμ᾽ ὀγδώκοντα μέλαιναι νῆες ἕποντο·
ἐν δ᾽ ἄνδρες πολέμοιο δαήμονες ἐστιχόωντο
Ἀργεῖοι λινοθώρηκες, κέντρα πτολέμοιο.

τῶν δὲ Ἀργείων οἱ προεστηκότες ὑπερβολῆι χαρέντες
ἐπὶ τῶι ἐγκωμιάζεσθαι τὸ γένος αὐτῶν ὑπὸ τοῦ ἐνδο-
ξοτάτου τῶν ποιητῶν, αὐτὸν μὲν πολυτελέσι δωρεαῖς
ἐτίμησαν, εἰκόνα δὲ χαλκῆν ἀναστήσαντες ἐψηφί-
σαντο θυσίαν ἐπιτελεῖν Ὁμήρωι καθ᾽ ἡμέραν καὶ
κατὰ μῆνα καὶ κατ᾽ ἐνιαυτόν, ⟨καὶ⟩ ἄλλην θυσίαν
πενταετηρίδα εἰς Χίον ἀποστέλλειν. ἐπιγράφουσι δὲ
ἐπὶ τῆς εἰκό⟨νος⟩ αὐτοῦ·

θεῖος Ὅμηρος ὅδ᾽ ἐστίν, ὃς Ἑλλάδα τὴν
   μεγάλαυχον
   πᾶσαν ἐκόσμησεν καλλιεπεῖ σοφίηι,
ἔξοχα δ᾽ Ἀργείους, οἳ τὴν θεοτείχεα Τροίην
   ἤρειψαν ποινὴν[29] ἠϋκόμου Ἑλένης.
οὗ χάριν ἔστησεν δῆμος μεγαλόπ⟨τ⟩ολις αὐτόν
   ἐνθάδε καὶ τιμαῖς ἀμφέπει ἀθανάτων.

348

and the island of Aegina, and Mases, Achaean lads,
their leader was Diomedes, good at the war cry—
Tydeus' son, with the force of his father, the son of
    Oineus—
and Sthenelos, glorious Capaneus' dear son.
With those two went Eurypylus, godlike man,
the son of Mekisteus, son of lord Talaos;
but the leader of all was Diomedes, good at the war
    cry.
With them there followed eighty dark ships,
and in them were ranged men skilled in fighting,
the linen-corslet Argives, goads of war.

The Argive officials were exceedingly delighted to hear
their race being praised by the most celebrated of poets.
They honored him with costly gifts, set up a bronze statue
of him, and voted to perform a sacrifice for Homer daily,
monthly, and yearly, and to send another one every fifth
year to Chios. On his statue they inscribed:

This is the godly Homer, who has adorned
    all of proud Hellas with his verbal art,
above all the Argives, who smashed Troy's god-built
    wall
    as restitution for what fair-tressed Helen did.
Because of this the people of this great city
    has set him here, and treats him with honors
    divine.

---

[29] ποινῆς cod.: corr. Barnes.

18   ἐνδιατρίψας δὲ τῆι πόλει χρόνον τινὰ διέπλευσεν
εἰς Δῆλον εἰς τὴν πανήγυριν. καὶ σταθεὶς ἐπὶ τὸν
κεράτινον βωμὸν λέγει ὕμνον εἰς Ἀπόλλωνα, οὗ ἡ
ἀρχή (Hymn. Ap. 1)·

μνήσομαι οὐδὲ λάθωμαι Ἀπόλλωνος ἑκάτοιο.

ῥηθέντος δὲ τοῦ ὕμνου οἱ μὲν Ἴωνες πολίτην αὐτὸν
κοινὸν ἐποιήσαντο, Δήλιοι δὲ γράψαντες τὰ ἔπη εἰς
λεύκωμα ἀνέθηκαν ἐν τῶι τῆς Ἀρτέμιδος ἱερῶι.

τῆς δὲ πανηγύρεως λυθείσης ὁ ποιητὴς εἰς Ἴον
ἔπλευσε πρὸς Κρεώφυλον, κἀκεῖ χρόνον διέτριβε
πρεσβύτης ὢν ἤδη. ἐπὶ δὲ τῆς θαλάσσης καθήμενος
παίδων τινῶν ἀφ᾽ ἁλείας ἐρχομένων ὥς φασι πυθόμε-
νος (Epigr. 17)·

ἄνδρες ἀπ᾽ Ἀρκαδίης[30] θηρήτορες, ἦ ῥ᾽ ἔχομέν
τι;

εἰπόντων δὲ ἐκείνων

ὅσσ᾽ ἕλομεν λιπόμεσθα, ὅσ᾽ οὐχ ἕλομεν
φερόμεσθα,

οὐ νοήσας τὸ λεχθὲν ἤρετο αὐτοὺς ὅ τι λέγοιεν. οἳ δέ
φασιν ἐν ἁλείαι μὲν ἀγρεῦσαι μηδέν, ἐφθειρίσθαι δέ,
καὶ τῶν φθειρῶν οὓς ἔλαβον καταλιπεῖν, οὓς δὲ οὐκ
ἔλαβον ἐν τοῖς ἱματίοις φέρειν. ἀναμνησθεὶς δὲ τοῦ

    [30] ἀπ᾽ Ἀρκαδίης cod., item Procl. et Anon. II, III: ἄγρης
ἁλίης Koechly.

350

1. THE CONTEST

After he had spent some time in the city, he sailed to Delos for the panegyris, and taking his stand at the Altar of Horns, he recited the *Hymn to Apollo*, which begins

> Let me call to mind and not neglect Apollo the far-
> shooter.

When the hymn had been recited, the assembled Ionians conferred joint citizenship on him, while the Delians wrote out the verses on a placard and dedicated it in the temple of Artemis.

When the panegyris broke up, the poet sailed to Ios to see Creophylus, and spent some time there; by now he was getting on in years. As he was sitting by the sea, they say he asked some boys who were returning from fishing,

> O huntsmen from Arcadia,[17] have we caught
> anything?

When they replied,

> The ones we caught we left behind, the ones we
> missed we carry,

he did not understand, and asked them what they meant. They explained that they had caught nothing on their fishing expedition, but they had de-loused themselves, and the lice they had caught they had left behind, but the ones they failed to catch they were still carrying in their clothes.

---

[17] "From Arcadia" makes no sense, and may be an ancient corruption for "of marine prey" (ἄγρης ἁλίης). But other Lives have the same reading, so it is likely to have stood in the *Certamen* from the start.

μαντείου, ὅτι τὸ τέλος αὐτοῦ ἥκοι τοῦ βίου, ποιεῖ τὸ τοῦ τάφου αὐτοῦ ἐπίγραμμα. ἀναχωρῶν δὲ ἐκεῖθεν, ὄντος πηλοῦ ὀλισθὼν καὶ πεσὼν ἐπὶ τὴν πλευράν, τριταῖος ὥς φασι τελευτᾷ· καὶ ἐτάφη ἐν Ἴωι. ἔστι δὲ τὸ ἐπίγραμμα τόδε·

ἐνθάδε τὴν ἱερὴν κεφαλὴν κατὰ γαῖα καλύπτει,
ἀνδρῶν ἡρώων κοσμήτορα, θεῖον Ὅμηρον.

1. THE CONTEST

Then he remembered the prophecy, that the end of his life had come, so he composed his own tomb inscription. And as he was returning from there, the ground being muddy, he slipped and fell on his side, and within three days, so they say, he died. He was buried in Ios, and this is the inscription:

> Here the earth conceals that sacred head,
> adorner of warrior heroes, the godly Homer.

ΗΡΟΔΟΤΟΥ ΠΕΡΙ ΟΜΗΡΟΥ
ΓΕΝΕΣΙΟΣ ΚΑΙ ΗΛΙΚΙΗΣ
ΚΑΙ ΒΙΟΥ

1 Ἡρόδοτος Ἁλικαρνησσεὺς περὶ Ὁμήρου γενέσιος καὶ
ἡλικίης καὶ βιοτῆς τάδε ἱστόρηκε, ζητήσας ἐπεξελ-
θεῖν ἐς τὸ ἀτρεκέστατον.

ἐπεὶ γὰρ Κύμη ἡ πάλαι Αἰολιῶτις ἐκτίζετο, συν-
ῆλθον ἐν αὐτῆι παντοδαπὰ ἔθνεα Ἑλληνικά, καὶ δὴ
καὶ ἐκ Μαγνησίης ἄλλοι τέ τινες καὶ Μελάνωπος ὁ
Ἰθαγένεος τοῦ Κρήθωνος, οὐ πολύφορτος ἀλλὰ βρα-
χέα τοῦ βίου ἔχων. οὗτος δὲ ὁ Μελάνωπος ἔγημεν ἐν
τῆι Κύμηι θυγατέρα Ὀμύρητος, καὶ αὐτῶι γίνεται ἐκ
κοίτης θῆλυ τέκνον, ὧι ὄνομα τίθεται Κρηθηΐδα. καὶ
αὐτὸς μὲν ὁ Μελάνωπος καὶ ἡ γυνὴ αὐτοῦ ἐτελεύτη-
σαν τὸν βίον· τὴν δὲ θυγατέρα ἐπιτρέπει ἀνδρὶ ὧι
ἐχρῆτο μάλιστα, Κλεάνακτι {τῶι}[31] Ἀργείωι.

2 χρόνου δὲ προϊόντος συνέβη τὴν παῖδα μιγεῖσαν
ἀνδρὶ λαθραίως ἐν γαστρὶ σχεῖν. τὰ μὲν οὖν πρῶτα
ἐλάνθανεν· ἐπεὶ δὲ ἤισθετο ὁ Κλεάναξ, ἤχθετο τῆι
συμφορῆι, καὶ καλεσάμενος τὴν Κρηθηΐδα χωρὶς
πάντων ἐν αἰτίηι μεγάληι εἶχεν, ἐπιλεγόμενος τὴν
αἰσχύνην τὴν πρὸς τοὺς πολιήτας. προβουλεύεται οὖν

2. (PSEUDO-)HERODOTUS
ON HOMER'S ORIGINS,
DATE, AND LIFE

Herodotus of Halicarnassus has produced this account of Homer's origins, date, and life, endeavoring to pursue the questions to the most accurate conclusion.

When the old Aeolian Cyme was being founded, there came together in it every kind of Hellenic people. Among those that came from Magnesia was Melanopus, son of Ithagenes the son of Crethon, not with a great deal of baggage, but with modest means. This Melanopus married at Cyme a daughter of Omyres, and from their union he got a female child, to whom he gave the name Cretheis. And Melanopus himself and his wife came to the end of their lives, but the daughter he entrusted to a man with whom he had much contact, Cleanax, an Argive.

Some time later it happened that the girl had secret intercourse with a man and became pregnant. At first no one noticed; but when Cleanax observed it, he was vexed at the occurrence, and summoning Cretheis to see him in private, he rebuked her roundly, adding that it put them to shame in the city. So he made the following plan for her.

---

31 Del. Wilamowitz.

περὶ αὐτῆς τάδε· ἔτυχον οἱ Κυμαῖοι κτίζοντες τότε
τοῦ Ἑρμείου κόλπου τὸν μυχόν· κτιζομένοισι δὲ τὴν
πόλιν Σμύρναν ἔθετο τὸ ὄνομα Θησεύς, μνημεῖον
ἐθέλων καταστῆσαι τῆς ἑωυτοῦ γυναικὸς ἐπώνυμον·
ἦν γὰρ αὐτῆι τοὔνομα Σμύρνα. ὁ δὲ Θησεὺς ἦν τῶν
τὴν Κύμην κτισάντων ἐν τοῖς πρώτοις Θεσσαλῶν,
ἀπὸ Εὐμήλου τοῦ Ἀδμήτου, κάρτα εὖ ἔχων τοῦ βίου.
ἐνταῦθα ὑπεκτίθεται ὁ Κλεάναξ τὴν Κρηθηΐδα πρὸς
Ἰσμηνίην Βοιώτιον, τῶν ἀποίκων λελογχότα, ὃς ἐτύγ-
χανεν αὐτῶι ἐὼν ἑταῖρος τὰ μάλιστα.

3   χρόνου δὲ προϊόντος ἐξελθοῦσα ἡ Κρηθηῒς μετ'
ἄλλων γυναικῶν πρὸς ἑορτήν τινα ἐπὶ τὸν ποταμὸν
τὸν καλούμενον Μέλητα, ἤδη ἐπίτοκος οὖσα, τίκτει
τὸν Ὅμηρον, οὐ τυφλὸν ἀλλὰ δεδορκότα· καὶ τίθεται
ὄνομα τῶι παιδίωι Μελησιγένεα, ἀπὸ τοῦ ποταμοῦ
τὴν ἐπωνυμίαν λαβοῦσα. τέως μὲν οὖν ἡ Κρηθηῒς ἦν
παρὰ τῶι Ἰσμηνίηι· προϊόντος δὲ τοῦ χρόνου ἐξῆλθε,
καὶ ἀπὸ ἐργασίης χειρῶν ὡρμημένη ἔτρεφε τὸ παιδίον
καὶ ἑωυτήν, ἄλλοτε παρ' ἄλλων ἔργα λαμβάνουσα·
καὶ ἐπαίδευε τὸν παῖδα ἀφ' ὧν ἠδύνατο.

4   ἦν δέ τις ἐν Σμύρνηι τοῦτον τὸν χρόνον Φήμιος
τοὔνομα, παῖδας γράμματα καὶ τὴν ἄλλην μουσικὴν
διδάσκων πᾶσαν. οὗτος μισθοῦται τὴν Κρηθηΐδα, ὢν
μονότροπος, ἐριουργῆσαι αὐτῶι εἴριά τινα ἃ παρὰ τῶν
παίδων ἐς μισθὸν ἐλάμβανεν. ἡ δὲ παρ' αὐτῶι εἰρ-
γάζετο, πολλῶι ⟨τῶι⟩[32] κοσμίωι καὶ σωφροσύνηι πολ-
λῆι χρωμένη, καὶ τῶι Φημίωι κάρτα ἠρέσκετο. τέλος
δὲ προσηνέγκατο αὐτῆι λόγους πείθων ἑωυτῶι συν-

The Cymaeans were just then colonizing the inner part of the gulf of the Hermus; the colony was named Smyrna by Theseus, who wanted to establish a memorial bearing the name of his own wife, for she was named Smyrna. Theseus was one of the leading Thessalian founders of Cyme, a descendant of Eumelus the son of Admetus, and a man of abundant means. There Cleanax placed Cretheis with Ismenias, a Boeotian who had been allotted a place among the colonists, and who was a great friend of his.

Some time later Cretheis went out with other women to a festival at the river known as the Meles; her time was due, and she gave birth to Homer, who was not blind but sighted. And she named the child Melesigenes, taking the name from the river. For the moment she was still with Ismenias. But some time later she left his house, and proceeded to keep the child and herself by manual work, taking employment from different people at different times, and she saw to her son's education as her means allowed.

Now there was in Smyrna at this time a man named Phemius, who gave boys instruction in reading and writing and the other humanities. He lived alone, and he hired Cretheis to card and spin bundles of wool that he got from the boys as school fees. She worked for him, displaying a high degree of modesty and decency, and Phemius was well pleased with her. Finally he approached her with the

---

32 Add. West.

οἰκεῖν, ἄλλά τε πολλὰ λέγων οἷς μιν ὤιετο προσάξεσθαι, καὶ ἔτι περὶ τοῦ παιδός, υἱὸν ποιούμενος, καὶ ὅτι τραφεὶς καὶ παιδευθεὶς ὑπ᾽ αὐτοῦ ἄξιος λόγου ἔσται (ἑώρα γὰρ τὸν παῖδα ὄντα συνετὸν καὶ κάρτα εὐφυέα), ἔστ᾽ ἀνέπεισεν αὐτὴν ποιεῖν ταῦτα.

5 ὁ παῖς δὲ ἦν τε φύσιν ἔχων ἀγαθήν, ἐπιμελίης τε καὶ παιδεύσιος προσγενομένης αὐτίκα πολλὸν τῶν πάντων ὑπερεῖχε. χρόνου δὲ ἐπιγενομένου ἀνδρούμενος οὐδὲν τοῦ Φημίου ὑποδεέστερος ἦν ἐν τῆι διδασκαλίαι. καὶ οὕτως ὁ μὲν Φήμιος ἐτελεύτησε τὸν βίον, καταλιπὼν πάντα τῶι παιδί, οὐ πολλῶι δὲ ὕστερον καὶ ἡ Κρηθηὶς ἐτελεύτησεν· ὁ δὲ Μελησιγένης ἐπὶ τῆι διδασκαλίαι καθειστήκει. καθ᾽ ἑωυτὸν δὲ γενόμενος μᾶλλον ὑπὸ τῶν ἀνθρώπων ἑωρᾶτο, καὶ αὐτοῦ θαυμασταὶ καθειστήκεισαν οἵ τε ἐγχώριοι καὶ τῶν ξένων οἱ ἐσαπικνεόμενοι. ἐμπόριον γὰρ ἦν ἡ Σμύρνα, καὶ σῖτος ἐξήγετο πολὺς αὐτόθεν, ἐκ τῆς ἐπικειμένης χώρας δαψιλέως κάρτα ἐσαγόμενος ἐς αὐτήν. οἱ οὖν ξένοι, ὁκότε παύσοιντο τῶν ἔργων, ἀπεσχόλαζον παρὰ τῶι Μελησιγένει ἐγκαθίζοντες.

6 ἦν δὲ ἐν αὐτοῖς τότε καὶ Μέντης ναύκληρος ἀπὸ τῶν περὶ Λευκάδα τόπων, καταπεπλευκὼς ἐπὶ σῖτον ἔχων ναῦν, πεπαιδευμένος τε ἀνὴρ ὡς ἐν ἐκείνωι τῶι χρόνωι καὶ πολυΐστωρ· ὅς μιν ἔπεισε τὸν Μελησιγένην μεθ᾽ ἑωυτοῦ πλεῖν καταλύσαντα τὴν διδασκαλίαν, μισθόν τε λαμβάνοντα καὶ τὰ δέοντα πάντα, καὶ ὅτι τὸ χώρας καὶ πόλιας θεήσασθαι ἄξιον εἴη αὐτῶι ἕως νέος ἐστί. καί μιν οἴομαι μάλιστα τούτοισι προσ-

proposal that she should live with him; among many other arguments that he thought would induce her, he referred to her child, saying that he would adopt him as his son, and that once educated by himself he would be a person of note (for he could see that the boy was intelligent and highly gifted); until he persuaded her to do so.

The boy was naturally endowed, and with the benefit of attention and education he quickly began to stand out far above the rest. When in time he reached manhood, he was nothing inferior to Phemius in learning. So it was when Phemius came to the end of his life, leaving everything to the boy; not long afterwards Cretheis died too, and Melesigenes was established as the teacher. Being now on his own, he attracted more notice, and earned the admiration both of the local people and of those foreigners who came in. For Smyrna was a trading center, and much grain was exported from there, as it was brought in from the surrounding country in great abundance; so when the foreigners stopped work, they used to spend time sitting in on Melesigenes.

There was among them at that period a shipowner Mentes from the Leucas region, who had sailed in with his ship for grain, an educated man for his time and a knowledgeable one. He persuaded Melesigenes to close his school and sail with him, for a wage and all found, adding that it was worth seeing countries and cities while he was still young. And I think that he was won over by this argu-

αχθῆναι· ἴσως γὰρ καὶ τῆι ποιήσει ἤδη τότε ἐπενόει
ἐπιθήσεσθαι. καταλύσας δὲ τὴν διδασκαλίαν ἐναντίλ-
λετο μετὰ τοῦ Μέντεω. καὶ ὅπου ἑκάστοτε ἀφίκοιτο,
πάντα τὰ ἐπιχώρια διεωρᾶτο, καὶ ἱστορέων ἐπυν-
θάνετο· εἰκὸς δέ μιν ἦν καὶ μνημόσυνα πάντων γράφε-
σθαι.

7   ἀνακομιζόμενοι δὲ ἐκ Τυρσηνίης καὶ {τῆς} Ἰβηρίης
ἀπικνέονται ἐς Ἰθάκην. καὶ τῶι Μελησιγένει συνέβη
νοσήσαντι τοὺς ὀφθαλμοὺς κάρτα δεινῶς ἔχειν, καὶ
αὐτὸν θεραπείης εἴνεκεν, πλεῖν μέλλων ἐς τὴν Λευ-
κάδα, καταλείπει[33] ὁ Μέντης παρὰ ἀνδρὶ φίλωι ἑωυτοῦ
ἐς τὰ μάλιστα, Μέντορι τῶι Ἀλκίμου Ἰθακησίωι,
πολλὰ δεηθεὶς ἐπιμελίην ἔχειν· ἐπαναπλώσας δὲ ἀνα-
λήψεσθαι αὐτόν. ὁ δὲ Μέντωρ ἐνοσήλευεν αὐτὸν
ἐκτενέως· καὶ γὰρ τοῦ βίου ἀρκεόντως εἶχε, καὶ ἤκουεν
εὖ ἐς δικαιοσύνην τε καὶ φιλοξενίην μακρῶι μάλιστα
τῶν ἐν Ἰθάκηι ἀνδρῶν. ἐνταῦθα συνέβη τῶι Μελησι-
γένει τὰ περὶ Ὀδυσσέως ἐξιστορῆσαι καὶ πυθέσθαι.
οἱ μὲν δὴ Ἰθακήσιοι λέγουσι τότε μιν παρ᾽ ἑωυτοῖς
τυφλωθῆναι· ὡς δὲ ἐγώ φημι, τότε μὲν ὑγιῆ γενέσθαι,
ὕστερον δὲ ἐν Κολοφῶνι τυφλωθῆναι· συνομολογοῦσι
δέ μοι καὶ Κολοφώνιοι τούτοις.

8   ὁ δὲ Μέντης ἀναπλέων ἐκ τῆς Λευκάδος προσέσχεν
ἐς τὴν Ἰθάκην καὶ ἀνέλαβε τὸν Μελησιγένεα· χρόνον
τε ἐπὶ συχνὸν συμπεριέπλει αὐτῶι. ἀπικομένωι δὲ ἐς
Κολοφῶνα συνέβη πάλιν νοσήσαντα τοὺς ὀφθαλμοὺς
μὴ δύνασθαι διαφυγεῖν τὴν νόσον, ἀλλὰ τυφλωθῆναι
ἐνταῦθα. ἐκ δὲ τῆς Κολοφῶνος τυφλὸς ἐὼν ἀπικνέεται

ment about all; for it may be that he was already thinking of setting his hand to poetry. He closed the school and sailed with Mentes. And wherever he went on each occasion, he observed all the local details and learned more by enquiry; and probably he also made written notes of everything.

Coming back from Etruria and Spain, they arrived at Ithaca, and it happened that Melesigenes developed an eye ailment and was in a very bad way. So that he could be looked after, Mentes, who was sailing to Leucas, left him with a great friend of his, Mentor, son of Alkimos, an Ithacan, entreating him to take care of him; he said he would pick him up on his return trip. Mentor tended him assiduously, for he had sufficient means, and much the best reputation of the men in Ithaca for uprightness and hospitality. It was there that Melesigenes enquired into and learned the story of Odysseus. The Ithacans say that it was then, among them, that he became blind; but as I maintain, he recovered on that occasion and became blind later in Colophon, and the Colophonians agree with me on this.

When Mentes sailed back from Leucas, he put in at Ithaca and picked Melesigenes up, and for a long time he continued to sail about with him. But when he came to Colophon, it happened that his eye ailment recurred, and he could not get rid of it but became blind there. From Colophon, as a blind man, he went to Smyrna, and in these

---

33 καταλείπει Wilamowitz: καταλιπεῖν codd.

ἐς τὴν Σμύρναν, καὶ οὕτως ἐπεχείρει τῆι ποιήσει.

9   χρόνου δὲ προϊόντος, ἐν τῆι Σμύρνηι ἄπορος ἐὼν
τοῦ βίου, διενοήθη ἀπικέσθαι ἐς Κύμην. πορευόμενος
δὲ διὰ τοῦ Ἕρμου πεδίου ἀπικνέεται ἐς Νέον τεῖχος,
ἀποικίην Κυμαίων· ὠικίσθη δὲ τοῦτο τὸ χωρίον ὕστε-
ρον Κύμης ἔτεσιν ὀκτώ. ἐνταῦθα λέγεται αὐτὸν ἐπι-
στάντα ἐπὶ σκυτεῖόν τι εἰπεῖν πρῶτα τὰ ἔπεα τάδε
(Epigr. 1)·

> αἰδεῖσθε ξενίων κεχρημένον ἠδὲ δόμοιο,
> οἳ πόλιν αἰπεινὴν νύμφης ἐριώπιδος Ἥρης[34]
> ναίετε, Σαιδήνης[35] πόδα νείατον ὑψικόμοιο,
> ἀμβρόσιον πίνοντες ὕδωρ θείου ποταμοῖο
> Ἕρμου δινήεντος, ὃν ἀθάνατος τέκετο Ζεύς.

ἡ δὲ Σαιδήνη ὄρος ἐστὶν ὑπερκείμενον τοῦ τε Ἕρμου
ποταμοῦ καὶ τοῦ Νέου τείχους. τῶι δὲ σκυτεῖ ὄνομα ἦν
Τυχίος· ἀκούσαντι δὲ τῶν ἐπέων ἔδοξεν αὐτῶι δέξα-
σθαι τὸν ἄνθρωπον, ἠλέησε γὰρ αἰτέοντα τυφλόν, καὶ
ἐκέλευσεν ἐσιέναι τε αὐτὸν ἐς τὸ ἐργαστήριον καὶ
μετέξειν ἔφη τῶν παρεόντων· ὃ δὲ ἐσῆλθε. κατήμενος
δὲ ἐν τῶι σκυτείωι, παρεόντων καὶ ἄλλων, τήν τε
ποίησιν αὐτοῖς ἐπεδείκνυτο, Ἀμφιάρεώ τε τὴν ἐξελα-
σίαν τὴν ἐς Θήβας, καὶ τοὺς ὕμνους τοὺς ἐς θεοὺς
πεποιημένους αὐτῶι, καὶ περὶ τῶν λεγομένων ὑπὸ τῶν
παρεόντων ἐς τὸ μέσον γνώμας ἀποφαινόμενος
θωύματος ἄξιος ἐφαίνετο εἶναι τοῖς ἀκούουσι.

10   τέως μὲν οὖν κατεῖχεν ὁ Μελησιγένης περὶ τὸ Νέον

circumstances he began to essay poetry.

Some time later, finding himself short of the means of livelihood in Smyrna, he decided to go to Cyme. As he journeyed across the plain of the Hermus, he arrived at Neonteichos, a Cymaean colony, founded eight years after Cyme. There it is said that he turned up at a cobbler's and recited these as his first verses (*Epigram* 1):

> Have respect for one in need of house and
>   hospitality,
> you that dwell in the steep city of fair-eyed Hera the
>   Bride
> on the lowest spur of high-forested Saidene,
> drinking the ambrosial water of the divine river,
> the eddying Hermus, born of immortal Zeus.

Saidene is a mountain lying above the river Hermus and Neonteichos. The cobbler's name was Tychios, and when he heard the verses, he decided to take the fellow in, as he felt pity for a blind man begging. He invited him in to the workshop and promised him a share of what there was, and he went in. As he sat in the cobbler's shop, with others also present, he would perform his poetry for them, *Amphiaraus' Expedition to Thebes*, and the Hymns that he had composed to the gods; and also by contributing comments on things that those present said, he made a great impression on his hearers.

So for the time being Melesigenes stayed around

---

34 νύμφης ἐρατώπιδος Ἥρης Hymnorum codd.: Κύμην ἐριώπιδα κούρην Vitae codd.

35 Ita fere Hymnorum codd. et Steph. Byz.: σαρδήνης et mox σαρδήνη Vitae codd.

τεῖχος, ἀπὸ τῆς ποιήσιος {γε}³⁶ τοῦ βίου τὴν μηχανὴν
ἔχων. ἐδείκνυον δὲ οἱ Νεοτειχεῖς μέχρις ἐπ' ἐμοῦ τὸν
χῶρον ἐν ὧι κατίζων τῶν ἐπέων τὴν ἐπίδειξιν ἐποιέετο,
καὶ κάρτα ἐσέβοντο τὸν τόπον· ἐν ὧι καὶ αἴγειρος
ἐπεφύκει, ἣν ἐκεῖνοι ἔφασαν ἀφ' οὗ ὁ Μελησιγένης
11 ἦλθεν αὐτοῖς πεφυκέναι. | χρόνου δὲ προϊόντος, ἀπό-
ρως κείμενος καὶ μόλις τὴν τροφὴν ἔχων, ἐπενοήθη ἐς
τὴν Κύμην ἀπικέσθαι, εἴ τι βέλτιον πρήξει. μέλλων δὲ
πορεύεσθαι τάδε τὰ ἔπεα λέγει (Epigr. 2)·

αἶψα πόδες με φέροιεν ἐς αἰδοίων πόλιν ἀνδρῶν·
τῶν γὰρ καὶ θυμὸς πρόφρων καὶ μῆτις ἀρίστη.

ἀπὸ δὲ τοῦ Νέου τείχεος πορευόμενος ἀπίκετο ἐς τὴν
Κύμην διὰ Λαρίσσης τὴν πορείαν ποιησάμενος· ἦν
γὰρ οὕτως αὐτῶι εὐπορώτατον· καί, ὡς Κυμαῖοι λέ-
γουσι, τῶι Φρυγίης βασιλῆι Μίδηι τῶι Γορδίεω, δεη-
θέντων πενθερῶν αὐτοῦ, ποιεῖ τὸ ἐπίγραμμα τόδε, τὸ
ἔτι καὶ νῦν ἐπὶ τῆς στήλης τοῦ μνήματος {τοῦ Γορ-
δίεω} ἐπιγέγραπται (Epigr. 3)·

ἔστ' ἂν ὕδωρ τε ῥέηι καὶ δένδρεα μακρὰ τεθήληι
ἠέλιός τ' ἀνιὼν λάμπηι λαμπρά τε σελήνη,
αὐτοῦ τῆιδε μένουσα πολυκλαύτου ἐπὶ τύμβου
ἀγγελέω παριοῦσι, Μίδης ὅτι τῆιδε τέθαπται.

12 κατίζων δὲ ἐν ταῖς λέσχαις τῶν γερόντων ἐν τῆι
Κύμηι ὁ Μελησιγένης τὰ ἔπεα τὰ πεποιημένα αὐτῶι

³⁶ Del. Wilamowitz.

Neonteichos, making his living from his poetry. The Neonteichians were still exhibiting up to my time the place where he used to sit and give performances of his verses, and they held it in great reverence. There was a poplar growing there which they said had grown up from when Melesigenes came to them. Some time later, however, being hard up and finding it difficult to feed himself, he decided to go to Cyme in the hope of doing better. Before he set out, he spoke these verses (*Epigram 2*):

> May my legs bring me soon to a respectful town:
> the heart of such men is willing, their devices the
>   best.

Setting out from Neonteichos, he reached Cyme by way of Larissa, for that was his easiest route. There, as the Cymaeans say, he composed this inscription for the Phrygian king Midas, son of Gordies, at the request of his kinsmen, and it is still inscribed on his memorial stele (*Epigram 3*):

> So long as water flows, and trees grow tall,
> and the sun rises and shines, and the bright moon,
> I shall remain here on this tear-stained tomb
> to tell wayfarers that Midas is buried here.[18]

At Cyme Melesigenes sat in the old men's saloons and performed the poems he had composed, and entertained

---

[18] This famous epigram is quoted by many authors. A longer version appears at *Certamen* 15.

ἐπεδείκνυτο, καὶ ἐν τοῖς λόγοις ἔτερπε τοὺς ἀκούοντας·
καὶ αὐτοῦ θωυμασταὶ καθειστήκεσαν. γνοὺς δὲ ὅτι
ἀποδέκονται αὐτοῦ τὴν ποίησιν οἱ Κυμαῖοι, καὶ ἐς
συνήθειαν ἕλκων τοὺς ἀκούοντας, λόγους πρὸς αὐτοὺς
τοιούσδε προσήνεγκε, λέγων ὡς εἰ θέλοιεν αὐτὸν δη-
μοσίηι τρέφειν, ἐπικλεεστάτην αὐτῶν τὴν πόλιν ποιή-
σει. τοῖς δὲ ἀκούουσι βουλομένοις τε ἦν ταῦτα, καὶ
αὐτῶι[37] παρήινεον ἐλθόντα ἐπὶ τὴν βουλὴν δεηθῆναι
τῶν βουλευτέων· καὶ αὐτοὶ ἔφασαν συμπρήξειν. ὃ δὲ
ἐπείθετο αὐτοῖς, καὶ βουλῆς συλλεγομένης ἐλθὼν ἐπὶ
τὸ βουλεῖον ἐδεῖτο τοῦ ἐπὶ τῆι τιμῆι ταύτηι καθεστῶ-
τος ἀπαγαγεῖν αὐτὸν ἐπὶ τὴν βουλήν· ὃ δὲ ὑπεδέξατό
τε καὶ ἐπεὶ καιρὸς ἦν ἀπήγαγε. καταστὰς δὲ ὁ Μελη-
σιγένης ἔλεξε περὶ τῆς τροφῆς τὸν λόγον ὃν καὶ ἐν
13   ταῖς λέσχαις ἔλεγεν. ὡς δὲ εἶπεν, ἐξελθὼν ἐκάθητο· | οἱ
δὲ ἐβουλεύοντο, ὅ τι χρεὼν εἴη ἀποκρίνασθαι αὐτῶι.
προθυμουμένου δὲ τοῦ ἀπαγαγόντος αὐτὸν καὶ ἄλλων
ὅσοι τῶν βουλευτέων ἐν ταῖς λέσχαις ἐπήκοοι ἐγένον-
το, τῶν βασιλέων[38] ἕνα λέγεται ἐναντιωθῆναι τῆι
χρήμηι αὐτοῦ, ἄλλά τε πολλὰ λέγοντα καὶ ὡς εἰ τοὺς
ὁμήρους δόξει τρέφειν αὐτοῖς, ὅμιλον πολλόν τε καὶ
ἀχρεῖον ἕξουσιν. ἐντεῦθεν δὲ καὶ τοὔνομα Ὅμηρος
ἐπεκράτησε τῶι Μελησιγένει ἀπὸ τῆς συμφορῆς· οἱ
γὰρ Κυμαῖοι τοὺς τυφλοὺς ὁμήρους λέγουσιν· ὥστε
πρότερον ὀνομαζομένου αὐτοῦ Μελησιγένεος τοῦτο
14   γενέσθαι τοὔνομα, Ὅμηρος, | καὶ οἱ ξένοι διήνεγκαν

his hearers in conversation, so that they became admirers of his. Seeing that the Cymaeans were receptive to his poetry, and drawing his hearers into familiarity with him, he made an approach to them, saying that if they were prepared to support him at public expense, he would make their city outstandingly famous. This was agreeable to them, and they advised him to go to the council and petition the councillors; they said that they themselves would support him. He followed their advice, and as the council assembled he went to the council room and asked the duty officer to take him in to the council. He undertook to do so, and at the appropriate moment he led him in. Melesigenes took his stand and made the speech about his support that he had made in the saloons. When he had spoken, he went out and sat down, while they deliberated what answer to give him. The man who had brought him in was keen, as were those councillors who had heard him in the saloons, but it is said that one of the law lords opposed his application, his chief argument being that if they decided to provide for *homēroi,* they would have a large, useless crowd on their hands. It was from then that the name Homer prevailed for Melesigenes, from his disability, for the Cymaeans call the blind *homēroi;* so that whereas he had previously been called Melesigenes, this became his name, Homer, and people from elsewhere disseminated it

---

37 αὐτῶι West: αὐτοὶ codd.: del. Wilamowitz.
38 Var. βουλευτέων.

ὅτε μνήμην αὐτοῦ ἐποιοῦντο. ἐτελεύτα δ᾽ οὖν ὁ λόγος
τῶι ἄρχοντι μὴ τρέφειν τὸν Ὅμηρον, ἔδοξε δέ πως καὶ
τῆι ἄλληι βουλῆι. ἐπελθὼν δὲ ὁ ἐπιστάτης καὶ παρ-
εζόμενος αὐτῶι διηγήσατο τοὺς ἐναντιωθέντας λόγους
τῆι χρήμηι αὐτοῦ καὶ τὰ δόξαντα τῆι βουλῆι. ὁ δὲ ὡς
ἤκουσεν, ἐσυμφόρηνέ τε καὶ λέγει τὰ ἔπεα τάδε (Epigr.
4)·

οἴηι μ᾽ αἴσηι δῶκε πατὴρ Ζεὺς κύρμα γενέσθαι,
νήπιον αἰδοίης ἐπὶ γούνασι μητρὸς ἀτάλλων.
ἥν ποτ᾽ ἐπύργωσαν βουλῆι Διὸς αἰγιόχοιο
λαοὶ Φρίκωνος, μάργων ἐπιβήτορες ἵππων,
5 ὀξύτεροι[39] μαλεροῖο πυρὸς κρίνοντες ἄρηα,
Αἰολίδα Σμύρνην ἁλιγείτονα, πότνιαν ἀκτήν,[40]
ἥν τε δι᾽ ἀγλαὸν εἶσιν ὕδωρ ἱεροῖο Μέλητος—
ἔνθεν ἀπορνύμεναι κοῦραι Διός, ἀγλαὰ τέκνα,
ἠθελέτην κλῆισαι δῖαν χθόνα καὶ πόλιν
    ἀνδρῶν·
10 οἱ δ᾽ ἀπανηνάσθην ἱερὴν ὄπα, φῆμιν ἀοιδῆς,[41]
ἀφραδίηι. τῶν μέν τε παθών τις φράσσεται
    αὖτις,
ὅς σφιν ὀνειδε<ίηι>σιν ἐμὸν διεμήσατο πότμον.
κῆρα δ᾽ ἐγὼ τήν μοι θεὸς ὤπασε γεινομένωι περ
τλήσομαι, ἀκράαντα φέρων τετληότι θυμῶι,
15 οὐδ᾽ ἔτι μοι φίλα γυῖα μένειν ἱεραῖς ἐν ἀγυιαῖς

[39] ὀξύτεροι West: ὁπλότεροι codd.
[40] πότνιαν ἀκτήν Scaliger: ποτνιάνακτον codd.
[41] ἀοιδὴν codd.: corr. Wolf.

when they spoke of him. Anyway, the conclusion of the magistrate's speech was that they should not support Homer, and the rest of the council was somehow persuaded. The presiding officer came and sat with him and explained the arguments that had been used against his application, and the decision of the council. On hearing this, he was disappointed, and spoke these verses (*Epigram* 4):

What a fate father Zeus made me prey to
when he fostered me, an infant on my modest
    mother's knees!
The city fortified at goat-rider Zeus' design
by Phrikon's host,[19] riders of furious steeds,
keener than ravening fire to decide the battle,
Aeolian Smyrna, seaneighbor, holy shore,
traversed by the bright water of holy Meles—
going forth from there Zeus' daughters, his glorious
    children,[20]
desired to celebrate a noble land and city of men,
but they in their folly refused the holy voice, the
    word of song.
Someone of them will realize when he suffers,
the one who decided my lot by way of insults.
Well, I shall bear the fate God gave me at my birth,
accepting failure with enduring heart;
but my dear legs no longer wish to stay

---

[19] Phrikon is presumably a legendary founder of Cyme, invented as one explanation of the city's epithet Phrikonis (chapter 38).

[20] The Muses.

Κύμης ὁρμαίνουσι· μέγας δέ με θυμὸς ἐπείγει
δῆμον ἐς ἀλλοδαπῶν ἰέναι ὀλιγηπελέοντα.⁴²

15   μετὰ τοῦτο ἀπαλλάσσεται ἐκ τῆς Κύμης ἐς Φω-
καίην, Κυμαίοις ἐπαρησάμενος μηδένα ποιητὴν δόκι-
μον ἐν τῆι χώρηι γενέσθαι ὅστις Κυμαίους ἐπαγλαϊεῖ.
ἀπικόμενος δὲ ἐς Φωκαίην τῶι αὐτῶι τρόπωι ἐβιότευ-
εν, ἔπεα ἐνδεικνύμενος ἐν ταῖς λέσχαις κατίζων. ἐν δὲ
τῆι Φωκαίηι τοῦτον τὸν χρόνον Θεστορίδης τις ἦν
γράμματα διδάσκων τοὺς παῖδας, ἀνὴρ οὐ κρήγυος·
κατανοήσας δὲ τοῦ Ὁμήρου τὴν ποίησιν, λόγους
τοιούσδε αὐτῶι προσήνεγκε, φὰς ἕτοιμος εἶναι θερα-
πεύειν καὶ τρέφειν αὐτὸν ἀναλαβών, εἰ ἐθέλοι ἅ τε
πεποιημένα εἴη αὐτῶι τῶν ἐπέων ἀναγράψασθαι καὶ
16   ἄλλα ποιῶν πρὸς ἑωυτὸν ἀναφέρειν αἰεί. | τῶι δὲ Ὁμή-
ρωι ἀκούσαντι ἔδοξε ποιητέα εἶναι ταῦτα· ἐνδεὴς γὰρ
ἦν τῶν ἀναγκαίων καὶ θεραπείης. διατρίβων δὲ παρὰ
τῶι Θεστορίδηι ποιεῖ Ἰλιάδα τὴν ἐλάσσω, ἧς ἡ ἀρχή
(fr. 1)·

Ἴλιον ἀείδω καὶ Δαρδανίην εὔπωλον,
ἧς πέρι πολλὰ πάθον Δαναοὶ θεράποντες Ἄρηος·

καὶ τὴν καλουμένην Φωκαΐδα, ἥν φασιν οἱ Φωκαεῖς
Ὅμηρον παρ' αὐτοῖσι ποιῆσαι. ἐπεὶ δὲ τήν τε Φωκαΐ-
δα καὶ τἄλλα πάντα παρὰ τοῦ Ὁμήρου ὁ Θεστορίδης
ἐγράψατο, διενοήθη ἐκ τῆς Φωκαίης ἀπαλλάσσεσθαι,
τὴν ποίησιν θέλων τοῦ Ὁμήρου ἐξιδιώσασθαι. καὶ
οὐκέτι ὁμοίως ἐν ἐπιμελίηι εἶχε τὸν Ὅμηρον· ὁ δὲ

in Cyme's holy streets: my great heart urges me
to go to a different people in my debility.

After that he left Cyme for Phocaea, laying a curse on
the Cymaeans that no poet of note should be born in the
place to glorify the Cymaeans.[21] Having reached Phocaea,
he lived in the same manner as before, performing poems
as he sat in the saloons. Now in Phocaea at this time there
was one Thestorides teaching boys to read and write, not a
good man. When he became aware of Homer's poetry, he
made an approach to him, offering to take him in and look
after him and feed him, if he was willing to set down in
writing the poems he had composed, and when he com-
posed more, always to bring them to him. When Homer
heard this he decided he should do it, as he was short of the
necessities of life and in need of care. While staying with
Thestorides he composed the *Lesser Iliad*, which begins

Of Ilios I sing, and Dardania land of fine colts,
over which the Danaans suffered much, servants of
the War god,

and the poem called *Phocais*, which the Phocaeans say
Homer composed among them. Now when Thestorides
had written down for himself at Homer's dictation the
Phocais and all the rest, he formed the plan of going away
from Phocaea, because he wanted to appropriate Homer's
poetry. And he was no longer so solicitous about Homer,

[21] This perhaps relates to the migration of Hesiod's father
from Cyme to Boeotia before the poet's birth.

---

[42] ὀλιγηπελέοντα West: ὀλίγον περ ἐόντα codd.

λέγει αὐτῶι τὰ ἔπεα τάδε (Epigr. 5)·

Θεστορίδη, θνητοῖσιν ἀνωΐστων πολέων περ,
οὐδὲν ἀφραστότερον πέλεται νόου ἀνθρώποιο.[43]

ὁ μὲν δὴ Θεστορίδης ἐκ τῆς Φωκαίης ἀπηλλάγη ἐς
τὴν Χίον καὶ διδασκαλεῖον κατεσκευάσατο· καὶ τὰ
ἔπεα ἐπιδεικνύμενος ὡς ἑωυτοῦ ἐόντα ἔπαινόν τε πολ-
λὸν εἶχε καὶ ὠφελεῖτο· ὁ δὲ Ὅμηρος πάλιν τὸν αὐτὸν
τρόπον διηιτᾶτο ἐν τῆι Φωκαίηι, ἀπὸ τῆς ποιήσιος τὴν
βιοτὴν ἔχων.

17   χρόνωι δὲ οὐ πολλῶι μετέπειτα ἄνδρες Χῖοι ἔμπο-
ροι ἀπίκοντο ἐς τὴν Φωκαίην. ἀκούσαντες δὲ τῶν
ἐπέων τοῦ Ὁμήρου ἃ πρότερον ἀκηκόεσαν πολλάκις
ἐν τῆι Χίωι τοῦ Θεστορίδεω, ἐξήγγελλον Ὁμήρωι ὅτι
ἐν Χίωι τις ἐπιδεικνύμενος τὰ ἔπεα ταῦτα γραμμάτων
διδάσκαλος κάρτα πολλὸν ἔπαινον ἔχει. ὁ δὲ Ὅμηρος
κατενόησεν ὅτι Θεστορίδης ἂν εἴη, καὶ παντὶ θυμῶι
ἐσπούδαζεν ἐς τὴν Χίον ἀπικέσθαι. καταβὰς δὲ ἐπὶ
τὸν λιμένα, ἐς μὲν τὴν Χίον οὐ καταλαμβάνει οὐδὲν
πλοῖον πλέον, ἐς δὲ τὴν Ἐρυθραίην τινὲς ἐπὶ ξύλα
παρεσκευάζοντο πλεῖν. καλῶς δὲ εἶχε τῶι Ὁμήρωι δι᾽
Ἐρυθρέων τὸν πλοῦν ποιήσασθαι, καὶ προσελθὼν
ἔχρηιζε τῶν ναυτέων δέξασθαι αὐτὸν σύμπλουν, πολ-
λά τε καὶ προσαγωγὰ λέγων οἷς σφέας ἔμελλε πεί-
σειν. τοῖς δὲ ἔδοξε δέξασθαι αὐτόν, καὶ ἐκέλευον
ἐσβαίνειν ἐς τὸ πλοῖον. ὁ δὲ Ὅμηρος πολλὰ ἐπαινέ-
σας αὐτοὺς ἐσέβη, καὶ ἐπεὶ ἕζετο λέγει τὰ ἔπεα τάδε
(Epigr. 6)·

who addressed him in these verses (*Epigram* 5):

> Thestorides, though many things come to mortals
> unexpected,
> there is nothing more unfathomable than the mind of
> man.

So Thestorides left Phocaea for Chios, and set up a school there; and by performing the poems as if they were his own, he enjoyed much praise and profit. Meanwhile Homer continued to live in the same style in Phocaea, supporting himself from his poetry.

Not long afterwards some Chian merchants arrived in Phocaea, and when they heard from Homer the poems that they had heard often before in Chios from Thestorides, they told Homer that there was someone in Chios performing these poems, a teacher of letters, and that he was enjoying much acclaim. Homer realized that it would be Thestorides, and he became very eager to get to Chios. He went down to the harbor, and though he found no vessel sailing to Chios, there were some men preparing to sail to the Erythrae area for timber. Homer was content to make his voyage by way of Erythrae, and he went and asked the sailors to take him as a passenger, with many enticing arguments likely to persuade them. They agreed to take him, and told him to embark. Homer thanked them profusely and went on board, and once he had sat down he spoke these verses (*Epigram* 6):

---

43 ἀνθρώποισι codd.: corr. Wilamowitz.

κλῦθι, Ποσείδαον μεγαλοσθενὲς ἐννοσίγαιε,
†εὐρυχόρου† μεδέων ἠδὲ ζαθέου⁴⁴ Ἑλικῶνος,
δὸς δ' οὖρον καλὸν καὶ ἀπήμονα νόστον
    ἀρέσθαι
ναύταις, οἳ νηὸς πομποὶ ἠδ' ἀρχοὶ ἔασιν.
5 δὸς δ' ἐς ὑπωρείην ὑψικρήμνοιο Μίμαντος
αἰδοίων μ' ἐλθόντα βροτῶν ὁσίων τε κυρῆσαι,
φῶτά τε τεισαίμην ὃς ἐμὸν νόον ἠπεροπεύσας
ὠδύσατο Ζῆνα ξένιον ξενίην τε τράπεζαν.

18   ἐπεὶ δὲ ἀπίκοντο εὐπλοήσαντες ἐς τὴν Ἐρυθραίην,
τότε μὲν Ὅμηρος τὴν αὖλιν ἐπὶ τῶι πλοίωι ἐποιήσατο·
τῆι δὲ ὑστεραίηι ἔχρηιζε τῶν ναυτέων τινὰ ἡγήσα-
σθαι αὐτῶι ἐς τὴν πόλιν, οἱ δὲ συνέπεμψαν ἕνα αὐτῶι.
πορευόμενος δὲ Ὅμηρος ἐπεὶ ἔτυχε τῆς Ἐρυθραίης
τρηχείης τε καὶ ὀρεινῆς ἐούσης, φθέγγεται τάδε τὰ
ἔπεα (Epigr. 7)·

πότνια Γῆ πάνδωρε, δότειρα μελίφρονος ὄλβου,
ὡς ἄρα δὴ τοῖς μὲν φωτῶν εὔοχθος ἐτύχθης,
τοῖσι δὲ δύσβωλος καὶ τρηχεῖ·, οἷς ἐχολώθης.

ἀπικόμενος δὲ ἐς τὴν πόλιν τῶν Ἐρυθραίων
ἐπηρώτησε περὶ τοῦ ἐς τὴν Χίον πλοῦ· καί τινος
προσελθόντος αὐτῶι τῶν ἑωρακότων καὶ ἐν τῆι Φωκαίηι
καὶ ἀσπασαμένου, ἔχρηιζεν αὐτοῦ συνεξευρεῖν αὐτῶι
19 πλοῖον, ὅπως ἂν ἐς τὴν Χίον διαβαίη. | ἐκ μὲν δὴ τοῦ

Hearken, Poseidon, powerful earth-shaker,
ruler of †broad-arena'd†[22] and of holy Helicon,
and grant a fair wind and a safe passage
to the sailors, the ship's escorts and commanders.
And grant that when I come to the foot of towering
    Mimas
I may find people respectful and righteous;
and may I punish the man who deceived me
and angered Zeus of Guests, and the guest-table.

When they reached the Erythrae area after a good voyage, for that night Homer bivouacked on the ship, but the next day he asked one of the sailors to conduct him into the town, and they sent one to escort him. As he made his way, finding the Erythraean terrain rough and mountainous, Homer uttered these verses (*Epigram* 7):

Mistress Earth all-bounteous, giver of sweet
    prosperity,
how well-contoured you are formed for some men,
and for others, with whom you are wroth, how
    lumpish and rough.

On reaching the town of Erythrae, he enquired about his passage to Chios; and when someone who had seen him in Phocaea came up and greeted him, he asked this man to help him find a vessel so that he could cross to Chios.

---

[22] We require a place name paired with Helicon. Compare Hymn 22.3, "Helicon and broad Aegae."

---

[44] ζαθέου Ruhnkenius: ξανθοῦ codd. Ante h.v. lac. stat. Wilamowitz.

λιμένος οὐδὲν ἦν ἀπόστολον· ἄγει δὲ αὐτὸν ἔνθα τῶν
ἁλιέων τὰ πλοῖα ὁρμίζεται, καί πως ἐντυγχάνει μέλ-
λουσί τισι διαπλεῖν ἐς τὴν Χίον, ὧν ἐδέετο προσελθὼν
ὁ ἄγων αὐτὸν ἀναλαβεῖν τὸν Ὅμηρον. οἱ δὲ οὐδένα
λόγον ποιησάμενοι ἀνήγοντο· ὁ δὲ Ὅμηρος φθέγγε-
ται τάδε τὰ ἔπεα (Epigr. 8)·

νᾶυται ποντοπόροι, στυγερῆι ἐναλίγκιοι αἴσηι
πτωκάσιν αἰθυίηισι, βίον δύσζηλον ἔχοντες,
αἰδεῖσθε ξενίοιο Διὸς σέβας ὑψιμέδοντος·
δεινὴ γὰρ μετόπισθεν ὄπις Διός, ὅς κ' ἀλίτηται.

ἀναχθεῖσι δὲ αὐτοῖς συνέβη ἐναντίου ἀνέμου γενομέ-
νου παλινδρομῆσαι καὶ ἐς τὸ χωρίον ἀναδραμεῖν ὅθεν
ἀνηγάγοντο καὶ τὸν Ὅμηρον καταλαβεῖν ἔτι[45] καθή-
μενον ἐπὶ τῆς κυματωγῆς. μαθὼν δὲ αὐτοὺς πεπαλιν-
δρομηκότας ἔλεξε τάδε (Epigr. 9)·

ὑμᾶς, ὦ ξεῖνοι, ἄνεμος λάβεν ἀντίος ἐλθών·
ἀλλ' ἔτι νῦν δέξασθε, καὶ ὁ πλόος ἔσσεται
ὕμιν.[46]

οἱ δὲ ἁλιεῖς ἐν μεταμελίηι γενόμενοι, ὅτι οὐ καὶ
πρότερον ἐδέξαντο, εἰπόντες ὅτι οὐ καταλιμπάνουσιν
ἢν ἐθέλοι συμπλεῖν, ἐκέλευον ἐσβαίνειν· καὶ οὕτως
ἀναλαβόντες αὐτὸν ἀνήχθησαν, καὶ ἴσχουσιν ἐπ'
20 ἀκτῆς. | οἱ μὲν δὴ ἁλιεῖς πρὸς ἔργον ἐτράπησαν· ὁ δὲ
Ὅμηρος τὴν μὲν νύκτα ἐπὶ τοῦ αἰγιαλοῦ κατέμεινε,
τὴν δὲ ἡμέραν πορευόμενος καὶ πλανώμενος ἀπίκετο
ἐς τὸ χωρίον τοῦτο ὃ Πίτυς καλεῖται. κἀνταῦθα αὐτῶι

There was no packet boat from the harbor, but he took him to where the fishing boats moor, and somehow fell in with a group who were about to cross to Chios. The guide went up to them and asked them to take Homer. They ignored him, and put out to sea, whereupon Homer uttered these verses (*Epigram* 8):

> Seafarer sailors, who share the horrid lot
> of the timorous shearwaters, with your unenviable life,
> respect the Zeus of Guests who rules on high:
> dreadful is Zeus' retribution that follows if one errs.

And after they had put out, it happened that a contrary wind arose, and they were blown back and beached at the spot from where they had set forth; they found Homer still sitting on the foreshore. When he became aware that they had been driven back, he said (*Epigram* 9):

> An adverse wind has come and seized you, sirs;
> but take me even now, and you'll have your sailing.

The fishermen repented of having refused to take him before, and saying that they would not leave him behind if he wanted to sail with them, they encouraged him to embark. So they took him on board, and set out; and they put in on an open shore. The fishermen then turned to their work. Homer stayed on the beach for the night, and next day he set off to walk. His wanderings brought him to the place called Pitys (Pine). As he was resting there for the night,

---

45 καταλαβεῖν Kassel, ἔτι Westermann: ἀναλαβεῖν ἐπι-codd.

46 Versiculos in prosam dissolutos restituit Barnes.

ἀναπαυομένωι τὴν νύκτα ἐπιπίπτει καρπὸς τῆς πίτυος,
ὃν δὴ μετεξέτεροι στρόβιλον, οἳ δὲ κῶνον καλέουσιν.
ὁ δὲ Ὅμηρος φθέγγεται τὰ ἔπεα τάδε (Epigr. 10)·

ἄλλη τίς σου πεύκη ἀμείνονα καρπὸν ἵησιν
Ἴδης ἐν κορυφῆισι πολυπτύχου ἠνεμοέσσης,
ἔνθα σίδηρος Ἄρηος ἐπιχθονίοισι βροτοῖσιν
ἔσσεται, εὖτ᾽ ἄν μιν Κεβρήνιοι ἄνδρες ἔχωσιν.

τὰ δὲ Κεβρήνια τοῦτον τὸν χρόνον κτίζειν οἱ Κυμαῖοι
παρεσκευάζοντο πρὸς τῆι Ἴδηι· καὶ γίνεται αὐτόθι
σίδηρος πολύς.

21   ἐντεῦθεν δὲ ἀναστὰς Ὅμηρος ἐπορεύετο κατὰ φω-
νήν τινα αἰγῶν νεμομένων. ὡς δὲ ὑλάκτεον αὐτὸν οἱ
κύνες, ἀνέκραγεν· ὁ δὲ Γλαῦκος ὡς ἤκουσε τῆς φωνῆς
(ἦν γὰρ τοῦτο ὄνομα τῶι νέμοντι τὰς αἶγας), ἐπέδρα-
μεν ὀτραλέως, τούς τε κύνας ἀνεκαλεῖτο καὶ ἀπεσόβη-
σεν ἀπὸ τοῦ Ὁμήρου. ἐπὶ πολὺν δὲ χρόνον ἐν θαύματι
ἦν, ὅκως τυφλὸς ἐὼν μόνος ἀπίκοιτο ἐς τοιούτους
χώρους, καὶ ὅτι θέλων· προσελθών τέ μιν ἱστορέει,
ὅστίς τε ἦν καὶ τίνι τρόπωι ἀπίκοιτο ἐς τόπους ἀοική-
τους καὶ ἀστιβέα χωρία, καὶ τίνος κεχρημένος εἴη. ὁ
δὲ Ὅμηρος αὐτῶι πᾶσαν τὴν ἑωυτοῦ πάθην καταλεγό-
μενος ἐς οἶκτον προηγάγετο· ἦν γάρ, ὡς ἔοικεν, οὐδ᾽
ἀγνώμων ὁ Γλαῦκος. ἀναλαβὼν δὲ αὐτὸν ἀνήγαγεν
ἐπὶ τὸν σταθμόν, πῦρ τε ἀνακαύσας δεῖπνον παρα-
σκευάζει, καὶ παραθεὶς δειπνεῖν ἐκέλευεν {ὁ Γλαῦ-
22   κος}.⁴⁷ | τῶν δὲ κυνῶν ἑστώτων καὶ ὑλακτούντων
δειπνοῦντας, καθάπερ εἰώθεσαν, λέγει πρὸς τὸν Γλαῦ-

there fell upon him that fruit of the pine that some call a whorl and others a cone. Homer uttered these verses (*Epigram* 10):

> Another pine puts forth a better fruit than yours
> on the peaks of Ida with its windy glens,
> where the War god's iron shall be among mortals
> on earth, when it belongs to Kebrenian men.

It was at this time that the Cymaeans were preparing to colonize Kebrenia near Mt. Ida; and much iron is produced there.[23]

Homer got up from there and went on his way, following a bleating of goats at pasture. When the dogs barked at him, he shouted out, and Glaucus, hearing his voice—this was the name of the goatherd—ran up hastily, called the dogs back, and shooed them away from Homer. For a long time he was in wonderment at how a blind man had found his way to such a place all alone, and what he wanted. He approached him and asked him who he was, and how he had found his way to uninhabited regions and trackless areas, and what he was after. Homer related all that had happened to him, and aroused his sympathy, for it seems that Glaucus was not an unfeeling man. He took him and led him to his steading, made up the fire, and prepared a meal, and putting it before him invited him to eat. When the dogs stood and barked at them while they ate, as they

[23] There was in that region in the time of Attalus I a mighty pine, some 67 metres tall and seven metres in circumference (Strabo 13.1.44).

---

[47] Del. Wilamowitz.

κον Ὅμηρος τὰ ἔπεα τάδε (*Epigr.* 11)·

Γλαῦκε βοτῶν[48] ἐπιόπτα, ἔπος τί τοι ἐν φρεσὶ
    θήσω·
πρῶτον μὲν κυσὶ δεῖπνον ἐπ᾽ αὐλείηισι θύρηισιν
δοῦναι· τὼς γὰρ ἄμεινον· ὁ γὰρ καὶ πρῶτος[49]
    ἀκούει
ἀνδρὸς ἐπερχομένου καὶ ἐς ἔρκεα θηρὸς ἰόντος.

ταῦτα ἀκούσας ὁ Γλαῦκος ἥσθη τῆι παραινέσει, καὶ
ἐν θαύματι εἶχεν αὐτόν. δειπνήσαντες δὲ διὰ λόγων
εἰστιῶντο· ἀπηγεομένου δὲ Ὁμήρου τήν τε πλάνην
τὴν ἑωυτοῦ καὶ τὰς πόλεις ἃς ἐσαπίκοιτο, ἔκπληκτος
ἦν ὁ Γλαῦκος ἀκούων. καὶ τότε μέν, ἐπεὶ ὥρη κοίτου
23 ἦν, ἀνεπαύετο· | τῆι δὲ ὑστεραίηι διενοήθη ὁ Γλαῦκος
πρὸς τὸν δεσπότην πορευθῆναι σημανέων τὰ ὑπὲρ τοῦ
Ὁμήρου. ἐπιτρέψας δὲ τῶι συνδούλωι νέμειν τὰς
αἶγας, τὸν Ὅμηρον καταλείπει ἔνδον, εἰπὼν πρὸς
αὐτὸν ὅτι διὰ ταχέων πορεύσομαι, καταβὰς δὲ ἐς
Βολισσόν (ἔστι δὲ πλησίον τοῦ χωρίου τούτου) καὶ
συγγενόμενος τῶι δεσπότηι ἀπηγέετο ὑπὲρ Ὁμήρου
πᾶσαν τὴν ἀλήθειαν, περί τε αὐτοῦ τῆς ἀπίξιος ἐν
θαύματι ποιεύμενος, ἐρώτεέ τε ὅ τι χρὴ ποιέειν περὶ
αὐτοῦ. ὁ δὲ ὀλίγα μὲν προσίετο τῶν λόγων, κατ-
εγίνωσκε δὲ τοῦ Γλαύκου ὡς ἄφρονος ἐόντος τοὺς
ἀναπήρους δεχομένου καὶ τρέφοντος· ἐκέλευε δὲ ὅμως
τὸν ξεῖνον ἄγειν πρὸς ἑαυτόν.

24   ἐλθὼν δὲ πρὸς τὸν Ὅμηρον διηγήσατο ταῦτα ὁ
Γλαῦκος καὶ ἐκέλευσεν αὐτὸν πορεύεσθαι, οὕτω γὰρ

normally did, Homer recited these verses to Glaucus (*Epigram* 11):

> Glaucus, overseer of livestock, let me put a saying in
>   your mind:
> first give the dogs their dinner at the yard gates.
> It is better so: that dog is the first to hear
> a man's approach, or a beast entering the stockade.

Hearing this, Glaucus was pleased with the advice, and wondered at the man. After their meal they entertained themselves with conversation, and when Homer related his travels and all the towns he had visited, Glaucus was astonished as he listened. For the moment, as it was time for bed, he took his rest. But the next day Glaucus decided to go to his master to tell him about Homer. Entrusting the pasturing of the goats to his fellow slave, he left Homer indoors, promising to come back shortly, and went down to Bolissos (which is near the place in question), met up with his master, and related the whole matter of Homer just as it was, treating his arrival as a marvel, and he asked him what to do about him. But his master accepted little of what he said, and condemned Glaucus as a fool for taking in and feeding the disabled. Nevertheless, he said he should bring the stranger to him.

Returning to Homer, Glaucus related this and told him he should go, for he would do well out of it; and Homer

---

48 βροτῶν ἐπιόπτα *Suda* (βοτῶν Küster): πέπων ἐπιών τι
Vitae codd.

49 πρῶτος West: πρῶτον Vitae codd.: πρόσθεν *Suda*.

εὖ πρήξειν· ὁ δὲ Ὅμηρος ἤθελε πορεύεσθαι. ἀναλα-
βὼν οὖν αὐτὸν ὁ Γλαῦκος ἤγαγε πρὸς τὸν δεσπότην.
διὰ λόγων δὲ ἰὼν τῶι Ὁμήρωι ὁ Χῖος εὑρίσκει ἐόντα
δεξιὸν καὶ πολλῶν ἔμπειρον· ἔπειθέ τε αὐτόθι μένειν
καὶ τῶν παιδίων ἐπιμελίην ποιέεσθαι· ἦσαν γὰρ τῶι
Χίωι παῖδες ἐν ἡλικίηι. τούτους οὖν αὐτῶι παρατίθε-
ται παιδεύειν, ὁ δὲ ἔπρησσε ταῦτα. καὶ τοὺς Κέρ-
κωπας καὶ Βατραχομαχίαν καὶ Ψαρομαχίην καὶ
Ἑπταπακτικὴν καὶ Ἐπικιχλίδας καὶ τἆλλα πάντα
ὅσα παίγνιά ἐστιν Ὁμήρου ἐνταῦθα ἐποίησε παρὰ
τῶι Χίωι ἐν Βολισσῶι, ὥστε καὶ ἐν τῆι πόλει περι-
βόητος ἤδη ἐγένετο ἐν τῆι ποιήσει. καὶ ὁ μὲν Θεστο-
ρίδης, ὡς τάχιστα ἐπύθετο αὐτὸν παρεόντα, ὤιχετο
ἐκπλέων ἐκ τῆς Χίου.

25   χρόνου δὲ προϊόντος δεηθεὶς τοῦ Χίου πορεῦσαι
αὐτὸν ἐς τὴν Χίον ἀπίκετο ἐς τὴν πόλιν· καὶ διδασκα-
λεῖον κατασκευασάμενος ἐδίδασκε παῖδας τὰ ἔπεα.
καὶ κάρτα δεξιὸς κατεδόκεεν εἶναι τοῖς Χίοις, καὶ
πολλοὶ θαυμασταὶ αὐτοῦ καθεστήκεσαν. συλλεξάμε-
νος δὲ βίον ἱκανὸν γυναῖκα ἔγημεν, ἐξ ἧς αὐτῶι
θυγατέρες δύο ἐγένοντο· καὶ ἡ μὲν αὐτῶν ἄγαμος
ἐτελεύτησε, τὴν δὲ συνώικισεν ἀνδρὶ Χίωι.

26   ἐπιχειρήσας δὲ τῆι ποιήσει ἀπέδωκε χάριν ἣν εἶχε,
πρῶτον μὲν Μέντορι τῶι Ἰθακησίωι ἐν τῆι Ὀδυσσείηι,
ὅτι μιν κάμνοντα τοὺς ὀφθαλμοὺς ἐν Ἰθάκηι ἐνο-
σήλευεν ἐκτενέως, τοὔνομα αὐτοῦ ἐναρμόσας ἐς τὴν
ποίησιν Ὀδυσσέως τε ἑταῖρον φὰς εἶναι, ποιήσας
Ὀδυσσέα, ὡς ἐς Τροίην ἔπλεε, Μέντορι ἐπιτρέψαι τὸν

wanted to go. So Glaucus took him and conducted him to his master. When the Chian talked to Homer, he found that he was clever and had wide experience, so he urged him to stay there and take care of his children; for the Chian had sons of age. So he entrusted them to him to educate, and Homer undertook the job. And the *Cercopes*, the *Battle of Frogs*, the *Battle of Starlings*, the *Heptapaktike*, the *Epikichlides*, and the rest of Homer's fun poems,[24] he composed there in the Chian's house at Bolissos, with the result that he now became renowned for his poetry in the city too. And as soon as Thestorides learned that he was there, he took sail and departed from Chios.

Some time later Homer asked the Chian to convey him to Chios, and he arrived in the city. He set up a school and began teaching boys his poems. He struck the Chians as very clever, and many became his firm admirers. After amassing sufficient means, he married a woman, from whom two daughters were born to him. One of them died unwed, the other he married off to a Chian.

When he turned his hand to poetry, he rendered his gratitude, firstly to Mentor the Ithacan in the *Odyssey*, for having tended him so assiduously when his eyes were ailing in Ithaca: he found a place for his name in the poem, making him a comrade of Odysseus' and writing that when Odysseus sailed to Troy he entrusted his household to

[24] On these titles see the Introduction to the Homeric Apocrypha above.

οἶκον ὡς ἐόντι Ἰθακησίων ἀρίστωι καὶ δικαιοτάτωι. πολλαχῆι δὲ καὶ ἄλληι τῆς ποιήσεως τιμῶν αὐτὸν τὴν Ἀθηνᾶν, ὁπότε ἐς λόγον τινὶ καθίσταιτο, τῶι Μέντορι οἰκυῖαν ποιεῖ. ἀπέδωκε δὲ καὶ Φημίωι τῶι ἑαυτοῦ διδασκάλωι τροφεῖα καὶ διδασκαλεῖα ἐν τῆι Ὀδυσσείηι, μάλιστα ἐν τοῖσδε τοῖς ἔπεσι (Od. 1.153–155)·

κῆρυξ δ' ἐν χερσὶν κίθαριν περικαλλέ' ἔθηκεν
Φημίωι, ὃς δὴ πολλὸν ἐκαίνυτο πάντας ἀείδων·
   {καὶ πάλιν}
αὐτὰρ ὁ φορμίζων ἀνεβάλλετο καλὸν ἀείδειν.

μέμνηται δὲ καὶ τοῦ ναυκλήρου μεθ' οὗ ἐκπεριέπλευσε καὶ εἶδε πόλιάς τε πολλὰς καὶ χώρας, ὧι ὄνομα ἦν Μέντης, ἐν τοῖς ἔπεσι τοῖσδε (Od. 1.180–181)·

Μέντης Ἀγχιάλοιο δαΐφρονος εὔχομαι εἶναι
υἱός, ἀτὰρ Ταφίοισι φιληρέτμοισιν ἀνάσσω.

ἀπέδωκε δὲ χάριν καὶ Τυχίωι τῶι σκυτεῖ, ὃς ἐδέξατο αὐτὸν ἐν τῶι Νέωι τείχει προσελθόντα πρὸς τὸ σκυτεῖον, ἐν τοῖς ἔπεσι καταζεύξας ἐν τῆι Ἰλιάδι τοῖσδε (Il. 7.219–221)·

Αἴας δ' ἐγγύθεν ἦλθε φέρων σάκος ἠΰτε πύργον,
χάλκεον ἑπταβόειον, ὅ οἱ Τυχίος κάμε τεύχων,
σκυτοτόμων ὄχ' ἄριστος, Ὕληι ἔνι οἰκία ναίων.

27   {ἀπὸ δὲ τῆς ποιήσεως ταύτης εὐδοκίμει Ὅμηρος περί τε τὴν Ἰωνίην, καὶ ἐς τὴν Ἑλλάδα ἤδη περὶ αὐτοῦ λόγος ἀνεφέρετο.}[50] κατοικέων δὲ ἐν τῆι Χίωι

Mentor, as the worthiest and most upright of the Ithacans.
In many other passages of the poem too he honored him by
making Athena take Mentor's form when she entered into
conversation with someone. He also repaid his teacher
Phemius for his upbringing and education in the *Odyssey*,
especially in these verses:

> And the herald placed the lovely lyre in the hands
> of Phemius, who far surpassed all in his singing,
> and he struck up the lyre for a fine song.

He also recalls the shipowner with whom he sailed out all
over and saw many towns and countries—his name was
Mentes—in these verses:

> I declare myself to be Mentes, the wise Anchialus'
> son, and I am lord over the Taphians, lovers of the
> oar.

He rendered thanks also to Tychios, the cobbler who
received him at Neonteichos when he came to his shop, by
embodying him in these verses of the *Iliad*:

> But Ajax came from nearby with his shield like a
> tower,
> his bronze one of seven hides, made for him by
> Tychios,
> the finest of leather workers, who dwelt in Hyle.

{From this poetic activity Homer was celebrated
around Ionia, and reports of him were now reaching the
Greek mainland.} Living as he was in Chios and celebrated

---

50 { } secl. West.

καὶ εὐδοκιμέων περὶ τὴν ποίησιν, ἀπικνεομένων πολλῶν πρὸς αὐτόν, συνεβούλευον οἱ ἐντυγχάνοντες αὐτῶι ἐς τὴν Ἑλλάδα ἀπικέσθαι· ὁ δὲ προσεδέξατο τὸν
28 λόγον, καὶ κάρτα ἐπεθύμει ἀποδημῆσαι. | κατανοήσας δὲ ὅτι ἐς μὲν Ἄργος πολλαί ‹οἱ›⁵¹ καὶ μεγάλαι εἶεν εὐλογίαι πεποιημέναι, ἐς δὲ τὰς Ἀθήνας οὔ, ἐμποιεῖ ἐς τὴν ποίησιν, ἐς μὲν Ἰλιάδα τὴν μεγάλην Ἐρεχθέα μεγαλύνων ἐν Νεῶν καταλόγωι τὰ ἔπεα τάδε (Il. 2.547–548)·

δῆμον Ἐρεχθῆος μεγαλήτορος, ὅν ποτ' Ἀθήνη
θρέψε Διὸς θυγάτηρ, τέκε δὲ ζείδωρος ἄρουρα·

καὶ τὸν στρατηγὸν αὐτῶν Μενεσθέα αἰνέσας ὡς πάντων εἴη ἄριστος τάξαι πεζὸν στρατὸν καὶ ἱππότας, ἐν τοῖσδε τοῖς ἔπεσιν εἶπε (Il. 2.552–554)·

τῶν αὖθ' ἡγεμόνευεν υἱὸς Πετεῶιο Μενεσθεύς.
τῶι δ' οὔ πώ τις ὁμοῖος ἐπιχθόνιος γένετ' ἀνήρ
κοσμῆσαι ἵππους τε καὶ ἀνέρας ἀσπιδιώτας·

Αἴαντα δὲ τὸν Τελαμῶνος καὶ Σαλαμινίους ἐν Νεῶν καταλόγωι ἔταξε πρὸς Ἀθηναίους, λέγων ὧδε (Il. 2.557–558)·

Αἴας δ' ἐκ Σαλαμῖνος ἄγεν δυοκαίδεκα νῆας,
στῆσε δ' ἄγων ἵν' Ἀθηναίων ἵσταντο φάλαγγες·

ἐς δὲ τὴν Ὀδυσσείην τάδε ἐποίησεν, ὡς Ἀθηνᾶ ἐς

⁵¹ οἱ add. Wilamowitz (is quidem post μεγάλαι).

for his poetry, with many people coming to hear him, those who made his acquaintance recommended him to go to mainland Greece. He was open to the suggestion, and very much wanted to travel. Realizing that he had composed many passages conferring high praise on Argos, but none on Athens, he inserted into his poetry, into the *Great Iliad*[25] to magnify Erechtheus these verses in the Catalogue of Ships:

> the people of great-hearted Erechtheus, whom once Athena
> nurtured, Zeus' daughter, and the grain-giving plowland bore;

and in praise of their commander Menestheus, that he was the best of all men at marshalling infantry and charioteers, he said in these verses:

> They in turn were led by Peteos' son, Menestheus.
> No man on earth has ever been his equal
> in arraying the horse and the warrior men;

and Ajax the son of Telamon and his Salaminians in the Catalogue of Ships he ranged with the Athenians, as follows:

> And Ajax from Salamis brought twelve ships,
> brought them and set them where stood the Athenian lines;

and into the *Odyssey* he wrote that Athena, after a conver-

---

[25] This unusual appellation distinguishes the poem from the *Lesser Iliad* mentioned in chapter 16.

λόγους ἐλθοῦσα τῶι Ὀδυσσεῖ ἐς τὴν Ἀθηναίων πόλιν
ἀπίκετο, τιμῶσα ταύτην τῶν ἄλλων πόλεων μάλιστα
(Od. 7.80–81)·

ἵκετο δ' ἐς Μαραθῶνα καὶ εὐρυχόρους ἐς
  Ἀθήνας,
δῦνε δ' Ἐρεχθῆος πυκινὸν δόμον.

29 ἐμποιήσας δὲ ἐς τὴν ποίησιν ταῦτα καὶ <τἄλλα>[52]
παρασκευασάμενος, ἐς Ἑλλάδα βουλόμενος ποιήσα-
σθαι τὸν πλοῦν προσίσχει τῆι Σάμωι. ἔτυχον δὲ οἱ
ἐκεῖσε τὸν τότε καιρὸν ἄγοντες ἑορτὴν Ἀπατούρια. καί
τις τῶν Σαμίων ἰδὼν τὸν Ὅμηρον ἀπιγμένον, πρότε-
ρον αὐτὸν ὀπωπὼς ἐν Χίωι, ἐλθὼν ἐς τοὺς φράτορας
διηγήσατο, ἐν ἐπαίνωι μεγάλωι ποιεύμενος αὐτόν. οἱ
δὲ φράτορες ἐκέλευον ἄγειν αὐτόν· ὃ δὲ ἐντυχὼν τῶι
Ὁμήρωι ἔλεξεν, "ὦ ξένε, Ἀπατούρια ἀγούσης τῆς
πόλιος καλέουσί σε οἱ φράτορες οἱ ἡμέτεροι συνεορ-
τάσοντα." ὃ δὲ Ὅμηρος ἔφη ταῦτα ποιήσειν, καὶ ἤιει
30 μετὰ τοῦ καλέσαντος. | πορευόμενος δὲ ἐγχρίμπτεται
γυναιξὶ Κουροτρόφωι θυούσαις ἐν τῆι τριόδωι· ἡ δὲ
ἱέρεια εἶπε πρὸς αὐτὸν δυσχεράνασα τῆι ὄψει, "ἄνερ,
ἀπὸ τῶν ἱερῶν." ὃ δὲ Ὅμηρος ἐς θυμόν τε ἔβαλε τὸ
ῥηθέν, καὶ ἤρετο τὸν ἄγοντα τίς τε εἴη ὁ φθεγξάμενος,
καὶ τίνι θεῶν ἱερὰ θύεται· ὃ δὲ αὐτῶι διηγήσατο ὅτι
γυνὴ εἴη, Κουροτρόφωι θύουσα. ὃ δὲ ἀκούσας λέγει
τὰ ἔπεα τάδε (Epigr. 12)·

sation with Odysseus, went to the Athenians' citadel, thus honoring this above other cities:

> And she came to Marathon and broad-arena'd
> Athens,
> and went in to Erechtheus' firm house.

Having made these insertions in his poetry and his other preparations, he was intending to voyage to mainland Greece, but put in at Samos. It happened that the people there were just then celebrating the festival of the Apatouria;[26] and one of the Samians, on seeing that Homer had arrived, having seen him previously in Chios, went and told his clansmen, commending him heartily. The clansmen said he should bring him along, so he went to Homer and said, "Sir, the city is celebrating the Apatouria, and our clansmen invite you to join them for the festival." Homer said he would, and went with the man who had invited him. On the way he encountered some women sacrificing to Kourotrophos[27] where the roads met, and the priestess, displeased at the sight of him, said, "You man, get away from the sacrifice." Homer took the words to heart, and asked his escort who it was that had spoken and to what deity the sacrifice was being made. He explained that it was a woman, sacrificing to Kourotrophos. On hearing that he spoke these verses (*Epigram 12*):

[26] A characteristically Ionian festival, concerned with the admission of new members to clans.

[27] A goddess concerned with the nurture of the young.

---

[52] ⟨ ⟩ add. Schadewaldt.

κλῦθί μοι εὐχομένωι, Κουροτρόφε, δὸς δὲ
  γυναῖκα
τήνδε νέων μὲν ἀνήνασθαι φιλότητα καὶ εὐνήν,
ἡ δ' ἐπιτερπέσθω πολιοκροτάφοισι γέρουσιν,
ὧν ὥρη μὲν ἀπήμβλυνται, θυμὸς δὲ μενοινᾶι.

31   ἐπεὶ δὲ ἦλθεν ἐς τὴν φρήτρην καὶ τοῦ οἴκου ἔνθα δὴ
ἐδαίνυντο ἐπὶ τὸν οὐδὸν ἔστη, οἱ μὲν λέγουσι καιο-
μένου πυρὸς ἐν τῶι οἴκωι, οἱ δέ φασι τότε ἐκκαῦσαι
σφᾶς, ἐπειδὴ Ὅμηρος τὰ ἔπεα εἶπεν (Epigr. 13)·

ἀνδρὸς μὲν παῖδες στέφανος, πύργοι δὲ πόληος,
ἵπποι δ' αὖ πεδίου κόσμος, νῆες δὲ θαλάσσης,
χρήματα δ' αὔξει οἶκον· ἀτὰρ γεραροὶ βασιλῆες
ἥμενοι εἰν ἀγορῆι κόσμος λαοῖσιν[53] ὁρᾶσθαι·
αἰθομένου δὲ πυρὸς γεραρώτερος οἶκος ἰδέσθαι.

εἰσελθὼν δὲ καὶ κατακλιθεὶς ἐδαίνυντο μετὰ τῶν φρα-
τόρων· καὶ αὐτὸν ἐτίμων καὶ ἐν θούματι εἶχον.
    καὶ τότε μὲν τὴν κοίτην αὐτοῦ ἐποιήσατο Ὅμηρος·
32 τῆι δὲ ἐσαύριον ἀποπορευόμενον ἰδόντες κεραμέες
τινές, κάμινον ἐγκαίοντες κεράμου λεπτοῦ, προσεκα-
λέσαντο αὐτόν, πεπυσμένοι ὅτι σοφὸς εἴη, καὶ ἐκέλευ-
όν σφιν ἀεῖσαι, φάμενοι δώσειν αὐτῶι τοῦ κεράμου
καὶ ὅ τι ἂν ἄλλο ἔχωσιν. ὁ δὲ Ὅμηρος ἀείδει αὐτοῖς
τὰ ἔπεα τάδε, ἃ καλεῖται Κάμινος (Epigr. 14; Hes. fr.
302)·

εἰ μὲν δώσετε μισθὸν ἀοιδῆς, ὦ κεραμῆες,

Hear my prayer, Kourotrophos, and grant that this
    woman
refuse the love and bed of younger men:
let her fancy be taken by old men grey at the
    temples,
whose vigor is blunted away, though their hearts still
    hanker.

When he reached the clan gathering and stood in the
doorway of the building where they were dining, some say
there was a fire burning within, but others that they only lit
one after Homer spoke the verses (*Epigram* 13):

A man's crown is his sons, a city's its walls;
horses adorn the plain, and ships the sea;
property enhances the house, and proud kings
as they sit in the gathering are a fine sight for the
    people;
but a burning fire makes the house a prouder sight.

Then he went in and reclined and ate with the clansmen,
and they honored him and admired him.

For that night Homer slept there. The next day, as he
went away, some potters, who were firing a kiln full of frag-
ile ware, saw him and called him over, as they had heard of
his skills, and encouraged him to sing for them, promising
to give him some of their wares and whatever else they
had. Homer sang them these verses, which are called *The
Kiln* (= *Epigram* 14):

If you are going to pay for my singing, O potters,

---

53 λαοῖσιν Ruhnkenius: τ᾽ ἄλλοισι codd.

δεῦρ᾽ ἄγ᾽ Ἀθηναίη, καὶ ὑπέρσχεθε χεῖρα
   καμίνου,
εὖ δὲ μελανθεῖεν κότυλοι καὶ πάντα κάναστρα,
φρυχθῆναί τε καλῶς καὶ τιμῆς ὦνον ἀρέσθαι,
5 πολλὰ μὲν εἰν ἀγορῆι πωλεύμενα, πολλὰ δ᾽
   ἀγυιαῖς,
πολλὰ δὲ κερδῆναι, ἡμᾶς δὲ δὴ ὥς σφας
   ὀνῆσαι.[54]
ἢν δ᾽ ἐπ᾽ ἀναιδείην τρεφθέντες ψεύδε᾽ ἄρησθε,
συγκαλέω δήπειτα καμίνων δηλητῆρας,
Σύντριβ᾽ ὁμῶς Σμάραγόν τε καὶ Ἄσβετον ἠδὲ
   Σαβάκτην
10 Ὠμόδαμόν θ᾽, ὃς τῆιδε τέχνηι κακὰ πολλὰ
   πορίζει·
†πεῖθε πυραίθουσαν καὶ δώματα, σὺν δὲ
   κάμινος
πᾶσα κυκηθείη, κεραμέων μέγα κωκυσάντων.
ὡς γνάθος ἱππείη βρύκει, βρύκοι δὲ κάμινος,
πάντ᾽ ἔντοσθ᾽ αὐτῆς κεραμήια λεπτὰ ποιοῦσα.
15 δεῦρο καὶ Ἡλίου θύγατερ, πολυφάρμακε
   Κίρκη·
ἄγρια φάρμακα βάλλε, κάκου δ᾽ αὐτούς τε καὶ
   ἔργα·
δεῦρο δὲ καὶ Χείρων ἀγέτω πολέας Κενταύρους,
οἵ θ᾽ Ἡρακλῆος χεῖρας φύγον, οἵ τ᾽ ἀπόλοντο·
τύπτοιεν τάδε ἔργα κακῶς, πίπτοι δὲ κάμινος,
20 αὐτοὶ δ᾽ οἰμώζοντες ὁρώιατο ἔργα πονηρά·
γηθήσω δ᾽ ὁρόων αὐτῶν κακοδαίμονα τέχνην.

then come, Athena, and hold your hand over the kiln:
may the cups turn a fine black, and all the dishes,
and be thoroughly baked, and earn the price they are
    worth
as they sell in quantity in the market and the streets,
and make good profits, and benefit me as it does
    them.
But if you turn to shamelessness and deceit,
then I will invoke all of the kiln gremlins,
Smasher and Crasher, Overblaze and Shakeapart
and Underbake, who does this craft much harm.
Invade(?) the fire-loggia and the rooms, may the
    whole kiln
be in turmoil, with the potters wailing loud.
As a horse's jaw munches, so may the kiln munch,
grinding up small all of the pots inside.
Come also you daughter of the Sun, witch Circe:
mix your wild drugs, and harm them and their work.
Let Chiron come, bringing his horde of Centaurs,
both those who escaped Heracles' hands and those he
    killed:
may they hit these works ill, and the kiln collapse,
and the men groaning watch the work of destruction.
I shall enjoy seeing their craft so bedevilled.

---

54 ἡμᾶς. . . σφας ὀνῆσαι R. M. Cook: ἡμῖν . . . σφι νοῆσαι
codd. (σφιν ἀεῖσαι Suda).

ὃς δέ χ᾽ ὑπερκύψηι, περὶ τούτου πᾶν τὸ
πρόσωπον
φλεχθείη, ὡς πάντες ἐπίστωντ᾽ αἴσιμα ῥέζειν.

33   παραχειμάζων δὲ ἐν τῆι Σάμωι, ταῖς νουμηνίαις
προσπορευόμενος πρὸς τὰς οἰκίας τὰς εὐδαιμονε-
στάτας ἐλάμβανέ τι ἀείδων τὰ ἔπεα τάδε, ἃ καλεῖται
Εἰρεσιώνη· ὡδήγουν δὲ αὐτὸν καὶ συμπαρῆσαν αἰεὶ
τῶν παίδων τινὲς τῶν ἐγχωρίων (Epigr. 15)·

δῶμα προσετραπόμεσθ᾽ ἀνδρὸς μέγα
δυναμένοιο,
ὃς μέγα μὲν δύναται, μέγα δὲ βρέμει, ὄλβιος
αἰεί.
αὐταὶ ἀνακλίνεσθε, θύραι· Πλοῦτος γὰρ ἔσεισιν
πολλός, σὺν Πλούτωι δὲ καὶ Εὐφροσύνη
τεθαλυῖα
5   Εἰρήνη τ᾽ ἀγαθή. ὅσα δ᾽ ἄγγεα, μεστὰ μὲν εἴη,
κυρβα‹σ›ίη δ᾽ αἰεὶ μάζης κατὰ καρδόπου
ἕρποι.[55]
νῦν μὲν κριθαίην εὐώπιδα σησαμόεσσαν

. . . .

τοῦ παιδὸς δὲ γυνὴ κατὰ δίφρακα βήσεται
ὕμμιν,
ἡμίονοι δ᾽ ἄξουσι κραταίποδες ἐς τόδε δῶμα,
10   αὐτὴ δ᾽ ἱστὸν ὑφαίνοι ἐπ᾽ ἠλέκτρωι βεβαυῖα.

[55] Sic Wilamowitz: κυρβαίη δ᾽ αἰεὶ κ. κ. ἕρποι μάζα fere
codd.

And whoever peeps over the top, may all his face
be scorched, to teach them all to behave decently.

He spent the winter in Samos, and at New Moon he
would go to the most well-favored houses and receive
something for singing these verses, which are called
Eiresione,[28] and there were always some of the local chil-
dren with him showing him the way (*Epigram* 15):

We take recourse to the house of a man of great
    means,
who has great resources and makes a great noise,
    ever prosperous.
Open of your own accord, doors, for Wealth will
    enter
in plenty, and with Wealth, flourishing Cheer
and welcome Peace. May the grain jars all be full,
and the mound of dough ever top the kneading
    trough.
Now [give us] beautiful barley meal laced with
    sesame

.   .   .   .

Your son's bride will come to you in a car,
hard-hoofed mules will bring her to this house:
as she weaves at her loom may she stand on a floor of
    electrum.

[28] The term properly refers to a branch hung with fruits and
cakes which boys brought to houses at Athens, and probably other
places, in an autumn ritual; they were supposed to bring prosper-
ity. See H. W. Parke, *Festivals of the Athenians* (London, 1977),
76; Walter Burkert, *Greek Religion* (Cambridge Mass., 1985),
101. On the present poem see the Introduction.

νεῦμαί τοι νεῦμαι ἐνιαύσιος ὥστε χελιδών·
ἕστηκ᾽ ἐν προθύροις ψιλὴ πόδας· ἀλλὰ φέρ᾽
αἶψα.
⟨ὑ⟩πέρ σε τὠπόλλωνος, ⟨ὦ⟩ γύ⟨ν⟩αι τι δός.[56]
κεἰ μέν τι δώσεις· εἰ δὲ μή, οὐχ ἑστήξομεν,
15 οὐ γὰρ συνοικήσοντες ἐνθάδ᾽ ἤλθομεν.

ἤιδετο δὲ τάδε τὰ ἔπεα ἐν τῆι Σάμωι ἐπὶ πολὺν χρόνον
ὑπὸ τῶν παίδων, ὅτε ἀγείροιεν ἐν τῆι ἑορτῆι τοῦ
Ἀπόλλωνος.

34   ἀρχομένου δὲ τοῦ ἔαρος ἐπεχείρησε πλεῖν Ὅμηρος
ἐς τὰς Ἀθήνας ἐκ τῆς Σάμου. καὶ ἀναχθεὶς μετά τινων
ἐγχωρίων ἀπηνέχθη ἐς τὴν Ἴον· καὶ ὡρμίσθησαν οὐ
κατὰ πόλιν, ἀλλ᾽ ἐπ᾽ ἀκτῆς. συνέβη δὲ τῶι Ὁμήρωι
καταπλέοντι[57] ἄρξασθαι μαλακῶς ἔχειν· ἐκβὰς δὲ ἐκ
τοῦ πλοίου ἐκοιμᾶτο ἐπὶ τῆς κυματωγῆς ἀδυνάτως
ἔχων. πλείους δὲ ἡμέρας ὁρμούντων αὐτῶν δι᾽ ἀπλο-
ΐην, καταβαίνοντες αἰεί τινες τῶν ἐκ τῆς πόλιος
ἀπεσχόλαζον παρὰ τῶι Ὁμήρωι, καὶ ἐν θαύματι εἶχον
35   αὐτὸν ἀκούοντες αὐτοῦ. | τῶν δὲ ναυτέων καὶ τῶν ἐκ
τῆς πόλιος τινῶν ἡμένων παρὰ τῶι Ὁμήρωι κατέπλω-
σαν παῖδες ἁλιῆες ⟨ἐς⟩[58] τὸν τόπον, καὶ ἐκβάντες ἐκ
τοῦ ἀκατίου προσελθόντες αὐτοῖς τάδε εἶπον· "ἄγετε ὦ
ξένοι, ἐπακούσατε ἡμέων, ἂν ἄρα δύνησθε διαγνῶναι
ἅσσ᾽ ἂν ὑμῖν εἴπωμεν." καί τις τῶν παρεόντων ἐκέλευε
λέγειν, οἳ δὲ εἶπαν· "ἡμεῖς ἅσσα εἵλομεν κατελίπομεν,

---

[56] Sic Wilamowitz: πέρσαι τῶι Ἀπόλλωνος γνιάτιδος *Suda*,
om. Vitae codd.

2. PSEUDO-HERODOTUS

I'll return, I'll return each year, like the swallow.
I stand at the porch, feet stripped,[29] so bring
  something quickly.
For Apollo's sake, lady, give us something!
If you will, well and good: if not, we won't wait about,
we didn't come here to make our homes with you.

These verses went on being recited in Samos for a long
time by the children when they went collecting at the feast
of Apollo.

At the start of spring Homer set out to sail to Athens
from Samos. But after sailing out with a local crew, he was
diverted to Ios. They did not moor at the town but on the
open shore. It happened that as Homer was sailing in, he
had begun to be poorly, and he disembarked and lay down
on the beach, in a weak state. They stayed at anchor for
several days because of unfavorable weather, and people
from the town kept coming down to pass the time with
Homer, and were impressed as they listened to him. As the
sailors and some of the townspeople were sitting with
Homer, some fisherboys sailed in at the place, and disem-
barking from their boat they came up and said, "Now, sirs,
listen to us and see if you can understand what we tell you."
Somebody encouraged them to go ahead, and they said,
"What we have done is leave behind whatever we caught,

---

[29] This is uttered in the person of the swallow which the chil-
dren carried round on their begging procession.

---

[57] καταπλέοντι Wilamowitz: κατὰ πολύ τι codd. (κατὰ τὴν
ὁδὸν Suda).
[58] Add. Wilamowitz.

ἃ δὲ μὴ εἵλομεν φέρομεν." οἳ δέ φασι μέτρωι εἰπεῖν
αὐτούς·

ἄσσ' ἕλομεν λιπόμεσθα· ἃ δ' οὐχ ἕλομεν
φερόμεσθα.

οὐ δυναμένων δὲ τῶν παρεόντων γνῶναι τὰ ῥηθέντα,
διηγήσαντο οἱ παῖδες ὅτι ἁλιεύοντες οὐδὲν ἐδύναντο
ἑλεῖν, καθήμενοι δὲ ἐν τῆι γῆι ἐφθειρίζοντο, καὶ ὅσους
μὲν ἔλαβον τῶν φθειρῶν κατέλιπον, ὅσους δὲ μὴ
ἐδύναντο, ἐς οἴκους ἀπεφέροντο. ὁ δὲ Ὅμηρος ἀκού-
σας ταῦτα ἔλεγε τὰ ἔπεα τάδε (Epigr. 16)·

τοίων γὰρ πατέρων ἐξ αἵματος ἐκγεγάασθε,
οὔτε βαθυκλήρων οὔτ' ἄσπετα μῆλα νεμόντων.

36   ἐκ δὲ τῆς ἀσθενείας ταύτης συνέβη τὸν Ὅμηρον
τελευτῆσαι ἐν Ἴωι, οὐ παρὰ τὸ μὴ γνῶναι τὸ παρὰ
τῶν παίδων ῥηθέν, ὡς οἴονταί τινες, ἀλλὰ τῆι μαλα-
κίηι. τελευτήσας δὲ ἐτάφη ἐν τῆι Ἴωι αὐτοῦ ἐπ' ἀκτῆς
ὑπό τε τῶν συμπλόων καὶ τῶν πολιητέων ὅσοι ἐν
διαλογῆι ἐγεγένηντο αὐτῶι. καὶ τὸ ἐλεγεῖον τόδε ἐπ-
έγραψαν Ἰῆται ὕστερον χρόνωι πολλῶι, ὡς ἤδη ἥ τε
ποίησις ἐξεπεπτώκεε καὶ ἐθαυμάζετο ὑπὸ πάντων· οὐ
γὰρ Ὁμήρου ἐστίν·

ἐνθάδε τὴν ἱερὴν κεφαλὴν κατὰ γαῖα κάλυψεν,
ἀνδρῶν ἡρώων κοσμήτορα, θεῖον Ὅμηρον.

37   ὅτι δὲ ἦν Αἰολεὺς Ὅμηρος καὶ οὔτε Ἴων οὔτε
Δωριεύς, τοῖς τε εἰρημένοις δεδήλωταί μοι καὶ δὴ καὶ

and what we didn't catch we're carrying." Or some say that they said in verse,

> The ones we caught we left behind, the ones we
> missed we carry.

When those present were unable to understand the utterance, the boys explained that in their fishing they had not succeeded in catching anything, but they had sat on the ground and de-loused themselves, and all the lice they caught, they left there, but all the ones they failed to catch, they were taking home with them. On hearing this, Homer spoke these verses (*Epigram* 16):

> That's because from such fathers' blood you are born,
> who had no rich allotments and grazed no countless
> flocks.

The result of this infirmity was that Homer died on Ios—not from his failure to interpret the boys' saying, as some suppose, but from his indisposition. Having died, he was buried on Ios, there on the shore, by his fellow sailors and those of the townspeople who had been in conversation with him. And the following elegy[30] was inscribed by the people of Ios at a much later date, after his poetry had spread abroad and become universally admired—it is not by Homer himself:

> Here the earth has covered that sacred head,
> adorner of warrior heroes, the godly Homer.

That Homer was an Aeolian, not an Ionian or a Dorian, I have shown above, and he also provides evidence as

---

[30] Not in fact an elegiac couplet, but two hexameters.

τοῖσδε τεκμαίρεσθαι παρέχει· ἄνδρα ποιητὴν τηλι-
κοῦτον εἰκός ἐστι τῶν νομίμων τῶν παρὰ τοῖς ἀνθρώ-
ποις ποιεῦντα ἐς τὴν ποίησιν ἤτοι τὰ κάλλιστα
ἐξευρόντα ποιέειν ἢ τὰ ἑωυτοῦ πάτρια ἐόντα. ἤδη
τοίνυν τὸ ἐνθένδε αὐτοὶ τῶν ἐπέων ἀκούοντες κρινεῖτε·
ἱεροποιίην γὰρ ἢ τὴν κρατίστην ἐξευρὼν ἐποίησεν ἢ
τὴν ἑωυτοῦ πατρίδι προσήκουσαν. λέγει γὰρ ὧδε (Il.
1.459–461)·

αὐέρυσαν μὲν πρῶτα καὶ ἔσφαξαν καὶ ἔδειραν
μηρούς τ᾽ ἐξέταμον κατά τε κνίσῃ ἐκάλυψαν,
δίπτυχα ποιήσαντες, ἐπ᾽ αὐτῶν δ᾽ ὠμοθέτησαν.

ἐν τούτοις ὑπὲρ ὀσφύος οὐδὲν εἴρηται ᾗ ἐς τὰ ἱερὰ
χρέονται· μονώτατον γὰρ τῶν Ἑλλήνων τὸ Αἰολικὸν
ἔθνος οὐ καίει ὀσφύν. δηλοῖ δὲ καὶ ἐν τοῖσδε τοῖς
ἔπεσιν ὅτι Αἰολεὺς ὢν δικαίως τοῖς τούτων νόμοις
ἐχρῆτο (Il. 1.462–463)·

καῖε δ᾽ ἐπὶ σχίζῃς ὁ γέρων, ἐπὶ δ᾽ αἴθοπα οἶνον
λεῖβε· νέοι δὲ παρ᾽ αὐτὸν ἔχον πεμπώβολα
χερσίν.

Αἰολέες γὰρ μόνοι τὰ σπλάγχνα ἐπὶ πέντε ὀβελῶν
ὀπτῶσιν, οἱ δὲ ἄλλοι Ἕλληνες ἐπὶ τριῶν. καὶ γὰρ
ὀνομάζουσιν οἱ Αἰολεῖς τὰ πέντε πέμπε.

38   τὰ μὲν οὖν ὑπὲρ τῆς γενέσιος καὶ τελευτῆς καὶ βίου
δεδήλωταί μοι. περὶ δὲ ἡλικίης τῆς Ὁμήρου ἐκ τῶνδ᾽
ἄν τις ἐπισκεπτόμενος ἀκριβῶς καὶ ὀρθῶς λογίζοιτο.
ἀπὸ γὰρ τῆς ἐς Ἴλιον στρατείης, ἣν Ἀγαμέμνων καὶ

follows. A man who is such a great poet is likely, when he describes social customs in his poetry, either to seek out the best ones or his own ancestral ones. Well, now you will be able to judge for yourselves by listening to his verses. To describe sacrificial ritual, he either sought out the best form, or the one that belonged to his own homeland. He says:

> They drew the heads back first, slaughtered and
>   flayed them,
> cut out the thighbones and covered them with fat,
> making a double fold, and laid raw meat on top.

Nothing is said here about the sacrificial use of the loin. The reason is that the Aeolian race is unique among the Hellenes in not burning the loin. He shows again in the following verses that he was an Aeolian and quite properly made use of their customs:

> The old man burned them on splinters, and poured
>   on the bright wine,
> while beside him the young men held the five-
>   pronged forks (*pempōbola*).

For it is only the Aeolians who roast the entrails on five prongs: the other Hellenes do it on three. And the Aeolians use *pempe* for "five" instead of *pente*.

I have now expounded the facts about his origins, his death, and his life. As to Homer's date, one can calculate it accurately and truly from the following considerations. From the expedition to Ilion which Agamemnon and

Μενέλαος ἤγειραν, ἔτεσιν ὕστερον ἑκατὸν καὶ τρι-
ήκοντα Λέσβος ὠικίσθη κατὰ πόλεις, πρότερον ἐοῦσα
ἄπολις. μετὰ δὲ Λέσβον οἰκισθεῖσαν ἔτεσιν ὕστερον
εἴκοσι Κύμη ἡ Αἰολιῶτις καὶ Φρικωνὶς καλεομένη
ὠικίσθη. μετὰ δὲ Κύμην ὀκτωκαίδεκα ἔτεσιν ὕστερον
Σμύρνα ὑπὸ Κυμαίων κατωικίσθη· καὶ ἐν τούτωι γίνε-
ται Ὅμηρος. ἀφ' οὗ δὲ Ὅμηρος ἐγένετο, ἔτεά ἐστιν
ἑξακόσια εἰκοσιδύο μέχρι τῆς Ξέρξεω διαβάσεως, ἣν
στρατευσάμενος ἐπὶ τοὺς Ἕλληνας καὶ ζεύξας τὸν
Ἑλλήσποντον διέβη ἐκ τῆς Ἀσίας ἐς τὴν Εὐρώπην.
ἀπὸ δὲ τούτου ῥηϊδίως ἐστὶν ἀριθμῆσαι τὸν χρόνον
τῶι ἐθέλοντι ζητεῖν ἐκ τῶν ἀρχόντων τῶν Ἀθήνησι.
τῶν δὲ Τρωϊκῶν ὕστερον γεγένηται Ὅμηρος ἔτεσιν
ἑκατὸν ἑξήκοντα ὀκτώ.

Menelaus organized it was a hundred and thirty years to the settlement of Lesbos by cities, it having been previously without city structure. After the settlement of Lesbos it was twenty years to the foundation of the Cyme known as Aeolian or Phrikonian. Eighteen years after Cyme, Smyrna was founded by the Cymaeans, and that was when Homer was born. From Homer's birth it is six hundred and twenty-two years to Xerxes' crossing, when on his expedition against the Hellenes he bridged the Hellespont and crossed over from Asia to Europe. From that point it is easily possible for anyone interested to reckon the time span by using the list of archons at Athens. And Homer was born a hundred and sixty-eight years after the Trojan War.[31]

[31] According to the author's reckoning Troy fell in 1270 BC, Lesbos was settled in 1140, Cyme was founded in 1120, Smyrna in 1102, and Homer was born in the same year. The genuine Herodotus, on the other hand, thought that Homer and Hesiod lived no more than four hundred years before his own time (2.53.2).

1   Περισσὸν μὲν ἴσως δόξειέ τισι πολυπραγμονεῖν περὶ
Ὁμήρου, ποίων τε ἦν γονέων καὶ πόθεν, ἐπεὶ μηδὲ
αὐτὸς ἠξίωσεν εἰπεῖν τὰ περὶ αὑτοῦ, ἀλλ᾽ οὕτως
ἐγκρατῶς ἔσχεν ὡς μηδὲ τὴν ἀρχὴν τοῦ ὀνόματος
ἐπιμνησθῆναι. ἐπεὶ δὲ ὡς πρὸς εἰσαγωγὴν τῶν ἀρχο-
μένων παιδεύεσθαι χρήσιμος ἡ πολυπειρία, πειρασώ-
μεθα εἰπεῖν ὅσα ἱστόρηται τοῖς παλαιοῖς περὶ αὐτοῦ.

2   Ἔφορος μὲν οὖν ὁ Κυμαῖος ἐν συντάγματι τῶι
ἐπιγραφομένωι Ἐπιχωρίωι (70 F 1) Κυμαῖον αὐτὸν
ἀποδεικνύναι πειρώμενός φησιν ὅτι Ἀπελλῆς καὶ
Μαίων καὶ Δῖος ἀδελφοί, Κυμαῖοι τὸ γένος· ὧν Δῖος
μὲν διὰ χρέα μετώικησεν εἰς Ἄσκρην κώμην τῆς
Βοιωτίας, κἀκεῖ γήμας Πυκιμήδην ἐγέννησεν Ἡσί-
οδον· Ἀπελλῆς δὲ τελευτήσας ἐν τῆι πατρίδι Κύμηι
κατέλιπε θυγατέρα Κριθηΐδα τοὔνομα, προστησάμε-
νος αὐτῆς τὸν ἀδελφὸν Μαίονα· ὃς διακορεύσας τὴν
προειρημένην καὶ τὴν ἀπὸ τῶν πολιτῶν ἐπὶ τῶι γεγο-
νότι δείσας κατάγνωσιν, ἔδωκεν αὐτὴν πρὸς γάμον
Φημίωι Σμυρναίωι, διδασκάλωι γραμμάτων. φοιτῶσα
δὲ αὐτὴ ἐπὶ τοὺς πλύνους, οἳ ἦσαν παρὰ τῶι Μέλητι,

3. (PSEUDO-)PLUTARCH
ON HOMER (I)

It may perhaps seem to some people superfluous to bother
about Homer's parentage and place of origin, seeing that
he himself did not see fit to speak of his personal details
but was so reserved as not even to mention his name. But
as a broad survey is useful as an introduction for those in
the early stages of education, let us try to state what the
ancients have recorded about him.

Ephorus of Cyme in the work entitled *Local History*,
attempting to show that he was a Cymaean, says that
Apelles, Maion, and Dios were brothers of Cymaean stock.
Dios because of debts migrated to Ascra, a village in
Boeotia, and there he married Pykimede and fathered
Hesiod. Apelles died in his native Cyme and left a daugh-
ter named Critheis, having made his brother Maion her
guardian: but the latter violated her, and fearing his fellow
citizens' condemnation in the matter, gave her in marriage
to Phemius, a Smyrnaean teacher of letters. She used to go
by herself to the washing places beside the Meles, and

ἀπεκύησε τὸν Ὅμηρον ἐπὶ τῶι ποταμῶι, καὶ διὰ τοῦτο
Μελησιγένης ἐκλήθη. μετωνομάσθη δὲ Ὅμηρος, ἐπει-
δὴ τὰς ὄψεις ἐπηρώθη· οὕτω δὲ ἐκάλουν οἵ τε Κυμαῖοι
καὶ οἱ Ἴωνες τοὺς τὰς ὄψεις πεπηρωμένους, παρὰ τὸ
δεῖσθαι τῶν ὁμηρευόντων, ὅ ἐστι τῶν ἡγουμένων. καὶ
ταῦτα μὲν Ἔφορος.

3   Ἀριστοτέλης δὲ ἐν τῶι τρίτωι περὶ ποιητικῆς (fr. 76
Rose) ἐν Ἴωι φησὶ τῆι νήσωι, καθ᾽ ὃν καιρὸν Νηλεὺς ὁ
Κόδρου τῆς Ἰωνικῆς ἀποικίας ἡγεῖτο, κόρην τινα τῶν
ἐπιχωρίων γενομένην ὑπό τινος δαίμονος τῶν συγχο-
ρευτῶν ταῖς Μούσαις ἐγκύμονα, αἰδεσθεῖσαν τὸ συμ-
βὰν διὰ τὸν ὄγκον τῆς γαστρός, ἐλθεῖν εἴς τι χωρίον
καλούμενον Αἴγιναν· εἰς ὃ καταδραμόντας λῃστὰς
ἀνδραποδίσαι τὴν προειρημένην καὶ ἀγαγόντας εἰς
Σμύρναν, οὖσαν ὑπὸ Λυδοῖς τότε, τῶι βασιλεῖ τῶν
Λυδῶν ὄντι φίλωι τοὔνομα Μαίονι χαρίσασθαι, τὸν δὲ
ἀγαπήσαντα τὴν κόρην διὰ τὸ κάλλος γῆμαι· ἦν
διατρίβουσαν παρὰ τῶι Μέλητι, συσχεθεῖσαν ὑπὸ
τῆς ὠδῖνος ἔτυχεν ἀποκυῆσαι τὸν Ὅμηρον ἐπὶ τῶι
ποταμῶι. ὃν ἀναλαβὼν ὁ Μαίων ὡς ἴδιον ἔτρεφε, τῆς
Κριθηΐδος μετὰ τὴν κύησιν εὐθέως τελευτησάσης·
χρόνου δὲ οὐ πολλοῦ διελθόντος καὶ αὐτὸς ἐτελεύτησε.
τῶν δὲ Λυδῶν καταπονουμένων ὑπὸ τῶν Αἰολέων καὶ
κρινάντων καταλιπεῖν τὴν Σμύρναν, κηρυξάντων τῶν
ἡγεμόνων τὸν βουλόμενον ἀκολουθεῖν ἐξιέναι τῆς
πόλεως, ἔτι νήπιος ὢν Ὅμηρος ἔφη καὶ αὐτὸς βού-
λεσθαι ὁμηρεῖν· ὅθεν ἀντὶ Μελησιγένους Ὅμηρος
προσηγορεύθη.

4   γενόμενος δὲ ἐν ἡλικίαι καὶ δόξαν ἐπὶ ποιητικῆι

there she gave birth to Homer at the river. Because of this he was called Melesigenes ("Meles-born"). His name was changed to Homer after he lost his sight, this being what the Cymaeans and Ionians called those with an ocular disability, because they need *homēreuontes*, that is, guides. So much for Ephorus.

Aristotle in Book 3 of his work *On Poets* says that on the island of Ios, at the time when Neleus the son of Codrus was leading the Ionian migration, a local girl was made pregnant by one of the sprites who dance with the Muses; ashamed of what had happened on account of her swelling belly, she went to a place called Aegina. Some freebooters came there on a raid and enslaved her and took her to Smyrna, which was at that time under the Lydians, and they gave her to the king of the Lydians, who was a friend of theirs, Maion by name. He grew warm towards the girl because of her beauty, and married her. As she was lingering beside the Meles, it happened that her contractions started, and she gave birth to Homer at the river. Maion accepted him and brought him up as his own, Critheis having died straight after the birth. But before much more time had gone by, he died too. When the Lydians were under pressure from the Aeolians, and decided to abandon Smyrna, the authorities announced that anyone who wished to accompany them should leave the city, and Homer, still an infant, said that he wanted to *homērein* (accompany): hence he was named Homer instead of Melesigenes.

When he reached manhood, having by now acquired

κεκτημένος ἤδη ἐπηρώτα τὸν θεόν, τίνων τε εἴη γο-
νέων καὶ πόθεν. ὁ δὲ ἀνεῖλεν οὕτως·

ἔστιν Ἴος νῆσος, μητρὸς πατρίς, ἥ σε θανόντα
δέξεται· ἀλλὰ νέων ἀνδρῶν αἴνιγμα φύλαξαι.

φέρεται δὲ καὶ ἕτερος χρησμὸς τοιοῦτος·

ὄλβιε καὶ δύσδαιμον—ἔφυς γὰρ ἐπ’
    ἀμφοτέροισιν—
πατρίδα δίζηαι· μητρὶς δέ τοι, οὐ πατρίς ἐστιν,
{μητρόπολις ἐν νήσωι ὑπὸ Κρήτης εὐρείης}[59]
Μίνωος γαίης οὔτε σχεδὸν οὔτ’ ἀποτηλοῦ.
ἐν τῆι σοὶ μοῖρ’ ἐστὶ τελευτῆσαι βιότοιο,
εὖτ’ ἂν ἀπὸ γλώσσης παίδων μὴ γνῶις
    ἐπακούσας
δυσξύνετον σκολιοῖσι λόγοις εἰρημένον ὕμνον.
δοιὰς γὰρ ζωῆς μοίρας λάχες· ἣν μὲν ἀμαυράν
ἠελίων δισσῶν, ἣν δ’ ἀθανάτοις ἰσόμοιρον
ζῶντί τε καὶ φθιμένωι· φθίμενος δ’ ἐπὶ[60] πολλὸν
    ἀγήρως.

μετ’ οὐ πολὺν δὲ χρόνον πλέων ἐς Θήβας ἐπὶ τὰ
Κρόνια (ἀγὼν δὲ οὗτος ἄγεται παρ’ αὐτοῖς μουσικός)
ἦλθεν εἰς Ἴον· ἔνθα ἐπὶ πέτρας καθεζόμενος ἐθεάσατο
ἁλιεῖς προσπλέοντας, ὧν ἐπύθετο εἴ τι ἔχοιεν. οἱ δέ,
ἐπὶ τῶι θηρᾶσαι μὲν μηδὲν φθειρίσασθαι δὲ διὰ τὴν
ἀπορίαν τῆς θήρας, οὕτως ἀπεκρίναντο·

[59] Versum om. Oenomaus ap. Eus. *Praep. evang.* 5.33.15.

a reputation for poetry, he enquired of the god who his parents were, and where he was from. He replied thus:

> There is an island Ios, your mother's home, which at
> your death
> will receive you. Only beware the young men's riddle.

There is also another oracle current, like this:

> Blessed and ill-starred one—for you were born to
> both—
> you seek your fatherland, but it's your mother's land,
> not your father's,
> not too close to Minos' country,[32] nor yet too far
> away.
> There it is your destiny to die,
> when from the tongue of boys you hear, perplexed,
> a song hard to fathom, uttered in devious words.
> For you have two allotted lives: one that is dimmed
> for your twin suns,[33] the other matching the
> immortals'—
> one for life, one for death; and in death you shall not
> age.

Not long afterwards, when he was sailing to Thebes for the Kronia, which is a musical contest that they hold there, he arrived at Ios. There, while sitting on a rock, he observed some fishers sailing up, and he asked them if they had got anything. They (having caught nothing but for lack of a catch de-loused themselves) answered:

[32] Crete.   [33] His eyes.

---

60 ἐπὶ West: ἔτι codd.

ὅσσ' ἕλομεν λιπόμεσθ', ὅσσ' οὐχ ἕλομεν
φερόμεσθα,

αἰνισσόμενοι ὡς ἄρα οὓς μὲν ἔλαβον τῶν φθειρῶν
ἀποκτείναντες κατέλιπον, οὓς δὲ οὐκ ἔλαβον ἐν τῆι
ἐσθῆτι φέροιεν. ὅπερ οὐ δυνηθεὶς συμβαλεῖν Ὅμηρος
διὰ τὴν ἀθυμίαν ἐτελεύτησε. θάψαντες δὲ αὐτὸν οἱ
Ἰῆται μεγαλοπρεπῶς, τοιόνδε ἐπέγραψαν αὐτοῦ τῶι
τάφωι·

ἐνθάδε τὴν ἱερὴν κεφαλὴν κατὰ γαῖα καλύπτει,
ἀνδρῶν ἡρώων κοσμήτορα θεῖον Ὅμηρον.

εἰσὶ μέντοι οἳ καὶ Κολοφώνιον αὐτὸν ἀποδεικνύναι
πειρῶνται, μεγίστωι τεκμηρίωι χρώμενοι πρὸς ἀπό-
δειξιν τῶι ἐπὶ τοῦ ἀνδριάντος ἐπιγεγραμμένωι ἐλε-
γείωι· ἔχει δὲ οὕτως·

υἱὲ Μέλητος Ὅμηρε, σὺ γὰρ κλέος Ἑλλάδι
πάσηι
καὶ Κολοφῶνι πάτρηι θῆκας ἐς ἀΐδιον·
καὶ τάσδ' ἀντιθέωι ψυχῆι γεννήσαο κούρας
δισσὰς ἐκ στηθέων, γραψάμενος σελίδας·
ὑμνεῖ δ' ἢ μὲν νόστον Ὀδυσσῆος πολύπλαγκτον,
ἢ δὲ τὸν Ἰλιακὸν Δαρδανιδῶν πόλεμον.

ἄξιον δὲ μηδὲ τὸ ὑπὸ Ἀντιπάτρου τοῦ ἐπιγραμ-
ματοποιοῦ γραφὲν ἐπίγραμμα παραλιπεῖν, ἔχον οὐκ
ἀσέμνως· ἔχει δ' οὕτως (Antip. Thess. *Epigr.* 72 G.–P.)·

All we caught we left behind, all that we missed we
carry.

The riddle meant that the lice they had caught they had
killed and left behind, but the ones they had not caught
they were carrying in their clothing. Unable to work this
out, Homer became depressed and died. The people of Ios
gave him a magnificent funeral, and inscribed this on his
tomb:

Here the earth conceals that sacred head,
adorner of warrior heroes, the godly Homer.

There are some, however, who endeavor to show that
he was a Colophonian, taking as their main piece of
evidence the elegiacs inscribed on his statue, which run as
follows:

Son of Meles, Homer, you gave glory to all Hellas
    and to your homeland Colophon for ever;
and from your breast with your godlike soul you
    fathered
    these two maidens, by writing out your texts.
One of them sings Odysseus' far-roaming return,
    the other the Dardanids' war at Ilion.[34]

Nor does the epigram written by the epigrammatist An-
tipater deserve to be passed over, as it is not unimpressive.
It runs as follows:

[34] The verses indicate a Hellenistic statuary group in which
the *Iliad* and *Odyssey* were represented as female figures and
daughters of Homer. So they were on Archelaus' famous relief
(the Apotheosis of Homer) and one or two other known monu-
ments; see *LIMC* iv(1).647–648.

οἱ μέν σευ Κολοφῶνα τιθηνήτειραν, Ὅμηρε,
  οἱ δὲ καλὰν Σμύρναν, οἱ δ' ἐνέπουσι Χίον,
οἱ δ' Ἴον, οἱ δ' ἐβόασαν εὔκλαρον Σαλαμῖνα,
  οἱ δέ νυ τὰν Λαπιθᾶν ματέρα Θεσσαλίαν,
ἄλλοι δ' ἄλλο μέλαθρον ἀνίαχον· εἰ δέ με
  Φοίβου
χρὴ λέξαι πινυτὰν ἀμφαδὰ μαντοσύναν,
πάτρα τοι τελέθει μέγας οὐρανός, ἐκ δὲ γυναικός
  οὐ θνατᾶς, ματρὸς δ' ἔπλεο Καλλιόπας.

5 γενέσθαι δὲ αὐτὸν τοῖς χρόνοις οἱ μέν φασι κατὰ
τὸν Τρωϊκὸν πόλεμον, οὗ καὶ αὐτόπτην γενέσθαι· οἱ δὲ
μετὰ ἑκατὸν ἔτη τοῦ πολέμου· ἄλλοι δὲ μετὰ πεντή-
κοντα καὶ ἑκατόν. ἔγραψε δὲ ποιήματα δύο, Ἰλιάδα
καὶ Ὀδύσσειαν· ὡς δέ τινες, οὐκ ἀληθῶς λέγοντες,
γυμνασίας καὶ παιδιᾶς ἕνεκα καὶ Βατραχομυομαχίαν
προσθεὶς καὶ Μαργίτην.

[Chapters 6–8 omitted.]

Some say Colophon was your nurse, Homer,
    and some fair Smyrna, and others Chios,
some Ios, some proclaim it prosperous Salamis,
    and some again the Lapiths' mother, Thessaly,
and others other homesteads. But if I should
    openly broadcast Phoibos' wise oracle,
the broad sky is your homeland, for you were born
    of no mortal mother, but of Calliope.

As to his date, some say he lived at the time of the Tro-
jan War, and saw it personally; others put him a hundred
years after the war, and other a hundred and fifty years
after. He wrote two poems, the *Iliad* and the *Odyssey*; and
as some say—incorrectly—he added the *Battle of Frogs
and Mice* and *Margites* by way of exercise and light relief.

ΠΛΟΥΤΑΡΧΟΥ ΠΕΡΙ
ΟΜΗΡΟΥ 2.1–4

1　Ὅμηρον τὸν ποιητήν, χρόνωι μὲν τῶν πλείστων
δυνάμει δὲ πάντων πρῶτον γενόμενον, εἰκότως ἀναγι-
νώσκομεν πρῶτον, ὠφελούμενοι τὰ μέγιστα εἴς τε τὴν
φωνὴν καὶ τὴν διάνοιαν καὶ τὴν τῶν πραγμάτων
πολυπειρίαν. λέγωμεν δὲ περὶ τῆς τούτου ποιήσεως,
πρότερον μνησθέντες διὰ βραχέων τοῦ γένους αὐτοῦ.

2　　Ὅμηρον τοίνυν Πίνδαρος μὲν (fr. 264 Sn.) ἔφη Χῖόν
τε καὶ Σμυρναῖον γενέσθαι, Σιμωνίδης δὲ (eleg.19.1)
Χῖον, Ἀντίμαχος δὲ (fr. 130 Wyss) καὶ Νίκανδρος (fr. 14
Schn.) Κολοφώνιον, Ἀριστοτέλης δὲ ὁ φιλόσοφος (fr.
76 Rose) Ἰήτην, Ἔφορος δὲ ὁ ἱστορικὸς (70 F 1) Κυ-
μαῖον. οὐκ ὤκνησαν δέ τινες καὶ Σαλαμίνιον αὐτὸν
εἰπεῖν ἀπὸ Κύπρου, τινὲς δ᾽ Ἀργεῖον, Ἀρίσταρχος δὲ
καὶ Διονύσιος ὁ Θρᾶιξ Ἀθηναῖον. υἱὸς δὲ ὑπ᾽ ἐνίων
λέγεται Μαίονος καὶ Κριθηΐδος, ὑπὸ δέ τινων Μέλη-
τος τοῦ ποταμοῦ.

3　　ὥσπερ δὲ τὰ τοῦ γένους αὐτοῦ διαπορεῖται, οὕτω
καὶ τὰ περὶ τῶν χρόνων καθ᾽ οὓς ἐγένετο. καὶ οἱ μὲν
περὶ Ἀρίσταρχόν φασιν αὐτὸν γενέσθαι κατὰ τὴν τῶν
Ἰώνων ἀποικίαν, ἥτις ὑστερεῖ τῆς τῶν Ἡρακλειδῶν

4. (PSEUDO-)PLUTARCH
ON HOMER (II)

The poet Homer, as he surpasses most others in antiquity and all others in ability, we naturally read first, with immense benefit to our eloquence, intellect, and knowledge of affairs. Let us speak about his poetry, after first briefly mentioning his origins.

Pindar called Homer both a Chian and a Smyrnaean, Simonides called him a Chian, Antimachus and Nicander a Colophonian, the philosopher Aristotle a native of Ios, and the historian Ephorus a Cymaean. Some have not shrunk even from making him a Salaminian from Cyprus, some have made him an Argive, while Aristarchus and Dionysius Thrax make him an Athenian. He is said by some to have been the son of Maion and Critheis, but by others of the river Meles.

Just as his origins are a matter of dispute, so is his date. The school of Aristarchus puts him at the time of the Ionian migration, which is sixty years after the return of

καθόδου ἔτεσιν ἑξήκοντα· τὰ δὲ περὶ τοὺς Ἡρακλείδας
λείπεται τῶν Τρωϊκῶν ἔτεσιν ὀγδοήκοντα. οἱ δὲ περὶ
Κράτητα καὶ πρὸ τῆς Ἡρακλειδῶν καθόδου λέγουσιν
αὐτὸν γενέσθαι, ὡς οὐδὲ ὅλα ἔτη ὀγδοήκοντα ἀπέχειν
τῶν Τρωϊκῶν. ἀλλὰ παρὰ τοῖς πλείστοις πεπίστευται
μετὰ ἔτη ἑκατὸν <τῆς Ἰώνων ἀποικίας, τινὲς δὲ καὶ
μετὰ τετρακόσια>[61] τῶν Τρωϊκῶν γεγονέναι, οὐ πολὺ
πρὸ τῆς θέσεως τῶν Ὀλυμπίων, ἀφ᾽ ἧς ὁ κατὰ Ὀλυμ-
πιάδας χρόνος ἀριθμεῖται.

4   εἰσὶ δὲ αὐτοῦ ποιήσεις δύο, Ἰλιὰς καὶ Ὀδύσσεια,
διῃρημένη ἑκατέρα εἰς τὸν ἀριθμὸν τῶν στοιχείων,
οὐχ ὑπὸ αὐτοῦ τοῦ ποιητοῦ ἀλλ᾽ ὑπὸ τῶν γραμματι-
κῶν τῶν περὶ Ἀρίσταρχον.

[61] <τῆς Ἰώνων ἀποικίας> add. Wolff, cetera West.

the Heraclids, the Heraclid affair falling eighty years after the Trojan War. But Crates' school puts him even before the return of the Heraclids, so that he would have been not a full eighty years removed from the Trojan War. Most authorities, however, believe that he lived a hundred years after the ‹Ionian migration, while some even put him four hundred years after the› Trojan War,[35] not long before the establishment of the Olympic Games, from which the dating by Olympiads is reckoned.

There are two poems by him, the *Iliad* and the *Odyssey*, each divided into the number of the letters of the alphabet, not by the poet himself but by the grammarians associated with Aristarchus.

[35] The transmitted text is impossible. My insertion is based on the similar passage in Tatian, *Oration to the Greeks* 31 (p. 32.8 Schwartz).

ΠΡΟΚΛΟΥ ΧΡΗΣΤΟΜΑΘΙΑΣ ΓΡΑΜΜΑΤΙΚΗΣ ΤΟ Ᾱ

ΟΜΗΡΟΥ ΧΡΟΝΟΙ, ΒΙΟΣ, ΧΑΡΑΚΤΗΡ, ΑΝΑΓΡΑΦΗ ΠΟΙΗΜΑΤΩΝ

1 Ἐπῶν ποιηταὶ γεγόνασι πολλοί· τούτων δ' εἰσὶ κράτιστοι Ὅμηρος, Ἡσίοδος, Πείσανδρος, Πανύασσις, Ἀντίμαχος.

2 Ὅμηρος μὲν οὖν τίνων γονέων ἢ ποίας ἐγένετο πατρίδος, οὐ ῥάιδιον ἀποφήνασθαι· οὔτε γὰρ αὐτός τι λελάληκεν, ἀλλ' οὐδὲ οἱ περὶ αὐτοῦ εἰπόντες συμπεφωνήκασιν, ἀλλ' ἐκ τοῦ μηδὲν ῥητῶς ἐμφαίνειν περὶ τούτων τὴν ποίησιν αὐτοῦ, μετὰ πολλῆς ἀδείας ἕκαστος οἷς ἠβούλετο ἐχαρίσατο. καὶ διὰ τοῦτο οἱ μὲν Κολοφώνιον αὐτὸν ἀνηγόρευσαν, οἱ δὲ Χῖον, οἱ δὲ Σμυρναῖον, οἱ δὲ Ἰήτην, ἄλλοι δὲ Κυμαῖον, καὶ καθόλου πᾶσα πόλις ἀντιποιεῖται τἀνδρός· ὅθεν εἰκότως ἂν κοσμοπολίτης λέγοιτο.

3 οἱ μὲν οὖν Σμυρναῖον αὐτὸν ἀποφαινόμενοι Μαίονος μὲν πατρὸς λέγουσιν εἶναι, γεννηθῆναι δὲ ἐπὶ Μέλητος τοῦ ποταμοῦ, ὅθεν καὶ Μελησιγένη ὀνομασθῆναι· δοθέντα δὲ Χίοις εἰς ὁμηρείαν Ὅμηρον

5. PROCLUS. CHRESTOMATHY I

HOMER'S DATE, LIFE, CHARACTER, CATALOGUE OF POEMS

There have been many hexameter poets; the chief among them are Homer, Hesiod, Pisander, Panyassis, and Antimachus.

As to Homer, it is not easy to state from what parents or place he sprang, for he has not said anything himself, and there is no agreement among those who have discussed him: because his poetry gives no express indication on these questions, each writer has indulged his inclinations with great freedom. Hence some have proclaimed him a Colophonian, some a Chian, some a Smyrnaean, some a man of Ios, others a Cymaean, and in general every city claims the man, so he might reasonably be called a citizen of the world.

Those who make him a Smyrnaean say that his father was Maion, and that he was born at the river Meles, and accordingly named Melesigenes, but after being given to the Chians as a hostage (*homēron*) he was called Homer.

κληθῆναι. οἱ δὲ ἀπὸ τῆς τῶν ὀμμάτων πηρώσεως
τούτου τυχεῖν αὐτόν φασι τοῦ ὀνόματος· τοὺς γὰρ
τυφλοὺς ὑπὸ Αἰολέων ὁμήρους καλεῖσθαι.

4   Ἑλλάνικος δὲ (fr. 5 Fowler) καὶ Δαμάστης (fr. 11 F.)
καὶ Φερεκύδης (fr. 167 F.) εἰς Ὀρφέα τὸ γένος ἀνά-
γουσιν αὐτοῦ. Μαίονα γάρ φασι τὸν Ὁμήρου πατέρα
καὶ Δίον τὸν Ἡσιόδου γενέσθαι Ἀπέλλιδος τοῦ Μελα-
νώπου τοῦ Ἐπιφράδεος τοῦ Χαριφήμου τοῦ Φιλοτέρ-
πεος τοῦ Ἰδμονίδα τοῦ Εὐκλέους τοῦ Δωρίωνος τοῦ
Ὀρφέως. Γοργίας δὲ ὁ Λεοντῖνος (82 B 25 D.–K.) εἰς
Μουσαῖον αὐτὸν ἀνάγει.

5   περὶ δὲ τῆς τελευτῆς αὐτοῦ λόγος τις φέρεται
τοιοῦτος. ἀνελεῖν φασιν αὐτῶι τὸν θεὸν χρωμένωι περὶ
ἀσφαλείας τάδε·

    ἔστιν Ἴος νῆσος μητρὸς πατρίς, ἥ σε θανόντα
    δέξεται· ἀλλὰ νέων ἀνδρῶν αἴνιγμα φύλαξαι.

λέγουσιν οὖν αὐτὸν εἰς Ἴον πλεύσαντα διατρῖψαι μὲν
παρὰ Κρεωφύλωι, γράψαντα δὲ Οἰχαλίας ἅλωσιν
τούτωι χαρίσασθαι· ἥτις νῦν ὡς Κρεωφύλου περι-
φέρεται. καθεζόμενον δὲ ἐπί τινος ἀκτῆς θεασάμενον
ἁλιεῖς προσειπεῖν αὐτοὺς καὶ ἀνακρῖναι τοῖσδε τοῖς
ἔπεσιν·

    ἄνδρες ἀπ᾽ Ἀρκαδίης θηρήτορες, ἦ ῥ᾽ ἔχομέν τι;

ὑποτυχόντα δὲ αὐτῶν ἕνα εἰπεῖν·

Others say he got this name from losing his sight, the blind being called by the Aeolians *homēroi*.

Hellanicus, Damastes, and Pherecydes trace his lineage back to Orpheus. They say that Homer's father Maion and Hesiod's father Dios were the sons of Apellis, son of Melanopus, son of Epiphrades, son of Chariphemus, son of Philoterpes, son of Idmonides, son of Eucles, son of Dorion, son of Orpheus. And Gorgias of Leontini takes him back to Musaeus.

Concerning his death there is a story current that goes like this. They say that when he consulted the god about keeping safe, his response was:

> There is an island Ios, your mother's home, which at
>   your death
> will receive you. Only beware the young men's riddle.

So they say he sailed to Ios and spent time with Creophylus, and when he wrote the *Capture of Oichalia* he gave it to him, and it is now current under Creophylus' name. And as he sat on a certain shore and observed some fishers, he addressed them and questioned them in this verse:

> O huntsmen from Arcadia, have we caught anything?

And one of them replied:

οὓς ἕλομεν λιπόμεσθ', οὓς δ' οὐχ ἕλομεν
φερόμεσθα.

οὐκ ἐπιβάλλοντος δὲ αὐτοῦ διελέσθαι τὸ αἴνιγμα, ὅτι
ἐπὶ ἰχθυΐαν καταβάντες ἀφήμαρτον, φθειρισάμενοι δὲ
ὅσους μὲν ἔλαβον τῶν φθειρῶν ἀποκτείναντες ἀπολεί-
πουσιν, ὅσοι δὲ αὐτοὺς διέφυγον, τούτους ἀποκομί-
ζουσιν, οὕτω δὴ ἐκεῖνον ἀθυμήσαντα σύννουν ἀπιέναι,
τοῦ χρησμοῦ ἔννοιαν λαμβάνοντα, καὶ οὕτως ὀλι-
σθόντα περιπταῖσαι λίθοις, καὶ τριταῖον τελευτῆσαι.
ἀλλὰ δὴ ταῦτα μὲν πολλῆς ἔχεται ζητήσεως, ἵνα δὲ
μηδὲ τούτων ἄπειρος ὑπάρχῃς, διὰ τοῦτο εἰς ταῦτα
κεχώρηκα.

6   τυφλὸν δὲ ὅσοι τοῦτον ἀπεφήναντο, αὐτοί μοι δο-
κοῦσι τὴν διάνοιαν πεπηρῶσθαι· τοσαῦτα γὰρ κατεῖ-
δεν ἄνθρωπος ὅσα οὐδεὶς πώποτε. εἰσὶ δὲ οἵτινες
ἀνεψιὸν αὐτὸν Ἡσιόδου παρέδοσαν, ἀτριβεῖς ὄντες
ποιήσεως· τοσοῦτον γὰρ ἀπέχουσι τοῦ γένει προσή-
κειν ὅσον ἡ ποίησις διέστηκεν αὐτῶν. ἄλλως δὲ οὐδὲ
τοῖς χρόνοις συνεπέβαλον ἀλλήλοις, ἄθλιοι δὲ οἱ τὸ
ἀνάθημα[62] πλάσαντες τοῦτο·

Ἡσίοδος Μούσαις Ἑλικωνίσι τόνδ' ἀνέθηκεν,
ὕμνωι νικήσας ἐν Χαλκίδι θεῖον Ὅμηρον.

ἀλλὰ γὰρ ἐπλανήθησαν ἐκ τῶν Ἡσιοδείων Ἡμερῶν·
ἕτερον γάρ τι σημαίνει.

---

[62] ἀνάθημα Wilamowitz: αἴνιγμα codd.

The ones we caught we left behind, the ones we
  missed we carry.

When he did not apprehend the solution of the riddle, that
they had had no success in their fishing expedition but had
de-loused themselves, and the lice they had caught they
had killed and left behind, while the ones that escaped
them they carried away, he became depressed, and went
away preoccupied, recalling the oracle, and in this condi-
tion he slipped and fell on a stone, and died two days later.
Well, these questions depend on extensive research, but I
have gone into them so that even in this you are not with-
out some knowledge.

Those who have stated that he was blind seem to me to
be mentally blind themselves, for he saw more clearly than
any man ever. And there are some who have written that he
was the cousin of Hesiod: they are no experts in poetry, for
Homer and Hesiod are as far from being related by birth as
their poetry is different. In any case, they were not even
contemporaries, and those who made up this dedication
were pitiful wretches:

Hesiod dedicated this to the Muses of Helicon,
having defeated in song at Chalcis the godly Homer.

They were led astray by Hesiod's *Days*—the passage
means something else.[36]

---

[36] The reference is to *Works and Days* 650–660, where
Hesiod records his victory in a poetic contest at Chalcis and his
dedication to the Muses of the tripod that he won as a prize.

7   τοῖς δὲ χρόνοις αὐτὸν οἱ μὲν περὶ τὸν Ἀρίσταρχόν
φασι γενέσθαι κατὰ τὴν τῆς Ἰωνίας ἀποικίαν, ἥτις
ὑστερεῖ τῆς Ἡρακλειδῶν καθόδου ἔτεσιν ἑξήκοντα· τὸ
δὲ περὶ τοὺς Ἡρακλείδας λείπεται τῶν Τρωϊκῶν ἔτε-
σιν ὀγδοήκοντα. οἱ δὲ περὶ Κράτητα ἀνάγουσιν αὐτὸν
εἰς τοὺς Τρωϊκοὺς χρόνους.

8   φαίνεται δὲ γηραιὸς ἐκλελοιπὼς τὸν βίον· ἡ γὰρ
ἀνυπέρβλητος ἀκρίβεια τῶν πραγμάτων προβεβηκυῖ-
αν ἡλικίαν παρίστησι. πολλὰ δὲ ἐπεληλυθὼς μέρη
τῆς οἰκουμένης ἐκ τῆς πολυπειρίας τῶν τόπων εὑ-
ρίσκεται. τούτωι δὲ προσυπονοητέον καὶ πλούτου
πολλὴν περιουσίαν γενέσθαι· αἱ γὰρ μακραὶ ἀποδη-
μίαι πολλῶν δέονται ἀναλωμάτων, καὶ ταῦτα κατ᾽
ἐκείνους τοὺς χρόνους οὔτε πάντων πλεομένων ἀκιν-
δύνως οὔτε ἐπιμισγομένων ἀλλήλοις πω τῶν ἀνθρώ-
πων ῥαιδίως.

9   γέγραφε δὲ ποιήσεις δύο, Ἰλιάδα καὶ Ὀδύσσειαν,
ἣν Ξένων καὶ Ἑλλάνικος ἀφαιροῦνται αὐτοῦ. οἱ μέν-
τοι γε ἀρχαῖοι καὶ τὸν Κύκλον ἀναφέρουσιν εἰς αὐτόν·
προστιθέασι δέ τινες αὐτῶι καὶ παίγνιά τινα· Μαργί-
την, Βατραχομαχίαν {ἢ Μυομαχίαν}, Ἑπτάπεκτον[63]
αἶγα, Κέρκωπας, Εἰς ξένους.[64]

63 Ἑπτάπεκτον Toup: ἔν τε πακτίον fere codd.
64 Εἰς ξένους West: κενούς codd.: Καμίνους Bergk: Κερα-
μέας Bossi.

424

5. PROCLUS

As to his date, Aristarchus' school puts him at the time of the Ionian migration, which is sixty years after the return of the Heraclids, the Heraclid affair falling eighty years after the Trojan War. But Crates' school takes him back to the Trojan era.

He was evidently old when he passed away, for his unsurpassed accuracy in material detail indicates an advanced age. That he travelled to many parts of the world can be inferred from his wide knowledge of places. We must also suppose a great abundance of wealth to have been at his disposal, for long journeys call for much expenditure, especially in those times when it was not the case that all seas could be safely sailed or that people could easily visit each other.

He is the author of two poems, the *Iliad* and the *Odyssey* (which latter Xenon and Hellanicus deny him). But the ancients also ascribe the Cycle to him, and some people add certain fun poems too: the *Margites*, the *Battle of Frogs*, the *Seven-times-shorn Goat*, the *Cercopes*, and *On Outsiders*.[37]

[37] The first of the "Epigrams" (pseudo-Herodotus' *Life*, 9) is found under this inept title in a number of manuscripts at the end of the *Hymns*.

HESYCHIUS MILESIUS

(*Suda* ο 251, iii.524.27 Adler)

1 Ὅμηρος ὁ ποιητής, Μέλητος τοῦ ἐν Σμύρνηι
ποταμοῦ καὶ Κριθηΐδος νύμφης, ὥς φησι Καστρίκιος
ὁ Νικαεύς· ὡς δὲ ἄλλοι, Ἀπόλλωνος καὶ Καλλιόπης
τῆς Μούσης· ὡς δὲ Χάραξ ὁ ἱστορικὸς (*FGrHist* 103 F
62), Μαίονος {ἢ Μητίου} καὶ Εὐμήτιδος μητρός· κατὰ
δὲ ἄλλους Τηλεμάχου τοῦ Ὀδυσσέως καὶ Πολυ-
κάστης τῆς Νέστορος. ἔστι δὲ ἡ τοῦ γένους τάξις
κατὰ τὸν ἱστορικὸν Χάρακα αὕτη· Αἰθούσης Θράισ-
σης Λίνος, τοῦ δὲ Πίερος, τοῦ δὲ Οἴαγρος, τοῦ δὲ
Ὀρφεύς, τοῦ δὲ Δρής, τοῦ δὲ Εὐκλέης, τοῦ δὲ Ἰδμο-
νίδης, τοῦ δὲ Φιλοτέρπης, τοῦ δὲ Εὔφημος, τοῦ δὲ
Ἐπιφράδης, τοῦ δὲ Μελάνωπος, τοῦ δὲ Ἀπελλῆς, τοῦ
δὲ Μαίων, ὃς ἦλθεν ἅμα ταῖς Ἀμαζόσιν ἐν Σμύρνηι
καὶ γήμας Εὔμητιν τὴν Εὐέπους τοῦ Μνησιγένους[65]
ἐποίησεν Ὅμηρον.

2 ὁμοίως δὲ καὶ κατὰ τὴν πατρίδα ἀμφίβολος διὰ τὸ
ἀπιστηθῆναι ὅλως εἶναι θνητὸν τῶι μεγέθει τῆς
φύσεως. οἱ μὲν γὰρ ἔφασαν γενέσθαι Σμυρναῖον, οἱ
δὲ Χῖον, οἱ δὲ Κολοφώνιον, οἱ δὲ Ἰήτην, οἱ δὲ Κυ-
μαῖον, οἱ δὲ ἐκ Τροίας ἀπὸ χωρίου Κεγχρεῶν, οἱ δὲ

426

6. FROM
HESYCHIUS OF MILETUS
INDEX OF FAMOUS AUTHORS

Homer, the poet, son of Meles, the river of Smyrna, and of
a nymph Critheis, as Castricius of Nicaea says; or as others
say, of Apollo and the Muse Calliope; or as the historian
Charax says, of Maion and Eumetis; or according to others,
of Odysseus' son Telemachus and Nestor's daughter
Polycaste. The sequence of his lineage according to the
historian Charax is as follows: from a Thracian woman
Aithousa Linus was born, from him Pierus, from him
Oeagrus, from him Orpheus, from him Dres, from him
Eucles, from him Idmonides, from him Philoterpes, from
him Euphemus, from him Epiphrades, from him
Melanopus, from him Apelles, from him Maion, who came
to Smyrna at the same time as the Amazons, married
Eumetis the daughter of Euepes, son of Mnesigenes, and
fathered Homer.

He is likewise indeterminate in respect of his home-
land, as his mighty talent made it seem incredible that he
was mortal at all. For some said he was born a Smyrnaean,
some a Chian, some a Colophonian, some a man of Ios,
some a Cymaean, some from a place Kenchreai in the

<hr>

65 Μελησιγένους Bernhardy.

LIVES OF HOMER

Λυδόν, οἱ δὲ Ἀθηναῖον, οἱ δὲ Αἰγύπτιον, οἱ δὲ Ἰθακή-
σιον, οἱ δὲ Κύπριον, οἱ δὲ Κνώσσιον, οἱ δὲ Σαλαμί-
νιον, οἱ δὲ Μυκηναῖον, οἱ δὲ Θετταλόν, οἱ δὲ Ἰταλιώ-
την, οἱ δὲ Λευκανόν, οἱ δὲ Γρύνειον, οἱ δὲ καὶ
Ῥωμαῖον, οἱ δὲ Ῥόδιον.

3   καὶ προσηγορεύετο μὲν κυρίως Μελησιγένης· καὶ
γὰρ ἐτέχθη παρὰ τῶι Μέλητι ποταμῶι κατὰ τοὺς
Σμυρναῖον αὐτὸν γενεαλογοῦντας· ἐκλήθη δὲ Ὅμηρος
διὰ τὸ πολέμου ἐνισταμένου Σμυρναίοις πρὸς Κολο-
φωνίους ὅμηρον δοθῆναι, ἢ τὸ βουλευομένων Σμυρ-
ναίων δαιμονίαι τινὶ ἐνεργείαι φθέγξασθαι καὶ συμ-
βουλεῦσαι ἐκκλησιάζουσι περὶ τοῦ πολέμου.

4   γέγονε δὲ πρὸ τοῦ τεθῆναι τὴν πρώτην ὀλυμπιάδα
πρὸ ἐνιαυτῶν νζ'· Πορφύριος δὲ ἐν τῆι Φιλοσόφωι
ἱστορίαι (fr. 201 Smith) πρὸ ρλβ' φησίν· ἐτέθη δὲ αὕτη
μετὰ τὴν Τροίας ἅλωσιν ἐνιαυτοῖς ὕστερον υζ'. τινὲς
δὲ μετὰ ρξ' ἐνιαυτοὺς μόνους τῆς Ἰλίου ἁλώσεως
τετέχθαι ἱστοροῦσιν Ὅμηρον· ὁ δὲ ῥηθεὶς Πορφύριος
μετὰ σοε'.

5   γήμας δὲ ἐν Χίωι Ἀρσιφόνην τὴν Γνώτορος τοῦ
Κυμαίου θυγατέρα ἔσχεν υἱεῖς δύο καὶ θυγατέρα
μίαν, ἣν ἔγημε Στασῖνος ὁ ὕπατος Κυπρίων· οἱ δὲ
υἱεῖς Ἐρίφων καὶ Θεόλαος.

6   ποιήματα δὲ αὐτοῦ ἀναμφίλεκτα Ἰλιὰς καὶ Ὀδύσ-
σεια. ἔγραψε δὲ τὴν Ἰλιάδα οὐχ ἅμα οὐδὲ κατὰ τὸ
συνεχές, καθάπερ σύγκειται, ἀλλ' αὐτὸς μὲν ἑκάστην
ῥαψωιδίαν γράψας καὶ ἐπιδειξάμενος τῶι περινοστεῖν
τὰς πόλεις τροφῆς ἕνεκεν ἀπέλιπεν, ὕστερον δὲ

428

Troad, some a Lydian, some an Athenian, some an Egyptian, some an Ithacan, some a Cyprian, some a Cnossian, some a Salaminian, some a Mycenaean, some a Thessalian, some an Italian, some a Lucanian, some from Gryneia, some even a Roman, some a Rhodian.

And he was called properly speaking Melesigenes, for he was born beside the river Meles according to those who make him a Smyrnaean by birth; but he was named Homer because of his being given as a hostage when the Smyrnaeans were threatened with a war against the Colophonians, or because when the Smyrnaeans were deliberating he spoke out through some divine impulse and gave them advice at an assembly debating the war.

He lived 57 years before the establishment of the first Olympiad, or as Porphyry says in his *Philosophical History*, 132 years before; and the Olympiad was established 407 years after the capture of Troy. Some record that Homer was born only 160 years after the capture of Ilion. But the said Porphyry makes it 275 years after.[38]

He married in Chios Arsiphone, daughter of Gnotor the Cymaean, and had two sons and one daughter. She became the wife of Stasinus, the chief magistrate of Cyprus. The sons were Eriphon and Theolaus.

His undisputed poems are the *Iliad* and the *Odyssey*. He did not write the *Iliad* all at once or in sequence, as it has been put together: he wrote each rhapsody and performed it as he went round from town to town to make a living, and left it there, and subsequently the poem was put

[38] Porphyry's dating agrees with that of the Parian Marble, and must go back to an older source. See Erwin Rohde, *Kleine Schriften* i.89–91.

429

συνετέθη {καὶ συνετάχθη} ὑπὸ πολλῶν, καὶ μάλιστα
ὑπὸ Πεισιστράτου τοῦ Ἀθηναίων τυράννου. ἀναφέρε-
ται δὲ εἰς αὐτὸν καὶ ἄλλα τινὰ ποιήματα· Ἀμαζονία,
Ἰλιὰς Μικρά, Νόστοι, Ἐπικιχλίδες, Ἠθιέπακτος ἤτοι
Ἴαμβοι, Βατραχομυομαχία, Ἀραχνομαχία, Γερανο-
μαχία, Κεραμεῖς, Ἀμφιαράου ἐξέλασις, παίγνια,
Οἰχαλίας[66] ἅλωσις, Ἐπιθαλάμια, Κύκλος, Ὕμνοι,
Κύπρια.

7   γηραιὸς δὲ τελευτήσας ἐν τῆι νήσωι τῆι Ἴωι
τέθαπται, τυφλὸς ἐκ παίδων γεγονώς. τὸ δὲ ἀληθές,
ὅτι οὐχ ἡττήθη ἐπιθυμίας, ἣ παρὰ τῶν ὀφθαλμῶν
ἄρχεται, καὶ παρὰ τοῦτο ἱστορήθη τυφλός. ἐπιγέ-
γραπται δὲ ἐν τῶι τάφωι αὐτοῦ τόδε τὸ ἐλεγεῖον, ὃ ὑπὸ
τῶν Ἰητῶν ἐποιήθη χρόνωι ⟨πολλῶι ὕστερον⟩, ὥς
φησι Καλλίμαχος (fr. 453)·

    ἐνθάδε τὴν ἱερὰν κεφαλὴν κατὰ γαῖα καλύπτει,
    ἀνδρῶν ἡρώων κοσμήτορα θεῖον Ὅμηρον.

66 Σικελίας codd.: corr. Pearson.

430

together by various people, above all by Pisistratus, the Athenian tyrant. Certain other poems are also attributed to him: the *Amazonia*, the *Little Iliad*, the *Returns*, the *Epikichlides*, the *Ethiepaktos* or *Iamboi*, the *Battle of Frogs and Mice*, the *Battle of Spiders*, the *Battle of Cranes*, the *Potters*, the *Expedition of Amphiaraus*, fun poems, the *Capture of Oichalia*, *Wedding Songs*, the *Cycle*, the *Hymns*, the *Cypria*.

He died old and is buried on the island of Ios, having been blind since childhood. The true version is that he did not succumb to lust, which begins from the eyes, and for this reason he was reported to be blind. There is inscribed on his tomb the following elegy, which was composed by the people of Ios long afterwards, as Callimachus says:

Here the earth conceals that sacred head,
adorner of warrior heroes, the godly Homer.

ΒΙΟΣ ΟΜΗΡΟΥ
(VITA ROMANA)

1   Τὸ μὲν ἄντικρυς εἰπεῖν διισχυρισάμενον τήνδε τινὰ
σαφῶς εἶναι τὴν Ὁμήρου γένεσιν ἢ πόλιν χαλεπόν,
μᾶλλον δὲ ἀδύνατον εἶναι νομίζω· ἀναγκαῖον δὲ κατα-
ριθμῆσαι τὰς ἀντιποιουμένας τῆς γενέσεως αὐτοῦ
πόλεις, τό τε γένος ἐξειπεῖν τὸ ἀμφισβητήσιμον τοῦ
ποιητοῦ.

2   Ἀναξιμένης μὲν οὖν (FGrHist 72 F 30) καὶ Δαμά-
στης (fr. 11 Fowler) καὶ Πίνδαρος ὁ μελοποιὸς (fr. 264
Sn.) Χῖον αὐτὸν ἀποφαίνονται, καὶ Θεόκριτος ἐν τοῖς
Ἐπιγράμμασιν (cf. A.P. 9.434)· ὁ δὲ Δαμάστης καὶ
δέκατον αὐτὸν ἀπὸ Μουσαίου φησὶ γεγονέναι. Ἱππίας
δὲ αὖ (FGrHist 6 F 13) καὶ Ἔφορος (70 F 99) Κυμαῖον· ὁ
δὲ Ἔφορος καὶ εἰς Χαρίφημον ἀνάγει τὸ γένος αὐτοῦ,
ὁ δὲ Χαρίφημος οὗτος Κύμην ᾤκισε. Τιμόμαχος δὲ
(754 F 2) καὶ Ἀριστοτέλης (fr. 76 Rose) ἐξ Ἴου τῆς
νήσου. κατὰ δὲ Ἀντίμαχον (fr. 130 Wyss) Κολοφώνιος·
κατὰ δὲ Στησίμβροτον τὸν Θάσιον (107 F 22)
Σμυρναῖος· κατὰ Φιλόχορον δὲ (328 F 209) Ἀργεῖος·
κατὰ Καλλικλέα δὲ (758 F 13) τῆς ἐν Κύπρωι
Σαλαμῖνος. Ἀριστόδημος δὲ ὁ Νυσαεὺς (FHG iii.307)

7. ANONYMUS I, LIFE OF HOMER (VITA ROMANA)

To assert outright that Homer's origins or city were such and such, I consider difficult, or rather impossible. But it is necessary to enumerate the cities that lay claim to his birth, and to set out the poet's controversial lineage.

Anaximenes, Damastes, and the lyric poet Pindar make him a Chian, as does Theocritus in his *Epigrams*; and Damastes says he was a tenth-generation descendant of Musaeus. Hippias and Ephorus, on the other hand, make him a Cymaean, and Ephorus even takes his lineage back to Chariphemus, who colonized Cyme. Timomachus and Aristotle have him come from the island of Ios; according to Antimachus he was a Colophonian, according to Stesimbrotus of Thasos a Smyrnaean, according to Philochorus an Argive, and according to Callicles, from Salamis in Cyprus. Aristodemus of Nysa argues him to be a Roman,

Ῥωμαῖον αὐτὸν ἀποδείκνυσιν ἔκ τινων ἐθῶν παρὰ
Ῥωμαίοις μόνον γινομένων, τοῦτο μὲν ἐκ τῆς τῶν
πεσσῶν παιδιᾶς, τοῦτο δὲ ἐκ τοῦ ἐπανίστασθαι τῶν
θάκων τοὺς ἥσσονας τῶν βελτιόνων ἡκόντων· ἃ καὶ
νῦν ἔτι φυλάσσεται παρὰ Ῥωμαίοις ἔθη. ἄλλοι δὲ
Αἰγύπτιον αὐτὸν εἶπον διὰ τὸ {ἢ} παράγειν τοὺς
ἥρωας ἐκ στόματος ἀλλήλους φιλοῦντας, ὅπερ ἐστὶν
ἔθος τοῖς Αἰγυπτίοις ποιεῖν.

3   πατρὸς δὲ κατὰ μὲν Στησίμβροτόν (107 F 22 adden-
dum) ἐστι Μαίονος τοῦ Ἀπέλλιδος καὶ μητρὸς Ὑρνη-
θοῦς ἢ Κρηθηΐδος, κατὰ δὲ Δείναρχον ⟨Κ⟩ρήθωνος,
κατὰ δὲ Δημοκρίνην Ἀλήμονος[67] κατὰ δὲ τοὺς
πλείστους Μέλητος τοῦ κατὰ Σμύρναν ποταμοῦ, ὃς
ἐπ' ὀλίγον ῥέων εὐθέως εἰς τὴν παρακειμένην θάλασ-
σαν ἐκδίδωσιν. Ἀριστοτέλης δὲ (fr. 76 Rose) ἱστορεῖν
φησιν Ἰήτας ἔκ τινος δαίμονος γεγεννῆσθαι τὸν
Ὅμηρον ταῖς Μούσαις συγχορεύσαντος.

4   περὶ δὲ τῶν χρόνων καθ' οὓς ἤκμασεν, ὧδε λέγεται.
Ἡρακλείδης μὲν οὖν (fr. 177 Wehrli) αὐτὸν ἀποδείκνυσι
πρεσβύτερον Ἡσιόδου· ⟨Π⟩ύρανδρος δὲ (FHG iv.486)
καὶ Ὑψικράτης ὁ Ἀμισηνὸς (190 F 5) ἡλικιώτην.
Κράτης δὲ ὁ Μαλλώτης (p.40 Wachsmuth) μετὰ
ἑξήκοντα ⟨ἔτη⟩ τοῦ Ἰλιακοῦ πολέμου φησὶν ἀκμάσαι·
Ἐρατοσθένης δὲ (241 F 9) μετὰ ἑκατὸν τῆς Ἰώνων
ἀποικίας·[68] Ἀπολλόδωρος δὲ (244 F 63) μετὰ ὀγδοή-
κοντα.

5   ἐκαλεῖτο δὲ ἐκ γενετῆς ⟨Μελησιγένης⟩ ἢ Μελη-

from certain customs that occur only among the Romans: firstly from the game of *pessoi*,[39] and secondly from the practice of inferiors rising from their seats when superiors arrive,[40] customs which are still preserved among the Romans. But others have said he was an Egyptian, because he portrays heroes kissing one another, which is an Egyptian custom.

His father according to Stesimbrotus was Maion son of Apellis, his mother being Hyrnetho or Cretheis. According to Dinarchus it was Crethon, and according to Democrines Alemon; but according to the majority it was Meles, the river of Smyrna, which flows for a short distance and then at once issues into the adjacent sea. Aristotle says the people of Ios record that Homer was born from a sprite who danced with the Muses.

As to the date when he flourished, the accounts are as follows. Heraclides makes him older than Hesiod, whereas Pyrander and Hypsicrates of Amisos make him his contemporary. Crates of Mallos says he flourished sixty years after the Trojan War; Eratosthenes, a hundred years after the Ionian migration; Apollodorus, eighty.[41]

He was called Melesigenes or Melesagoras from birth,

[39] A board game, mentioned in *Odyssey* 1.107.
[40] As in *Iliad* 1.533.
[41] This information is confused. Eratosthenes dated Homer a hundred years after the Trojan War; Apollodorus put him a hundred years after the Ionian migration. See Felix Jacoby, *Apollodors Chronik* (Berlin, 1902), 98–107.

---

[67] Δημόκριτος et Δαήμονα *Certamen* 3.
[68] τῆς Ἰώνων ἀποικίας del. Jacoby.

σαγόρας, αὖθις δὲ Ὅμηρος ἐλέχθη κατὰ τὴν Λεσβίων
διάλεκτον ἕνεκεν τῆς περὶ τοὺς ὀφθαλμοὺς συμφορᾶς·
οὗτοι γὰρ τοὺς τυφλοὺς ὁμήρους λέγουσιν. ἢ διότι
παῖς ὢν ὅμηρον ἐδόθη Βασιλεῖ, ὅ ἐστιν ἐνέχυρον.
τυφλωθῆναι δὲ αὐτὸν οὕτω πως λέγουσιν· ἐλθόντα
γὰρ ἐπὶ τὸν Ἀχιλλέως τάφον εὔξασθαι θεάσασθαι τὸν
ἥρωα τοιοῦτον ὁποῖος προῆλθεν ἐπὶ τὴν μάχην τοῖς
δευτέροις ὅπλοις κεκοσμημένος· ὀφθέντος δὲ αὐτῶι
τοῦ Ἀχιλλέως τυφλωθῆναι τὸν Ὅμηρον ὑπὸ τῆς τῶν
ὅπλων αὐγῆς· ἐλεηθέντα δὲ ὑπὸ Θέτιδος καὶ Μουσῶν
τιμηθῆναι πρὸς αὐτῶν τῆι ποιητικῆι. ἄλλοι δέ φασι
τοῦτο αὐτὸν πεπονθέναι διὰ μῆνιν τῆς Ἑλένης ὀρ-
γισθείσης αὐτῶι διότι εἶπεν αὐτὴν καταλελοιπέναι
μὲν τὸν πρότερον ἄνδρα, ἠκολουθηκέναι δὲ Ἀλεξάν-
δρωι· οὕτως γοῦν < . . . >,[69] ὅτι καὶ παρέστη αὐτῶι,
φησίν, νυκτὸς ἡ ψυχὴ τῆς ἡρωίνης παραινοῦσα καῦ-
σαι τὰς ποιήσεις αὐτοῦ, [καλῶς δὲ] εἰ τοῦτο ποιήσοι
πράξοι·[70] τὸν δὲ μὴ ἀνασχέσθαι ποιῆσαι τοῦτο.

6   ἀποθανεῖν δὲ αὐτὸν λέγουσιν ἐν Ἴωι τῆι νήσωι
ἀμηχανίαι περιπεσόντα, ἐπειδήπερ τῶν παίδων τῶν
ἁλιέων οὐχ οἷός τε ἐγένετο αἴνιγμα λῦσαι. ἔστι δὲ
τοῦτο·

        ἅσσ' ἕλομεν λιπόμεσθ', ἅσσ' οὐχ ἕλομεν
            φερόμεσθα.

[69] Lacunam stat. Wilamowitz.
[70] καλῶς δὲ et πράξοι West: spat. vac. litterarum fere vii et
πρόσχοι cod.

436

but later he was spoken of as Homer in the Lesbian dialect on account of what happened to his eyesight, for they call the blind *homēroi*. Or it was because as a boy he was given to the Great King as a *homēron*, which means a surety. They say his blindness came about in this way: he went to the tomb of Achilles and prayed that he might behold the hero as he was when he went out to join the battle arrayed in his replacement armour.[42] When Achilles appeared to him, Homer was blinded by the dazzle of the armour; but Thetis and the Muses took pity on him and honored him with the gift of poetry. Others, however, say he suffered this disability as a result of the wrath of Helen, who was angry with him because he said she had deserted her former husband and gone with Alexander. So at any rate < . . . says >,[43] that the soul of the heroine actually appeared standing before him in the night, advising him to burn his poems, as he would be < all right > if he did so; but he could not bear to do it.

They say he died on the island of Ios after finding himself helpless because he was unable to solve a riddle of the fisherboys. This is it:

> What we caught we left behind, and what we missed
>   we carry.

[42] See the description in *Iliad* 19.364–398.
[43] An author's name has fallen out.

καὶ αὐτοῦ ἐπὶ τῶι τάφωι ἐπιγέγραπται ἐπίγραμμα τοῦτο·

ἐνθάδε τὴν ἱερὴν κεφαλὴν κατὰ γαῖα καλύπτει,
ἀνδρῶν ἡρώων κοσμήτορα θεῖον Ὅμηρον.

7. ANONYMUS I

And on his tomb is inscribed this inscription:

Here the earth conceals that sacred head,
adorner of warrior heroes, the godly Homer.

ΓΕΝΟΣ ΟΜΗΡΟΥ
(VITA SCORIALENSIS I)

1 Ὅμηρος ὁ ποιητὴς υἱὸς ἦν κατὰ μέν τινας Μαίονος
καὶ Ὑρνηθοῦς, κατὰ δὲ ἐνίους Μέλητος τοῦ ποταμοῦ
καὶ Κριθηΐδος νύμφης. ἄλλοι δὲ αὐτοῦ τὸ γένος εἰς
Καλλιόπην τὴν Μοῦσαν ἀναφέρουσιν. φασὶ δὲ αὐτὸν
Μελησιγένη ἢ Μελησιάνακτα κεκλῆσθαι, τυφλω-
θέντα δὲ αὐτὸν ὕστερον Ὅμηρον κληθῆναι· οἱ γὰρ
Αἰολεῖς τοὺς τυφλοὺς ὁμήρους καλοῦσιν.

2 πατρίδα δὲ αὐτοῦ οἱ μὲν Σμύρναν, οἱ δὲ Χίον, οἱ δὲ
Κολοφῶνα, οἱ δὲ Ἀθήνας λέγουσιν. περιιὼν δὲ τὰς
πόλεις ᾖδε τὰ ποιήματα· ὕστερον δὲ αὐτὰ Πεισίστρα-
τος συνήγαγεν, ὡς τὸ ἐπίγραμμα τοῦτο δηλοῖ·

> τρίς με τυραννήσαντα τοσαυτάκις ἐξεδίωξεν
>   δῆμος Ἐρεχθειδῶν καὶ τρὶς ἐπεσπάσατο,
> τὸν μέγαν ἐν βουλαῖς Πεισίστρατον, ὃς τὸν
>   Ὅμηρον
> ἤθροισα σποράδην τὸ πρὶν ἀειδόμενον·
> ἡμέτερος γὰρ ἐκεῖνος ὁ χρύσεος ἦν πολιήτης,
>   εἴπερ Ἀθηναῖοι Σμύρναν ἐπωικίσαμεν.

3 φασὶ δὲ αὐτὸν ἐν Ἴωι τῆι νήσωι διὰ λύπην

440

8. ANONYMUS II
THE LINEAGE OF HOMER
(VITA SCORIALENSIS I)

The poet Homer was the son according to some of Maion and Hyrnetho, according to others of the river Meles and a nymph Critheis. Others take his lineage back to the Muse Calliope. And they say he was named Melesigenes or Melesianax, but later after becoming blind was called Homer, as the Aeolians call the blind *homēroi*.

As to his homeland, some say it was Smyrna, some Chios, some Colophon, and some Athens. He used to go round from town to town reciting his poems, and subsequently Pisistratus gathered them together, as this epigram shows:

> Thrice I was tyrant, as many times the Erechtheid
>   people
>   chased me out, and thrice called me back,
> Pisistratus great in counsel, who gathered Homer
>   that previously was sung in scattered form;
> for that man of gold was a citizen of ours,
>   if you grant that we Athenians founded Smyrna.

They say he died in the island of Ios, starving himself to

ἀποκαρτερήσαντα τελευτῆσαι διὰ τὸ μὴ λῦσαι τὸ ζήτημα τὸ ὑπὸ τῶν ἁλιέων αὐτῶι προτεθέν. ὁ μὲν γὰρ ἐπιστὰς ἤρετο·

ἄνδρες ἀπ' Ἀρκαδίης ἁλιήτορες, ἦ ῥ' ἔχομέν τι;

οἱ δὲ ἀπεκρίναντο·

ὅσσ' ἔλομεν λιπόμεσθ', ὅσσ' οὐχ ἕλομεν
φερόμεσθα.

ἐπιγέγραπται δὲ ἐν τῶι μνήματι αὐτοῦ οὕτως·

ἐνθάδε τὴν ἱερὴν κεφαλὴν κατὰ γαῖα καλύπτει,
ἀνδρῶν ἡρώων κοσμήτορα, θεῖον Ὅμηρον.

death in chagrin at not solving the problem put to him by the fishers. For he went up and asked:

> O fishermen from Arcadia, have we caught anything?

And they replied:

> All that we caught we left behind, all that we missed we carry.

On his memorial is inscribed:

> Here the earth conceals that sacred head,
> adorner of warrior heroes, the godly Homer.

ΑΛΛΩΣ (VITA SCORIALENSIS II)

1   Ὅμηρος ὁ ποιητὴς πατρὸς μὲν ἦν Μέλητος, μη-
τρὸς δὲ Κριθηΐδος, τὸ γένος κατὰ μὲν Πίνδαρον (fr.
264 Sn.) Σμυρναῖος, κατὰ δὲ Σιμωνίδην (eleg. 19.1)
Χῖος, κατὰ δὲ Ἀντίμαχον (fr. 130 Wyss) καὶ Νίκανδρον
(fr. 14 Schn.) Κολοφώνιος, κατὰ δὲ Βακχυλίδην (fr. 48
Sn.) καὶ Ἀριστοτέλην τὸν φιλόσοφον (fr. 76 Rose)
Ἰήτης, κατὰ δὲ Ἔφορον (70 F 99) καὶ τοὺς ἱστορικοὺς
Κυμαῖος, κατὰ δὲ Ἀρίσταρχον καὶ Διονύσιον τὸν
Θρᾶικα Ἀθηναῖος. τινὲς δὲ καὶ Σαλαμίνιον αὐτὸν
εἶναί φασιν· ἄλλοι δὲ Ἀργεῖον· ἄλλοι δὲ Αἰγύπτιον
ἀπὸ Θηβῶν.

2   τοῖς δὲ χρόνοις κατὰ μέν τινας πρὸ τῆς τῶν
Ἡρακλειδῶν ἐγένετο καθόδου, ὥστε ἕνεκεν τούτου
γινώσκεσθαι ὑπ᾽ αὐτοῦ τοὺς ἐπὶ Ἴλιον στρατεύσαν-
τας· τὰ γὰρ ἀπὸ τῶν Τρωϊκῶν ἐπὶ τὴν κάθοδον τῶν
Ἡρακλειδῶν ὀγδοήκοντα ἔτη. τοῦτο δὲ ἀπίθανον ὑπ-
άρχει· καὶ γὰρ αὐτὸς ὁ Ὅμηρος ὑστεροῦντα πολλοῖς
χρόνοις ἑαυτὸν ἀποδείκνυσι λέγων (Il. 2.486)·

ἡμεῖς δὲ κλέος οἶον ἀκούομεν, οὐδέ τι ἴδμεν.

9. ANONYMUS III
(VITA SCORIALENSIS II)

The poet Homer's father was Meles, and his mother was Critheis. By birth he was according to Pindar a Smyrnaean, according to Simonides a Chian, according to Antimachus and Nicander a Colophonian, according to Bacchylides and the philosopher Aristotle from Ios, according to Ephorus and the historians a Cymaean, and according to Aristarchus and Dionysius Thrax an Athenian. Some even say he was a Salaminian, others an Argive, and others an Egyptian from Thebes.

As to his date, according to some he lived before the return of the Heraclids, so that those who took part in the expedition to Ilion could have been known to him, the time from the Trojan War to the return of the Heraclids being eighty years. But this is implausible, for Homer himself shows that he lived long afterwards when he says

> But we only hear the report, and have no personal knowledge.

τινὲς δὲ λέγουσιν αὐτὸν τῆς Ἰωνικῆς ἀποικίας ἀπολεί-
πεσθαι ἔτεσιν ἑκατὸν πεντήκοντα.

3 οὐδὲν δὲ αὐτοῦ θετέον ἔξω τῆς Ἰλιάδος καὶ τῆς
Ὀδυσσείας, ἀλλὰ τοὺς Ὕμνους καὶ τὰ λοιπὰ τῶν εἰς
αὐτὸν ἀναφερομένων ποιημάτων ἡγητέον ἀλλότρια
καὶ τῆς φύσεως[71] καὶ τῆς δυνάμεως ἕνεκα. τινὲς δὲ
αὐτοῦ φασιν εἶναι καὶ τὰ φερόμενα δύο συγγράμ-
ματα, τήν τε Μυοβατραχομαχίαν καὶ τὸν Μαργίτην.

4 τὰ δὲ ποιήματα αὐτοῦ τὰ ἀληθῆ σποράδην πρότε-
ρον ᾀδόμενα Πεισίστρατος Ἀθηναῖος συνέταξεν, ὡς
δηλοῖ τὸ φερόμενον ἐπίγραμμα ⟨τὸ⟩ Ἀθήνησιν ἐπιγε-
γραμμένον ἐν εἰκόνι αὐτοῦ {τοῦ Πεισιστράτου}. ἔχει
δὲ ὧδε·

> τρίς με τυραννήσαντα τοσαυτάκις ἐξεκύλισεν
>   δῆμος Ἐρεχθῆος καὶ τρὶς ἐπηγάγετο,
> τὸν μέγαν ἐν βουλαῖς Πεισίστρατον, ὃς τὸν
>   Ὅμηρον
> ἤθροισα σποράδην τὸ πρὶν ἀειδόμενον.
> ἡμέτερος καὶ ἐκεῖνος ὁ χρύσεος ἦν πολιήτης,
>   εἴπερ Ἀθηναῖοι Σμύρναν ἐπῳκίσαμεν.

5 πλανηθέντα δὲ τὸν Ὅμηρον ἐν Ἰθάκῃ πολύν φασι
διατρῖψαι χρόνον· καὶ πολλὰς χώρας ἀμείψαντα ἐν
Ἴῳ τῇ νήσῳ τελευτῆσαι ἐκ τοιᾶσδε αἰτίας. καθημέ-
νου γάρ ποτε τοῦ Ὁμήρου ἐν αἰγιαλῷ, τυφλοῦ αὐτοῦ
ὄντος, αἰσθέσθαι ἁλιέων παρερχομένων, πρὸς οὓς
εἶπεν·

Some say that he lived a hundred and fifty years after the Ionian migration.

Nothing is to be acknowledged as his apart from the *Iliad* and *Odyssey*: the *Hymns* and the rest of the poems attributed to him are to be reckoned alien, in regard both to their nature[44] and their effectiveness. But some say that those two current compositions, the *Battle of Mice and Frogs* and the *Margites*, are his.

His poems—the genuine ones—were formerly recited in scattered form, and it was Pisistratus of Athens who arranged them together, as is shown by the well-known epigram that is inscribed at Athens on his statue. It runs as follows:

> Thrice I was tyrant, as many times Erechtheus'
>   people
>   bundled me out, and thrice brought me back,
> Pisistratus great in counsel, who gathered Homer
>   that previously was sung in scattered form.
> That man of gold too was a citizen of ours,
>   if you grant that we Athenians founded Smyrna.

They say that Homer travelled abroad and spent a long period in Ithaca; and that after passing through many places he died on the island of Ios from the following circumstance. Homer was sitting one day on the beach—he was blind—and he became aware of some fishers approaching, to whom he said:

44 Or (with Wilamowitz's emendation) diction.

---

71 φράσεως Wilamowitz.

ἄνδρες ἀπ᾽ Ἀρκαδίης ἁλιήτορες, ἦ ῥ᾽ ἔχομέν τι;

τοὺς δὲ ἀποκριθέντας εἰπεῖν·

ὅσσ᾽ ἕλομεν λιπόμεσθ᾽, ὅσσ᾽ οὐχ ἕλομεν
φερόμεσθα.

τὸ δὲ λεγόμενόν ἐστι τοιοῦτον· ἐπειδὴ γὰρ οὐδὲν ἦσαν ἔχοντες τότε ἐξ ἀλείας, ἐφθειρίζοντο, καὶ οὓς μὲν ἔλαβον ἐκ τῶν φθειρῶν φονεῦσαι καὶ μὴ ἔχειν, οὓς δὲ οὐκ ἔλαβον ἐν τῆι ἐσθῆτι περιφέρειν. οὐ νοήσας δὲ τὸ λεγόμενον, ἀπὸ θλίψεως ἐτελεύτησεν ἐν Ἴωι τῆι νήσωι. ἔθαψαν δὲ αὐτὸν μεγαλοπρεπῶς οἱ Ἰῆται, χαράξαντες ἐπὶ τῶι τάφωι τὸ ἐπίγραμμα τοῦτο, παρ᾽ αὐτοῦ ζῶντος ἔτι γεγραμμένον εἰς αὐτόν·

ἐνθάδε τὴν ἱερὴν κεφαλὴν κατὰ γαῖα καλύπτει,
ἀνδρῶν ἡρώων κοσμήτορα θεῖον Ὅμηρον.

9. ANONYMUS III

O fishermen from Arcadia, have we caught anything?

And they replied:

> All that we caught we left behind, all that we missed
> we carry.

The meaning is this: as they were on that occasion without anything from their fishing, they de-loused themselves, and those of the lice that they had caught, they had killed and no longer had, while those they had not caught they were carrying about in their clothing. But he, not understanding the utterance, died from depression on the island of Ios. The people of Ios gave him a magnificent funeral, and carved on his tomb this inscription which he had written for himself while still alive:

> Here the earth conceals that sacred head,
> adorner of warrior heroes, the godly Homer.

APPENDIX ROMANA

A

1   Τὰ παρατιθέμενα τοῖς Ὁμηρικοῖς στίχοις Ἀρισταρχεία σημεῖα. ἀναγκαῖον γνῶναι τοὺς ἐντυγχάνοντας.

διπλῆ ἀπερίστικτος	>
διπλῆ περιεστιγμένη	⸖
ὀβελός	—
ἀστερίσκος καθ᾽ ἑαυτόν	※
ἀστερίσκος μετὰ ὀβελοῦ	※—
ἀντίσιγμα	⊃
ἀντίσιγμα περιεστιγμένον	Ͽ·
κεραύνιον	Τ

>   ἡ μὲν οὖν διπλῆ ἀπερίστικτος παρατίθεται πρὸς τοὺς γλωσσογράφους ἢ ἑτεροδόξως ἐκδεξαμένους τὰ τοῦ ποιητοῦ καὶ μὴ καλῶς· ἢ πρὸς τὰς ἅπαξ εἰρημένας λέξεις, ἢ πρὸς τὰ ἐναντία καὶ μαχόμενα, καὶ ἕτερα

---

45 By this title I designate further material from the prolegomena to the D scholia on the *Iliad* in cod. Rom. Bibl. Nat. gr. 6, the manuscript from which the first Anonymous Life is taken.

10. APPENDIX ROMANA[45]

A

The Aristarchean signs placed beside lines of Homer. (Must be identified by those who encounter them.)[46]

Diple undotted	>
Diple dotted	⍮
Obelos	—
Asterisk by itself	※
Asterisk with obelos	※—
Antisigma	)
Antisigma dotted	)·
Keraunion	T

> The diple undotted is placed by a line with reference to the glossographers or others who have interpreted the poet's words in an idiosyncratic and erroneous way; or with reference to words occurring only once, or to contra-

[46] Aristarchus' critical signs, found sporadically in some papyri and medieval manuscripts of Homer, were the subject of treatises by Aristonicus and others. Similar summaries to the present one are found in a few other Greek and Latin sources. See Wilhelm Dindorf, *Scholia Graeca in Homeri Iliadem* I (Oxford, 1875), xlii–l.

σχήματα πάμπολλα καὶ ζητήματα.

⸖   ἡ δὲ περιεστιγμένη διπλῆ πρὸς τὰς γραφὰς τὰς Ζηνοδοτείας καὶ Κράτητος καὶ αὐτοῦ Ἀριστάρχου καὶ τὰς διορθώσεις αὐτοῦ.

—   ὁ δὲ ὀβελὸς πρὸς τὰ ἀθετούμενα ἐπὶ τοῦ ποιητοῦ, ἤγουν νενοθευμένα ἢ ὑποβεβλημένα.

※   ὁ δὲ ἀστερίσκος καθ᾽ ἑαυτόν, ὡς καλῶς εἰρημένων τῶν ἐπῶν ἐν αὐτῶι τῶι τόπωι ἔνθα ἐστὶν ἀστερίσκος μόνος.

※—   ὁ δὲ ἀστερίσκος μετὰ ὀβελοῦ, ὡς ὄντα μὲν τὰ ἔπη τοῦ ποιητοῦ, μὴ καλῶς δὲ κείμενα ἐν αὐτῶι τῶι τόπωι, ἀλλ᾽ ἐν ἄλλωι.

Ɔ   τὸ δὲ ἀντίσιγμα καθ᾽ ἑαυτὸ πρὸς τοὺς ἐνηλλαγμένους τόπους καὶ ἀπαίδοντας.

Ɔ·   τὸ δὲ ἀντίσιγμα περιεστιγμένον παρατίθεται ὅταν ταυτολογῆι καὶ τὴν αὐτὴν διάνοιαν δεύτερον λέγηι.

Τ   τὸ δὲ κεραύνιον ἔστι μὲν τῶν σπανίως παρατιθεμένων, δηλοῖ δὲ καὶ αὐτὸ πολλὰς ζητήσεις πρὸς ταῖς εἰρημέναις.

τούτων δὲ ἁπάντων τῶν σημείων ἡ ἀκριβεστέρα γνῶσις ἐν ταῖς βίβλοις τῶν συγγραψαμένων περὶ τούτων, καὶ εἴ σοι φίλον ἐπιζήτει παρὰ τῶν τεχνικῶν.

2

>   τῆι διπλῆι χρῆται Ἀρίσταρχος πρὸς ἱστορίαν καὶ σχηματισμοὺς καὶ ἑτέρας ποικίλας χρείας.

⸖   τῆι δὲ περιεστιγμένηι πρὸς Ζηνόδοτον τὸν διορθωτήν.

dictions and inconsistencies, or to many other figures and problems;

$\dot{>}$ the dotted diple with reference to readings of Zenodotus and Crates,[47] and of Aristarchus himself and his editions;

— the obelos for what is athetized in the text, that is, what is spurious or interpolated;

✳ the asterisk by itself, to signify that the verses are apposite in the place where the asterisk alone is put,

✳— whereas the asterisk with obelos signifies that although the verses are Homer's, they are not apposite in that place but in another.

Ɔ The antisigma by itself is used for passages that have been transposed and are out of accord;

Ɔ· the dotted antisigma is placed where he repeats himself and expresses the same idea a second time.

T The keraunion is one of those that are rarely deployed; it too signifies many sorts of problem besides those already mentioned.

For all these signs, more detailed knowledge is to be found in the volumes of those who have written about them, and if you care to, you can seek it out from the specialists.

> The diple is used by Aristarchus with reference to mythology, figures of speech, and diverse other purposes;

$\dot{>}$ the dotted diple with reference to the editor Zenodotus;

[47] Aristarchus frequently criticized Zenodotus' readings; much less often those of his own contemporary, Crates of Mallos.

— τῶι δὲ ὀβελῶι πρὸς ἀθέτησιν.

※— ἀστερίσκωι δὲ σὺν ὀβελῶι πρὸς τὸ εἶναι μὲν τοὺς στίχους Ὁμήρου, κεῖσθαι δὲ ἐν ἄλλωι τόπωι καλῶς, οἷς καὶ ἀστερίσκος μόνος παράκειται.

Ͻ τῶι δὲ ἀντίσιγμα καὶ τῆι στιγμῆι, ὅταν δύο ὦσι διάνοιαι τὸ αὐτὸ σημαίνουσαι, τοῦ ποιητοῦ γεγραφότος ἀμφοτέρας, ὅπως τὴν ἑτέραν ἕληται· τῶι δὲ χρόνωι καὶ αἱ δύο εὑρέθησαν, οὐκ ὀρθῶς ἔχουσαι.

※ τῶι δὲ ἀστερίσκωι μόνωι χρῆται πρὸς τοὺς αὐτοὺς στίχους οἳ κεῖνται ἐν ἄλλοις μέρεσι τῆς ποιήσεως καὶ ὀρθῶς ἔχοντες φέρονται, σημαίνων ὅτι οὗτοι καὶ ἀλλαχοῦ εἴρηνται.

B

1 Ἡ δοκοῦσα ἀρχαία Ἰλιάς, λεγομένη δὲ Ἀπελλικῶντος,[72] προοίμιον ἔχει τοῦτο·

Μούσας ἀείδω καὶ Ἀπόλλωνα κλυτότοξον,

ὡς καὶ Νικάνωρ μέμνηται καὶ Κράτης ἐν τοῖς Διορθωτικοῖς. Ἀριστόξενος δὲ ἐν αʹ Πραξιδαμαντείων (fr. 91a Wehrli) φησὶ κατά τινας ἔχειν·

Ἔσπετε νῦν μοι, Μοῦσαι Ὀλύμπια δώματ᾽ ἔχουσαι,

[72] Ἀπελλικῶντος Schimberg (-ῶνος Ribbeck): ἀπ᾽ ελικῶνος cod.

—   the obelos for athetesis;

※—   the asterisk with obelos to signify that the lines are Homer's but are found more appositely in another passage, where the asterisk alone is placed;

Ɔ   the antisigma and the point, when there are two sentiments with the same meaning, the poet having written down both, intending to make his choice between them, but subsequently both were transmitted by mistake.

※   The asterisk alone he uses where the same lines occur in another part of the poem and they are correctly transmitted (in the present place), to indicate that they have been used elsewhere too.

B

What is considered the old *Iliad*, the one known as Apellicon's, has this proem:

Of the Muses I sing, and Apollo of the famed bow,

as recorded both by Nicanor and by Crates in his *Text-critical Notes*.[48] Aristoxenus in book 1 of his *Praxidamanteia* says that according to some it had:

Tell me now, Muses who dwell on Olympus,

[48] Apellicon of Teos was a book collector who died in 84 BC; Sulla brought his library to Rome. The peculiar *incipit* found in his *Iliad* had apparently already been quoted by Crates, who predated Apellicon. Nicanor was a grammarian of the second century AD.

ὅππως δὴ μῆνίς τε χόλος θ' ἕλε Πηλείωνα
Λητοῦς τ' ἀγλαὸν υἱόν· ὃ γὰρ βασιλῆϊ χολωθείς.

2   τὴν δὲ ποίησιν ἀναγινώσκεσθαι ἀξιοῖ Ζώπυρος ὁ
Μάγνης (FGrHist 494 F 3) Αἰολίδι διαλέκτωι· τὸ δὲ
αὐτὸ καὶ Δικαίαρχος (fr. 90 Wehrli).

3   αἱ μέντοι ῥαψωιδίαι κατὰ συνάφειαν ἤνωντο, κορω-
νίδι μόνηι διαστελλόμεναι, ἄλλωι δὲ οὐδενί.

how it was that wrath and anger seized Achilles
and Leto's glorious son; for he, angry with the king
(etc.).

Zopyrus of Magnesia considers that the poem should
be read in Aeolic dialect, and so does Dicaearchus.

The rhapsodies were joined up continuously, being
demarcated by a coronis alone and nothing else.[49]

[49] A coronis is an ornamental marginal symbol used in ancient
manuscripts to mark the beginning of a new poem, excerpt, etc.

INDEX TO THE HOMERIC HYMNS AND APOCRYPHA

References are to the Hymns where not otherwise specified. The *Battle of the Weasel and the Mice* is here referred to as *Gal.* (*Galeomyomachia*), and the *Battle of Frogs and Mice* as *Batr.* (*Batrachomyomachia*).

459

INDEX

INDEX TO THE
LIVES OF HOMER

Composed in ZephGreek and ZephText by
Technologies 'N Typography, Merrimac, Massachusetts.
Printed and bound by Edwards Brothers, Ann Arbor, Michigan
on acid-free paper made by Glatfelter, Spring Grove, Pennsylvania.